Empire Under Glass

Empire Under Glass

A NOVEL

Julian Anderson

Faber and Faber
BOSTON • LONDON

First published in the United States in 1996 by Faber and Faber, Inc.,
53 Shore Road, Winchester, MA 01890

Library of Congress Catologing-in-Publication Data

Anderson, Julian.
    Empire under glass : a novel / Julian Anderson.
       p.   cm.
    ISBN 0-571-19884-8
    1. Aged women—Fiction.   2. Mothers and daughters—Fiction.
    I. Title.
    PS3551.N372E47   1996
    813′.54—dc20   95-25592
                                                                                CIP

Jacket design by Hania Khuri

Printed in the United States of America

FOR GREGORY

For support while working on the manuscript,
I am grateful to the Ohio Arts Council.

1

Underwater

ALL THIS HAPPENED because my dear friend Jackson Pancake took me up in his plane for a spin. Going AWOL from the Sunset Home, we were heady with adventure, and I had no sense of danger. Jackson guided us up and out toward Hayfields House, "site of skirmish," as he so happily informed me, bouncing us down on the short strip ten minutes later, "circa seventeen eighty-one." Revolution seemed the right theme for our July outing.

After the tour of the house, we picnicked in a pasture with some cows and their flies. We didn't talk as we arranged our little meal of pooled resources: thermos of decaf, Tupper of applesauce, potato salad from the grocery's deli section, cottage cheese, a Baggie of carrot pennies, a French loaf already thoughtfully sawed into rounds, and some intimidatingly green Granny Smiths to dig our dentures into for dessert. It was a meal noisy with nature, not human talk. My spirits had sunk as low as rain clouds from encounters in the farmhouse. Jackson was put out with me, I could see, for balking at his hobby. His smile seemed remote as I offered the little smuggled treat of my friend Evangeline's citizenship cake, smeary with toxic reds and blues.

As soon as we lifted off again, I fell asleep—I was that tired. I was dozing on the way to Conflux, but opened my eyes just as we hummed back over my daughter's farm, clearly outlined by her tumbleweed hedges. Looking down, I could see people moving around on the ground like beetles: my daughter, my son-in-law, the twins.

"Drop a bit," I shouted to Jackson above the engine's thrum. He circled lower. There they were, busy following their own trajectories on earth: as far from me as I had ever felt, yet so exposed. I could have lobbed tomatoes down with impunity—but it was all so beautiful . . . it was all so beguiling and attractive that, hanging half out of the plane as we were, we must have winged too low in one of our swoops and—engine failure—nose-dived in.

Down, down I come, like glist'ring Phaeton, quoted my irrelevant brain—*down, down* into the abrupt, shocking cold of the water's murky welcome as it swallowed me whole. In the darkness, time slowed, memory meandered, and I felt an alert peacefulness. There, at the bottom of Marjorie's muddy fishpond, I lay almost horizontal among algae. Thoughts like vivid fish fanned themselves across my nose. I was not dead. I was not even particularly frightened, strangely, though I considered in the abstract that I might not reach the surface again. But death was a preoccupation of the young, and at my age you worried about the little things: what your husband's name had been, how much the post office charged for an aerogramme. Also—and the memory of this rushed in clear and strong—I had fallen through ice once as a girl; in some ways my whole life had been lived in closed time.

I became aware of soft mud shifting lightly under my skin, my right arm pinned beneath me, weeds playing over my nose. On casting my eyes about, I recognized the true strangeness of my predicament. I raised myself on an elbow and found I was breathing real air. I was sitting as though in a bathtub, in about four inches of pond water. Above me arced a bubble through which poured shafts of greenish light. I reached out as best I could in my cramped posture and pressed against this surface—a hard, transparent plastic material that resisted a shove with official conviction. Somehow I had been thrust beneath the windshield of the plane that, like me, had become detached. Sinking, it had fallen over me, providing an air pocket and a view of waterlogged sky.

As I resettled myself, drawing up my extremities more symmetrically, my heart's weak valve fluttered in horror. Had I dislodged that bubble securing me, in would have poured all the pond! At that, I felt the full danger in trying to free myself. And even if I had trusted myself to swim, past eighty you hesitate to undertake spontaneous heroism. I would sit it out, I decided, confident that above me rescue was at hand. I tried some shallow breathing. Surely an old lady didn't require much oxygen . . .

Jackson! With a shiver of panic, I looked around for signs of my friend. My one true friend, I thought; he must not end here. Through the fine dust that rose up like steam from the mud bottom, I saw something that might have been he—a long blur, rising up. It was an eerie moment, seeing what I thought was his body lift vertically upward while I remained trapped, below, and in that moment I knew the anguish of the living seeing off the dead. Or vice versa. Logically, it should have been the other way around. I assured myself, neither of us would die; I had risen once before from the bottom of a lake, and now that Jackson was escaping upward, my own rescue was bound to follow. In the meantime I'd sit—literally—tight. Too tight. I regretted the extra sandwiches at lunch and felt the constriction of even my lightweight girdle.

In times of distress, you need your handbag. Mine, loyal friend, rested against my foot. I tugged it toward me, onto my lap, where it lay sodden and abashed, poor thing, as though it were to blame. That colossal purple pocketbook was one of my prize finds. I bought it last spring for three dollars at the home's Bring-N-Buy. It was pure leather, and so carefully looked after by Mrs. Rotweiler, bent over with osteoporosis on the fourth floor, that inside it even had its original yellowed tissue paper and a little plastic comb. Mrs. Rotweiler was one of the wealthy ones at Sunset, the widow of the Conflux Bus System's president. When she hopped by on her ultra-lightweight walker, she hardly lifted an eyelid in my direction.

I felt odd meeting her when I was carrying her accessory, but I didn't get out much and I needed a bag. Actually, I preferred neutral shades in my suits, and the outspoken smartness of the purple bag made me a little self-conscious about taking it on visits to Marjorie. My daughter was devoted to some sartorial principle that had to do with spontaneity, heartfeltness, and irony. Taste she held in suspicion. Bargains qualified only if Marjorie could show the items off to the family with guffaws. Sometimes I recognized a tasseled hat or weasel-biting-weasel stole adorning her as items my own generation might ourselves have chosen to wear with all decorum to the cinema. It distressed me to see my daughter giggling at my past. On the other hand, regarding my own purple bag, I did need something that could stand up to my friend

Evangeline's Italian leather purse. Being Canadian, one is chary of display, but when the two of us got ourselves up for chess, I felt comparisons were silently made in my Greek friend's favor. Even at breakfast, Evangeline Ypsilanti looked as though she were on her way to a wedding. Overdressing was of course a faux pas, except that she didn't know it, so she won again.

I struggled with that big catch on the bag. Things got stubborn underwater. With some effort I opened it and checked inside for my vital possessions: a hand mirror told me I was still a large-nosed old lady who, wig having come off somewhere on the way down, should run a comb through her hair. Mrs. Rotweiler's little one lost some teeth in my tangle, but I smoothed out the worst of the mess and gave it some guidance on how to dry, then applied my hot poinsettia lipstick, one cast off by Mrs. Ypsilanti, who had a Mediterranean color sense: nothing matching, everything bright. Still, I was glad for it, as the greenish-brownish light filtering down made me look like a blancmange. I'd given up powder and rouge, and any foundation had crumbled long ago, so I was only lips now by way of artifice, and those were as thin as ticking stripes. My tactful little hand mirror observed the home improvements without comment.

As I replaced these objects, I stirred around inside my bag and, now with some time on my hands, checked what trash I'd collected. Sorting through the scraps was a task I disliked, mainly because of my eyes. Farsightedness I felt was a cure for romanticism and aesthetic reverie. It explained the persnicketiness of old people to whom the landscape was not a haze of sensation but a clearly defined set of objects at various distances. The morning's cows had been pleasant, but they had not sent me into gyrations of quatrains. One literally gained perspective as one's eyeballs shrank. For close work, too, you lost patience. It was just so hard to get it far enough away to look at properly. I had little interest in receipts, old lists depressed me, and Jackson's postcards, somehow in my bag, reminded me of our run-in.

The first part of the trip had gone off without a hitch. As we rolled away down the strip, Jackson turned knobs and flipped out a pair of sunglasses against his chest. "Let's get this baby off the ground," he said, amusing me: behind an engine the straitlaced Jackson turned Hollywood flying ace.

With a light bounce, we picked up speed and were suddenly pointed over the windsock into depthless sky. And there I was at eighty-one, borne up as if by my heart's own little propellers. I was flying thigh to thigh with a man who'd been to Wallawalhalla Island. This fact meant a lot to me. People at the home never grasped our attraction: what could that large, aloof lady in summer suits find to talk so long about in the lobby with that mountaineer, yes, that buzz-topped, leathernecked ex-mailman from East Tennessee? But at our age, local accents and poll booth preferences mattered as little as brands of antacids. The point was, Jackson knew Walla. In giant America, even in a place with as much regional flavor as Conflux, N.C., a little pinprick of land like that got lost. When I mentioned the island where I had spent the most important summer of my youth, no one was sure if Wallawalhalla was in the South Atlantic or the North Sea—except Jackson. He needed never refer to the bougainvillea's panicles pouring over porches, the volcano at the island's far end, the rumored platoons of white ants ready to carry us all away—he had been there, and that was enough for me. At his side, admiring the deftness of his large hands pulling controls, I wondered if he ever felt as helpless in the new world as I did. I suspected he did not and wondered at the source of his optimism.

"Hayfields," he cried, ten minutes up, pointing to a gray blur amid corn fields.

"Fine," I said, ready to try to like what he did. How blithely I let him fly me right into old torment.

The guide at the site, in her revolutionary-era skirts, Adidas shoes, and bonnet clamped down over perm, showed us around with a prepared patter. Jackson quizzed her about hinges and paced out hallways. On the second floor landing she raised her arm to a framed embroidery. "Elysian Fields mourning picture," she said. "Are you familiar with these?"

She asked Mr. Pancake and me, the only people at the house that hot morning, to stand in a bedroom doorway and note how the spare figure in white, leaning so spinelessly over the tombstone in the scene, suddenly, viewed in the landing mirror, disappeared. Studied directly, there he stood; but in the mirror—gone. Direct—figure; mirror—gone.

"Now notice the tree," she instructed.

We looked. An angel's head, invisible when viewed directly, appeared in the mirror, stuck in the lollipop tree. It was as though the mirror were the other world, and figure turned to ghostly angel in the glass. This was remarkable in itself as stitchery, but something about the face caused my pulse to skid.

"Beautiful work," said Jackson brightly. "I wonder who the man was."

"This manner of embroidery was part of a young lady's training," our guide answered. "Now turn around and note the decor of the guest room. The coverlet depicts the apotheosis of General George Washington."

I hung back, still scrutinizing the embroidered face, which glowered at me, featherstitched. I knew it all too well; it was that rogue Roddy Borders, impersonating an angel. I struggled for air and clutched at anything to hold me up. A candlestick clanged, and, deep in conversation, they turned—guide's face livid, Pancake's ashen—as I slid to the floor.

I regained my composure on a pew down in the cellar gift shop. The guide brought me a paper cup of water, which I sipped quietly, waiting, catching my breath while inside I was sinking. Trying to close off that nasty moment on the landing, I vented some silent anger at Jackson who was bent over the glass counter, inspecting mementos. Why an upright, sensible man who needlepointed pictures, suitable for hanging, of eagles and mountains, would be so taken with hokey memorabilia, I couldn't understand.

Then my anger turned like a gyroscope back on myself; Roddy Borders's angel face ate through my thoughts like acid. His plunge into the Indian Ocean had plagued my life, and now I'd come face to face with him, in America of all places, in a lesser-known historic house not twenty miles from Conflux. And he knew it was me. He had tracked me down, and by the spell of his evil eye, or some inexact irony, it was I who next found myself underwater, at the bottom of my daughter's cold and copper-colored pond, waiting, hoping for rescue. This encounter pitched me curvy right up against myself. I could have used a little mercy.

I missed Jackson at the bottom of the pond. A fish—a bass, I wagered by its lips, wide like a smoker's—tried speaking without sound to me through my Plexiglas shell. It looked concerned. Perhaps it mistook me for a giant sea turtle. I smiled and waved to reassure it, and returned to thumb through the fistful of odds and ends I'd gathered from the interior of my purse.

The little bracelet I thought I'd misplaced, the gold charm bracelet with a locket in the shape of a heart that broke open like a book: there it was, its chain snaking around a pen at the bottom of the bag. I was glad to find it, as I wanted to leave it to my granddaughter. I pried it open and looked at the tiny picture: my mother as a girl, with wide forehead, piled blonde hair, pleasant almost-smile. At the click of the shutter had she broken into a grin, or, equally possible, turned sullen? I made an arthritic attempt to wrap the bracelet around my wrist. Jessica would like the picture, I knew. She'd inspect it closely and fantasize, just as I had done as a child, about the image under glass and gain . . . well, the answer was a closed book to me.

The accumulation of things weighed one down. White ants on my old island were thought by those who believed in them to chew through Renaissance drawings in less than half an hour and leave only a few shreds, too chalky to swallow, lying on the sand. How restful to stop trying to salvage the past that keeps disappearing on one. Progress—why not just let it happen? Now that was a relaxing thought!

But my mind fanned backward all the same. As a young girl I'd nearly drowned once, falling through the ice of my best friend's pond. They'd pulled me up at the last moment, gasping and angry; I'd known peace at the bottom of the water and it was hard to return to the world, chill and breezy, where my friend's eyes shrank back from me, unsmiling, while her suspect German father revived me with wet, moustacheprickly, coffee-fumed breaths.

My life might have closed there, at the age of twelve, and spared me anguish that sometimes seemed to outweigh the joy, yet I had gone on making mistakes for nearly seventy years. Underwater, I seemed for a short time safe from the accusations in Roddy Borders's ghosting face, but its appearance seemed the final pushing upward of the lava that I had kept under the crust since Walla; the past was about to erupt. I wished Jackson were there under my bubble so I might explain it all to him: my girlhood, Walla, and why I lived in disguise at the Sunset Home, and hoped—sixty years after the fact—for absolution, before the oxygen ran out.

2
Canada

How My Life Began as a Colony

WHEN LITTLE I, infant Viola, sucked my toes in southern Ontario, Canada was still colored red. Empire spread like a fever across the forehead of the North American continent, like a rash through Africa, like measles over the Pacific. A few years later, Miss Gloria Tillotson, the teacher of grades three through five, tapped at the points of interest on the map she unscrolled and the six squirming rows of boys and girls droned after her the names of red places: Tanganyika, Gold Coast, British Guyana. My lunch dreams interrupted, I borrowed a red crayon from my very best friend, Felicity, and took momentary pride in the waxy ease with which the Empire bled across the page. Miss Tillotson explained that, safe in Ontario, in a confederation, we at the Bremen Primary School were twice blessed. Two great leaders looked over us. She pointed to the framed rotogravures above the blackboard—one the jowly king, the other, Canada's own skinny prime minister, Robert Borden: Santa and helpful elf.

At home, the top floor of the Travelers' Arms Hotel, which my father himself had designed, Aunt from the red homeland looked after me. She had lived with us since I was a baby. From the patchwork of her family lore, I pieced together the story of how my father, lured to Canada, had trained as an architect in Toronto, then, as young and unsettled as the first years of the century, had taken a job on the tiny outpost of Empire in the Indian Ocean called Wallawalhalla Island. He designed an officers' club, into which he poured his soul. It must have been a happy time for him, because in less than a year he also married a very beautiful girl, from an American family with Canadian roots and royalist leanings. They quickly produced one child—me, a thin,

13

yellowish baby with the curious deformity of two left feet. But at that point Aunt's story lost momentum. Shortly after my birth on Walla, my mother died. She had not died of anything particular, Aunt said; she just died. That sometimes happened. Probably a fever, she conceded when pressed.

My father lost heart. He returned to Ontario with the squalling baby me under his arm and settled down to accomplish nothing much in life. Toronto relations being either too ancient or too masculine for the job of looking after a widower and left-footed babe, Aunt had uprooted herself from her village near Hull and accepted the post as caretaker in the new world. Out of her trunk she unpacked Swedish exercise clubs and spinsterish pride. She took pains to remind me of my heritage. While my father's sculptures of Greek goddesses gloomed in the halls, Aunt hung lurid prints of nursery rhymes in my room. My early fears were peopled with the old woman beating all her children at the toe of the shoe, the Knave of Hearts running off with the tarts, Polly Flinders among the cinders, and a most macabre Humpty Dumpty toppling to his death. I grew quite attached to these unhappy people and took their woes to heart. Aunt read me Dickens till she was hoarse. London seemed to me more real than any place in Canada. Aunt heard this reprovingly but admitted, "It is."

Aunt had little interest in and no answers about my feet. "Nature's way of doing things that day," she said, running a washcloth between my two sets of toes all pointing east.

"Did I inherit them from someone?" I persisted.

"Not that I would know of. Character and reputation—those are what you should concern yourself with, Viola, not which side your toes are on."

Still, my feet were in fact something of a handicap, and the reason much later that I met Harry Bagg. As a child I learned to walk straight by overstressing the motion of my right leg. Running and games of tag were less possible, hopscotch being the only sport in which I excelled. An orthopedic specialist in Toronto who studied my feet with profound silence, finally declared, "They're not even the *same* foot. They are two completely *different* left feet! This one has wide spacing, and this one's a thin, bony thing with poorly articulated metatarsals." He had been eating peppermint, which I smelled on his breath as he accused me, "This defies the binary principle of human genetics!"

"Whatever that means," said Aunt. "My goodness!"

"It means," he almost shouted at us, "things are supposed to come in pairs! Your feet, your hands, your ears are all mirror images of each other! It's one of life's organizing principles!"

"It's not my fault," I reminded them.

"Can't something be done?" asked Aunt. She was looking around at cases of pointed instruments and was worrying, I knew, of the train we'd have to catch, of my father's pork chops still to be cooked. She found me a toffee in a corner of her pocketbook, as the doctor, shaking his head, fitted me out with a brace that wrapped around my arch, ankle, and calf, and provided some false toes that flexed on the outside of my foot.

This worked in principle but proved a problem at shoe stores. "I'm not about to pay for one pair size three medium and the other four extra wide just so that brace can get its own shoe," Aunt whispered emphatically when the salesman had gone behind the curtain for another pair. "You'll make do with what Nature intended." Thereafter in shoe stores I tried on only the left shoe, one size too large, and bought the pair. At home we stuffed tissue paper into the toes of the other shoe so that it more or less fitted, and from the outside no one suspected the cause of my slight limp and tendency to fall sideways. The procedure planted in my mind my lifelong desire to disappear into the world's mirroring regularity.

If my feet were an immediate worry, Aunt's short, flat statements of fact concerning my parents' early life comprised the mystery of my childhood. I studied a picture of Mother in the locket I kept in a match-box, the only piece of her jewelry I owned. Her features seemed strange and delightful; I had inherited my father's family's dark hair and gray eyes, designed for a mundane and practical life, whereas Mother's bright face radiated faith in high ideals. Her father had been an American. Perhaps it was her American blood, I thought, all that extra oxygen of freedom and democracy, that accounted for her beauty. I set my hopes on her light hair and robin's-egg eyes. She seemed a creation of spun sugar, what we called grandma's hair, all sweet and brittle pastels.

Her picture, exemplifying Beauty, led me into friendship with Felicity MacIntosh. Born in East Anglia, at the source of all the red, Felicity had come at the age of seven to Heino and Gudrun Brenneke, who farmed wheat and raised pigs outside of town. Felicity was termed a Home Child, an English orphan adopted by Canadians in those years to save them from the streets. When she sat in the desk behind mine in grade two, I fell in love and immediately brought her home to show her off to Aunt. "She looks identical," I insisted, holding out the locket miniature to Aunt for comparison.

The childless Brennekes, filing their application for a Home Child, had expected a muscular boy to help with the livestock. They readjusted however. Mrs. Brenneke braided ribbons through Felicity's yellow hair. Mr. Brenneke read English books aloud to her; he had a taste for Shakespeare and Walter Scott. In short order Felicity learned the Brennekes's Prussian dialect. Perched on a volume of *Duden's Encyclopedia* at mealtime, she said grace: *Danket dem Herrn, denn Er ist immer so freundlich* . . . She told me she prayed at night for Sir Robert Borden, King Edward, and the Kaiser.

Aunt encouraged our friendship. As a rule, there were no occasions at our house; everything that would ever happen had already done so. Holidays, marked by the bellhop and three chambermaids with custard creams and shiny party hats and streamers roaming the corridors and smashing the gong, were passed by us in gray idleness. On Christmas Day my father went out as usual and returned past my bedtime, leaving Aunt and me to broil a tired chicken and silently fletcherize. But when Felicity visited, Aunt spread out a tablecloth and baked a cake. Craving sweets in those days, I held vigil in the kitchen, ready to mix batter and lick spoons and oversee the addition of the maple syrup, its secret, wonderful ingredient. Aunt predictably underbaked, burned, or omitted something, so the Empire Cake she offered my friend was more a curiosity and symbol of welcome than an item for consumption. I felt grateful to Aunt for trying.

"Tell about the cake," I urged.

Aunt obliged. Empire Cake was a family secret, devised by my grandmother, mother's Canadian mother, before confederacy. She had been a girl at the time of the Prince of Wales's first trip abroad. He had been but a young man himself and made a great impression in Ontario with his good humor and energy. My grandmother offered a recipe of her own devising to celebrate his arrival in our town. The Prince took several slices.

"Tell Felicity what he said," I prompted Aunt.

"He said, 'And who is the great bakeress?' And then Viola's granny stepped forward. 'Sir,' she said and curtsied. 'And what do you call it?' he said. 'I call it Empire Cake, sir, in honor of your inspection of this part of the Empire.' And the Prince said, 'Jolly good,' and then he said, 'I want the receipt. I shall have this in Windsor on my return to remind me of the potential that lies in Canada.'"

"Is that how royalty really talks?" asked Felicity. She had the kind of face that never changed expression. She also seemed indifferent to the cake's condition. Grateful, Aunt and I often invited her over after school. Once Aunt made the mistake of asking our guest to say grace. *"Danket dem Herrn . . ."* Felicity began. "Quite," interrupted Aunt, absentmindedly buttering my friend's toast. "And I'm sure any words will reach the right ears." That was in 1912, before the Kaiser had made trouble and our town, Bremen, had to be renamed Balmoral.

The Brenneke's stiff little pony usually fetched Felicity all by himself when the school bell rang, but when I was expected, Mr. Brenneke drove the wagon down and, grunting at our weight, heaved us up onto the rig beside him. Ordering our boots off at the door, Mrs. Brenneke, angular in an apron, met us, list in hand. We had to polish copper bowls, dig wax stubs out of candlesticks, haul out garbage to their sullen hog, Cassandra, whose prickly face reminded me of Mr. Brenneke's own. I felt overworked but useful on their farm. Time hurried them hard.

Christmas 1912. The Brennekes's scrubbed kitchen table turned into a factory of confections. My passion for sweets met with hard tempta-tion as Felicity and I constructed a gingerbread house, dipping tooth-picks into colored sugar to draw the tiles of the roof. Mr. Brenneke, with his whiskers and barn smell, spent the afternoon trudging around in his boots, banging at the walls with a hammer.

"Bad news from the Fatherland," Felicity remarked. Tasting tiling-sugar on a fingertip, she looked up. "Germany," she explained, just a shade sarcastic at my confusion.

On Saturdays, under a rosebush in the schoolyard, Felicity and I pulled down rosehips from the stalks above, poked twigs into them and made stick dolls with round red heads. On one such Saturday morning my Hermione was hopping along, hop hop hop, humming "Rule Britannia," and chanced upon Felicity's Frau Ilse, who was very stylish in a broad-brimmed maple-leaf hat. Frau Ilse, in greeting, made a curtsy, which, being too violently gracious, broke my lady's twig back. *"Ach,"* cried Frau Ilse. *"Ach, du lieber!"* Hopping up and down in panic, Frau Ilse fractured both legs.

Our game was suddenly not fun. I picked off Hermione's head and chewed the bitter fruit. In silence Felicity dug a shallow grave and stuck Frau Ilse in. It was 1913. Sir Robert Borden had returned from London. Factories were dying huge lots of khaki, and men walked about, conscious of their newly measured, vulnerable physiques.

We became serious and productive that year. In school we learned to turn a heel and count off stitches. Miss Tillotson had even the boys knitting scarves. Every Wednesday evening, Aunt buttoned up in her warm coat and walked down to her meeting of the Daughters of the Empire. They were large, serious ladies, intent on rolling bandages and sniffing out spies. They had furious teeth and heavy shoes that left black prints in the snow.

Easter 1914. I carried home eggs colored by the Brennekes and placed them in a bowl. Felicity and her mother, working with tiny brushes plucked from Cassandra's back, had painted motifs—gold stars, gold candles—over the Prussian blue. The eggs shone like precious gems in our white enamel bowl, the prettiest sight in the house.

"But impractical," Aunt said, collecting up the eggs with both fists. "What's happened to that nice Jenny Abbott at school?"

My father suddenly stepped into the room, carrying a newspaper, which I knew was a disguise, for he must have been listening. "We can't have you going to and fro with that family. They could be spies."

I stared: my father, holding his newspaper upside down and telling me that Felicity who painted Easter eggs would sabotage a submarine, and Aunt, looking down with a sad remoteness, as frail and misled as women in the Dickens novels she read. I saw it suddenly. The Empire had got hold of them; they were washed in red.

As I declared loyalty to my friend, Aunt and her associates tried to lure Felicity away from Brenneke dangers. They offered her piano lessons with Frieda McKay, Miss Tillotson's married sister. And they used me as bait; Felicity must come as often as she liked, Aunt insisted, tucking her second-best quilt around my mattress. Felicity often spent Friday night with me, and I would walk her home on Saturday, stopping on the way for a half-hour of skating on the Brennekes's secluded pond.

The Daughters of the Empire joined the effort to save my friend from the Huns. Aunt escorted Felicity and me one chill April night to their Wednesday meeting. The ladies had taped posters around the hall showing unsexed Anglo-Saxons in helmets. Mrs. McKay played "Once to Every Man and Nation" like a dirge. Clearly the Daughters of the Empire knew which was the good, which the evil side. Someone urged Felicity to describe to the gathered her hometown, hoping to spark some patriotism, but when she began telling how she'd wrapped up her feet in newspaper against the snow, Mrs. McKay took charge and struck an F-major chord, and a stoutly off-key "God Save the King" silenced the speaker. Felicity smoldered beside me, eyes level and unrelenting. The hotel's cook passed around hickory-nut coffee. By accident or design, we girls were also given mugs; I sipped adulthood—acrid, hot, compromising. Coward or convert, I held my mug up to my face and mouthed the words.

It's not easy to share a quilt with someone when you're no longer on speaking terms. All night Felicity lay facing the wall while I lay facing the door. The next morning, grip in hand, ice skates around her neck, she announced she would be returning home posthaste. That was the actual expression she used, a legacy of the Brennekes's reading.

"But," I began, trying to hold her back. "I'm coming skating."

"Next Saturday," she said. Her squint unnerved me past argument.

Rain was hazing the air, and the street lamps, still lit, cast the stone storefronts along Main Street in woolly grayness. Felicity, in her best gray cloak, refused my offered raincoat and started off, arms swinging fiercely, as if we'd never been friends. Later in the morning, burning toast, Aunt called her a spoiled, willful girl, and I invited Jenny Abbott over, out of spite.

I did go skating with Felicity, for one last and memorable time, but more disturbing even than falling through ice on the following Saturday was standing in the street outside my front door that morning, watching my friend disappear, unprotected, in the drizzle, black ice skates looped over her neck like dead birds. In my rejected raincoat, head and hands warm in red flannel lining, I stood by, full of hurt at her arm-swinging stride out of town, as she left me gas-shadowed to take up my life as a colony—and wonder how my mother's pastel picture had betrayed me.

World Without Men

*B*EFORE THE ARMISTICE, my town of Bremen was a world without men. Women operated the trolleys, ushered you to your seat in the cinema, peeled off dollar bills behind glass at the bank, while small girls nursed gruesomely wounded dolls. The few old men and boys around town seemed like discount merchandise, no good for fighting or feeding families. For Jenny Abbott and me, it was the best time we'd known; we planned our bright careers.

At home, Aunt took charge as my father's silence had become a philosophical position. No one needed an architect in the war years, and though Father went out every day in his suit, he looked insincere; his face twitched, his unbrushed hair stood on end, his interpretation of shaving made islands of whiskers over his cheeks and patchy scabs on his chin. Clearly he expected no clients. His briefcase, I knew from snooping, was weighted with not blueprints but luridly colored cook-books. It was a hungry time.

I rejoiced when he stayed out late. Aunt and I then had the run of the house. Sometimes I could persuade her to wear the necklace she had recently inherited from Great-Aunt Eustacia in Toronto, the matriarch of my father's family. When her sons emigrated to Upper Canada, she had followed, to keep them in line, and had brought with her the strand of heavy amber, which was passed down the female line and comprised the family jewels.

Not much pleased Aunt, but she did like the ambers. Together we fingered them in their box. Like glass drawer knobs and a china washbasin painted with daffodils, they were the stuff of my earliest memories of Toronto visits. Taller than any of her sons, and resembling the Eiffel Tower, Great-Aunt Eustacia caused even wayward Cousin Rudolph to jump to his feet when she entered a room. All my family's tightly strung pride had hung suspended in the folds of her neck. This strand of dark amber, the color of apricot jam, was twenty inches long and lustrous from lifetimes of service. Great-Aunt Eustacia had inherited them, Aunt told me, from a grandmother who had married a Prussian merchant who had bought them from a trader who knew the man who had unearthed them from a primeval Baltic forest, and had passed them dutifully down the female line, along with heart murmurs and literal-mindedness. Each bead seemed to signify, sufficient unto itself, some virtue: poise, wisdom, gravity. And strung together they gathered a force as mighty as the red moons of Jupiter.

The ambers were a match for any occasion. I remembered Aunt Eustacia lifting them up and letting them drop, clacking darkly together, to emphasize her breathy imperviousness to chaos. The motion seemed to say that she ran the family, if not the world. She squeaked them quietly with a twist as she studied a birth announcement. She tugged them in a circle around her neck as she explained, leaning back in a deck chair, the exact kinship remove of Cousin Rudolph to myself. As I took a nearsighted look at the insects trapped inside, she would watch me through lids at half-mast and comment, "Those creatures got caught in there thousands of years ago, like the poor people at Pompeii." Not every bead, but perhaps every third contained evidence of a long lost insect kingdom—sometimes a wing or claw only, sometimes the entire crouched creature, perhaps a soldier in mid-battle or a worker with foodstuff still between its teeth, preserved for eternity by the drop of resin that, honeylike, had trapped it in its empire under glass.

"They're not a precious stone, not like diamond," Aunt advised me, carefully coiling the beads into their box, "but they have intrinsic value." She meant, I felt, a force kept in check, visible but protected in its power. Intrinsic value, her lowered eyes suggested, belonged also to our female line.

Aunt more than deserved the beads. Always fearful of her brother's intellect and proud of his black moods, she made it her job to spare me from him. She would whisper over her stack of ironing, "He's just re-

turned. He's overtired. If you want to play, go out the back door—now."
Overtired was her code word for foul-tempered, as if she could excuse her brother's moods by some virtuous fault like overwork. She never complained, but seemed rather to expect his pointed silence at meals and find it the way of all men. She had never married and regarded men, I imagined, like modern art—inevitable but not to her taste.

Aunt thrived on duty. Bosomless, she looked like a child in the beads, but on those evenings when my father stayed out, she wore them as if they were a seal of office. At an early age I decided that good and evil, friend and foe, were easily distinguished along gender lines, but the discriminating virtues in the beads' wearer could ward off all danger. Thus decorated and alone in a state of heady potential, we did little more than roll bandages and knit scarves, but the air in the parlor seemed wide open for democracy.

Aunt had run our house with deference, walking sideways around my father, but during the war she came into her own. Always efficient but socially shy, she now held Empire meetings in our own parlor and found a career in good works. The pressure of national emergency quickened her fingers as she turned heels of countless khaki socks. And rationing made bloom a hidden talent for improvisation. Aunt reveled in hardship; her spirits rose with adversity. It seemed that life held a purpose for her at last beyond her timid housekeeping. People noticed her on the street as if she had been an old movie suddenly colorized.

My own life's goal at that time was to find a friend like spun sugar. It was not Jenny Abbott's fault to be on the winning side in a tale that favored the underdog, and Jenny matched up to my specifications— strawberry blonde, though her eyes were deep olive green. Her narrow, solemn face promised respectability despite occasional irreverent remarks. She had a small, sweet voice and a stillness admired by adults. A bonus for me, Jenny was fatherless. I hung back from houses in which fathers returned all of a sudden from work, called for their family's attention, swung the children around, charging the air with their largeness. Visits to Jenny's house held no threat of male intrusion. We turned her dollhouse into a hospital for the wounded and played undisturbed all afternoon and into evening's dark.

Mrs. Abbott ran the family bakery. A feisty widow, she prettified her force with a piping of sugar. There was something regimented about mother and daughter; they wore matching sailor dresses all year round. Even their little baked goods, the rows of chocolate cookies and ladyfingers and eccles cakes, lined themselves up on trays, ready for maneuvers. How could Mrs. Abbott have laid her hands on so much sugar in wartime? Despite rationing she made bloom like easy creations from a magician's hat the sweets that gained her bakery fame and caused my own hungry, wakeful mind to wander at night over the vision of cupcakes, doughnuts, marble cake, cookies under the display case.

Crossing through the bakery on our way upstairs to Jenny's room of an afternoon, I was snared in a complex web of sensation—coffee and hot milk and melting chocolate and lemon, draping me like elegant, invisible robes. Under the display counter, the creamy centers of eclairs hung in eggy suspension, firm, cool dollops under glossy chocolate awnings, the Black Forest cake opening up in symmetrical wedges, revealing its spongy middle, and sugar cookie upon sugar cookie, lightly scattered with jimmies, ready to give of itself with a hard crunch and melting crumb.

When invited by Jenny's mother, very occasionally and always without warning, to pick a treat, *one* treat, a kind of paralysis gripped me. I could hardly decide, so overwhelming the choices, so strong my desire. To pick one seemed almost greater torture than to have been denied all. I might have disciplined myself against all inclination, to stroll by the counters without a glance on my way upstairs, but the encouragement—obligation, really—to choose one, only one, kept revving the engines of desire. Time and again I experienced what seemed a cruel trick: first the magic of the bakery's aromas—confectioners' sugar, lemon, egg white, ground hazelnut—and then the grateful excitement at being allowed to choose by Mrs. Abbott's regimented gesture, then the unexpected, inexplicable confusion of disappointment when, having licked a greedy tongue through the jam of a filled doughnut, the choice had been made, my sweet was in hand, and I had once again lost access to that sugary wonderland. Its power under glass mocked me instead. I learned only in later years that complete denial could be more freeing than allowing oneself even one small bite, but I paid a price for that lesson.

Mrs. Abbott, like a dachshund after weasels, coveted my family's Empire Cake. Perhaps she encouraged Jenny's friendship with me in the hopes of one day securing the recipe. "Your aunt's not much for kitchenry, eh?" she would suggest sweetly, holding a tray of day-old doughnuts under my nose. "Now, it's cinnamon she uses. Isn't it?"

I warned Aunt, "If you're out for spies . . . look in Abbott's Bakery."

Aunt ignored this. Deep in her bones she believed in genetic superiority; she regarded blonde Jenny as an ideal friend for me and kept close tabs on Mrs. Abbott's intentions for Jenny's future. A year into the war, our schooling had become a problem. Miss Tillotson had enlisted in the Red Cross and was sent off to France. The school found a series of part-timers, but it was like trying to get an education in the lobby of a bank, with a new teacher revolving in, printing her name on the blackboard, and revolving out again. After close consultation, Mrs. Abbott and Aunt sent us up to Morcombe's School for Girls in Toronto, where we boarded during the week and came back on the train Friday evening.

The school accommodated twenty girls from good families. It was run in an upright old house by spinster triplets, the Misses Morcombe. Miss Faith Morcombe, headmistress, taught English, history, and piano, Miss Hope Morcombe sewing and chemistry, and Miss Charity Morcombe, who had a secret passion for chewing gum, French and basketball. The girls who had gone before us, in loose dresses, hair in buns, featured in photographs of the basketball teams lining the walls, had all settled down as wives to men in the professions, but in the unmanned landscape of the war years, Jenny and I gave little thought to marriage. We wanted to work. The idea of wearing suits to an office and earning money seemed an exotic adventure, and to that end we spent much post–lights-out time in a closet, practicing shorthand.

When Mr. Lydgate hired us that summer for his law firm, long days and dull memos had no place in the fantasy of independence Jenny and I wove for ourselves over malteds on our lunch break. We had joined the company of women who were holding the fort. Newsreels extolled our commitment and dedication. We compared favorably to the women pictured on war posters with their hair bound in scarves.

But for us the war came to an end all too soon. In the summer of

1919 Jenny and I were ex-stenogs, replaced by the boys in khaki who were given first dibs at employment. We tossed about for other occupations. Jenny occasionally helped at Abbott's, but her mother felt that a Morcombe's education placed Jenny beyond the shop. We tried our best to be useful: we helped Aunt entertain uniformed stragglers with tea in tiny cups whose overly pink roses we'd painted ourselves. Yawns lengthened our faces as we nodded helpfully at their plans to raise pigs now that they were home again. As Mr. Lydgate would not take us back though we begged, we hung in a limbo between postwar parlor efforts and petit point. In desperation we looked for something—*anything*— new to do.

It was Jenny's idea, not mine, one day the following spring, to borrow the black Ford car parked outside Mr. Lydgate's office. We were ambling through the town center with a swish discouraged at Morcombe's, edgy with energy, foot to the gas but going nowhere. At the newly updated war memorial, we stopped and took an appraising look. Most towns had not set up memorials yet; ours was way ahead, thanks to a local family whose artist son had already finished commissions in Toronto. Bremen's—now Balmoral's—memorial was tastefully small. A boy cast in bronze leaned vacant-eyed over a gun, his flat helmet tipped to one side. He was mounted on a pedestal that tilted slightly in earth newly disturbed, planted round with petunias. A plaque at the bottom catalogued in block letters the names of our region's dead.

I'd been to the unveiling the week before, a ceremony that had included music by three men in kilts who tangled up their music stands but eventually provided the crowd with "Keep the Home Fires Burning" and other cheerless tunes. Amidst that patriotic fervor, as the mourning Mrs. McMurphy laid a wreath of evergreens at the base of the memorial, I thought of her son Tommy's scaly eyelids. In grade four he had proudly turned them inside out for any watching girls. Alive, Tommy might have grown up to plow corn fields or wash dishes; dead, he claimed our full, all-stops-out grief. Why did we honor him so?—and yet we did. I had caught my balance on Aunt's thick arm; I had a sense that the world was tipping and tilting underfoot, that what we held for true was not and maybe Aunt's steadfast faith in the war could explain this paradox. But Aunt looked only mournful and proud and not in a mood to discuss it. The mayor, meanwhile, voice still weak from a bout of flu, spoke of Tommy McMurphy's heroism. I listened carefully for clues to the mystery of hero-making. His words made me proud for that moment of the very earth on which I stood. His rhetoric nudged aside the niggling knowledge that Canada was only a dominion. On that day patriotic fervor seemed sufficient unto itself.

Helping in her mother's shop in preparation for the post-unveiling mob, Jenny had missed the ceremony. When we stopped on that idle day a week later to inspect the memorial, she gave the pedestal a kick and murmured, "Blotto."

I took a more critical look at the soldier. "Just demented," I decided, "like most boys that age."

Satisfied, we moved on. The yearning-to-be-test-driven Ford car was parked off the square, directly in our path as Jenny and I strolled up the sidewalk. It was a huge piece of shiny black transportation, with delicate balloon tires. We patted the hood, warm from the sun. We peeked through an open window and breathed like smelling salts the scent of rich leather upholstery.

"Lydgate's nephew," said Jenny, always a font of doughnut-coaxed information. "Junior's joining the firm. There're the keys. On a pink rabbit's foot."

I looked at Jenny; we looked at each other; a new world beckoned. Why not? No one was going to buy us a car, give us a job, or help us toward a life of any interest whatsoever. This knowledge gnawed at us and, like some worm in the brain, disturbed our judgment. We slid onto the slippery seats. Jenny claimed the driver's spot by virtue of having once been driven in a cousin's car. For me, the sensation was all new. As Jenny inspected the crank at the front end, I jiggled up and down, entranced by the springy seats, the tiny vase in which was shriveling a rosebud, the isinglass windows that redecorated the outside world in elegant shades.

With just a few false starts, Jenny impressed me by cranking up the engine.

"Where to?" she cried.

"Anywhere!" Anywhere; the world outside the windshield seemed smoky and tranquil, untouched by drying sun and dwindling time.

"Watch out!" my friend declared. She sounded unlike herself, older and brassy. Which may have been the result of something in the car itself. Within a minute, we knew our Ford car was possessed by evil spirits. It reared up and out of its parking spot into King Street, bounced by a milk wagon, scaring the driver, and then took the bit in its teeth. Jenny could do nothing but give it its head as the demon car steered right over the curb onto the grassy square. It was clearly set on flattening several stands of daffodils under its patterned tires. Jenny whooped in distress. I made a grab at the wheel and, failing to gain control, stomped Jenny's foot on the brakes hard. But the car had targeted the unknown soldier and took off full tilt. Nothing could arrest our breakneck charge across the square—except an obstacle of brass and stone newly planted in the center.

Amid sudden silence, broken glass, wheels spinning, up-ended, we came to a stop. We were sitting sideways, high up above the lawn. A look down showed the bronze young man who stood for all young men who had given their lives for us in the Great War, now lying completely horizontal. And through smoke Mr. Lydgate, his nephew, and several other citizens were striding our way, faces full of the God-awful truth.

It was a tactless accident. Father locked the door to his study and refused to speak to me. I sat on a low hassock in the front parlor and listened to Aunt's complaints as she sewed summer slipcovers. A row of pins between her lips gave her the look of a martyr to some strange domestic torture. "Vizzy," she said, voice muffled, "you're getting wild."

"Yes," I agreed. I sat with my arms clasped tightly around my knees. I was worried about myself.

"What are we going to do with you? What? Tell me."

"I don't know," I confessed. "Send me up to Toronto?"

She sniffed. "You'll stay right here, where Aunt can keep an eye on you."

Jenny and I were not permitted to meet for a month. Forbidden even to venture out of the hotel, I spent my days roaming our three rooms, looking out the window, rereading about the unhappy childhoods of characters in Dickens, playing solitaire.

Meanwhile, however, in the Abbott's bakery, plans were fomenting. One afternoon I chanced to overhear a conversation between Aunt and Mrs. Abbott, who had stopped by with day-old bread for Aunt's pudding. They had met at the hotel kitchen's back door, and on my way to check our pantry for fruit, I heard Mrs. Abbott's sweetly emphatic voice rising up to me. She was telling Aunt, "It's my late husband's cousin Emma, on an island not far from India. Her husband's ex-army, a photographer on an *excavation*. So exciting! She wrote—I have the letter in the shop—Jenny and some friend might like a *working holiday*. An archaeological dig in progress needs girls for typing, steno. A place called Wallawalhalla."

At the name, my heart jumped inside my chest. *Wallawalhalla.* Blood pounded so hard in my ears I could scarcely hear. Through the rush of pulse, I listened for Aunt's reply. She sounded dubious as she asked, "What's this place like?" I heard more in this question than Mrs. Abbott could. Wallawalhalla—mythical in my childish mind, the island where so long ago my then unthinkably young parents had met, where I'd been born, where my mother had died. Her locket miniature was my only link to her story. Now Walla's name filled me with a yearning that made me tremble.

"Quite tolerable climate, I understand," Mrs. Abbott was saying. "There's a volcano. Some trouble with ash in the air. Rumors of white ants. No natives—they all left for better climes years ago. And now a rich American has organized a dig. Hopes to find—some utopia, I believe that's the word. They still need women to do the paperwork. Personally, Miss Monroe . . ." Mrs. Abbott's voice sounded a note of criticism. "It might not be a bad thing at all for these girls to travel, to see something of the Empire, work for their keep."

"Hmm," said Aunt. From my listening post, I heard budging and rejoiced.

Over Friday's dinner of cheesed broccoli the topic eventually came up. Father and Aunt had apparently already discussed and approved of the scheme. A letter had gone out to Walla. Jenny and I were to live with Mr. and Mrs. Borders, members of the dig. They could provide us with a comfortable room and meals in exchange for part of our salaries, and could be counted on to chaperone appropriately. "This is necessary," Aunt explained with cautious, hiccoughing animation, "because of all the men around." I tried my best to look solemn, hesitant, responsible.

Up in my room, I pulled all my shoes from my closet and with wild tears began packing.

Just before I left, Aunt surprised me by coming into my room one evening, holding the family ambers up between her hands as if she'd never seen them before. "Take them," she mumbled.

"But aren't you going to wear them still?"

"I'll be going back home now, what with you grown up. Who else would I leave them to? You might as well have them now."

They were as heavy as a line of jellyfish. I held them carefully, but could not bring myself yet to put them on. As a small girl, I had longed for the day when I would clasp around my neck those mysterious, honey-colored stones. When Aunt handed the beads over, however, on the eve of my grown-up life, which would for the first time include men, the beads' glow seemed to emanate less from the magic of their contents than from the power claimed for them through close propinquity to aunt after aunt. With the help of those beads, I felt sure that I could take on the search for the mother I imagined all in white, leaning like a Sargent lady against a mirrored mantel; I could handle the contingencies of grown-up life, and take on those errant creatures—men.

I was glad to be wearing the necklace the first night on the train. Jenny and I were traveling unchaperoned from Dundas to Vancouver, a journey of many days on our own recognizance. Two young women, struggling with hat boxes, were fair game to strangers. If ready to try out Fords at home, I relied on the respectability of my necklace as we swayed upright that first night. I felt its weight and remembered Great-Aunt Eustacia's patient explanation of the family tree that always seemed like some magical plant. I counted on the power and shaded protection of my breeding.

At exactly six o'clock, Jenny and I balanced down a tightrope of corridor to the dining car and collapsed at the first empty table. Ontario passed by our window, but I was more interested in our fellow travelers. Across the aisle two gentlemen, already seated, glanced at us with a look I took for chivalry; they were there for us. I touched my beads.

Fresh trout was featured on the menu. I assured the waiter I'd have the fish. I ordered spinach to impress him. Jenny, on the other hand, flipped to the dessert list. Crème caramel, she announced, fruit soup, then apple torte à la mode. I blushed for the waiter, but he jotted down her requirements without comment.

When I saw my plate, I picked at the spinach as my friend spooned into cherry soup. My sole comfort was that the gentlemen across from us also had trout on their plates. In quick feints I observed them. The younger, a wearer of gold-rimmed spectacles, wiped gravy from his moustache like someone sealing an envelope. He spoke to the elder traveler with such politeness his lips hardly moved. The older gentleman gave slight nods. They leaned toward each other, discreet to a fault: I caught not a whisper of their talk. This behavior was too well-bred for businessmen, I decided. The younger man's long fingers tapped the napkin at a spot of water on his trousers with a particularness that confirmed my suspicions: they must be scholar colleagues, or uncle and nephew of independent means. They pursued some hobby like geology that obliged them to travel west.

I felt fortunate to have spotted them. Their presence, even as strangers, reassured me. A single man traveling alone would have remained closed to us, even suspect, but these two, revealing their niceness in conversation together, seemed as upright as the columns of a bank. We could lean on them. They would be our refuge in times of baggage mix-ups, etcetera.

I tried to convey this happy news to Jenny, but my friend was busy digging through caramel. I sighed a weary Aunt Eustacia sigh. My gentlemen, meanwhile, exsected bones from their fish, and I realized things were changing. Nineteen years old, in heirloom jewelry, I was leaving behind youthful folly and heading out toward life. The path was as clear and measured and straight as the tracks now bearing us toward Manitoba's pastures.

Our tall waiter returned as I was savoring this new maturity. He set down Jenny's order of apple pie and turned to our gentlemen's table. The elder gentleman discreetly slid some bank notes onto the waiter's salver and dismissed him with a nod. I guessed the tip was generous by the way the waiter bore it out, draped like the sacraments.

Two minutes later, though, he was back, with the conductor puffing up behind. Their voices, too low to understand, confronted my favored pair. The uncle spotted his forehead with a napkin, a gaucherie

I forgave but noted. Strain, I saw, was hardening the nephew's features; his expensive spectacles slid down his nose unchecked.

Heart racing, I sought Jenny's eye. She raised her fork in slow motion as we monitored the events unfolding. First, the waiter, who, I noted weirdly, with his brush of black hair bore a strong resemblance to my Cousin Rudolph, lifted up a lavender bank note. It was a ten-dollar bill bearing King George's profile. Rudolph held it like a dirty sock and shook it. The nephew looked away. Then, dipping the money into a water glass, Rudolph rubbed the paper across the tablecloth. The conductor growled. What I saw I stared at, trying to understand a way around it. There by the saltcellar was a short purple smear. The uncle was staring at it, too, but the nephew jerked his head abruptly toward the window, which now featured only twilight. Guided to his feet by the conductor's grip on lapels, the uncle sputtered some pink indignation that all of us watching saw through. The nephew followed him, escorted, up the aisle, face as sealed as a casket.

"Counterfeiters," whispered Jenny. "What a swell adventure!"

I smiled vaguely, inwardly appalled. Only moments before, two wealthy gentlemen had sat offering us protection with their good manners. Now their napkins lay on top of their plates, soaking up lemon and tartar sauce. The short, straight smudge—the remains of King George's face—connected a water goblet and a saltcellar in a meaningless dot-to-dot. Of all the passengers on board I might have picked for solace, I had settled on two well-dressed swindlers. This knowledge disturbed me deeply. The tracks rushing under me felt like carpet swept from beneath my feet in some cruel magic trick. I sensed for the first time the danger of my own bad judgment. And I blamed the beads. They had me by the throat.

3

Wallawalhalla

A New Life

⸎

W ALLAWALHALLA ARCHED UP on the horizon like a whale out of
the water, a little volcano of courage in the vast Indian Ocean,
spouting fountains of a mind-stripping sulfur stink toward us. We had
docked in Bombay and disembarked from the vast *Empress of Canada*,
changing onto a sturdy little freighter on which we were wedged among
mailbags, mail-order furniture, and crates of potatoes bound for Walla.
Though the crossing in the lush liner had offered many comforts, Jenny
and I had hoped to lose some of our fellow travelers in India. No such
luck. The pinch-faced little boy, who on board had lingered with intent,
mounted the gangplank with his war-torn nanny right ahead of us, on
their way to Walla, too. As were the young men who shuffled and gig-
gled as we tried to pass. But the last leg of the journey, if uncomfortable
and peopled by ex-pats, provided the excitement of arrival. On deck
that afternoon, Jenny and I held down our hats in the warm sulfur wind
and watched with pride as the little bulge grew larger: our island! our
paradise! our new-found land!

As we churned nearer, inch by inch, the sea that swirled beneath
the metal sides of our ship changed from a deep violet to patchy greens
and browns. We worked into the harbor, the mouth just deep enough for
our boat, into a pure, clear blue so crystalline that beneath the surface
we could watch the course of orange fish flirting with our barnacles.

During the trip from Bombay, we had struck up casual acquaintance with the man acting as purser, one Harry Bagg, a tall and private
man, who we knew was somehow attached to the Walla excavation. He
leaned on the rail near us during docking operations and recited with a
crooked smile: "'Yonder lies our young sea-village . . . Art and Grace are

less and less: Science grows and Beauty dwindles . . . roofs of slated hideousness!' Not to mention the stench."

"Oh," I said, undeterred in my enthusiasm, "I don't see any slate." I was determined that cynicism would not spoil our arrival. We could make out the modest skyline that was Walla Town: white wooden houses with wide porches, a small wooden church in the squared Norman style, and up on the hill a tattered windsock. And as we neared I felt a thrill of celebration as the small crowd at the dock cheered and clapped.

We swayed on tipsy sea legs down the gangplank to the dock. Jenny spotted her relations and called, "Hello, hello!" and her cousin Roddy Borders and his wife, Emma, moved forward, greeting us, stiff-handed, on schedule. They looked delicate and perfect in their tropical whites, though neither smiled; an air of ordered unhappiness hung about them. I was introduced but found myself wordless, struck dumb by Borders's elegant good looks: golden hair combed back in slow waves, eyes as blue as some frozen Ontario lake, nose and cheekbones and chin all conforming to a gentleman's agreement of chiseled perfection. By contrast, his wife seemed small and negligible. Her hair was piled up on the top of her head in an untidy knot. Her wide-set eyes pleaded, *Oh, don't look at me— Roddy's the pretty one!*

Indeed, his face held me so, that it was all I was worth to stand beside their enormous black car and pay attention to the talk. "We'll have to wait for your baggage," Borders was explaining. "That'll suit you nicely, won't it, my dear?" he shouted at his wife above the noise on the dock.

"Roddy," she tried and stopped. She disappeared behind her scarf as if in purdah.

"My wife quite admires the seafarers," Borders explained. His wife's face turned away to the sea, stone hard. He continued, however, singing, "'Never weather-beaten sail more willing . . .' Not your cup of tea, Viola?!"

"I like cars," I said with studied innocence. I heard sarcasm and taunting in his tone, yet, as if under the influence of some drug, my heart raced to the sound of his voice.

He guffawed. "So we hear!"

"Yours is a Morris Cowley?" I persisted.

"It's Miss Bartram's. Local crackpot, she is, lets me borrow it. Inherited it, as it were, from a nephew, blown up at Passchendaele."

I thought about this. "Is Miss Bartram part of the, um, excavation?"

With a disparaging action of his long throat, Borders brought up phlegm and spat. "A hanger-on. Wouldn't you say, lady-wife?"

"Personal reasons," she whispered. They both looked uncomfortable.

"She likes it here, then?" I tried out, hoping to find someone who did.

"Mmm," they said, oddly united for a moment.

Borders offered, "She's ordered a little harpsichord, against all reason. Madness at this latitude. We should see if it's come."

An alarming stream of wicker hampers and wooden crates was being pulled up by a small crane from the hull and set on the dock. How had we ever stayed afloat?

Jenny, yawning lightly, remarked, "It's like waiting for a cat to vomit some specific piece of hairball."

"She's a harmless fool, our Miss Bartram," Borders said, not having quite heard Jenny's remark.

While under the spell of his looks, which off-balanced me every time I turned to him, I suppressed my discomfort for a time at his tone. "What exactly have you dug up?" I asked my host as we waited.

"Not much. Walls, mainly. Some evidence of canals. That sort of thing. A brooch or two. Clay pipe. Hard to date. Possibly fourth century, B.C. Found some mummies a few days ago. Been dusting them down."

"Aren't mummies always in pyramids?"

"No." He tucked our arms under his and laughed gaily. "You girls! Did you chat with our archaeologist coming over on the boat? I saw him getting off with you. Bagg?"

"Mr. Bagg's the archaeologist?"

"Sam Kinver's in charge, of course, officially, but he's always running off, family matters, etcetera. He's just back from the Hebrides. Next week it's Cairo. Bagg's the brains behind the dig. Quite a crackpot on the topic. Kinver's nanny was coming over with the son, just out of school."

"Oh, we saw the nanny. That was his son?" I said.

"Spoiled little brat," said Jenny. "He tried to put mirrors under our skirts when the wind blew!"

"Poor woman won't last long. They never do. Kinver's wife has given up trying, stays at home in Arizona full-time. They've got more money than you could stuff into a mountain. Of course, what they want is some claim to good blood. Kinver goes around saying he's eighth cousin thirteen times removed to Alfred the Great, isn't that right, my dear?"

"Henry the Second."

Our suitcases finally popped out of the hull. "Going over the top," said Borders, when we pointed them noisily out. No harpsichord for Miss Bartram, but assured that the next boat would bring it, we all climbed into the car, fitted ourselves into capacious motoring robes and bonnets and set off.

High sun nearly blinded me, but I looked with excitement. The sand, grass, sea, sky swept before us in horizontals of ochres, azures, and olives. Borders pointed out the buildings: houses, post office, and little store, all left over from more languid outpost days. "Ahh! Ohh," Jenny and I murmured at these, passing like scenes in a stereopticon, with the added effects of sandy wind and sulfur heat.

All the while, a hard little substance, like a stone in the tire, clicked through the sights and voices of the ride. I knew nothing of marriages, was unaccustomed to poking behind social façades, but I felt disjuncture as we bounced along, Mrs. Borders in the backseat with Jenny and me, down the Strand Road toward their house at the very end of town. Uncle Roddy—we *must* use their Christian names—called back, falsely hearty, "Know your geography, girls?"

We demurred.

"Wallawalhalla Island is about the size of Hamilton Bay—if you can picture land as water for a moment, water as land. Been to Hamilton, you two?" he asked, referring to a steel manufacturing town south of Toronto.

"No," I emphasized.

"Yes," said Jenny.

Borders nodded, swerving around some branches. "I mention Hamilton Bay," he called back, "for the interesting reason that Walla is built on a volcanic lake. Rather deep and not the place for attractive girls to wash their . . ."

"Roddy," interrupted Mrs. Borders.

"*Stockings*. And there's Mt. Walla at the far east end, makes some little rumblings now and again. You've noticed the smell? But we're here to excavate, are we not? Kinver the American got the rights to the spot for the Arizona Museum, quite excited by some garbage pits he's uncovered. Too bad for you young ladies, dig has encroached on the old officers' club."

Leaning forward, I asked timidly, "What do you *do* exactly on the dig? Just dig?"

"Me? Photographer. Bagg sketches the finds, but I have to get shots of everything *in situ*. Nothing moves till I've got it on celluloid. Show you my new Kodak. Like to pose for me, girls? Fancy yourselves as pin-ups?"

Embarrassed, we said nothing, though the thought of that handsome man taking my picture, his ice-blue eye trained on me through a camera lens, filled me with a certain horrified excitement. I indulged in the fantasy until Emma Borders broke the silence with a burst of energetic chat. Tightening her scarf with each question, she asked mechanically: "You haven't said anything about the trip. How is your mother, Jenny? Aren't the stars magnificent at sea?"

The Strand was almost the only road on the island. As we drove along with sea grass blocking much of our view on either side, Borders pointed out Miss Bartram's cottage, a tiny pointed Gothic structure with gingerbread around the overhang. We slowed over a pothole by her gate, and a tall, wild-haired old lady shot up from behind a yew hedge, brandishing hedge clippers. "*Qui va la?*" she shouted, then stared at me hard, her smile freezing with surprise. Eyes on me, she said, "Where's my harpsichord?"

"Next boat," Borders shouted back.

She did not return our wave as Borders pumped us right into more potholes. I was wondering at her odd examination of me when a break in the trees revealed an immense square building. Part of it was a heavy sandstone structure with neoclassical proportions; figures stood around the roof. Part of it seemed more like a fortress, with heavy scaffolding at the corners.

"The old officers' club. Magnificent, no?" Borders declared.

I ventured, "Why is it covered with scaffolding?"

"Kinver's promised repairs to the building. Looks a bit like Dundurn Castle."

"My father worked as an architect here, some twenty years ago."

"Name of . . . ?"

"Monroe. Same as me." A thought occurred to me with breathless force: "Did you know him?"

"We've been here only two years," Emma Borders interjected. She seemed vaguely annoyed, and pulled her scarf more snugly around her chin as she looked out to sea.

Borders remarked, "There's some talk of a dance this Saturday, in the foyer. The rest of the place is crumbling and off-limits. These girls will be breaking more hearts than they could back in Bremen, eh, dearest?"

"I'm not sure they want to break hearts, dearest."

"Don't give me that bloody insipid talk!" Borders's roar upended us, sending spasms through my insides. "All girls are good for is breaking some hearts before they go sour."

The club moved behind us, and we rode on in stone silence. I felt ever tenser, my insides knotting hard with the unexpressed sense that we were their burden, that we would further fray an already unraveling union. But as awful as the car ride felt, at least we were stable and moving; I dreaded ever reaching our destination, fearing combustion if we stopped in one spot together. I glanced at Jenny; her jaw line was set and unmoving.

Borders pointed out the volcano, just visible as we rounded a bend. At the bottom of a hill he tooted the horn. "Here we are, girls—Egrets!" It was a wide, forbidding house with broad verandahs on two sides and a low, shading roof.

"I thought I'd put them in the green room," Aunt Emma told her husband.

I thought he had not heard until he half turned and shouted, "Then do it, do it, woman! Don't consult me about flower pots in paradise!"

Jenny and I froze. People's marriages were full of these mysteries, and I knew that what one saw were misleading shards from which one could reconstruct only vaguely the actual shape and color of the union's design. Thus, things might not be so bad as they seemed, I tried to believe as I stepped stiffly down. Still, I wished they'd keep it to themselves.

Like an octopus, Borders wrapped long arms around our suitcases and started with them fast up the steps. We mounted more slowly behind, lending a hand to the unsteady Emma. Furniture and potted plants crowded the verandah. "We had a macaw," she said, waving to an empty wicker cage. "It's better off now."

By contrast to very bright sun outside, the interior seemed remarkably underlit, shaded as it was by the verandah on three sides of the house. Inside, the air was stifling. We might have been in a crypt.

"Tea," said Aunt Emma with a small clap of her hands, which I thought at first might bring a servant but turned out only to be her own stiff display of enthusiasm. And, of course, there were no locals on Walla; no one but Canadians would live in such heat, under the constant threat of carnivorous white ants.

I hoped Emma would bring back with her something large and substantial to eat; I was famished and ready, after ship fare, for some treats. Too giddy to sit while she went off to boil water, Jenny and I paced around that very English room.

"It's like Miss Faith's study," I remarked to Jenny. I wondered if Borders had grown up in so lavish a setting, if his wife, from Montreal, weren't stretching a bit as mistress of this grandeur.

"Groan," Jenny answered with a tight grin, then, "Oh, how pretty!" bumping into the piano. As her hand fell on the first notes of a Scott Joplin tune that girls always played during lunch at Morcombe's, the familiar notes came out as "De dee de *clung*..." The piano gave a nasty reverberation at the back. Jenny tried again, "Do do *clang clung*..."

Aunt Emma hurried indirectly into the room toward Jenny. I stepped out of her way and lowered myself into a ladder-back chair. "I may not have mentioned," Aunt Emma said, breathless. "They tend to chew..." Her voice broke off with the splintering of wood; I had fallen right through the bottom of the chair. "Oh, gracious, Viola, you must be careful!"

I was only slightly bruised but felt assaulted. After an all-too-paltry cup of tea I was ready to unpack in private. Our room, airy and papered with a rosebud print that buckled and sagged just a little, gave off to the verandah, and thus afforded us a wide view of the ocean. We unpacked ourselves into invisibility in the high bureaus—bird's eye maple, brought over from Canada, lined with tin against creatures of the night. The room looked much like a room back home, caught at a moment of intensive cleaning. The four-poster bed stood away from the walls, with netting draped down from its canopy.

When Jenny and I climbed in for the night, Aunt Emma placed bowls of water at the foot of the bed. "To guard against crawling insects," she said. Outside the barred windows swung long sponges. "They're soaked in water," Emma explained. "They hang and dangle, you see, and the air picks up coolness as it flows in. Good night, girls." As an afterthought, she bent and deposited a dry kiss on each of our foreheads. "Go to sleep," she said, suddenly gruff. "Tomorrow we'll see about your jobs."

Under netting, side by Jenny's perspiring side, away from walls for the air, hoping for wind to stir those wet weeds, sinuses stripped by sulfuric air, trying to put the oddness of the place out of my mind by agreeing with Jenny about the great kindness of our hosts, I fell at last into a hungry, restless sleep and dreamed that Emma Borders was my own lost spun-sugar mother.

The following morning an unfamiliar bird's call woke me just moments before Emma brought in breakfast on small tin trays. I had pictured her more the reclining type, vaporish, arriving at equilibrium only by noon. "Is it all right?" she asked anxiously. "I'm unused to girls and their appetites and regular meals and such. You wouldn't prefer a cooked breakfast? Should I do an egg? I think we must have an egg somewhere . . ." She propped a tray on Jenny's lap set with a saucerless cup half-filled with tea only one fine shade darker than old bath water. "Your mother wrote you favored a light repast."

Aunt must have said I had a hearty appetite, for my tray was crammed with random treats, special Scottish rough-cut marmalade, gooseberry jam, and Greek honey made from thyme. Between the jars were propped three diagonally cut slices of burned bread. "This looks fine," I said with forced enthusiasm. I just felt grateful that I had not been given Jenny's tray.

My friend, poking under a large stained linen napkin, discovered her own triangle of toast. She tactfully joined in with my smiling. Aunt Emma hovered and drifted in the doorway.

"Where's Uncle Roddy this morning?" asked Jenny, chewing slowly, trying to make it last. "Taking pictures so early?"

"Oh," said Aunt Emma, as if reminded of something. "They found another mummy late yesterday. He had to go look into it. Down at the site. They haven't quite dug it up yet."

I passed some marmalade over to Jenny. "Mummies . . ." I said, half-remembering my dream.

"Let's go have a look!" Jenny cried, passing me a spoon for the honey.

Aunt Emma agreed, unsure. "Young girls need exercise. I must remember that. We can look into your jobs later. But first I want you to finish up everything on your plates."

This wasn't hard to do, unfortunately. I hoped someone else would be organizing lunch. "The toast," I ventured when we were alone, "must be a special size."

"She's preoccupied," Jenny reminded me. Evidently we were going to be gracious and discreet. I knew this was right, but it was lonely to find my partner in crime suddenly taking the ethical high road.

Later in the morning, when the sun had already turned the air heavy and yellow, Jenny, Aunt Emma, and I chaperoned each other to the site. It was a pleasant walk down the Egrets' drive, flanked by tall plants ripe and unknown to me that spread their colors over our horizon. Birds, also unfamiliar, circled and cawed overhead, gnats swarmed like low-flying clouds, and we guarded our legs against bites with chemical-smelling anti-insect wraps. After weeks at sea, it felt good to stretch my legs on solid ground, and the whiteness of the sand underfoot added a kind of magical lightness to our stride.

We followed a road that swerved picturesquely toward the club, then ended abruptly with rubble piles and a field of tarpaulined pits staked off in an enormous triangle. At the edge of the pit a small crowd had gathered, mostly ladies like ourselves whom we joined, trying to crane our necks and appear restrained at the same time. Down inside were stooped and scraping about fifteen sweat-soaked young men, while another two rolled wheelbarrows of earth up the bank. Through the dirt floor I could see the line of stone that marked the top of walls. At one end of a long pit lay a row of ancient stone coffins in various states of uncover, like holiday makers at a beach.

Kneeling over them was Borders, shiny Kodak slung on his back, measuring things with a tape. Sketching beside him was the man I recognized from the boat: Harry Bagg. Neither paid attention to the crowd; they were engaged in serious business.

I looked at the spot where the coffins lay, the dampish earth older than any of us, relentlessly silent. "What does it mean?" I whispered to Aunt Emma. "Is it important?"

Her eyes seemed broadly unfocused as she turned to me for a moment as if to brush away a mosquito. Frowning, she said, "He's muddied his shirt. I'll have to iron another when he comes back for lunch. *And* he's got a cut on his hand!"

I glanced uncomfortably at Jenny, but she was determined, it seemed, to find nothing amiss. Aunt Emma's attention to her husband's appearance was interrupted at that moment by the lady crowd.

"Riveting," said a Mrs. Tennyson, introducing herself and daughter Henrietta. She was a large woman whose corset gave her squared-off corners and a bosom like a bookshelf. Later Aunt Emma explained that she and her daughter were destitute and dependent on a son in England, but when Mrs. Tennyson and Nettie thrust themselves on us in greeting, they seemed more in command than the archaeologists. "Just got here?" Mrs. Tennyson inquired. "You'll find the pickings slim, but girls these days can't be choosy. Not after a war. I wish you both the best of luck. Nettie, you know, has already caught the eye of darling Dr. Glover."

"Sam Kinver's godson," added Nettie, buttoning on slim gloves. "He's sweet." She added, "I hope you dance. We're having a hop at the old club tonight, if you can come."

We were joined just then by Miss Bartram of the gingerbread house. Like the Tennysons and Aunt Emma, she was wearing, I noted, the long white dress, round-bosomed and lace-trimmed, of the old regime, as if there had been no war, King Edward were alive and well, and everyone still read Browning aloud. Walla time ran behind, I realized, and stretched to accommodate inclinations more readily than

North American clocks knew how. This seemed a good thing. It promised me better odds for recovering my mother's own past time.

Miss Bartram looked less wild without her pruning shears, even coolly scientific on the edge of the pit, advancing her theory: "The white ants mummified the bodies. They do things like that, having the power to paralyze. We haven't met officially," she said, singling me out. "Anthea Bartram—though I know of course who you are. Welcome to our little paradise. You must explain yourself sometime, Viola. I've had warnings about you in my tea. The white ants are preparing to swarm, Emma. They're looking for a queen, and they'll take surrogates, you know." To Aunt Emma, she advised sharply, "These girls mustn't wander about."

Nettie Tennyson, I noticed, was making rude faces behind Miss Bartram's back. Her mother answered stoutly, "Of course they are carefully chaperoned, thank you, Miss Bartram, so I don't think we'll be bothered by your ants, and now, I think we should be getting back . . ."

"You know, they took that girl hostage once," Miss Bartram insisted, turning to me. She stood so close that I could see the dark rings around her eyes' irises and her gluey eyelashes. "It was quite some time ago. Before I came out. They're due for another swarm. And of course they work in the dark. They sniff out where things are, being blind, mostly," she continued. "They're also apt to chew down living creatures, same as if a man were a leg of your piano."

"Just how big are they?" I asked.

"Miss Bartram," interjected Aunt Emma and, taking Jenny and me by the hands, tugged us away.

"Come to tea!" called Miss Bartram after us. "Especially you, Viola. I'll tell you all about our little colony."

"Don't forget the dance," Nettie reminded us.

"What time?"

She shrugged happily. "Whenever!"

The dance, Aunt Emma explained later as we fanned ourselves in the parlor after the exertion of the walk, was a little celebration to welcome the incoming boat and try out the new ladies—Jenny and me and the Kinvers's new nanny. Sam Kinver had had to import men to do the digging, mostly soldiers left over in the east after the war, about twenty of them. They were naturally pleased with mail from home and the new tins of tea, bottles of maple syrup, and jars of Robertson's marmalade sent by English cousins, and what better way to express their joy than a formal dance in stiff, hot clothes? And we would see inside the famous Wallawalhalla club, designed by my own father.

Back from the dig, bathed beyond clean, wafting a lemony fragrance about his manly person, Borders stopped into our room as we were dressing. We had little warning to cover up. Unconcerned, he flipped a tie around on itself and said, "Our club's a grand monument—one of the great architectural undertakings of the Far East. Special moment, girls!"

It was hard to tell if he were genuine or sarcastic as his voice, even shouting "Fire!" in a hotel would, I suspected, have been edged with irony. It gave him, for me, a peculiar attractiveness, seeming to indicate as it did some hidden turnings in his thinking, some closeted notions that one might open on dark hinges. I was not even deterred in my admiration when I saw his eye catch sight of his image in our dressing table's mirror and linger there a moment too long, in appreciation.

Aunt Emma scuttled in immediately behind him, newly polished shoes in hand. "I scraped most of the mud off," she apologized.

"You can see your face in *those*," I said, trying to hold him with wittiness, but my idea of a romantic hero turned with his wife without comment to complete their wardrobe next door.

Jenny and I had brought our long white graduation dresses to wear for formal occasions, and being of the old style they of course fitted right in. We helped each other with the hooks and eyes like baboons grooming, and chatted about our experiences so far. Work had been put off for more important things, and I was in no hurry, nor was Jenny, to get down to typing.

Jenny stuck some bougainvillea in her hair and studied the effect in the mirror. I clasped Aunt Eustacia's ambers round my throat. "This is it!" Jenny whispered. "Off to meet our futures!"

"Well, *maybe*," I said, stalling, but also stirred by her theatrics.

Jenny and I, joined by Aunt Emma in a fringy shawl, climbed into the backseat of Miss Bartram's car, conveniently not yet returned to her, with Borders at the wheel. Aunt Emma evidently preferred the backseat to the front, seeming to count herself among the children on board.

As we drove right through the gates I got a close-up of the much-admired club with its heavy stonework. It reminded me—and why should this come to me as a surprise?—of the hotel in Bremen in which I had grown up.

"Travelers' Arms," said Jenny before me. "Exactly that string of long windows and pointy dome on top."

"The foyer's octagonal," Borders and I said in unison, surprising each other. Borders might have been describing the hotel's lobby as he elaborated, "It's decorated to resemble a Muslim interior, a sort of tent canopy supported by spears."

"Just like your hotel," said Jenny.

"Well," I reminded them, struggling to control my voice, "there's a good reason for that—my father designed them both." A shiver passed down my arms as I imagined my father, full-haired and hopeful in those honeymoon days.

"Otherwise," said Borders, ignoring me, "Georgian. Had some trouble with parts crumbling. Bagg wants to organize repairs. Talks about organic structure, nature, that sort of thing. Wants to do Gothic stuff—towers, turrets. He's a trained architect, actually. Archaeology's just a sideline. You may have met him on the crossing."

"Mr. Bagg," I said, "doesn't like slate." I added, "Isn't Gothic a little *outré?*"

"Couldn't tell you. Bagg's the one with harebrained notions of the club as the moral code or some rot. Personally, I think our moral code's sunk so low that a skyscraper in New York couldn't restore it. It's dog eat dog. Or dog play with dog's wife. What do you say, Mrs. Borders? Nothing, per usual."

He parked the car and led us to the door but stayed outside to smoke with some of the men. He was still in a huff, which I put down to strain over the current finds. I wondered if he had official business, disguised as aimless chat, with some of the diggers. I was caught off guard by the vista of them—those strong, browned men in white evening dress, grouped together on the lawn in heroic attitudes like statues.

"Come along, girls," Aunt Emma urged, heading us through the front columns into the octagonal room. I walked forward with an odd mixture of pride and regret: this was my own father's crumbling triumph, with its spear-columns arranged around the circle and the ceiling a plaster drapery, painted crimson, that hung in heavy swags edged in gold. The dance committee had been hard at work. Paper streamers described scallops along the walls; chairs and sofas—massive, late Victorian—had all been pushed back to the wainscoting to allow for dancing. An enormous rug had been rolled back to the end of the room, where it lay like a long yule log and exposed the wide floor-boards. Under a plaster swag some musicians blew odd notes down their instruments, tuning up. Brass sconces cast wide arcs of yellow light onto the faces of the guests. I looked them over. These, according to Jenny, were the men of our future.

After my misapprehensions on the train to Victoria, I was on guard. On the sea voyage over we'd been chaperoned by friends of my Cousin Rudolph's, but at Bombay our escorts had disembarked and waited only long enough to get us onto the boat to Wallawalhalla before setting off on business in the city. We had chatted with the purser in his booth, but when the first mate greeted us in a narrow passage and offered to show us the ship, I invented an ankle sprained on mailbags.

Jenny seemed less troubled by the potential for danger with men. As we stood up straight and surveyed the hall that second night on the island, she suddenly gave a wave and cried, "Look, it's Roger!" The first mate, leaning on a pedestal, returned a mild salute but did not bestir himself. After my anxiety, this casualness struck me as almost insulting. Jenny was not without alternatives, however, and a smile in the direction of another young man with bright blue eyes quickly gained her a dance request.

"Hold this," she said, handing me her shawl. "It's the fox-trot."

"How lovely, there's Claralise," said Emma vaguely and swayed toward the Tennysons.

So I was left on my own, against the wall, under swags, unable to dance with my over-balancing feet. It was, I felt, standing awkward and alone, spirits falling like mercury after sundown, some signal to me: I would never move into life's gay present, would never abandon myself to the tempo, but would be conscripted forever to the margins—all by virtue of feet that were not mirror reflections.

As I stood feeling sorry for myself, up strode Harry Bagg with an ungainly piston limp I had not observed on shipboard. Punch cups tipped and spilled in his hand as he asked, "Now, why aren't you dancing, Miss Monroe from Ontario?"

I smiled back with unexpected pleasure, my mind still on his strange walk. I had liked him on the crossing, as little as we'd seen of him. He had a plain, flushed, but friendly face, with a beaky nose and formal manner that made him seem older than he was and put me at ease. Acting as purser in the absence of such on board, he'd been helpful to us. He had that kind of mind in conversation as well: you got a quick accounting, be it money or historical fact. From his booth he had offered an interesting and male alternative to chats with the timid Kinver nanny, who had stuck to our sides like tooth cream. Sitting behind his little glass window, tallying rolls of coins, Harry Bagg had explained how he was a farmer's son, from Caledonia, near my own town of Bremen. Like a meter on a taxicab, his talk was overlaid with his steady counting, making me a little nervous while amazing me with his powers of concentration. With spare and modest words he gave me to understand that he had shown clear promise early—in reading and drawing. He had quickly outstripped his teachers, and with their urging, had been financed to Cambridge, where he had read history, always especially alert to archaeological news.

He was only sixteen and apprenticed to an architect uncle when the war broke out. On shipboard once he described his visit to the Crystal Palace just before his unit had been deployed to France. He cited Ruskin as saying that nothing of iron could be called architecture. Such a contrast, he exclaimed, "the exhibition of Syrian treasure housed within that great greenhouse." Somehow, there, he'd heard of Kinver's dig, and the desire to come to Walla had fueled him through the war.

Five years my senior, Harry Bagg on board ship had seemed to me as ancient as a kindly uncle; we had batted back and forth badminton-weight flirtations. Now at the club, hobbling towards me with his kindly limp and cups of punch, tie off center, he looked young and unsure. "Don't you approve of dancing?" he persisted, fitting the cup into my hand. His forefinger brushed against mine in an unanticipated thrill of intimacy.

Heart racing, I answered, "It's nothing like that. It's—I don't hold with the notion that things come in twos."

He had, I noticed, an intriguing smile, which he shone on me for a brief moment, like a searchlight. "Don't you now?" he said softly. "What things? All things? Do we, in your opinion, overstate the duality of life: good and evil, night and day, man and woman, the quick and the dead? It's a rebel notion!" He laughed, suddenly intoxicated with his own talk, but not unconscious, I felt, too, of the cut of my dress or my fine ambers. I sipped, silenced by the overkill of his response, and followed him to a little grouping of sofas.

"The sum," he remarked.

I thought he was speaking metaphorically, drawing on mathematics, and was impressed once again by the subtlety of his mind. "The sum of experience," I replied, trying to keep pace, "is greater than its parts."

His pulled in his upper lip. "The Somme," he said, "was where I injured my leg. My reason—less profound than yours—for staying off the dance floor."

"Oh," I said, stiff with my gaffe, unable suddenly to look anywhere but at his leg. Etiquette failed me for a moment: should I invite him to sit?

Oblivious to my discomfort, he leaned against a sofa back and explained his limp in more detail. "Shot in the thigh by a German boy, not more than sixteen. Damned thing never exploded."

He paused, and I decided to risk it. I swept my hand toward one of the green chairs. "Please," I said.

"Thank you," he said and sat, and I felt as dizzy and happy as if I'd been lifted by an elevator right up to the top of Chicago's famous Wainwright Building.

Harry Bagg, on sitting, crossed the wounded leg over the other so that it stuck straight out in the air like a diving board. This did not seem unusual to him, however, and so I pretended it was fine with me, too. I looked at the stiff leg and realized this was one of the first times, apart from the arrival on the boat, that I'd seen him outside his glass box. He seemed very different. "Does it hurt much?" I asked.

"When it rains," he replied comfortably, "gives me a twinge, that's all. So this is the perfect climate." His voice, slow and kind, gave me the feeling that I was a very old lady. It was pleasant in an odd way. I looked around, expecting Aunt Emma to chaperone, but she was drifting toward the little buffet table where two tanned diggers, muscular in formal wear, shifted at each end, bored but on hand to pour coffee and punch. Aunt Emma placed a single berry on her plate and smiled vaguely at the bouncy little fat man beaming at her as he held out his cup to overflowing punch.

"Sam Kinver," said my escort, following my eye. "Dig's sponsor. Just returned."

"Oh!" I exclaimed. "He's *American!*"

Harry Bagg looked amused. "Let me top you up."

I sat watching him cross stiffly to the buffet table. I located Jenny's back; she was in animated, swaying, conversation with some masculine-type person unfamiliar to me. Her dress struck me as rather gossamer and her hair curled with a russet shine. I wondered, as Mr. Bagg began his formal limp back, two glasses in hand, if I too might be mistaken for a heroine in a novel. It was an exciting notion.

Harry, I tried out in my mind's ear as he seated himself and began talking about invasions. I didn't try to keep the place names apart. The punch was playing fast and loose in my circulatory system, naively ready to welcome strangers aboard its little falukhas and steer them along on a friendly ride up to the top of my head, out my oddly gesticulating arms, down new canal routes right to the ends of my toes.

Suddenly, feeling unusually happy, I wanted to dance. The band's fox-trot was urging me up, and I thought perhaps I could hop through several popular moves, but Mr. Bagg held his ground. The bullet lodged in his thigh, he explained, had never exploded. "Have to be careful with the quick-step," he said with a flicker of irony intriguing enough to make up for his refusal. "You hide your limp well," he added, which I was amazed to see he intended as a compliment.

"Sorry?" I said.

"Why did you come out to Walla?" he continued with embarrassed, spotlit interest.

I paused, then tried out a truth on him. "I'm a native, actually."

He raised an eyebrow. "In what sense?"

"I was born here."

"Oh," he said, recovering. "That's quite another matter. No one is a native of Walla."

"Why not, if I was born here ..."

"Yes, but to be a native means *incorporation*, taking Walla into yourself, letting yourself into Walla."

"I think a dictionary would disagree."

"I wouldn't rely on a dictionary to tell me who I was! So, you've come to Walla because you imagine you are a native."

"For a change, really," I answered, annoyed by his tone.

"From what?"

I had to think, which I both resented and enjoyed. "Systems of thought," I finally offered. It sounded good, though somehow beyond my own understanding.

"Intellectual freedom?" suggested Mr. Bagg, resettling his legs, prepared to talk at some length on this topic.

"Something like that."

"Toppling dead gods?"

"I suppose." It sounded blasphemous, but I was flattered by his interested overreading of my answers. I wondered if this made him more gullible or me brighter than I'd thought.

He mused, "What will you think when you've been here a month?"

"I plan to like it."

"Will you have the courage to admit it if you don't? It's a messy place, you know. Seething with discontent and personal desire. Something happens to our kind in the tropics. Canadians are not made for volcanic zones. Too trusting for poor visibility. We don't know what to do with things we can't see. Or can see but can't reach."

I dismissed all this enigmatic chatter. "Well, it seems very agreeable to me. And everyone's been extremely kind."

He studied me for a moment, then turned to another topic. "Lots of theories about Walla, you know. You'll meet Miss Bartram, who's convinced we're sitting on the last of Lemuria, the lost continent. Surely you've heard the theories. What was up is now down, and what's down was once up. Just imagine the map of the world in vertical reverse.

Where there's now Canada would have been a great ocean, and the Atlantic would have been land. All of the ocean around us would once have been a continent, and now only this tiny island is left of that land-mass—the last little tip of Lemuria."

I swallowed back a feeling of seasickness. "Hmm," I said, nodding. With this, he was off, explaining the Lemuria theory in detail, his eyes wandering occasionally with a mild, flattering interest from my neck—I touched my ambers—to my shoulders, long slim arms, to the lace at the hem of my dress, to my high white-strapped shoes.

And as he talked, turning me to alabaster with his approving scrutiny, I was likewise taking in Harry Bagg: square chested, down sloping green eyes, hair receding at the temples but enough to brush thickly back. Very clean-shaven, in the style of the day, he sat neatly upright, the one stiff leg like a ramrod supported by the other. It was not the debonair and world-traveled pose of a romantic lead; it was the posture of an inveterate bookworm whose brain raced while his body rested. You could count his virtues as if they'd been medals: accuracy, a mind that struggled to hide its light under a bushel of convention, and a playfulness that tagged at its prey like a cat's paw. He had a glow, an animation I'd not previously appreciated in the little chats Jenny and I had shared with him on shipboard. It was as if that purser's glass box had now opened and I had let out the real Harry Bagg, with something of the farm about him, but traveled, and wounded, and with a capacity to roll around in, double, and divide ideas like mercury. It was his talk that absorbed me the most; my mind lingered on his words, happy to learn new facts, feeling opened and pleasantly teased toward knowledge.

"Plato's description of Atlantis," he was saying, "fits neatly with Euhemerus's island of Panchaea. Now, one wonders why ..." As I nodded encouragement I was imagining my hand rising to smooth his lapel, pulling loose my interlocutor's crooked little tie.

"Dr. Paul Schliemann," he continued, encouraged by my smile. "Perhaps you know of his article a few years ago in the *New York American*? His grandfather, the famous Heinrich, passed down to him a bronze bowl, he claims, found with the Treasure of Priam. You know about this? The inscription, in Phoenician, reads 'From King Cronus of Atlantis'!"

"Hmm!"

"Quite. Which would prove Cronus to be human, not divine, something that rather appeals," he said with a squint and pause of irony. Then his face pulled suddenly conversational. "Say," he said. "Mrs. Borders is rather fond of Mr. Kinver, eh? I wonder if they're talking genealogy. It's his best subject. He knows all about cousins removed."

I paused and swallowed hard. We both turned our heads toward the buffet table where I realized Emma, over green eggs, in her near-sighted politeness, was inspecting something, a scar or tattoo, on Sam Kinver's arm. Then she pulled at her shawl and spread out the fringe, as if explaining the macramé knots of that item. They looked like a pair of ladies in a dressmaker's shop. I remarked, "I think she needs friends."

He looked unsure, then laughed suddenly so hard that his drink fountained out of his mouth. "Oh, dear!" he said, happily spotting up the wetness on his knee. "I was just thinking of Miss Bartram. She's a sort of friend to Mrs. Borders, I believe, but they're probably not good for each other. Don't get Miss Bartram on the subject of white ants. She'll have you packing in a trice."

"She has mentioned them already, actually."

"Anthea Bartram," he explained, sober again, and regarding me with kind helpfulness. "One of the dearest creatures on this island. I'm very partial to her. She reminds me of a cat we had at home who would stalk mops and brooms just for the pleasure of it. And like most people on this island, she's afraid of something. She has conceived great dangers in natural wildlife. There are rumors that enormous white ants, presumed to live in the volcano at the east end, once carried a young woman off to their den, which is quite impossible given their size, but Miss Bartram seems to be waiting around for them to do the same with her. She wouldn't think of leaving Walla and its imminent dangers."

"Except now she thinks the ants might take Jenny or me."

"Well, I certainly wouldn't allow that," said Harry, settling the matter with a smile. "So don't let her alarm you. She's only trying to keep her life exciting. The ants are a kind of solution, you might say, especially if your name were Constantine Cavafy. Greek poet whom I met in Alexandria. One of the moderns, by virtue of turning back to the richest part of the past. What I admire. But then, your name isn't Cavafy, is it? No. You, young woman, on the brink of your life, are traveling incognito, but who knows what destiny your name will bring you. Think: you are at this moment living your own future's past. Beware."

I nodded slowly, mesmerized, and at the same time aware of how dull he must find me. For my part, I felt what an alcoholic must feel at the first mouthful of whiskey: a craving for something I had not until then known I so urgently needed. "What do you fear, Mr. Bagg?" I asked.

"Oh, that's just a theory, not to be taken literally," he replied, brushing heavily at the spot on his trousers. His refusal to confide felt as if a door, opened to me, had suddenly closed, until I considered that perhaps only I had thought it open in the first place, that talk I had understood as intimate had all been rhetorical.

Interrupting us at that moment came Jenny, bleary faced and supported, necessarily, it seemed, by the arm of the blue-eyed young man. They were flushed with physical exertion. "You've missed the dancing!" she chided us, plunking down right next to Mr. Bagg. "Hi, sailor!" she said, "Remember me?" and gave his upstretched knee an unnecessary pat. I waited for him to swing his leg aside but he did not, glancing instead with interest at her hand lying there, as if some unusual leaf had dropped from a branch overhead.

"This is Robin Glover," Jenny said to me. "Physician."

Dr. Glover, lighting a cigarette, moved forward in his seat.

"Don't get up," I warned.

The doctor sat back and grinned shyly at me. "Evening, Bagg," he said, nodding to my escort between flicks of his lighter.

Mr. Bagg was rolling his drink, upright and nervous. I thrust about for a conversational gambit. "Mr. Bagg was just explaining to me many fascinating facts about the island's history."

Dr. Glover glanced at Jenny, who let loose a roll of giggles like pearls off their string. I fell into a moral silence—for Mr. Bagg, Dr. Glover, and myself. "I'm tired," I declared, with operatic yawns. "Let's get some air, Jen."

"Let her finish her nightcap first," said the doctor.

"The only nightcap Jenny needs is one for her head," I quipped, and heard with a flash of shameful recognition Miss Charity's tones.

"Come back soon," said the doctor as he lit my escort's cigar. The men didn't seem to notice the staginess of all this. Supporting Jenny by the waist, I pivoted us toward the doors, feeling the burden, as much as Jenny's ninety-seven pounds entailed, of maintaining decorum as we exited from the glorious neoclassical hall crumbling around us. Respectability was the word I would throw in my friend's face when we'd cleared the foyer.

"We came to rescue poor you," Jenny said to my surprise. "After the last two-step."

"What do you mean?"

"You missed the best, most glorious, most fabulous dance, Vizzy, dear thing, being nice to that overly educated prig. Robin says he makes a point of rescuing people from the Boring Bagg. It's a pun, by the way — you can laugh."

I was fully silenced, dumbstruck, as we stepped into the dark night. I felt Jenny's effort to focus her eyes on me. "You didn't really *enjoy* his company, did you?"

"Jenny," I said, getting my breath under control, "you used to chat with him as much as me on the boat. He was *interesting*. I *do* like him."

"History of the island . . ." Her voice trailed off into a giggle. "I'm sleepy."

"I'm sure," I said, and felt so full of new thoughts and sorrows that I could say no more. I just wanted to get us home.

Borders had never appeared at the dance, was not visible around on the grounds, and as our source of transport, he was vital. I knew no one else to ask, and I didn't dare pinch Miss Bartram's car, what with our poor driving record. It was going to be, I realized, looking into the long dark, quite a hike back to Egrets. I felt in some way, though, that we deserved it.

Once outside the club's circle of light, I removed our shoes and stockings to save them from the mud and made Jenny carry them. I didn't mind going barefoot in the dark where no one would see my feet. Punch still humming something lightly sad and romantic in my head, I undertook the walk as penance.

The road held danger from creatures on the prowl, but with the moon lighting our path, we had suffered only a few scratches from sea grass when the sound of a motor stalled behind us, and Miss Bartram's voice scolded, "At this time of night! All alone! Unchaperoned! Where is your dear aunt? Whence the manners of your young men? What of morals nowadays?" All this came without expectation of reply so I stepped docilely into her car, propped up Jenny, and heard the reprimands like a pleasant waterfall.

"Hello, Miss Bartram," I acknowledged when her tirade had subsided.

As we rode along I realized that we were not on the Strand Road but had turned off and were bouncing on a much less-traveled roadbed. "Miss Bartram?" I didn't want to seem ungrateful. "Miss Bartram, are you sure of the way?"

"Want to show you something," she said. In the dark I could see her point forward, and squinting hard, I spotted the height of Mt. Walla ahead. It rose quiet and grand.

I whispered, "Gosh."

"The volcano," she said. "But that's not what we're here for." She braked abruptly, lurching Jenny and me up to the windshield and back again hard in our seats. "Look down there, at the water."

I strained to see in the blackness what seemed to be a party in progress, out in the water—skittish movement of forms, phosphorescent glimmering. "What is it?" I asked. I could see nothing that I could be certain of, but imagined, my mind still full of the party at the club, fashionable merrymakers, with martinis held above splashing in tight swimsuits.

"The Night of the Dead," came her answer.

I cleared my throat, shivering slightly in the cool air, knowing I was in the company of a lady not renowned for credibility, watching something altogether weird. "The Night of the Dead?" I was hoping to jog her along.

"The white ants. They have great respect for Time, and the forgetfulness we all suffer as we chew along into the future."

"Those are white ants down there?"

"Their ritual of remembrance. I'm always touched by it. In ways it runs so counter to their nature, yet they endeavor to honor the past. They dress in white feathers and spend the night in the shallows of the bay moving pebbles from one side to the other. It's symbolic, you see."

"Golly."

Miss Bartram suddenly cranked the engine. "Home, girls!" she said. As we started back toward the Strand Road, she said, "It's not something many people have seen, Viola dear. Press that into your keepsake book to remind you of Walla days."

I heard the rub of irony as she spoke, but her stern profile gave me no further clues to her real feelings. In her silence for the rest of the trip, though, I sensed she had been affected by the sight. Jostling along, thinking of my evening, I considered: white ants were out there, a force as great and unknowable as death or men, or my dead mother's history, or my own best interests, or the fears and desires of all the people cloistered on Walla, and I had preparation for none of it.

Attempt at Empire Cake

⤜∞⤛

I N THE MORNING, on raising my head into that yellow air, I wondered first: were we caught in a science project in Miss Hope's laboratory? Opening my eyes I found Jenny settling herself comfortably back in bed with a huge hot water bottle on top of her head. She looked like a Renaissance doge.

"Besides which," she said as I tottered to the chamber pot—she had been talking for some time, it seemed—"your friend Bagg and Baggage can't dance with that awful leg. And he has tunnel vision from the war, I happen to know. Fact." She looked at me out of the corner of her eye. "Could you ever actually *kiss* a man with such spotty skin? Uggh!"

I doused myself with cold water and brushed my fuzzy teeth. I tried to sound casual. "Of course he has some physical problems. We were talking about them." Lying on top of the counterpane, I took up a book but could not concentrate. I was keeping at bay the memory of my wildly unsuitable ideas concerning Mr. Bagg.

Jenny broke into a laugh and caught herself back. "He agreed he looked like a fence post?"

I stayed in our room with Jenny all morning, pretending to keep her company, just glad to have some time to regain my balance. Aunt Emma moved briefly in and out precariously with trays of tea and toast, unsure how to manage us. Uncle Roddy was already down at the site, she said, and I felt a kind of easing of tension mixed with disappointment; I would have liked to have seen him, to have discovered what he ate for breakfast—egg or porridge or toast—to hear his opinion of the dance, to see what he would wear that day. It gave me a tingly feeling of excitement to be sharing a roof with such a man. Despite myself, I kept thinking Aunt Emma a very ill-matched mate for him. No wonder he was sometimes sharp with her. Roddy Borders needed someone much younger, with more spark.

"He'll be back for lunch?" I asked.

"You know, I don't know! I forgot to ask! And I suppose it depends on what they turn up. Now, as for you girls, we could see about your jobs, or wait till tomorrow, if you'd rather."

I said nothing, confused by the laxness of these arrangements. Jenny answered for us, "Let's wait till tomorrow. We're bushed."

"You're unused to drink, I expect," Aunt Emma began.

Here it comes, I thought, bracing myself for the lecture.

"Me?" said Jenny with a pout. "I had one small cup of that punch."

"Overstimulated, I expect," Aunt Emma hurried to correct herself. "It's the air on Walla, tends to enervate. You must try to stay calm. Everyone should try to stay calm," she said, spreading down the corner of the counterpane with frantic little strokes. And that was all that was said about my friend's behavior.

"Where are we going to work?" I asked.

"Well," she began, brightening, glad to be of factual help. "Jenny, you're going to Dr. Glover's office. He's terribly nice, Jenny. The Tennysons are rather fond of him. So are Roddy and I. Oh, yes, you met him at the dance . . . And he needs someone for filing, that sort of thing. And Viola, we thought you could go to the laundry to sort, but Mr. Bagg has asked specifically for you in his office . . . So, that's very nice."

"Oh, yes," I said quickly, heart thumping, unsteady. "Sure."

As she closed the door, Jenny grinned at me. "Lucky you. Shoulder to shoulder with the walking encyclopedia." Then she took out her embroidery, laid it on top of her chest, and went off into a gentle doze. I saw her life's history right then and there, as if featherstitched in the center of the hooped cloth: if Nettie snared Dr. Glover, Jenny would marry a Toronto lawyer. She would keep a tidy brick house with walled garden. I could expect a yearly Christmas card with photograph picturing well-brushed children—boy, girl, boy, girl—coming down a staircase as rhythmically predictable as footsteps, taller each year. Only I, wild and unpatterned, left footed and large handed, could have imagined romance with the cerebral Harry Bagg, could long to see

Roddy Borders spooning porridge into his handsome, curling mouth. What was happening to me? My intention of recovering my mother's trace was being sidetracked all too quickly by men.

Of the two of us lying in bed, Jenny seemed the one destined for mild trouble and sure pardon, while I would be forever fettered by decorum and its attendant vice—real trouble. I sensed disturbingly that my passions were not to be trusted; I had no inborn pattern for life. I didn't know how to flirt; I had no lexicon to the language men spoke to women. What did Mr. Bagg's request mean? On that morning watching out the window as the sun pearled over the sea I felt that something wild was coiled in me, ready to spring, and I would have to work very hard to follow the course effortlessly steered by my hungover friend.

We dozed and embroidered the day away. The morning air next day seemed thicker than ever as Jenny and I readied ourselves for our jobs in town. "Volcano's acting up," said Aunt Emma. "Blowing ash around a little this morning." She was fanning herself abstractly on the verandah as we came out dressed in our old Lydgate suits.

"I thought it was dormant," I said.

"Mm," was all the answer I got. She was still in peignoir and looked so limp I half-wondered if *she* were drunk. I noticed she was watching the moving blur in a jar on the table beside her: bees darting and buzzing inside the glass. "They want to get out," she whispered to me and a sob caught in her throat. She looked up at us with a face bereft of hope. "They've been trapped in there since early morning. They so want to get out . . ." Tears trickled over her cheeks.

I studied the situation, walked to the table, took up the jar, unscrewed the lid, and with one motion scattered the bees into the air where they zigzagged fast off into the cover of bushes.

"What . . . have . . . you . . . done?" sobbed Aunt Emma outright, sitting up. Just then Miss Bartram toot-tooted for us from the high seat of her car. She had accepted the task of conveying the newly arrived clerical staff to our respective places of employment.

"I've let them go, of course," I said. "Whoever trapped them? It was unthinkably cruel."

"But out in the world," cried Aunt Emma, chin swinging downward to her bony chest with each sob. "How will they manage? They'll die, and we'll never know of it! No one will mourn them..."

"I'm sorry..." I began, utterly confused. "But I don't see the point..."

"When should we be back?" Jenny interrupted. "Miss Bartram's waiting."

"Oh, I don't know..." sighed Aunt Emma, looking out to the sea. "By two? For lunch?"

"Yes. Why not?" She gave an indistinct wave of her fan.

"Important day, girls, eh," remarked Miss Bartram as we climbed into her backseat. "Work of national urgency. Building the Empire, and all that. Or digging one up. Excited?"

I didn't approve of her sarcasm. "I'm looking forward to doing something," I informed her evenly. "We've just been sort of tourists until now."

"Nothing wrong with a bit of work. Nothing wrong with a rest, either. Jenny, this is where you get off. Ah, and here's the good doctor to hand you down, polite young man that he is. Hello, Doctor. Here's your ward. Jenny's to get back to Egrets for her lunch by two, young man. Can't let her miss her shepherd's pie. What with shepherds so scarce on the island and hard to trap."

Dr. Glover, looking seven feet tall, had, I saw in morning light, a face like an inclined plane. He blushed and replied with a creaky, "Yes, Miss Bartram." He looked abashed at having Jenny beside him at the door to his little practice, as though he had been publicly handed a concubine. His evening brashness had all been bluff; clearly he was already smitten. I wondered what Mrs. Tennyson would do about it as I called out, "Bye," to my friend. She chose to ignore me, preferring a more casual half wave in our general direction while murmuring something to Robin Glover, bending to hear.

"And on to Harry Bagg's little abode," said Miss Bartram.

Her attitude a mystery to me, I felt obliged to ask as we bounced over a pothole, "Miss Bartram, are you happy on Walla?"

"About as happy as a yoked ox."

"Then why do you stay on?"

"Because I *am* as happy as a yoked ox! You young people with your lives ahead of you think you can switch and change and decide how everything will turn out in advance. You can't. Remember that. But you can adjust to how things go. And there's a certain freedom in confinement, don't you find?"

"I'm not confined," I reminded her firmly.

Miss Bartram murmured, "Hmm," but gave no further answer as we pulled up outside a wooden hut with a low overhanging roof.

"This is it?"

"This is it. He seems to spend late morning off-site, just figuring."

And there was the figuring Harry Bagg himself, to my embarrassment, standing solidly in the doorway, hand on hip, perspiration darkening his shirt, watching with remote amusement as we disencumbered ourselves of our motoring robes.

"I understand you know all about columns and pediments, Miss Monroe," he said, offering me a hand down. "We're digging for some."

"Oh, let us not to the marriage of true minds admit pediments," misquoted Miss Bartram, neatly cutting off what I heard as a patronizing challenge. I wondered at this new side to Mr. Bagg. No longer the amiable escort of the club, he had become the brisk and abrasive expert archaeologist. Suddenly his age seemed much greater than mine and my general standing much lower. My antennae sensed danger. My approach to men, a passive resistance that I invented before Gandhi, had worked well with my father; I resolved that morning to keep out of Harry Bagg's way.

"Let's go in," Miss Bartram insisted. "I want to see how this young man wastes his day. Oh, fun!" she cried as entering we encountered in the dusty-smelling room a high drafting table covered with rolls and scrolls and instruments of surgical precision.

"What a lot of pictures!" I exclaimed. Around the walls were architectural drawings and photographic enlargements of coigns and cornices tacked on top of them, all neatly at right angles to each other.

"Buildings. One of my passions, apart from the past."

"What is this one?" I asked of a postcard of an enormous structure that caught my eye.

"Don't you know?" he said with a strained smile.

"I know!" cried Miss Bartram. "I was there! The Crystal Palace. New York. Eighteen fifty-three. I was in my nurse's arms but remember it to this day!"

"Actually," said Harry Bagg, "this is the original, Paxton's, eighteen fifty-one. Most dreadful structure of the century. Can't even call it architecture. A giant greenhouse!"

"Was it full of silly doohickeys like the one in New York? Lamps that looked like storks mating? That was one I loved! Mind you, I was only about six months old at the time!"

"Viola may not know that it housed the Great Exhibition of the Works of Industry of All Nations. May industry decline as a result." He added with distinct pleasure, "My great disappointment in life is that I was born too late to see the Exhibition. I would have blown the place up there and then and saved civilization from such debasement!"

Feeling the need to defend my family's shrinking turf, I hurried to remind them, irrelevantly, "My father was an architect, you know. Trained in Toronto. I'm sure he had a postcard of this in his shaving mirror."

"I don't see why he would have. As architecture, a disaster."

"But I'm sure he did," I said, hot over accusations I did not understand.

"I'll just leave you two chatting, then," Miss Bartram interrupted brightly, and tying on her bonnet, stepped back into her car. "Mr. Bagg, come see me and bring your music. My harpsichord is here at last and I'm going home to practice. Let's hope the ants haven't carted it off yet!"

"Well," I said, embarrassed, turning my attention again to the wall in the vacuum wake of her departure. "That Crystal Palace is certainly very shiny."

"It was enormously difficult to build," Harry instructed me, leaning an elbow on a filing cabinet. "But it is not real architecture. Real architecture looks to the past and molds it into some form that suits the needs of the present. Like Darwin's theory of evolution. It must happen slowly and definitely with the greatest care to style. No, the Crystal Palace redeemed itself by housing a most glorious exhibit of Layard's Syrian finds. You know of them, surely? Two enormous rooms and a huge palace façade." His flat face flushed for a moment, remembering. "Ceremonial hall, royal chamber, images of winged, human-headed lions, Gilgamesh the lion killer, friezes of martial and hunting scenes from the days of King Assurnasirpal himself, walls reconstructed of

Babylonian brick. That's a glazed variety with colors used in no other ancient architecture." Awe hushed his voice.

"Oh," I whispered. "It sounds lovely."

"Yes. It changed my life. I was working in my uncle's architectural firm when I walked through that exhibit two years ago, and in the royal chamber, who should I meet but Sam Kinver."

He had told me all this once before, on the boat, but now I thought about it all more personally. I said, "I wish my life would take such a turn."

"It might. It could at any moment."

I didn't feel much conviction, though. If any force were to intervene to shape my life, I considered, it would have to be my own. Settling myself at my workbench, where I was supposed to make lists of objects in a shoe box, I found another postcard of the Crystal Palace. Surprised, I challenged him, "You must like it, to have these pictures all around."

Harry Bagg's face swelled red, like someone about to blow the trumpet. "If I do it's a failing," he sputtered. "A little private flaw. Something I don't myself understand that draws me to it. Perhaps it's my sense of humor getting in the way. You and I have been born too late, you know. All we can do is dig up the past and grieve."

"Well," I said, annoyed by these home truths that I somehow could not dispute. "The future's just as exciting."

"We'll make do," he said softly. "Maybe on Walla at least we can hold progress at bay, eh?"

I looked at him, confused. I wondered if progress was what he feared.

"Panchaea," he said with a new surge of excitement. Though surprising that he didn't feel the need to get some work done, it was interesting to see him so excited as he explained, "Panchaea. The island utopia of the Indian Ocean described by Euhemerus around three hundred B.C. My dear, I have a notion we might be digging up quite a treasure right underfoot. Would you sharpen those pencils? Let's get to work! I have to go down site in half an hour."

When Jenny and I arrived back at Egrets by two, tired and dusty, Emma Borders had changed into a dark cotton dress and almost set the table. Neither she nor I made mention of the bee incident. As Jenny and I helped her with the last of the plates, set out more knives, and sat, she seemed strangely uninterested in our morning's labors, or rather interested only in fits and starts. "You must tell me *everything!*" she insisted, handing a bowl of greasy-looking soup down to Jenny. "No holding back!" But when Jenny started to describe Dr. Glover's many intricate tools, or I tried to convey Harry Bagg's interest in architecture, Emma Borders just stared at the tablecloth and seemed to go limp. When I added, "He's looking for an ancient utopia," she brushed a lock of hair from her temple and said, "Goodness, what a lot of work that must be."

After lunch I learned the reason for her distraction, at least that day's reason. After the washing up, we went back to our room to prepare our wardrobes for the following day and write letters. Aunt Emma took Jenny off to show her something and, returning, commenced hovering again. I'd just begun a letter to Aunt:

> *Dearest Aunt, I hope these lines find you in good health and comfortably situated once again in your little cottage, which I am sure you will enjoy very much after twenty years away.*

Emma Borders was watching me with tiny twisted smiles. "I'd like to talk to you, Viola," she said when I looked up. "Just for a moment, dear. It won't take long."

"What is it?" I said, too loudly, gripped by panic.

Rather than reassure me, her eyes moved floorward. "Let's sit on the verandah. Jenny, we'll just be . . ."

Jenny knew. I could tell by the way she never stopped rolling her socks over the opened drawer. As I followed Emma Borders down the hall, my mind formulated the worst. I had worked myself up enough that when we finally sat and Aunt Emma—I must call her Aunt, she reminded me—smoothed my hands in her small cold ones, I braced to hear my fate. She said quietly, "It seems that your dear aunt . . ."

I sucked breath hard. "What?"

Her eyes were round and palely glittering. Her voice cracked as she told me, "The ship . . . sank."

"Oh . . ." sounded from the base of my throat. I looked over the verandah. The winds swished the trees back and forth, moving the heat like yellow blankets in the sky. A macaw, perhaps the one who had escaped, called out to us from the other end of the house. I had imagined Aunt waist-deep and muddy in her Yorkshire garden by now. The shock was that she had never made it back. "Oh," I said and slumped against Emma Borders's shoulder. I was trying to remember her, that bony personage whom I realized I had loved the most of anyone in the world, though I had spent her time with me dreaming of a lost mother; I was trying to understand Aunt's fate. Anger and frustration and disbelief and a kind of numbing certainty struggled against each other. Mostly I felt an overwhelming remorse: she had given all those years to tending me, not her choice, and lost her own life at the very moment when she might have had it back. Her history seemed one given to disappearance; only for that brief time during the war had Aunt been truly visible, found what she desired. Now she was under the sea.

"Your father's written. His letter," Aunt Emma said, drawing it from her pocket. The familiar, stingy italic handwriting brought forth slow tears as I felt what of course had always been true. I was all alone, all alone on an odd spot of land on the wrong side of the world.

Aunt Emma stroked my arm as if I were an animal with sharp teeth. "You're grown up now. Your father isn't well, is he?"

I tried to think. I wondered what she might have heard from Jenny's mother. "He's getting older."

"He's going up to relatives in Toronto."

This seemed irrelevant, but in my vulnerable state everything mattered, everything counted. "Yes. I see," I murmured. Then I read her meaning. My father had no interest in my returning. He did not want me. Though this could not have been a surprise, but still I felt a dull blow, like pressure on a bruise. Aunt Emma paused a moment. "Your job now is to find a really nice husband," she counseled.

"Right." I was ready to agree to any plan.

"Because financially . . ." Her voice trailed off. "Without an income, you know . . . Apparently your father . . ."

"Yes," I repeated. "There was never much."

"Of course, your job will support you, for your stay with us."

Something about the way she said it made me ask, my heart hardening for a moment, "Do you require more?"

"Oh! Good heavens! At least for the moment, Mr. Borders feels. We'd never ask a penniless . . . And after a while, you'll find someone . . ."

"Yes," I whispered again. And I earnestly determined I would.

At first, though, I could do nothing at all. I sat on the porch the rest of the evening, slept little, found I needed my full strength and concentration just to get into bed. Jenny delivered a message down to Harry Bagg the next day that I would return soon, following bad news. If he expected a stiff upper lip and an iron will to work, it was of no consequence to me what he thought. I needed to fall apart a little.

For many days, Jenny and I spoke only about the most obvious things. In the dark before sleep I remembered my old home, thought of my father all alone, and noticed little of the world around me. Mourning is difficult without a body; I could not fully believe my loss, so I hung in limbo for several weeks, moping without hitting bottom. I imagined myself ghostlike, drifting outside our house in Bremen, peering in through the windows at my father smoking his pipe and sketching in his notebook, and Aunt, every bit as alive as when I had left, hemming a tablecloth. Gradually this vision blurred and was replaced by a hard conviction that I must never go home again.

I spent long solitary hours in the front parlor, my head in a book whose pages I didn't turn. I sought comfort from tangibles. The spirit of Aunt seemed suddenly to inhabit objects about the room, and everything British reminded me of her. A certain brass eight-day clock on the mantel of the false fireplace mesmerized me. My mother, I knew from Aunt, had brought with her dowry just such a clock, a lacquered brass timepiece with tall glass dome that my father had brought back to Bremen on his mournful return. It had stood on a bookcase in our parlor, its tick-tock plaguing me the winter I lay with scarlet fever on the chesterfield.

My mother's presence I had felt in the island's white sands. Now Aunt joined her in infinite absence, in the form of the clock. Straight, stiff, rough-handed Aunt, who had given the third score of her years to tending me. Time's treachery seemed evident in the steady ticking of the clock on the Borders's mantel. It did not have the sense to stop now that everyone was gone.

I watched that clock, the base decorated with its gold balls rotating first to the left, then to the right, like dancers in a minuet, and I felt at each shift in direction a melancholy readjustment of perspective on my state. It seemed to me as I sat there watching the dance, that *clockwise* I was a fortunate guest of the Borders—but *counterclockwise* had no means of support beyond their uncertain kindness; that *clockwise* the Borders were generous people—with *counterclockwise* interior strains I'd begun to sense; that *clockwise* I was a girl with an open future—which *counterclockwise* could sink me into the Tennysons's trap of poverty. This way, that way, swung my mood. I wished only for what I knew I could not have—the stillness and permanence of the blue world around my mother's face in the miniature. Time was all to blame. I sat on and on till the dance itself slowed and stopped. No one dared intrude to wind it up. Something like satisfaction replaced my previous regret; I stared at stopped time, then, aware that my vigil had ended, found the key on the mantel and steadily wound up the clock.

I was just fitting on the glass dome when Aunt Emma and Jenny stuck their heads into the parlor and suggested timidly that I accompany them on a Sunday visit down to the Tennysons. I looked at them. "Yes," I whispered. "All right. Why not?" They were so surprised by my change of heart that they bumped each other in their rush to get my hat and reticule. Jenny buttoned on my shoes as if I were Cinderella.

We had tea, tea, acrid tea in Mrs. Tennyson's purple, heavily wall-papered parlor. They were not part of the dig, I learned from Aunt Emma on the way down, but rather leftovers from the island's previous life as naval base. Captain Tennyson, it seemed, and his two sons had been lost in high waves off the island some years before, and the lady Tennysons waited out their time on Walla as being the most economical solution in their now straitened circumstance, while the third son, sent back home to Harrow, found a situation.

Mrs. Tennyson seemed steam driven, large, puffing, and full of opinions. Nettie, by contrast petite and pale, sitting with her knees touching Jenny's—they had grown chummy in my absence, I noticed—seemed to have stored up all her mother's longings for a girl child and flowered out with femininity in every possible direction. She wore only the frilliest dresses, and at a time when bosom was unfashionable, Nettie could not help but protrude. She confessed, blushing, that she was a devoted subscriber to and quoter of and cutter-outer of the paper dolls in *Godey's Lady's Book.* I never saw Nettie perspire. Despite all that, I liked her. A desire to be useful gave her face an almost melancholic appeal. "Darjeeling will cheer you up," she whispered as she passed me my cup. "And dressing more brightly. Yellow raises the spirits of persons suffering from melancholia, Robin Glover says. Do you think that is possibly what you're suffering from?"

"Quite possibly," I admitted. "Among many things."

"Yellow," she advised again. "I'll order you some fabric if you like. We can get it quite reasonably through friends in Delhi."

I smiled and said nothing, but appreciated her genuine attempt to help, even as it made me feel more outside the Walla lady world than ever. Tea had always been my favorite meal, with its promise of cakes and sweetmeats, but the comfort I derived from the visit was bitter-sweet. As I did not know the Tennysons, I sat apart on a low ottoman and rested my head in my hand. Nettie passed around one plate of suspiciously dry-looking eccles cakes and another of Bath buns. I took something onto my plate and stared out to sea. The water looked as flat as a mirror.

Sitting there, ankles shackled in my posture of politeness, I thought nostalgically of good smells from my childhood: porridge heavily salted on cold mornings, jams boiling on the stove, my maternal grandmother's famous Empire Cake baking with the timer ticking down to tea time. The batter with its hint of maple smelled of delicious things to come: a country full of promise and full-running sap. Surely, had my mother ever baked the cake, it would have tasted sweeter than ambrosia. The promise always failed poor Aunt. I remembered her panicked flight round the kitchen as smoke signaled from the oven in a message you didn't have to be an Indian to read. I chewed Mrs. Tennyson's dry Bath bun without thought to the present and considered: the Empire Cake recipe must be somewhere among my things, written out in my Royalist grandmother's own spiky hand. For the first time in weeks, it seemed, I had a wish and a plan: I would bake that cake.

"I believe we've cheered you up," Mrs. Tennyson puffed at me. "You look almost pleasant, Viola. Though you have such a serious, long nose. Doesn't she have a serious, long nose, Mrs. Borders? I'm going to lend you my Browning, Viola, *The Ring and the Book*. It's about a murder. I don't waste my time on penny-dreadfuls; this is first-rate."

"Lovely," I said quietly, laying the heavy book by my feet.

I waited through the visit and, back at Egrets, hunted feverishly through my belongings. The recipe was the one thing I had from my mother's family: tangible, renewable, incorruptible. Hadn't I put it away for safety in a sweater pocket before my trip? Where was the pullover I'd worn collecting branches fallen from our maple tree after an April storm? Where was that recipe so familiar to me from Aunt's yearly attempts, my grandmother's looped handwriting bespattered with decades-old batter dropped in a pause of tasting? Twice, three times through my bureau drawers and tin box of accouterments turned up no recipe. I gulped air in frustration. It was as if the meaninglessness of life in death now teased me with this disappearance of the one small thing I craved. Defeated, I sat on the edge of the bed and sobbed.

Then stubborn determination took hold again. I was resolved to bake the cake no matter what. I would wing it. When I had cooled my face into respectability with the water in the pitcher, and smoothed my hair and felt safe that I could speak of this event in my life without causing embarrassment to myself or my hosts, I made my way to the parlor.

"Aunt Emma," I began.

She was sitting with Borders on the loveseat. I noted that the seat's fabric was chewed around the tacks. A broken leg had been replaced with a flat stone. The two looked up, constructing smiles, and Borders's fingers smoothed off his wife's arm; his grip left its clench on the lawn of her sleeve. A sheet of pain dropped from her face. She held out her hands to me. "Darling Viola. What can we do to cheer you?"

Distressed by the strange scene I'd interrupted, I looked out the window to answer as calmly as I could, "I'd like to do some baking, please. I'd like to make a cake." I would trust in faith and memory and the spirit of my mother on this island to guide me. "I'll need lots of butter," I added.

The kitchen was a brick cave behind the main house. All the ingredients were kept in tins that I had to open with the end of a screwdriver. I found an abundance of crockery, mixing bowls, spoons, a whole tea service in a very pretty rose pattern, a couple of giant industrial-sized stirrers, a meat grinder, a tin opener, ceramic measuring cups, even a juicer. As I worked I felt something of Aunt's assurance as she'd instructed her "help," Mrs. Callahan, about weights and measures. I could hear Mrs. Callahan responding with her own opinions: don't buy from Mr. Mercer, his meats are low grade, order from the man down Dundas way. I sifted the flour, and felt better. Doing something gave me back memories, and with them, confidence.

Aunt Emma flitted in the doorway, watching. I tried to ignore her. What were her intentions, I wondered, as I poured the flour. I didn't know what to say, so said nothing and pretended much concentration with leveling the surface of the measuring cup. I was working off inspiration: four eggs, a half pound of butter, two cups of flour, sifted. My hot cheeks might have been from the oven, though really they drew their redness from embarrassment at my sheer ignorance of life.

"We'll just let it bake, now," I said as I began clearing up. To my surprise and distress, Aunt Emma scurried in and began spotting up with a wetted finger the excess flour and droppings of butter and sugar. Beads of batter disappeared like gumballs down her throat. Her greed or hunger was so extreme that, in fascinated horror, I felt too paralyzed even to acknowledge it. It matched, even exceeded, any I had known.

"There," I said when this sudden act of ravenous housekeeping had ended and she was just touching around the mixing bowl with her fingers. "There, now," I said as a sign for her to stop. "An hour and we'll see how it has turned out."

I waited out on the verandah, too agitated to sit. Aunt Emma joined her husband in the parlor. I could hear Borders's hard voice raising objections and her tiny efforts at appeasement. I didn't know the subject of their discord, but I hoped that somehow my cake would draw them once more into harmony. Baking it had calmed my own upheaval. The smell led me into recesses of memory that were mixed with images of Aunt tangling the strings of an apron around her bony middle and dreams of Mother, mistress of Empire Cake, herself a confection. I had high hopes. We would all enjoy a good tea together—my dream for peace among the peoples of the earth, specifically those hungering under Egrets's roof. What more could they want?

I returned to work out an icing when the "Well, well, well," of a familiar voice interrupted me. It sent a nervous shudder down my spine. "And how are we progressing?" Borders drew a slender finger through my icing and pulled it over his lower lip. "Mm. Talked to Harry Bagg down at the dig this morning."

"Yes?"

"Seems pleased with your work."

"It's interesting, what he's doing." I was trying to breathe normally, to concentrate on my job at hand.

"Unlikely he'll find fame and fortune."

I considered. "I don't think he's after them."

"No. His mind's on that damned column. Sam Kinver's ready to pack up, what with nothing turning up and Harry Bagg obsessed with old gods. Failed at architecture, failing at archaeology . . . what can you expect?"

"He's a very good architect, I believe."

"Canada needs forceful independent go-ahead, not prettified sky-lines." He stood with a hand on his hip, prepared to set me straight. "To tell you the truth, I consider him dangerous!"

"How could he be *dangerous?*"

"Isn't a company man. He has all sorts of fuzzy notions of honor and national character and the lessons of the past. If I gave him an order to shoot at the enemy, and the enemy suddenly mentioned liking a particular Egyptian pyramid, Harry would be thrilled, put away his gun, and try to negotiate some compromise, believing the fellow sal-vageable. He gets form and content confused. It's shallow thinking after all, isn't it, to take admiration of a pyramid as a sign of moral fiber, or— let's be more specific—to ignore the artifacts you're turning up, not to mention the gold, because you're looking for a column that most likely doesn't exist?"

I couldn't think of an argument to what must be faulty logic, though it echoed in some regards my own annoyance with Harry, who so far had not understood that I needed a husband. Not wanting to appear disloyal, I shifted ground. "But if you think Canada needs independent thinkers, and you just said he *wasn't* a company man, then he must be what Canada needs."

He looked annoyed at this. "The right sort of independent thinkers. Men who can lead the country forward. Not erect fake Tudor castles all over Sam Hill and wallow around in some notion of civilization's decline. So you're baking a cake," he observed. Even in the dark of the kitchen I could feel how tired and unshaven and wrung out he was. He gave a rough laugh as he sat on a stool. After a moment he said, "They're loaded, you know. The white ants."

I paused.

"Gold," he supplied.

"Oh!" I laughed lightly. "Herodotus!"

He threw me into hurried beating as he almost shouted at me, "They stockpile all the valuables that wash up. They have treasures so rare one suitcase full and your fortune would be made. *Mine*, I should say!" The throaty laugh was beginning to strain my nerves. I felt that perhaps Jenny's uncle had come a little unhinged in the subcontinental sun.

He watched me with a curious wistfulness, stoop shouldered on his stool. "Let me lick the spoon," he said. His tongue traveled the length of the handle and around the spoon's bowl with silent enjoyment; he watched me watching him. "It's good," he whispered with an infinitesimal raise of an eyebrow. "Not great, but good enough." His eyes narrowed on me.

I wiped my hands on the chintz apron. "If you're done with that."

He ran the spoon prisoner-fashion back and forth on his knees, then handed it docilely over. "They say there's more treasure stored inside that volcano than all the museums in the world. And that an American woman is down in there, directing operations."

"Who says that?"

He looked surprised. "It's just a story. Why? Interested in joining her?"

"You don't think it could be true?"

"Don't buy anybody's myths. They go for cheap."

Of course, the cake collapsed. Something important, whatever was needed to make it rise, had been omitted. When I opened the tomb-oven, expecting treasure, and saw instead a charred, pancake failure, inert in its metal tin, I might have been looking at the remains of the women in my family, so despondent did I feel with renewed grief for all the time beyond my grasp.

Diminishing Elephants

⤬

W ORKING SIX FEET from Harry Bagg, plotting, dusting, sorting pottery fragments in boxes, I listed code numbers and made him tea. We talked a little but we both were thinking hard, he about the past, I presumed, and I about how to honor it. In my own small way I was determined to leave the island a better place than I had found it. I did not know just what that might entail, but I would do it, in the name of Aunt and in the spirit of my long-dead mother. Grief had forged in me this resolve.

Harry's habit was to start early at the site, then come back up to his hut by nine and do figuring, cataloguing, and plotting till lunch break around one, the hours when I worked for him. More and more, however, I wanted to go down to the site itself, to be part of the uncovering. The dig was turning up new things every day, Harry told me: pots, amphorae, spears, gold jewelry, bones, cooked and raw. Some dated back one or two hundred years B.C., others were more recent. The dusting down of the trace of walls, originally convincing him that he had found the site of Panchaea, had yielded no golden column. The walls outlined a space that contained artifacts from the span of a millennium. "It's like digging in a garbage pit," Harry complained. "You've found some nice things, though," I said, to comfort him, but even the prettiest pottery bowls with feet failed to rouse Harry from his frustrated musing. "We have to go deeper," he told me, eyes glazed with fatigue. Occasionally he tacked up on the wall a new drawing of the island Panchaea, based on the descriptions he read aloud to me, translating from the Greek as he went, in the world history of Diodorus Siculus, an extant fragment from Book Six.

"Euhemerus," he explained, voice lowered as if revealing family secrets. "Euhemerus's account, circa three hundred B.C., of Panchaea describes the chief monument on the island as a golden column on which are inscribed the deeds of Uranus, Zeus, and Cronus, described as kings of the island, not yet gods. That means they were just people originally. It's just like the divine right of kings being challenged in western Europe in the Middle Ages, you see? The column would prove that there are no gods. People have just attributed godlike powers to ordinary human beings." He stretched his legs out and seemed almost asleep in thought.

"Is that what you want? To prove that there is no God?" Though interested, I was taken aback. I had pictured a husband as someone with whom one attended church on major holidays.

"God or gods," he said. An idea seemed to propel him out of his chair. He strode around the room like a wind-up toy, full of energy but with nowhere to go. "I want to show that there is no such thing as God's will or predestination. That there is no reason for complacency in the face of wrongdoing. That we really are the captains of our fates!"

"Mmm," I murmured, watching him raise and lower the venetian blinds, in awe of his electric zeal. I wondered how this fitted in with my own little project. It gave me a kind of heady pleasure to imagine myself in charge of my fate.

"You see," he continued, "the past can actually free us from traditional thought. Because tradition is all short-lived anyway. It's all invented at some point, so it can just as easily be disinvented or reinvented."

I looked at him and picked at my thumbnail. I was aware of feeling hungry for lunch, but also in the midst of something I shouldn't miss, though I hardly knew what to ask. "Go on," I said.

"Take Scottish tartans," he said. "Dress Stewart, Ancient Campbell. You'll find that *ancient* is relative if you do a little research. No one paid much attention to all that till the last century, did they?"

"Didn't they?"

"No. Or take your Christmas tree. Your wassail song. Your Easter bunny. Absolutely modern. So, the lesson is to debunk tradition when it gets in the way. The more distant past can actually move us into a better future."

I sat back, breathless. "Huhn! You think that you and Mr. Kinver can do all that by digging up the ground around the club?"

His face twisted with confusion and amusement. "No. Sam Kinver has no interest in the column or Panchaea, actually. He's looking for Atlantis, but," he smiled broadly, "he wouldn't mind proving his family descended from Zeus, I think. He's always trying to push his family tree back a generation!"

As this was a joke, I tried to look amused, but I felt mostly dazed— by Harry's sudden revelations, which were revelations of his own heart's desire, by the outpouring of information more detailed than any in Miss Hope's world history class, and by a sense that I was standing on more than an oriental carpet of the unknown past. Under my feet old worlds were still at work with promise of capture or release.

I sharpened my pencils, but before I lost Harry to his reading again, I felt I needed to say something of my own mission. "I'm going to work for goodness, too, Harry," I explained. "I won't tolerate the injustice of the status quo."

Looking up from Diodorus, his face was as blank as the sea.

"I just thought you should know," I said. "I want to make this island a utopia, too."

"Oh," he said, frowning. "Good!" He bent his head again to his book then surfaced a moment later, just to comment with a sweetness that surprised me, "Then we're in this together!"

I nodded, suddenly shy and anxious to get down to work. But I had little mind for my tasks. Being with Harry, I considered, was like going through heavy weather: clouds giving to sunlight with strong winds and rain, all happening fast. Studying the pictures on the walls, the great iron beams and glass panels of the Crystal Palace beside the column of Panchaea, reminded me of his curious regret in life, as well as his mission for Walla, and excused him for single-mindedness on the job.

I wondered in those first weeks, in long moments of idleness, turning on a high stool, not wanting to disturb him, why he had asked me to work for him. We seldom talked, and I had fairly little to do except study his profile as he sat at his high drawing table, reading, or marking quick lines against a ruler he raced like a fast-action Ouija tripod around his paper. Once, too bored to stop myself, I broke the silence with the information, "Mr. Borders thinks the white ants are hoarding gold. Are they really, really big?"

Harry smiled. "Size twelve."

"No, honestly."

"Hoarding gold? I doubt it," he answered politely. He laid down his pencil. "In his Indian travels Herodotus mentions something of that sort, of course. That's where he gets it. Your host would like to find a reason to play the warrior. First-rate photographer, but caught behind the lens. Rather likes his own image, too, doesn't he?" His small laugh was unconvincingly congenial, as if he regretted these remarks. He pulled a tattered book from a row on his shelf and with some flipping around found a passage. "Herodotus. I'll translate: 'In this sandy desert are ants smaller than dogs but bigger than foxes.' All right . . . 'These ants live underground, digging out the sand just like ants in Greece and they look very much like Greek ants,' and so on. Our brand lives in the volcano, according to Miss Bartram. 'The sand they are digging contains gold.' This is the part Roddy Borders likes to read. 'Nothing is quicker than these ants, and if the Indians,' or Canadians, 'did not move quickly ahead of them while the ants were preoccupied with their gold-digging, not a man would escape alive.' So you see."

"But you don't believe in them."

"Belief plays no part. I've never seen them, that's true, but really they don't interest me. In fact, we seem to be on quite opposite sides in the matter of using the past; they'd like to chew it all down and turn it into building blocks, while I'd like to get right to the heart of antiquity and reconstruct it."

"Except the parts of the past you don't want."

He gave me a narrowed look of respect. "Except those parts, and the white ants are welcome to them. Now, let's get you home."

I never looked forward to the morning's end, even with its promise of lunch and a rest. Harry had begun to escort me back before going on down to the site, but we spoke little on the walk. Our view as we walked eastward was the volcano Mt. Walla, sending up occasional clouds that Harry assured me meant nothing more than a sneeze in the pathology of the landscape but which seemed to me to be signal warnings over the Borders's house. Not only was something wrong at Egrets, I had begun to see, but my position now as quasi-orphan seemed to be straining my hosts' hospitality. When Harry paid me my weekly wages, I gave what had been agreed upon to Emma. Without looking at me or acknowledging the payment, she hurried the money into a skirt pocket. For a moment, I thought of offering more, but then practicality set in and I knew I must also save for my own security; I had no way of knowing when I might be asked to leave.

My friendship with Jenny, too, seemed to be slipping out of my grasp. I felt, in my fragile state, that all Jenny's talk had about it a happiness, an excitement at surface charms, mixed with a persistent reference to Bremen and what people would be doing there. In a different way, I missed Bremen, not our small rooms at the top of the Travelers' Arms, nor our routine lives, the stone storefronts and cold rain, but Aunt, whom I could still not imagine as dead, and also what I felt had been our friendship, Jenny's and mine.

We were out on a walk with Nettie Tennyson one Saturday, when Nettie suddenly stopped, perched herself on a rock, and unlacing her boot, shook out sand. "What pretty toes!" exclaimed Jenny, stopping too. Nettie rolled off her stocking and extended her slim foot with silent agreement. Jenny cried, "Vizzy, doesn't Nettie have the loveliest little feet!" Then Jenny herself had to join in the show of toes, pulling off both boots to foil Nettie's feet even more favorably. They leaned back on the rock and held two perfect pairs of feet skyward, while Jenny gave commentary: "My toes are so short, like grubs, but yours are long and so neatly fitted together, and your arch is high, like a little Japanese bridge. They should use your foot as a model in shop windows. Viola, have you ever seen such neat little feet?!"

No, I had to agree, abashed and unmoving in my left-footedness down the sand. No, never had I seen such pretty feet, feet that mirrored each other in calm self-sufficiency. I cursed them silently till their owners had tied up the laces again, and I felt as we set off that the foot exhibition had set them apart from me. From then on I felt like their clumping escort, tolerably amusing but outside a magic twosomeness.

Missing and mourning our old meeting of minds, I also felt embarrassed by Jenny's obvious preoccupation with the external trappings of her cousins' lives. I grew easily bored with her endless comparisons, her observations of minutiae. I felt excluded, too, as my own first impressions of the Borders were of sorrow and despair. I found no words with which to bring Jenny back. My long face must have bewildered her into greater permutations of happy chatter. She must have felt, meanwhile, that she was fitting in well.

On Walla, I privately observed, women could be as brainless and ornamental as the long-necked sea birds that flocked in on the occasional breeze to rest in some long flight and roll in the ants' insecticidal secretions before taking off again, except that the ladies of Walla had nowhere to go. Emma Borders sat at home to receive visitors who never came. If etiquette was the religion of Canada's first families, here the ladies became fundamentalists, and Emma Borders's name should have been up for beatification.

When we could persuade her to let us out, she stuck close. It was hard to say who was chaperoning whom. We bolstered her on walks; she was fragile, tall and narrow, teetering, ankles as small as a baby's wrists. We monitored her drinking at whist games, diluting her capfuls of gin with the lemonade Jenny and I drank through silver straws. She had contracted a cough that seemed to collapse her upper chest, to which she frequently applied a narrow hand, wreathed with rings.

"Part of my family's estate," she explained, mistaking my concern for interest in the jewelry. "I wear my wealth. Nothing much else to show for it. Not that I need money, we're so comfortable here," she added, somewhat gratuitously, I thought. Besides which, I had not been looking at her jewelry but at the green and yellow bruises that ringed her wrists.

As I helped her on with her wrap one afternoon after a luncheon visit with the Tennysons, I started at purple marks on either side of her throat. "Oh," she cried lightly, a hand reaching up. "I walked into the parlor door last night! I'm so accident-prone!" Nettie Tennyson and her mother joined Jenny in social smiles. I hid my face, busy arranging my *topi*.

One evening Aunt Emma retired from our game of pinochle early because of a sprained wrist. "So clumsy," she exclaimed, and it was true that she seemed always to be tripping, or pricking her finger on a needle; at the same time, no one moved with a finer fear of disturbing the lightest particle in the universe. When she was out of earshot, I whispered to Jenny, "Don't you feel it? They are so unhappy."

My friend, whose edges were being softened by the lapping waters of Walla society and who seemed to be adopting Nettie Tennyson's syntax, took it as unfair criticism of her cousin's wife. "Could it be jealousy or ennui from which you are suffering?" she asked, aggressively snapping down a match in her solitaire.

I stood thinking of these mysteries, and my own strange fate to have come to this island just as my home gave way, to be living under the same roof as a man so alarmingly attractive as Roddy Borders, while Jenny was herself quite untroubled. "Look," she lied comfortably, shuffling the cards and sticking them back into their box. "I hate it, too, but what can we do? Aunt Emma's a dear and Uncle Roddy's a pussycat and I'm sure we'll all get on like gangbusters!"

I looked away from the window to Jenny, blankly, as I realized how flat her face had become for me. "Don't you feel it?" I said. "That something's wrong here? She's not right for him."

She explained, "Aunt Emma's lonely."

Lonely was not the word I would have chosen. I didn't know whether Jenny meant something else or really referred to a condition I had overlooked. "That," I continued. "And just general problems. Also with your uncle."

"Vizzy," she said, as if she were Miss Morcombe in her mahogany office, registering disappointment over my six weeks' report, "she lost her faith. Back in Canada. Two years before they came out, Aunt Emma was terribly devout. Anglican, of course. And she lost it."

"How?"

"Mother said she was going round in Toronto one afternoon, shopping and whatnot. And suddenly in the coat department of Simpson's, she no longer believed."

I stared, waiting.

"Full stop," said Jenny. "All those coats like mortal shells, is how she explained it."

I cast my eyes around the room. *To be or not to be* offered itself unhelpfully in the place in my brain that struggled for answers.

Jenny pursed her lips and nodded. "It's affected her."

"Of course," I said. In my own state of grief postponed, I took it as a personal warning. "Of course," I ventured, remembering Harry Bagg's excitement over the golden column. "She could chart her own destiny."

"Well," said Jenny efficiently, as though she'd already considered this option and discarded it, "I think she consulted several clergymen. She relies on my uncle now for everything, you see." She patted the box of cards over her yawning lips. "Let's call it a day."

Part of my mind built a little pedestal for Roddy Borders while the other part puzzled over the frailty of Emma, with her strained wrists, turned ankles, eyes black from walking into open cupboards. I worried over the case of Aunt Emma the way at a stranger's house for dinner a child might worry the peas around on the plate, circling a knife through them, pushing them to the rim with a fork, growing bored with the nearsighted tedium, slightly nauseated at the smell of the bright-skinned enemy, and altogether angry with the project that must be achieved, of somehow disguising thirty green peas on a broad white Minton plate.

When I came upon Aunt Emma the next morning struggling to open a jar of marmalade, I nearly cried out, there in the bright kitchen, for I saw not what Jenny had comfortingly tried to persuade me of, a woman in her mid-forties struggling with religious incertitude, but some clothing stitched together over an emptiness that refused to acknowledge itself.

She turned. Her face seemed unformed and afraid. "What? Is something the matter? What are you looking at?"

"Nothing," I whispered. Turning away in tears I headed back to our bedroom, crawled under the covers with the snoring Jenny, and tried to sleep off my fears. My emotions were too pent up for rest, though. Perhaps Aunt Emma held a terror for me because I felt in some way my own hopes at risk. There seemed little to lay my trust in, apart from the miniature of my mother, of whose life and fate I could find no trace.

The following Saturday night Nettie came up to Egrets, and we girls hooked up each other's dresses again for another dance. "I want someone with some go to him," said Jenny as we sat in the parlor waiting for Miss Bartram to drive us to the club.

"Mr. Bagg's a nice person, bit of a loner, though," said Aunt Emma with effort, an arm over her eyes; she had a headache.

"I think Dr. Glover's terribly kind," said Jenny. "A fellow was in the other day with bunions and Dr. Glover handled his feet so tenderly. He's making special orthotics."

I looked at her with surprised respect. She was suddenly conversant about sutures and bandages and astringent cleaners.

"Robin Glover's interested in me, you know," Nettie reminded her, "but I quite fancy your uncle." She noted my eyebrows rising up. "He's the kind of man who can get things done."

"Of course he's taken," I reminded them in a hush, embarrassed to think of my own attraction, alarmed at her easy confession in front of Emma of the secret I'd kept closely guarded.

"Very go-ahead," agreed Jenny. "And such a nice face."

"That's putting it mildly. And muscular," added Nettie. They broke into giggles. Unnerved, I watched Aunt Emma's mouth pull lightly in a smile. She obviously had not heard. "There's Miss Bartram," she said.

Roddy Borders almost knocked my breath away in the mornings, carrying his towel and shaving cup down the hall, swinging in his dressing around the corner, with the firm and blonde-haired calves of his legs visible in their naked stride. When I should have veered discreetly back into my room, I hesitated. He turned slightly and gave me minute lifts of his chin, eyes brightly seeking out mine to confirm some suspicion he held. He knew I was observing him. It both exhilarated and embarrassed me to know he knew. Was it for me he would walk past our door still buttoning his shirt, a triangle of furry chest yet evident? The struggle to appear unaffected taxed my energy whenever I found myself with him, alone or with others.

I had thought this my own private reaction, though, until at the dance I noticed for the first time what a universally charismatic effect he had on people—men and women. They seemed charmed with him by compulsion, helpless to his smile. He moved with a glow and seemed to leave a hazy residue of happiness on those he favored.

Harry Bagg had warned me about Borders's interest in the island's gold. I felt sure he was capable of dangerous acts and I could not suppress a certain rising anger even as I felt myself in awe of Roddy

Borders's striding entrance at the club, his quiet nods at the lady packs. "Could you trust him, though?" I suggested to Nettie, who was watching him with keen concentration.

"Upper Canada," she said, as if that explained it all.

He aroused admiration by virtue of his sheer presence. Sauntering in immaculate whites around the foyer, casual and easy, with an elastic smile, Roddy Borders walked above the earth's surface. He seemed only slightly less than a god.

"He looks as though he could work magic," breathed Nettie over her cup of punch.

"Black magic," added Jenny, as though that were a greater accomplishment.

Once I looked closely, I saw that to my enormous surprise, even Harry Bagg, like a tamed duck, seemed under his spell. His kneeless walk attempted, unsuccessfully, Borders's sprung strut; he tried out the tight jaw, and mimicked Borders's habit of flicking his hair off his forehead with a twist of the neck. On Harry Bagg it looked like a muscle spasm.

"Has he got a tick?" asked Nettie, sending us into giggles.

Meanwhile on that evening Harry Bagg, happily oblivious to my fascination with Borders, again presented me with his formal, social side, sidling up with spare cups of punch, which seemed his usual gambit, gallant and useful at the same time. Pleased, I accepted his invitation to sit out the fox-trot.

His first words surprised me. "I don't like many people," he said, "but it's always a pleasure to see your face. It's so reassuring."

It was spoken as fact, not flattery. "I do have a calm sort of face," I agreed.

Harry Bagg smiled into his punch with warm pleasure.

Later, when we were dancing a slow waltz, he continued, "It's the roundness and the—" He paused, turning to look at me better under the lamp that hung on the wall. "There's a serenity," he said. "Do you believe in God?"

"Not very much. I believe in the past. I think people were better then."

"I see." He sounded preoccupied, as though he'd lost interest. He surprised me by suddenly agreeing with vigor. "So do I. If you dig to the right level."

"I wish I had religious faith. It seems to help people. Perhaps if I'd lived through an earthquake," I said, "or volcanic eruption, or had my best friend hit by a bus—"

"No," he interrupted quietly. "It doesn't help."

"My mother died on this island," I told him, and found myself excited to speak of it.

"Odd," he remarked, but asked no questions. "Do you miss her?"

His voice, direct and quiet, touched me to the core. No one had asked me this before, and the sheer wealth of pent-up emotion caused a mini damburst that washed my face with sharp tears. I stopped dancing and pulled away from him to say, "I do, very, very much. But how can it be? I never even knew her!"

He seemed untroubled by my behavior. "It doesn't matter," he said. "I miss things, too, that I never saw. The building of the Parthenon, the erection of Stonehenge, Leif Ericson's discovery of Newfoundland, Queen Victoria's coronation." He calmly wrapped an arm around my waist again, took up my hand and led me back into the slow waltz. "You're not just mourning your mother," he whispered. "You sense, as I do, that we've come too late."

"Well," I said, looking at his ear at close range, a perfect pink shell. "I think it's mainly my mother I miss. And my aunt."

"No. No. It's the past that we've lost, an age of hope and faith. You and I will never live in real time. What we do won't truly matter."

"I see," I whispered back. My head on his shoulder, told that my mistakes and yearning were of small consequence, to the steady *thuck thuck* rhythm of his heart, I felt peaceful. As others pranced around us, we seemed just to bend slowly; the experience to me was like being shaded by a tree, a maple in southern Ontario, that rocked and rustled in the wind. My upbringing told me I should be ashamed of my outburst, but nothing in his manner rebuked me. Instead my sorrow seemed to put him at ease and join us in a way our polite conversation never had.

"Harry," I began, as we swung around a corner stacked with chairs. I stopped, as there sat Emma Borders beside Roddy, both with their eyes on us. Emma seemed faintly interested in seeing me dance, while Borders sat like an Alsatian that, alert to a painful supersonic whistle, was straining at orders not to attack. Harry murmured a faint *hello* and moved us out of range again.

"I haven't danced in years," he said lightly.

"Nor I," I said. I was working hard at keeping my balance, and so far my foot was holding its own.

He laughed. "The two of us should be in a special room for the crippled, shouldn't we!" He quickly backpedaled, sensing my distress. "I meant that only in the nicest way."

"I don't see how you could."

"We're set apart. I think so, anyway." As the music moved up and around and back into the tonic, my partner looked down at me with curiosity. "Something's going to happen to me," he remarked. Looking into his face close-up, I read for the first time anxieties, undisclosed fears, passions submerged beneath that astounding assortment of hacked features and stiff hair. He read my face, too, and the lines in his fell slack.

"What's going to happen?" I asked. "Something bad? Are you sure?"

"Miss Bartram saw it in my teacup. Not necessarily bad, she said. But it will change my life. It's true." He gave me a twisted look. "And that's that. The present moves in of its own accord, doesn't it? Just like the legendary termite tunnels. It comes building around you, despite what you hope or want."

Having no sense of what he might mean, I had trouble finding some comforting answer. He studied my stammering as though a smile were all I had meant to convey, and that gesture in and of itself told me he was the sort of man I could love, who felt already no embarrassment at a smile exchanged in human sadness, at the quiet that surrounded our careful, clumsy waltzing. A low *zing* of current ran between us. I rested my head on his shoulder and found how comfortable that spot was. My hand on his chest fingered his pearl shirt studs, and we danced on with the slow grace that had soothed me from the first. As the music ended, he lifted my hand up to Roddy Borders as if presenting a wafer to the faithful, whispering to me, "You are a little sad and bewildered now, but you have a great potential for happiness, I think."

Before I could answer, Borders was pushing me around the floor in a close and puffing embrace. He seemed put out. "Not a man to trust," he said. "Look at his features. The face is the man. He's all bark. You want a fellow with some bite."

I didn't dignify the remark with an acknowledgment, once again paralyzed by the conflicting emotions that Roddy Borders aroused in me: social confusion and animal attraction. I tried to detach myself intellectually from the feel of his long legs pressing mine as we swung around the maple floor, his smell of sweat and lemon, his cheek's stubble that scratched my ear and neck, his brisk move into shadow that set us to mouth-to-mouth combat, soft and firm, till I struggled away, trembling, bewildered.

I tried to concentrate instead on Harry. "All bark" brought to my mind the image of a grand deciduous tree—with the rush of sap inside. The exchange with Harry Bagg had been, it seemed, like the sudden break of sun through a high-canopied forest. Mostly we worked in shade, we men and women, it seemed, and even a small ray graced the whole forest. I felt I had a real companion, who even in silence would share my sense of the world. I had looked to Harry Bagg as someone to marry me, and now I found that, when I disregarded my edgy alertness to Roddy Borders, I loved him—Harry was my man.

The happy tension increased between us. I worked with new commitment and interest in his goals. The sun shining into his little study seemed to bathe the two of us in drowsy calm. But while I made tea and copied data into notebooks and studied the notion of entwining my fate with Harry Bagg's, I sensed increasingly the shadow life at Egrets where Roddy Borders watched me watching him, and Emma lay gazing at the sky.

One evening toward the end of June, Borders was on the verandah, checking through his recent photographs from the dig. From my room I could hear his tenor voice gliding across the refrain of "Loch Lomond." He had been working in the darkroom off the kitchen all afternoon. The work must have gone well, I deduced from his song. I was alone with him as Jenny had gone off with Aunt Emma and Nettie to watch the preparations for a carnival entertainment down the Strand. It was a little operation of rickety tents and weather-beaten contortionists that traveled around the subcontinent and Pacific rim. Their annual stop on Walla apparently constituted one of the island's few diversions.

I had felt disinclined to walk down with them, claiming fatigue but secretly aware that declining would leave me alone in the house with Borders. It seemed a dangerously exciting option. Under guise of resting, I wandered at loose ends around our bedroom, picking up objects—large conch shells with pink lustrous linings, a mahogany alarm clock with a little pipping bell. Harry Bagg, without ceremony one morning, had presented me with five brass elephants, which I placed in diminishing size along the mantelpiece like the death of a bad idea.

I imagined Harry objectively, as though trying on a new blouse. He would probably be walking through the last of the day's digging, instructing the workers, "Scrape your loose." The findings were still not encouraging: a clay pipe, bones of a dolphin, a monkey's jaw, but no sign of the column of Zeus, Cronus, and Uranus. Rumor in the camp, I learned from Jenny, who'd heard it from Robin Glover, had it that Kinver was impatient and threatening to pack up soon, not wanting, in his words, to "throw good money after bad." Harry, of course, being Harry, held firm. I thought, as I arranged the elephants, for all his reputed stubbornness and obsession with Panchaea, he represented something I liked very much. He was not afraid to be a diminishing elephant.

"Viola!" called Roddy Borders's tenor, still on key, interrupting my thoughts. "Viola, come out here! Join me!"

What I had wanted—time by myself with him—seemed so easily attained I could only congratulate my good organizational powers as I threw my pointelle cardigan around my shoulders, loosely, so as not to hide the lovely polished cotton of my summer dress, bought with the last of Cousin Rudolph's birthday money at Eaton's just before the trip out. I started down the hall that smelled richly of wood oils and a sweetness I later knew was local bug spray, the precursor of Flit, thinking he saw for himself that I was worthy of him, that Emma was no match to me: helpful, heavy haired, twenty. Not proud to acknowledge this, I thought of myself as a realist. He was, I imagined, my other half, my counterpart. Blonde like my mother where I was dark, blue-eyed where I was brown, outgoing and forward-looking where I was tied to the past, aggressive and physical where I was reserved, Roddy Borders embodied the lost side of my heritage; with him I could become whole. He and I would now share stolen moments, in silence or in talk, never referring directly to our attractions but sealing our bond with a touch or glance before his wife returned. I was trying to step lightly and muffle the heavy, executioner's *tack, tack* of my new shoes across the teak boards, when from the shadows someone stepped ahead of me, blocking my path. Borders had rounded the corner of the hall, filled it with his vertical slimness, a silk ascot tied around his neck. His smile accordioned sideways, like a glow worm.

"What a pretty frock. You must come out and keep me company on the verandah." I looked at Jenny's elegant cousin, face distorted and florid. "With the sea's refreshing salt airs, the scent of jasmine and bougainvillea trellises clinging to your breath . . ."

He was drunk. He clapped twice and looked as though he might throw himself into the opening steps of a tango, then he subdued into the caricature of a gentleman. "Mango juice, Viola, my little niece, let us wayfarers, lonely ones, with too much time on our hands, share a cup . . . ?" Accepting his arm, I returned the cheap smile.

On the verandah he snatched at his trousers' knees to sit and pulled his rocker close up to mine. A thrill zinged like tiny lightning through me as his hand first brushed my wrist, then came to rest, large and warm, on top of my own.

"A young woman," he began, "alone in the wilds of Walla, walwala, wawal, wa . . ." He gave a downward push so that my chair rocked to his rhythm. The pressure of his hand on mine, which might have been avuncular, was a shade too firm, but an attempt at extrication I realized might suggest distrust. I desired his good opinion too much to risk offense.

"With you and Aunt Emma and Jenny and all the diggers stationed here," I reminded him, "we're hardly alone . . . Oh," I interrupted myself, spotting the pictures on the railing, "are those your photographs?" *Let's get impersonal.* My hand was by then feeling trapped and starting to hurt under the weight of his.

With a sly smile, he passed me the stack of photographs. Hand freed, I examined them with relief. They were glossy, black-and-white, finely focused images on paper the size of index cards. On top was a carefully labeled picture of an amphora. It was one I myself had dusted in Harry's office. Now I marveled at how beautiful it seemed in a photograph, set apart. The next picture showed the outline of the stone wall I'd seen emerging on my visits to the site. It, too, as a photograph, held a mysterious power. The third, a piece of metal with a ruler laid beside it for scale, looked more important than I knew from Harry it would be to the quest. The fourth—my heart jumped to my throat—the fourth was a man, utterly naked, standing sideways, the closer leg resting on the rung of a chair while his face turned coyly toward me. I knew the man: it was Harry Bagg. At least, I thought it was he, though the shock cast a film over my vision. I dared not understand the image before my eyes, yet the notion of seeing him so catapulted my heart around in my chest and I hardly knew what I desired.

"You like it?" whispered Roddy Borders's warm breath on my ear.

Stunned, I quickly turned to the next picture and met with another shock: a naked, hefty-thighed woman lying on a bed, lifting her arms up to dangle a necklace between her bosoms. Averting my head, I pushed the prints into Borders's lap.

He said, with a smile, "The lady was someone here before you, a governess for the Kinver boy. She had to leave. Too bad." He laid the stack to one side. His face, when I dared to glance up at it, had changed, blackened; his mobile mouth made a hard downward line. "You'd look very pretty on a bed like that, pearls, which," he said, appraising me, "need the caress of a woman's flesh to glow. Same as a woman needs a man. But you know all about that, don't you?"

I could not shake my head, my neck was so stiff with fear. Carefully, he reached for his glass, drained back half, and gave me another of his gentlemanly smiles gone agutter. Then, before I could pull away, he leaned over and I felt rubbery lips creeping up my neck like a crab. Courtesy and shame rebuking me all the while, I pushed him away, pressing a hand hard against the rough linen of his jacket. Leaning across me, he bore down on the chair's arm and sent me almost flying over the verandah in the sudden dive and duck as the runner warped over the wooden floor.

Then he stopped. I sat upright, ready to think I'd misunderstood. I breathed out, watching as, satisfied for a moment, he reached for the tumbler, tossed back the remainder of the drink, and, wild-eyed, began again: half stood, crouched, over, down, with his full weight upon me, his chest pressing mine, his astringent breath hovering over my ear, my hair, my neck, my chest, pinning my arms, as, whimpering, I struggled to free myself, press him off, while the chair, off kilter, tilted and rocked, till with one great thrust of my weight, it threw us forward and back and forward. My assailant stepped back, backward over the railing, and crashed to the ground. I struggled from the rocking chair and stood looking down on him, paralyzed for a moment with alarm and confusion. He lay motionless.

Thinking to bring a glass of water or a blanket, any of a number of items that my frightened mind suggested, I retreated into the house, grabbed a velvet cushion from the chesterfield, and hurried out again. The body that had so long entranced me lay still on the grass. I knelt and laid my head on top of the starched chest. *Ka-thump, ka-thump* frightened me at being so close. My own pulse off kilter, I did the only thing I could think of: I dragged him up the steps, head bumping each riser, and pulled him across the porch, upside down, his hair catching leaves fallen from bougainvillea, foot knocking the doorsill with a solemn *thud* that brought a moan from his throat. Through the house I pulled him, to the parlor chesterfield, heaved him onto it, stuffing the pillow and photographs behind him, arranging his arms and legs out straight. Then I retreated to my own room, where I scrubbed my face and hands, took off my Eaton's dress, sat down on the bed, breathed in once hard, and howled.

When Aunt Emma and Jenny came home, I met them in my dressing gown, *The Ring and the Book* in hand for camouflage. I had freshened my face and combed my hair, though I felt soiled and spent. They noticed nothing, however, and just glanced casually toward Borders. His breathing was shallow. I prayed he was only asleep.

"Out long?" asked Aunt Emma, lifting her hat off her hairdo. "Ow!" She sucked a finger.

"For some time."

"He works so hard," said Jenny, bending over him and patting his hand. "Poor, poor Uncle Roddy. Tuckered out."

"Had a nice time?" I asked Jenny as she readied for bed.

"Lovely. Harry Bagg met us afterward and gave us *gin and tonics!* You should have come. Don't mope around here all the time."

"You're right," I said.

"He's really quite sweet. I know what you see in him. And there's going to be a lovely booth with ducks, fake ones, and a man selling big fluffy balls of grandma's hair. I haven't had that in years—so sticky on the cheeks!" For once the rush of her simple commentary seemed like good news. Unwilling to change the mood, to intrude ugliness and conflict into her easier world, I sat under the sheets, listening in silent gratitude.

The next day Roddy Borders was out before the rest of us woke, spending the afternoon in the darkroom, and entering the house late in the evening. Apart from my own sudden sense of revulsion for him and disgust with myself, things remained as before, with Aunt Emma bruising herself in doorways, Jenny busy with Nettie and Robin Glover, and me feeling grateful to Harry and studying often my mother's miniature, longing to walk into that world under glass where strife and tension vanished in cloudless grace.

Afraid to stay in the house again by myself, I agreed two evenings later to accompany Jenny and Aunt Emma down to see the carnival in action. Borders was sitting astride a chair, cleaning his new Kodak, when Jenny and I appeared in the parlor, *topis* in hand.

"Gracious!" said Aunt Emma. She moved out from behind the curtains, where it appeared she'd been hiding, and straightened a strand of hair. "Can it be time to go?"

Borders took aim through the camera at each of us in turn. "Does Viola plan to eat a live chicken?" he inquired. "Or will Jenny be swallowing fiery spuds on a stick this evening?"

"It will be fun to walk down," suggested Aunt Emma, buttoning on her shoes.

I said, "I want some grandma's hair."

"Oh, yes, I haven't tasted grandma's hair in years," repeated Emma, brightening.

"Why don't you just chew your own?" asked her husband with a sweet grin.

"I fancy that shooting gallery," said Jenny. "With moving targets."

"Oh, yes!" cried Aunt Emma.

A small belly laugh from Borders did not convince me of any amusement. "You!" he called to his wife. "You couldn't shoot a target. You'd take up the cause of the little moving ducks and cry before you pulled the trigger. Watch her, girls, she's soft as butter. You might lose her in the sun if you set off now."

"We'll wait on the porch," I told Aunt Emma, eager to get out of the house.

"She's unwell," I said to Jenny outside, as we tied on our hats.

"It's overbreeding," said Jenny. "The stock weakens, and you get Aunt Emma—overrefined and skittish."

"She's not a cow," I said.

Jenny just laughed. "If she were, she'd be put out to pasture!"

"Jenny!" But my friend, as usual, was just joking. Merriment at our outing had now taken hold, and the world for her teemed with light nonsense.

I felt for a time betrayed, by what seemed Jenny's abandonment of niecely duties, by Emma's obstinate deceit. Things were very wrong. Aunt Emma was wearing round sunglasses behind which I sensed her eyes had not slept. She was coughing and had tied a large green silk scarf around her neck. "One of my chills," she said. On the down slope of tiny roller coaster, the scarf fluttered too hard, slipped through the knot of her fingers, and exposed for one brief, horrible moment, before she grabbed at it and the shutters closed again on that flash I'd had of her secret married life: a thin trace of red, as though a cord had pulled around the narrow drape of throat that trilled with an unsure passage of blood from heart to brain. All this I saw in an instant on the roller coaster, as Aunt Emma turned her head and the scarf blew out, then was caught up again, but I knew, by her timid blue eyes glancing behind dark glasses, by her hand, thin and cold, patting my own hand suddenly, the pleading smile that twitched at her lips, that she knew I knew and that I was agreeing by silence to say nothing.

I was so weighed down that I felt no forward motion when we stepped off the ride. I stood to one side, unable to move. Jenny pressed out behind me and pulled us, her aunt on one arm, me on the other, and called, "There's the booth! We must try the ducks!" A miracle, I felt, that someone felt excitement in this confused array of pleasure contrivances.

The shooting gallery featured a plaster basin at one end, painted deep blue, decorated with wildflowers. A blue tent arching overhead made a perfect happy sky for seven celluloid ducklings who, motherless and without a compass, bobbed at random on the water. It was not an easy task, standing some ten feet back, toes behind a chalk line, trying to swing the hoop up into the basin to ring a duck. It was, in retrospect, a rather silly game, but I was peculiarly attracted to those celluloid birds, appalled at the gleeful snaring of them. The prize: one of the teddy bears that were strung up like convicts behind the ticket-taker.

Aunt Emma was seized by a sudden urge to buy ten rings. She planted her size five-and-a-half-double-A feet anxiously behind the line and pulled an arm back to let fly. She was unused to sport, and I distrusted her enthusiasm. I pictured her hurling the hoops across the space like deadly haloes, decapitating the ticket-taker standing there by the water. But as I waited, braced, nothing happened. Aunt Emma lowered her arm, stood fingering the hoops she'd bought. In the stillness of anticipation, we the waiting heard her long sigh as she walked toward the little blue-lit pond.

"Behind the line," warned the man in charge. Men from the dig waiting behind us were murmuring some impatience.

Aunt Emma threw him a glance as she continued her amble down to the water. "Look," she said conversationally to the man, peering close. "It's *our* island, isn't it?" Always slightly farsighted, I could see that someone had painted a coastline on the back of the plaster basin, and it did look like Walla, with the club's domed roof central to the modest skyline, and a threateningly fiery rendition of our volcano at the far end. Aunt Emma shook her hand in the highly tinted blue water. Two fat little yellow representations trembled nearby and spun away. "Come back!" she whispered with a catch in her throat. Two diggers exchanged looks. "I won't hurt you," we heard her insist as she made a grab at a duck that bobbed down and up. It collided with a fellow duck as Aunt Emma, on tiptoe, crying out, "Come back!" threw herself into the water—right over the basin's edge like a diving bell.

"What's this?" cried the ticket man, forehead twitching. He might have said more, but I didn't hear, as two of the diggers and I were already poolside, pulling at legs and hair amid ducklings circling and bumping, turning Aunt Emma's head sideways, alarmed by her closed eyes, jerking her heavily from the water, over the plaster edge, supporting her upright with an arm around her waist.

"Tropical fever," advised the ticket-taker. "It affects the ladies."

We stretched her out on the sawdust. Some water trickled out of her slack mouth as her eyes opened, unfocused, unfriendly.

"Could be the sun," said one of the diggers, trying to lift her upright.

"That's it," I whispered. "Overtired."

Jenny on one side, me on the other, a digger behind, we pulled her up enough for her narrow feet to take some of the weight and her legs to waggle forward. As we stepped measure by measure out of the tent, her clothing dripped and dragged in the dust. People must have gawked but I looked at no one, panicking still, the question running through my mind: had she really tried to drown herself?

Out into the shadows of the afternoon, Jenny said with practical wisdom, "We'd better get home."

We were breathless with carrying Aunt Emma, who though thin was not a small person and was lending little help to the effort. The sun overhead was hot enough to smelt rock, and my spirits were flagging at the thought of the length of sand ahead, through the park, to the Strand Road, up to Egrets, when a cheerful *toot toot* startled us. Turning, we faced the dusty front end of a Morris Cowley, the owner herself sitting tall behind the wheel.

"Our deus-ex-motorcar," I said to Jenny, who smiled agreeably; she had forgotten all her Latin.

"Hop in," Miss Bartram cried in her hectic, abstracted way. "Which direction are you headed? Poor thing, Emma. You look quite peaky. And wet."

"Egrets," said Jenny. "Please, if it's not out of your way."

"You girls are always in need of rescue. You must learn to fend for yourselves! Discovered the fate of your mother yet, Viola?"

"No."

"Tried the volcano?" Miss Bartram shifted gears several times and we were off. "Egrets!"

There were no egrets on Wallawalhalla. This occurred to me on the bumpy drive back, in the bizarre way things do, irrationally in context of my other preoccupations, but the notion began to irritate me, that the house where I was living and to which I was returning the ailing Emma Borders, née Satterfield, was a fabrication. But Egrets dominated the view at the end of the Strand Road, and there was no denying that at least as a great wooden structure with porches and porticoes and birds of passage flying off its roof like figures in a glockenspiel, Egrets more than existed. And, that being so, we pulled Aunt Emma up the steps and through a dark entrance hall into the parlor.

"Come hear us play, Mr. Bagg and me," called Miss Bartram, walking backward down the front steps. "We've worked up a partita duet."

"Thanks," I called and waved back. "We're very grateful."

"He's been asking. I promised him you'd come," she said.

"It's the heat," Jenny was telling me, pulling a photograph from a frame, bending over her aunt and fanning her with a tattered picture of Aunt Emma herself as a graduate. "She's so fair. This heat could knock a stone off its feet." She paused to examine the photograph. "So pretty back then. All in white."

As we wrapped Aunt Emma in a light blanket, anxious to cover her as we began the undressing, she sat stiff and expressionless.

"How do you feel?" I asked, pulling off a shoe and tipping out the water onto the dusty carpet.

"What?"

"How are you feeling? Better? That was a nasty accident."

She shook her head. "No," she whispered. "No." It was a firm denial of everything—us, life, the world.

Once nearly drowned myself, aware of its confusions, I avoided the subject. Jenny brought in dry undergarments and a change of skirt and blouse, which we, without help from the inert and seemingly ungrateful Aunt Emma, managed to fit around her. Jenny was less concerned than I was about leaving her to recover in the parlor. "Uncle Roddy should be in soon," she said. "He's developing, out in the darkroom."

"We should tell him," I said.

"No," whispered Aunt Emma. "He mustn't be disturbed. He's a genius, you know. The greatest man on earth."

"Sshh. You need to rest," Jenny said, slipping the picture back in the frame and setting it on a table.

"I can't rest," Emma whispered. Her voice seemed to scratch at the haze that separated her from us. I looked from Jenny to Emma, hand draped across her eyes, exhaling noisily next to a small portrait of herself as a young woman, in the white dress of her school graduation, before any Roddy Borders demanded a wife, before her faith wandered beyond her range in the Simpson's coat department. It was one minute before six. The eight-day clock in its domed globe, swinging in its dance, pulled its hands up for a moment, poised to spring on us new counts of treachery.

Inside Miss Bartram's House

*T*HE NEXT MORNING, while Jenny was slipping into her camisole, hopping into stockings, ready for a day at Dr. Glover's, I lay in bed, thinking of Harry, wondering where my rookie heart was taking me. Aunt Emma had evidently recovered. Her footsteps were tapping along the hall, bringing us, I imagined, some burnt toast, when we heard the ratchety pull of the doorbell. The footsteps faltered, moved away. After a time, Aunt Emma, *topi* in hand, opened our door with a tap. She seemed ill. A yellow bruise edged above her collar, a blue one shone through white powder by her ear. She looked me up and down with dull confusion. "A gentleman caller," she whispered, pulling off her gloves. "Mr. Bagg has dropped by. You girls get your clothes on."

We wrapped dressing gowns around ourselves in time decently to greet the largely angular Harry Bagg fingering the parlor piano. "Just dropping by," he repeated. He had evidently rehearsed the phrase. "This needs tuning, eh? Not the climate."

I nodded, giddy at finding him there. "I'm just on my way down to work," I said. "We were about to breakfast."

"I'll wait and walk you," he said. "I was up early, walking, thinking, and wanted to bring you this." He held out a stalky plant. "Native to the western shore of the island. Thought it would interest you." It was tall and spiky and had a blossom like a weak-chinned face.

"Pee-U!" said Jenny, clamping a hand on her nose. "It stinks—like rotten meat!"

"Flies love the smell," Harry said, pointing proudly down into the throat. "It's like an aphrodisiac."

"A what?" Jenny brightened, checking Harry's reaction. He ignored her.

"It gets them to go down in there and then traps them with all its sharp spikes that point—do you see?—downward." He stepped toward me. "It won't bite *you*," he said, smiling, his idea of a tease.

In the aftermath of the scare with Roddy Borders, I felt all the more grateful for Harry Bagg's friendship. Though Jenny might think him as plain as the plant he held out for me to admire, might find his endless fascination with the past a dull parading of facts, I knew I needed him. And wanted to hear his voice discussing things new to me and to discover with time, I hoped, the consequence of his mind's busy rustlings. Looking at his earnest face and steady hands outstretched, I told myself that much between a man and a woman might remain hidden, but I praised my fortune in finding a mate made of maple, and tried to feel the shade of his mind, to imagine the sweet sap beneath the bark. Looking him over, I spoke a silent, curious *yes*.

The idea of marriage made me nervous, though. To attach myself to a man from Caledonia, intellectual, with a limp and an obsessive, unalterable interest in life B.C.; it seemed like burying myself alive. *Can this union succeed?* an advice column might headline our case. I tried to make a list of our qualities. I determined that Harry and I shared a geographical past, we liked digging up antiquity, we believed that history drifted toward decline, and we were dedicated to working against the current. There my list came to an end, and I doodled sunflowers in the margin and smiled to recall his energy, bad jokes, unapologetic honesty. Still, as much as Harry and I talked and bantered, there seemed often no way into him. I sometimes felt as lonely in his company as I did in Jenny's, though not as sad. Permanent entrance to a man was perhaps as sealed as the Egyptian tombs Harry had described to me; no light shone on his inner life behind what he declared more or less officially as his passions and goals. The door opened for a moment on treasures, then locked shut again. In contrast to Roddy Borders, the minute to minute for Harry seemed to leave no mark; the present just barely existed for him. Yet I existed, it encouraged me to realize. He was courting me, surely, with his visits and he offered my only hope to a settled life. Otherwise, I'd decided, I would become, with some training, a schoolteacher. I tried to picture myself as Miss Faith Morcombe, cameo pinned at my throat, or Miss Charity, shooting baskets in a gym filled with noisy girls. But I doubted I could pull it off. Teaching did not suit me temperamentally; it took someone more hopeful about the future. Harry was my chance. And if sometimes frustrated, I could not stay away; a little electric current inside me seemed to be hooked up with magnets ready to charge toward his iron lure.

While Jenny and Nettie spoke endlessly of Robin Glover's upright character and Roddy Borders's Grecian nose, I kept thoughts of Harry to myself. My future was too risky a business to offer up as chitchat. My inner preoccupations separated me in an invisible way that my friends did not mention but clearly perceived. They no longer expected me to join in their strolls along the beach or make up a foursome at the Tennyson bridge table. Though the separation was mostly of my own making, I needed guidance I could not get from my friends or the delicate Emma Borders, who sat working her embroidery, taking shallow breaths.

One day, seated near her, darning up some holes in my good stockings, which had been eaten through by something in the night—and I didn't want to speculate what—I asked her if she'd ever heard of my mother. "Her father was in the Navy, stationed here. About twenty years ago."

"How lovely!" remarked Aunt Emma and looked up, illuminated from within by some notion that I was telling her happy news.

"She died here," I added, but her expression remained fixedly beatific. Observing the lightness of her hair, her eyes, her almost porcelain complexion, I realized how closely she resembled my mother's miniature. On a whim, I fetched it from my room.

She held it close to her weak eyes. "Isn't that lovely! This is your mother? How lucky you are! A thing of beauty is a joy forever, or so they say. And what a handsome little frame!"

Whatever I had hoped for did not happen. She handed the picture back with such a tremble that it fell into her lap and we both had to rummage around amid the embroidery threads and her full skirt to retrieve it. "So clumsy!" she whispered. "Take care of that, Vizzy. Relations never fail you."

As I dropped the picture into my pocket and took up my darning, I felt more then ever bereft of conversation and companionship. I remembered Miss Bartram's invitation to tea and suddenly desired to see inside her queer little house that looked like a Brothers Grimm gingerbread cottage; I needed to consult her about my future with Harry; I wanted to discover the reason she seemed to single me out; I wanted to ask what she knew about my mother.

With a visit to Miss Bartram in mind, on the following day I tried baking another Empire Cake. It rose, at least. I spread it with white boiled icing and added some bougainvillea blossoms around the top. The cake smelled sour but looked pretty as I packed it into a little tin box. "Come on with me," I said to Jenny. "She's so nice," I added.

Jenny declined. "Nettie's invited me down to a tiddlywinks. Robin Glover should be there. You go on, though," she said. She looked pale as she sorted through her postcard collection. Pictures of Niagara Falls and Banff and Victoria littered the floor. She was homesick, I saw, moved by her effort at cheerfulness.

"Another time, then," I said.

"She's a tiresome woman," Emma Borders said on the verandah, embroidery hoop shading her eyes. "My only friend here, you know, but always predicting doom. People should be more thoughtful."

Within twenty minutes of quick walking, I arrived, headachy from the sun and soaked with perspiration, at Miss Bartram's gate. The steeply pitched roof of her house, called Nuremberg Cottage, I learned from the little sign painted on the gate, defied the needs of the climate and contrasted spookily with the lush vegetation around. I was not sure I wanted to go in. I shook the dust off my hem and kicked my shoes through her yew bushes a few times to clean them. From the porch I caught the *ting, ting* of delicate plucking—her newly installed harpsichord. I mustered some courage. The doorbell jangled atonally over the sound.

"Who is it?" Miss Bartram barked, and when I identified myself, there was a heavy rattling of metal locks along the height of the door before she opened it. "Hoofed it, did you?" she asked first thing, towering over me on her tottering high-heeled pumps. She was dressed all in black. "I'm in mourning," she explained before I could answer her question. "My ancestors at Agincourt."

"But I thought that had taken place in October. Shakespeare . . ."

"One honors as one can. *Old men forget,* but not old women. That's our fate. Like elephants. Come in, come in. You made a cake? How charming! I never touch sweets. It's a pleasant walk, isn't it? Mr. Bagg's given me some dreadfully complicated pieces that I'm beating my brains over. Walking—you're a nonconformist, like me. Though," she added, leaning over me, "I wouldn't advise much walking after dark. The white ants . . ."

"No," I agreed to stop her from telling me about the ants.

She did anyway. "When there's this much rumbling in Mt. Walla, you know the ants are distressed. They might do *anything!*"

She brought out a tray with cups and saucers and a teapot, no two of the same pattern. In casting my eyes around the room, I was surprised by the odd assortment of objects—limbs of statues, metal spears, paving stones, broken plates—like properties backstage in a theater. The house was much smaller than Egrets, and her main room looked not so much like a Toronto parlor as an auction house. There was an enormous chesterfield with two broken legs propped on books, a deteriorating wing chair, two leather ottomans, a headless bronze sculpture with stubs of arms outstretched.

"You dust and spray," Miss Bartram complained, pouring out, "but they carry off everything. Or drop things off you'd never want. Lock your windows! One morning I found among my rhubarb a great Viking shield! Nicely preserved, bits glued firmly back on. That's it—I've hung it over the fireplace—as a warning!"

I followed her pointing finger to a huge flat, circular wooden shape studded with metal hanging over the hearth. Beside it were framed prints that caught my eye.

"Etching is my passion," she said, noting my interest.

I moved close up to inspect. "You did these?" One print was a fine architectural drawing of an interior. I recognized the Walla club's paneled foyer, decorated with domestic debris: a bonnet, an open book, a lady's boot, a lap rug, a hair ribbon.

Miss Bartram whispered excitedly, "It happened one evening, at dusk. A sudden attack by the white ants. Species *Termites*. Before my time. I myself have triple locks on all my doors. And a dead bolt. They carried off the dead, parts left intact. And one young woman, whom they crowned their queen triumphant!"

"Hmm," I said as politely as I could, unnerved by her vehemence.

We sipped Lapsang souchong. "How are the Borderses treating you?" she asked.

I hesitated. "Aunt Emma is very kind. And Uncle Roddy."

Miss Bartram slammed down her cup so hard some mended chips sprayed out onto the carpet. "Stop calling him 'uncle,' if just in my house. Your relations are far grander and worthier than the likes of him."

Taken aback, I said, "What do you know about my relations?"

"Well," Miss Bartram answered, working her mouth around, smiling strangely as though caught out in an untruth but still sticking by it, "I have my theories about you, you see. Breeding shows. My teacups tell some tales." Her eyes narrowed. "You never knew your mother, did you?" Lifting up the lid of the teapot, she looked in and said, "You had no idea, I gather."

I hesitated. "Of what?"

"That you were that unfortunate young woman's child. Your mother, my dear, is the Empress of the White Ants."

I stared at her. My mind reeled. I considered the possibility for less than a second before reason stamped its angry foot. I put down my cup with a trembling hand and stood. "Thank you, Miss Bartram, but I see it's getting late . . ."

"Sit down. You don't believe me."

She looked harmless enough for me to say, with abrupt relief, "No. No, I don't as a matter of fact."

"Pish posh. That's up to you." She looked defiant. "Something to eat? Your cake is, ah, perhaps lacking in something? Tell me about the dig."

"They don't seem to be turning up anything much. A few mummies. No gold column yet."

"Harry's mistaken about all that. He should be on the lookout for lemur bones."

"I beg your pardon?"

"Lemurs. Little nocturnal animals, name comes from the Latin *lemures,* meaning ghosts. I think your archaeologists would do well to consider that this island is part of the lost continent of Lemuria." Miss Bartram sped into an explanation she seemed annoyed at giving. "What is now dry land was once under water, and what is now under water was once dry land. It's good practice, just to get things in perspective. Just think of the world in color reverse: the sky as white, the sand as blue; or try size: people as tiny creatures scratching around in dirt, and ants as great masters of earth's destiny. But we'll get to that later. Lemuria, now: down goes up, up goes down, which is why you find lemurs in both India *and* Madagascar. How did they possibly get there? By walking—over dry land, every bit of which is now under the sea, except Wallawalhalla, the last bit of land bridge. So, a lemur jawbone, a lemur thigh bone, and we're home free! Unless you're afraid to think of places shifting over time. Unless you're silly enough to overlook lemurs in your search for gods."

"I think Harry told me something of this when we met," I answered, unwilling to walk onto her minefield.

"Harry Bagg's not afraid of ups and downs." Miss Bartram leaned hard toward me, cup to her chest. "He's afraid of the past."

And as if on cue, Harry Bagg crossed the porch with that lopsided gait, bearing a musical score. "Hello, Viola," he said and shook my hand warmly, as if I had not seen him already in his little office that morning.

"Hello," I said, feeling both joy and confusion. Afraid of the past? I would have thought, if anything, afraid of the future. Harry Bagg, now to my mind my future fiancé, was saving me from the terrible unknown and was, it suddenly struck me, perhaps the greatest unknown of all. Everything he did I determined to observe.

He set the score on the harpsichord and, standing, ran his fingers over the plucking keys. After a short interlude of scales, he stretched out in one of Miss Bartram's chairs, in the process of unstuffing itself, crossed his boots, rested his hands over his middle, and said to me, "How are you getting on? All right?" I was grateful when Miss Bartram handed him a plate to see him chewing my cake without obvious politeness. He wiped his fingers on his handkerchief. "How's that allegro, Miss Bartram?"

"Oh, I'm struggling. But play for us, Harold! What a treat, Viola, to have a musical man in the house. It organizes the vibrations."

Harry Bagg immediately installed himself at the harpsichord. I could see he felt quite at home there, that the two had a routine established whereby Harry played while Miss Bartram worked on some score of her own at the table. In a chair by the window, I studied my secret intended: from the left, from the right, from behind as he carefully fingered through the repertoire of Bach he knew by heart. He played with a light deliberateness, almost mechanically. He was very exact. His fingering brought from the instrument pluckings as subtle as a lute's.

Miss Bartram looked up after a while, hot with concentration. "You know, I've got a tin cabinet, came in on the last boat. Protects the instrument from the ants. I've been sleeping in here to keep them away from it. If you could just help me put it in place."

"Certainly, Miss Bartram. I'll have that slice, Vizzy, if it's homeless," said our visitor, eyeing my cake, glad to do me the favor. "Then we'll get your cabinet."

Said cabinet, a kind of metal hut with a hinged door, something like a doghouse for a St. Bernard or a giant cake tin, we carried in from her porch and fitted over the harpsichord. The result was like lowering a jar over a bee: as Harry tried out a scale, the widely reverberating buzz suddenly became a flat and localized hum, and, so to speak, lost its sting. Harry's fingering sounded metallic and tuneless, but he kept on, striking dead notes and double dead notes as it wound down and down. It seemed an absurd device as it spoiled the very sound Miss Bartram had worked so hard to bring to Nuremberg Cottage, but Miss Bartram regarded the tin hut with quiet satisfaction.

Suddenly getting up as Harry played on, she nodded to me, and dropped in my lap a weighty tome, one volume of a set of ragged-spined encyclopaedia. "*Termes,*" she whispered. "I want you to read this. We call them white ants, but they aren't ants at all. Termites is what one should technically say. And this book does not cover our branch of the family. They're like the distant cousins in Debretts, important to us but not included by the genealogists."

Under *Termes* I found brief descriptions and a few illustrations that quite put me on edge, as I sat, legs folded up, almost levitating with discomfort. Against my will, I learned about the insects' colorless appearance, their complex system of passageways, the queen at the center who lay like a great slug with distended abdomen, moved around, licked, and fed by the workers, just laying eggs. The book talked of workers decomposing the riffraff thrown up against the walls of the mound. I whispered over to Miss Bartram, who had returned to her score, "They chew up everything that lands on the beach?"

Miss Bartram smiled politely. "Did you get to the part about the glue? Look up *nasuti.*"

Nasuti. Soldiers, almost jawless, had long snouts housing a gland that could squirt a glue over its enemies, rendering them paralyzed or actually stuck together. "Good heavens," I breathed.

"It's quite a serious matter, though no one around here will listen. You know about the massacre, and one young woman was taken away to be queen!" She looked at me intently. "You know why you're here, don't you?"

Was this a theological question? Did Miss Bartram have psychic revelations for me? "To discover the secrets of the past," I replied unsteadily.

"Well, there's an original idea. What secrets exactly and why should one discover them?"

"Well, Mr. Bagg wants to prove that Zeus was king. And Mr. Kinver wants to find Atlantis. That, or trace his ancestry back to classical times. And Mr. Borders wants to photograph right down to the molecule everything they dig up—."

"Gold," she interrupted. "The answer, dear child, is *gold.* We're here to get rich. Samuel Q. Kinver can't afford his houses and horses and hunts without some inflow of the stuff, and he's determined to have it, but even more determined to establish himself as the discoverer of the lost Atlantis, which he is not about to find on Walla! It's your so-called uncle who's just after gold. The first nasty nuggets turned up in the sixteenth century when a lucky Dutchman was blown over to Walla by winds. He took back a chunk of gold as big as a chamber pot, I'm told. Red gold, as they call it in the medieval tales. Very valuable stuff, if that's the stuff you value. And we all seem to. And we've been looking for it ever since. Has something to do with the volcano. Gold forged under specific geomorphic conditions, etcetera, etcetera. Herodotus mentions it."

"I thought the volcano was dormant."

"Rumbles now and again. But it did its work, apparently. If they could only find the rest of the gold. If there is any. Personally, I think Jerry van Dutchman probably stumbled across the only bit. But I'm being tedious. More tea?"

We sat in silence some minutes as the new leaves steeped, Harry's steady climbs and circlings back a counterpoint to my troubled thoughts. I whispered so as not to disturb the pot, "You certainly aren't here for gold, Miss Bartram."

"You're quite right. I just stay on to protect and warn people. I have a drafty little place near Boston, inherited from my father's family. It dates from before the Revolution, which practically makes it un-American! I was keeping house for him out here before he died. I am the last of the line, since my nephew was killed in the war. I could go back anytime, but one stays on." Her mouth went into train tracks again as she looked me over, knowingly. "Well!" she breathed. "Surely Mr. Bagg is thirsty. Ask him to come out for some tea."

I peeked through the little door at his back. "Tea, Harry?" It was dark inside, lit only by a small lantern that cast a white light over the pages of music and the black keys and turned the contours of his face skeletal.

He gave a businesslike nod to the page and at the end of a line, emerged. Straightening like a ladder unfolding, he smoothed down the lacquered hair, lifted up his shoulders to a right angle, and lowered himself into a wing chair. "Fine instrument," he said just before the first hefty forkful of cake muffled his speech. I cut more to have at the ready. Watching him, I noted that he ate the way the prime minister waved— stiff armed, up and down.

Harry knew all about virginals and harpsichords and had a way of starting in on the topic as if we had been discussing it mutually all along. "Of course," he began, with a dubious, weighing, critical tone, enjoying his judgments, "the very finest were built by the Rucker brothers." He raised an eyebrow at me knowingly. "Antwerp. Of course, many instruments have been made to resemble the Ruckers's. And the exterior may indeed be quite similar, but the tone quality gives it away the instant one commences to play. Construction of the soundboard. Not to mention the frame points."

"Hmm, frame points," I said. I hoped that I'd get interested in harpsichords after a while. I'd heard that a couple often started out strangers and grew to resemble each other. Somehow, with Harry, I doubted that would happen. I imagined rather that I would have to care for him like a demanding houseplant, something stationary, requiring vigilance and steady watering. Or perhaps a grandfather clock: tall and wooden, with one or two stiffly moving parts and a ticking in tireless meter. I would dust, consult, but never hope to move it myself, one puny girl. Or, I added, stringing along metaphors to pass the time as he stooped inside the cake box again, he was buried treasure, a Pandora's box, and I wondered what I might find inside. And what did Harry understand about *me?*

When he folded up his music and declared himself ready for a swim off Devil's Peak, I got up, too, but Miss Bartram seemed anxious for me to stay. "Don't you want to know more of your heritage?"

"Miss Bartram . . ." I said, "it's *not* my heritage," but I could not stop her. The white ants were clearly her best subject.

"Don't imagine," she began, and I sat down again, resigned. "Don't imagine that the termites dine as we do, my dear, on chicken and eggs and some spinach on the side. No. They grow mushrooms in little moonlit gardens. The mushrooms provide tasty vitamins, a little treat at breakfast time, but more importantly, so I understand, they break up the woody beds on which they grow. Then the termites feed off the wood. Do you see? There are lunar groves of fungus. The workers huddle under the mushrooms, moistening and pruning them, rather like sunbathers applying lotion under beach umbrellas, as it were. Ha! If you look closely at the humus around the mushrooms, you might spy a polished toe of a boot poking out or a man's finger resting beside the trunk of the smooth morel—so I'm told."

I gaped mentally but tried to keep from Miss Bartram the extent of my shock at these descriptions. "Go on," I said.

"The termites' tunnels change in style from the classical to the medieval," Miss Bartram continued. "Like the dripping dungeon stuff you read about in *Morte D'Arthur*. Behind a great metal door, complete with little grill window, is the royal suite. It's like walking into another kind of garden, not of flowers or mushrooms but of light. Reds ricocheting off bare white walls and low-slung chairs, brilliant blue searing the floor with a long ribbon of eerily overdone river, greens illuminating the figures recumbent on a divan."

"How could there be any light?" I didn't ask the more obvious—how did Miss Bartram know these things—for fear of offending her and inciting more volatility.

"Glass," she explained. "They've restored a window from the Hagia Sophia, Constantinople, from glass bits washed up."

"I see."

"I know glass, incidentally, being myself from a family of glaziers. One of my ancestors worked on the Prophets, in the Augsburg Cathedral. No doubt you've seen them."

I confessed, "I've never been to Europe."

"Don't bother. If you stay in Wallawalhalla long enough you'll find all you need of past civilization. Most of it has been destroyed and washes up here eventually." She considered for a moment, dipping her toast into her cup. "People always like Windsor Castle. The Louvre is said to have some good pictures. *Mona Lisa* . . . Or do you prefer the modern stuff? What's left standing is hardly worth that long trip—rain, mediocre guides, lice-infested hotels, German tourists who hiss at you, 'Be qviet, vee vant to hear our guide!' My cousin and I did the tour before Walla. Of course the Bristol is the only place to stay. In Salzburg the Bristol Hotel was really all we saw, it rained so much. How did Mozart keep his spirits up? No wonder he died young."

"And what do they do down there actually?" I asked, fascinated by the original, awful topic.

"The termites? They have long conversations about all sorts of things."

"But, but they can't *talk!*"

Her eyes wobbled for a moment in confusion, then the answer came. "Ouija board. Very clever they are about Anglo-Saxon poetry. Experts on meter. They chew to the rhythm of 'The Seafarer,' going right through life rafts in a single night if they keep the pace." I balked at this nonsense, stifling a guffaw, but she went on. "The ones who chew things up stuff the remains into the bottom of the volcano, and it melts or smelts in the lava or whatever is down there. Steam vents. Your Uncle Roddy," she burst at me suddenly with fiery eyes, "thinks that's what turns into gold. He gave a little scientific lecture on this subject, which of course you and your friend missed, having had the wisdom to arrive some days following. Oh yes, he's got it worked out! All the detritus washed up on Walla, he claims, the debris of centuries, gets chewed into tiny bits, stuffed down the volcano, and changed by the heat into a peculiar form of gold. He had us sit on hard benches in the dark while he pushed magic lantern pictures back and forth across one of the intact walls of the club to prove his point. He was trying to get us excited about plunging down into the volcano ourselves and hauling out the loot."

"Is there really gold there?"

"No." She pulled herself up stiff. "But there's very much more! At Mt. Walla's bottom, it is rumored, are the remains of centuries of foreigners to the island. Goodness knows why Harry and his crew aren't excavating there. Wallawalhalla, formerly Whitsun Isle, as you know from your geography, was the stopping-off point, even the destination, and according to Greek scrolls, the origin of most of the Western world. All seas flowed to Walla, and all oceans flowed out, so with this ebb and flow the Phoenicians, Greeks, Romans, Norsemen, Welsh explorers, Portuguese going the wrong way to the North Pole, all seaborne folk steered naturally toward the island. Even *Mayflower* Pilgrims made a short stop, a little off course, but the passengers, having packed for a long voyage anyway, insisted on getting their money's worth by detouring down to the land of their forebears before pushing on to the New World. Even then they were concerned with their origins. No wonder Sam Kinver's so caught up in his genealogy.

"And at the bottom of the volcano are papyrus scrolls, so I understand, much of the lost library of Alexandria, carried back by the Humbolt current and other streams to the source of knowledge; rune stones leaning heavily against Ionic columns, while Phoenician mastheads work mouth-to-mouth resuscitation with gargoyles on Viking ships; treasure from Benin, Icelandic manuscripts, Chinese bronze.

Deep diving on a Sunday morning, Viola, my dear, you would have your choice of services—at a stave church, or a temple to Dionysus, a Gothic cathedral, or a synagogue, or a staid Norman chapel where a painted Mary's wooden nipple is nuzzled by a rococo stone Jesus, all open and visited by pious catfish and observant eels, murmuring catechism, feeding on lichen from Lapland, fungae of the Acropolis, counting off beads that float upward to the surface as they fan through the stations of the cross."

I set a small slice of cake on my saucer, where some drops of tea softened and crumbled it. A little numbed by this nonsense, I tried to make light of the usefulness of such a pond. I mumbled, "I wish I could push Uncle Roddy into that volcano."

Rubbing her cookie thoughtfully along her cheek, Miss Bartram remarked, "It's a mystery your Aunt Emma stays on with him." I looked at her stained teeth as she confided, "I think she's hoping to find her faith here, you know." Her smile was almost smug. "Perhaps she thinks it will wash up!"

At this I felt a kind of hopeless sorrow slip over me like a net. Would circumstance capture me, too, as it had poor, skittish Emma Borders? I sighed, for her, for me, for mad Miss Bartram, for all of us trapped on Walla.

My hostess suddenly took my cup and, turning it, studied the contents. "What's this about a man?"

I blushed. "I don't know what you're talking about."

She looked at me closely till I confided, trying to sound natural, "I've got to get married. Sometime."

My hostess put the cup down so hard it sounded a note. "You're not in trouble, are you?"

"No! Nothing like that." I busied myself with folding my napkin into various triangular shapes. "I'm supposed to make my own way. Aunt Emma advises me to find a husband."

"That's one solution," she agreed. "Anyone in particular?" Her voice was sharp-edged.

"It's not my idea!"

"Oh?" She sat back and looked at the ceiling with a faint smile, as if working a brain teaser. "I've never been married myself, but if I should: someone kind. With a harmonious nature. Someone who hits the notes right ninety percent of the time. Some people think good blood lines protect the children. That can go awry, of course. Hemophilia." She looked at me closely. "You do know the Facts? You haven't come for me to—."

"No!" I fairly shouted. In truth, I had only the vaguest understanding of the Facts, but I certainly did not want Miss Bartram setting me straight. "Do you think I could have more tea?"

"Most importantly," she said as she poured out dregs into my cup, "discover what one single trait you cannot live without, and when you find that—stick to him like a tick. Have you never fallen in love?"

I swished my tea about, mortified.

Miss Bartram leaned forward suddenly. "Let me look at that." Upturning it in the slop jar, she inspected the dregs. "Quite a lots of news today! I see," she began slowly, "Mt. Walla. It's erupting."

"Do you see marriage in my future?"

She turned the cup around and examined it closely, then handed the cup back to me with a puzzled expression. "Let me run you home in the motor."

As we chugged up the hill to Egrets, she said, "Harry Bagg's not as simple as he seems, is he? Shell-shocked, you know. The war took the starch right out of him. Though his mind still ticks over like a taxicab. Not always really in this world. If I were thirty years younger . . ." She turned to me with a look that made me want to sink right through the floorboards. "On the other hand," she said slowly, "he's one of those rare men for whom age is an attraction. I wouldn't fuss too much about marriage. Just follow your heart. Though," she said and smiled with nervous suppression of something that flickered around her face, "I wouldn't go to extremes!"

"No," I said, finding her mysteriousness disagreeable. "No, I'm afraid I don't."

Miss Bartram brought the Morris to a standstill under a shady stand of sea grass. Turning, she asked with banked emotion, "Aren't you the least bit curious about your mother?"

"What do you mean?"

"As daughter of the empress, you must beware!"

"I'm no such thing," I argued, annoyed that her mad notions included me personally. "That story, the woman kidnapped, it's just apocryphal."

Miss Bartram, stiff-backed, started up the car. "Such a vocabulary! Well, you may think whatever you will, naturally, but if I were you—specifically *you*—I'd tread carefully! No one becomes an empress without a little ambition. Wild natures are inherited. The ants have their eyes on you—they are lurking at every turn!"

Untoward Events

ONE AFTERNOON DOWN at the site, a mummified baby crocodile turned up, stuffed with papyrus scraps. Word of this find traveled quickly through the island. Harry fairly stuttered with excitement, and Borders went into seclusion, developing his film and enlarging in the darkroom behind the house for long hours at a stretch. Aunt Emma left trays for him by the door of what she could manage (leftover oatmeal, cold vegetable soup, popcorn), and at night I thought I heard stirrings in the hallway, but we saw him little during the day. When I mentioned this to Harry, he said first with careful respect, "Passion. Wonderful thing to be so caught up. Actually," he then conceded, "the fragments seem to give new evidence of gold deposits. Which, of course, is why he's here. Oh, well!"

"But it's as though he's in hiding."

"Hm," Harry said, not looking up from typing a report to Sam Kinver, who had gone off to Delhi for two weeks, "your aunt weighs him down . . ."

"Oh, dear," I said, my confused sympathies swinging back to Roddy Borders as lone male in a house full of noisy women.

"Though he seldom complains," Harry added.

Blushing at the memory of the odd photograph Borders had shown me of Harry—had it really been Harry? naked like that?—I tried to mention, "Roddy Borders is not really . . ."

"Not really what?"

I took a few shallow breaths. "There's something . . . The way he affects people . . ."

Harry did not look up. After a moment, he said quietly, "Yes."

Clearly neither of us would say more. I could not tell what Harry understood, but I felt at least there was a link of sympathy between us on the subject, and I was less alone in my fear.

With all the excitement over the crocodile, I wanted to work down at the site itself. But Harry objected: "You're made of delicate stuff."

"I'm as strong as an ox," I countered. "I did all the plowing at home." This lie gained me time at the site, which suited me better than office work. I liked scraping, scraping, the mindless repetition, in which present time gave no trace of itself beyond the slow creep of shadows like the cover of a book closing over the pit. Even the dust that coated my hands and cheeks and tongue and turned my tropical whites a sepia tint seemed part of some physical reality that momentarily appeased my yearnings. "I feel I'm really here," I explained, shielding my eyes to see Harry as he stopped over my section, checking the progress.

"But do you want to be?" he asked, testing me.

"That's not the point. Since I am, then I want to feel it."

That the dig was going badly in no way dampened my enthusiasm. I scraped happily alongside the ex-soldiers, perspiring in more layers of clothing and denying myself a sip from the hide jug at the edge of the site until they had all begun to drink; powerful thirst made that sun-warmed water the most refreshing I had ever tasted. For me the dig was a tonic; I arrived early, full of energy, in the cool before the sun was fully up, and scraped right into early afternoon, undeterred by tedium or flies or the sulphur wind or scorching sun. In the afternoon when I laid my tools in the trench and straightened muscles that felt bruised with stooping, and stretched the tarpaulin back over the pit, everything took on a golden tint; I was worn to the bone, but I had spent my day digging in treasure-studded ground I wanted to claim as my own, and my life seemed justified.

For Harry and Mr. Kinver, however, watching from above, our unearthings—a few bones, crockery shards, spearheads, one plain pot, the skull of a lemur—brought only afternoon discouragement. Harry's voice as he called down to us, "Scrape your loose, time to close up shop," sounded daily more tired.

The dig was seldom our topic when in the cool he called on me up at Egrets, his new pattern. He played everything by the rules. Lifting off his pith helmet he pushed his hair back like someone smoothing out a document to sign. Jenny spent most of her free time down at the Tennysons's, so Harry and I were chaperoned by Aunt Emma, who lay never far away, picking at embroidery. She laughed weakly when we asked to look at her progress, saying, "Oh, I had to take it all out." I rebelled inwardly at her pose as Penelope, stalling progress till her husband appeared. I had seen enough below the surface of her marriage to object to her playing the role of adoring and devoted wife. The falseness of it disturbed me.

Seated side by side, changed into our freshest whites, Harry and I made conversation. Our union, possessing little outward glamour, I told myself, would be based on an exchange of intellectually stimulating thoughts, shared interests, and solid values. We were virtuous people: Harry lived in a cerebral realm beyond the complexities of daily temptations, and I, more earthbound, struggled to master my desires and less generous thoughts, to work hard, to look for the good in others. I had once been party to a Ford car joy ride, but thumbing through my little-used prayer book, I could not think of one truly grievous crime I had ever committed. I was smugly content in our twosomeness.

Sometimes, having had enough of his lectures on the ancients, I would urge him toward talk about things closer at hand. "I bet you were the clever boy at school," I baited him.

"The fat boy," he confessed with a grin.

"Goodness!" cried Aunt Emma. "You're skin and bones now."

"Piggy—that was my nickname."

"Redheaded and chubby," I said, happy to imagine this. "And top of the class."

"I had an interest in ancient history even then. My mother tells a story of how she found me early one morning when I was four years old, wrapped in a sheet and seated in the parlor wing chair. I announced to her, 'I am Apollo, the sun god, waiting to greet the dawn.'"

"Delicious!" laughed Aunt Emma.

"I think I quite alarmed her." Harry smiled, a little surprised that his life could amuse, but I was not satisfied with crumbs. I pressed for more: his family, his undergraduate days. He obligingly described his older sisters' ill-fated fishing expeditions, his own high jinks over college walls, but he seemed happiest to return to the subjects of lost worlds. His yen for utopia struck me at times as downright hurtful, if I allowed myself to take it all too personally; wasn't he enjoying life more now that he'd found *me?* Wasn't love supposed to color one's world with shades of joy? If so, then why did he strive always to uncover something apart and unrelated to himself or me?

"You're possessed," I accused him one evening, in exasperation. "You have Cronus on the brain."

Harry looked pleased. "And aren't you always thinking of your lost parent?" he countered. "Aren't you intent on becoming a Wallan?" He rubbed a dry hand across my jaw. I studied him in admiration and surprise. It felt both unfamiliar and pleasant, like undressing for a skinny-dip, to have someone know such secret things about yourself.

In fairness, I had to admit that my infatuation with Harry Bagg, for all its excitement and promise, had not diminished my preoccupation with discovering the fate of my mother. Her trace hallowed the island for me. There seemed no real remains to identify her with Walla—no stone in the small Canadian cemetery on the way to the dig, no sign of her in Mrs. Tennyson's velvet photograph album, no memory of her in the mind of anyone now on the island. I had no source of information beyond Aunt's brief stories, no patron, no plans for excavation, and my search seemed permanently stalled, but I never lost the pang of not having known her myself, of wishing still in some way to become her. I even played with a fantasy that she was still alive, the American woman Miss Bartram believed kidnapped and held a willing hostage by the termites; perhaps my mother was even now happily embroidering in the royal suite. I wanted to but could not share this absurd idea with Harry; I didn't know him well enough. With regret, even as we stared into each other's eyes as the greens and reds around us blared in the evening's longest rays, I recognized our apartness.

Harry's experience differed fundamentally from mine. Just as he could not risk a leap, I considered, because of the bullet in his leg, he would not undertake strong personal emotions. He could not even admit an attraction, so obvious to me, for the Crystal Palace. Layard's Syrian treasures had hurled him toward his current work, but the building's glass casing had captured his horrified heart. The many pictures tacked on the wall announced plainly what he would not. Would he ever fly in the face of Ruskin and admit his liking for the oversized greenhouse? He rode like a child, backward on time's hayrack. Recognizing this, knowing it when he did not, I felt an ironic tenderness toward him. This was what a marriage was like, I thought: a catalogue of each other's foibles, collected and secretly filed.

We grew accustomed to a household without Roddy Borders. Harry was dropping by most afternoons to help me feed flies to my plant, Aunt Emma picked at her needlework, and I supplied lemonade. Jenny's play to capture the imagination of Robin Glover through a tireless generation of illnesses — red spots along her hairline, mysterious fainting spells and fevers, a muscular twitch at her elbow — was being countered by unending invitations from Mrs. Tennyson and Nettie for Jenny to stay down at their cottage. Oh, but she must! they insisted; she would be more comfortable, they wanted her nearby. If they couldn't put an end to her symptoms at least they would route Dr. Glover back to Nettie's home court. I'd see them all together sometimes taking the air along the Strand Road, Robin Glover pushing Jenny in a wicker wheelchair flanked by Mrs. Tennyson on the left, Nettie on the right.

In the midst of all this, Uncle Roddy finally emerged from piecing together papyrus clues in his darkroom to raid our domestic peace predawn. I awoke to hear him arguing with Aunt Emma in their bedroom. A loud smash was followed by another, even louder and certainly deliberate. Coward, when I thought the coast was clear, I tiptoed to the kitchen to cook myself some oatmeal — and ran right into him. He looked worse for wear — a four-day stubble roughed up his pale face; his eyes gleamed with what seemed hunger but might have just been lust.

"I've found it," he whispered. "I'm on to it . . ." He stepped toward me, smiling crookedly, taking hold of my shoulders in a way that by slight degrees clamped down tight.

"Don't," I whispered, my back up against the broom closet. The warmth and confidence of his hands on my shoulder, the way they molded to my form and pressed with restrained desire, unbalanced me even as the door handle pressed painfully into my right kidney. "Don't *touch*," I pleaded.

Squinting, he dropped his arms just in time for Aunt Emma,

entering on soft slippers, to find husband and paying guest staring at each other like cats angling to strike. "What do you need, darling?" she whispered. I stared in horror at the blood that trickled from the corner of her left eye and spotted, spotted the floor as she stood.

"Oatmeal," I stuttered. Of course I assumed *darling* meant me. "I . . . can't find it . . ."

Borders turned and pumped himself a glass of water.

Emma queried tentatively, "Have you finished your work, dearest? Will you be joining us for luncheon? There's potted ham."

He turned, aggressively amused. "Tomorrow's my birthday, woman!"

"Oh! How could I have forgotten . . . ?" Then she noticed the puddle of red collecting at her foot. She seemed confused by it and stepped back.

"I'll bake a cake," I said, helpless.

"Lovely," cried Aunt Emma in her wispy morning voice.

"Not another charred thing," said Borders.

"No digging today, Viola," interrupted Aunt Emma. "Just bake!"

I baked. This time I added more eggs to try to get the thing aloft. Jenny was still visiting the Tennysons, recuperating from yellow dots on her left thumb. I stood in the back kitchen all that ashy-aired day, pouring out sugar, sifting flour, beating eggs, measuring components, hoping for the best. I baked under what I felt was a heavy threat of unspecified harm, either to myself or Emma Borders or both.

Emma, tidying up later, brought in the remains of the crockery caught in the morning's domestic dispute: pieces of a teacup. She gave me a vague smile. "Lovely," she said all round to everything in the kitchen. "Some people will be dropping by tomorrow. Roddy had to go out . . . they've found a glass necklace, I hear. We'll have a tea for his birthday tomorrow." She laid the broken pieces on newspaper. They comprised a cup from her best Staffordshire set, white with a pretty blue and gold border pattern. "May I?" she asked, finger poised over my batter. "This is how the white ants do it, I hear from Anthea Bartram," she said, shy but determined. Like someone planting seeds, she deposited beads of paste along the raw edges of the porcelain. She pressed two shards together, held them with her fingers and advanced the work with the next pair of joining bits. "It was part of my dowry," she explained as if apologizing. "One feels a certain sentimental attachment..."

Logic prompted me to intervene—her task was hopeless—but her sheer concentration impressed me. I had not previously seen in her such perseverance. Did I have such faith in the restoration of order, such commitment to harmony? I had to admit to myself, I sometimes felt less sympathy for Harry Bagg's limp than annoyance—as I also felt about my own lopsided gait. Harmony of heart could not always depend, though, on symmetry of tangibles.

Returning to the kitchen later in the day, I pulled back the oven door, and—the cake stood upright and golden in its pans. I pulled it out and prayed against its collapse. To my relief and surprise, it continued to look like a cake, cooling first in its pans, then overturned on a rack as I, humming, began the icing. The Staffordshire cup, all but perfectly mended, lay drying on its side as I worked. It seemed that between us Emma Borders and I could restore the world.

Satisfaction over these small accomplishments gave way that night to unnamed fears when Aunt Emma and I retired to our rooms. Uncle Roddy had not emerged yet from the darkroom. His light burned on inside the hut. Jenny was still at the Tennysons's, recuperating; the yellow spots were fading, but Robin Glover felt she should be cautious. This left Aunt Emma and me alone at Egrets. Emma had gone vaguely off to bed after nine and filled the hall with inefficient snores. I felt a leaden responsibility of guarding her. Miss Bartram's talk of white ants had alarmed me, and Uncle Roddy's odd behavior seemed a sign of a world out of sync. I selected the largest of my lineup of brass elephants—a chunky fellow the size of a grapefruit, with a trunk curved up—as a weapon. Lying rigid in bed, I kept the elephant clenched in my right hand, just under the coverlet, ready to throw at or bash anything that moved.

Scarcely asleep an hour, I was awakened by a stifled scream. I sat up, my heart racing. I listened for a moment. What I had thought were Aunt Emma's tenser snores I realized after a moment were muffled shouts. Finding my slippers in the moonless dark, I crept down the hall, pausing outside the master bedroom. From inside came sounds of a struggle—a woman's short, sharp cries; a man's arched whispers —then a sudden collapse of something heavy, followed by frantic sobs. Sudden light vee'd into the hall and Roddy Borders strode past me; the room's brightness made me invisible to him. His neck's angle and his stiff stride warned me that I must not come under his scrutiny, not now. As he passed along the hall, I held my breath. He opened the door to the drawing room, giving me a moment to scuttle back to my room, pull the covers up, and, shaking, grip the elephant tightly. I found no reassurance in its chill weight.

Under the covers I tried to slow my breathing, but even the blood thrashing through my ears tricked my hearing. Footsteps? Did I hear or imagine them tapping down the hall, toward my room? Why, my inner voice frantically queried, why, of all nights, was Jenny malingering at the Tennysons's? Why?—leaving me alone—a muscleless, half-grown woman with useless feet, trying to lift a small brass elephant above the coverlet and take aim.

A shape in the heavy darkness, blacker than emptiness, moved into the room and paused. "You!" it whispered. "You."

I froze at the sound of his voice. My senses shut down. All I saw was hard danger; all I smelled was his sharp sweat as he closed in toward where I lay; all I heard was his hoarse voice, and, arms aching, I brought myself upright. "Don't!" I warned, my voice choking. Then I noticed that a second figure disturbed the darkness. The two blurred to one with a shout and struggle, then something heavy swung out and struck the dresser. My speeded-up heart informed all my parts: I could save us. I parted the netting, took aim, hurled straight, overhand, heard the blunt *bump* and *thud*, and saw the blackness drop to the floor.

In the timeless moment that followed, I realized someone was calling out, "Vi! Viola!" The shock of Emma's voice focused my mind. I slipped out of bed. The darkness was still too great to make out what I instinctively knew. Hurriedly, with trembling fingers, I lit a candle. Emma was slumped against the maple dresser, right hand clutching her left upper arm. Her face in the candle's light looked haggard. From her left hand hung—I lowered the candle and drew breath in shock—a heavy camera on a strap: her husband's new, favored Kodak.

"Viola," she said, and her face directed my candle still farther downward, to the heap at her feet. It was the doubled-over figure of the attacker, hers and mine: Roddy Borders. "I've killed him," she whispered to me. Her voice snagged on itself. "I picked up what lay closest! The camera. His camera! I thought he was a burglar, Vizzy!"

Her voice, quavering near hysteria, sent a panicked shiver down my legs. At the same time I marveled at her coolness in covering up with the burglar story. Unable to consider even defending myself, I cried out, "No! I struck him! With my elephant! I killed him!"

The Kodak dropped to the matte rug with a dull *thunk* beside the body. "No," she said, more softly, suddenly practical and under control. "You hit *me*."

Moving my candle close I saw that her hand was pressed on a running wound; blood as black as ink in the night oozed through her fingers, over the folds of her cotton nightgown. "I did that?" I cried. "I hit your arm?"

She almost smiled. We looked down at the man at our feet. "Dearest Vizzy," she said, and her hanging left hand reached out spastically and wrapped around mine.

"It's over," I whispered to comfort her, "it's all over ..."

She let out a low hiss like a deer frightened in the dark and pressed her face against my heaving shoulder.

"I heard a sound, something stirring ... You know Uncle Roddy's been working late." I explained all this, breathlessly careful, to Dr. Glover as he wrapped gauze around Aunt Emma's arm some hours later. He had passed by early to collect Nettie's bathing costume, somehow left on the porch at Egrets, and found Aunt Emma and me sitting in the parlor, changed into dark dresses, pale, sipping strong tea.

A few hours earlier, Aunt Emma's arm tied with my ripped pillow-case, we had donned macs and gum boots and with much effort lifted the body to the back door, where Aunt Emma stood guard while I fetched the wheelbarrow from under the darkroom's overhanging roof and heaved the body in. This had been my job, with Aunt Emma's arm dangling and her generally rundown condition. His unwieldy weight angered me into a swearing panic. I could not look at what we had done, but what I'd always heard proved true: adrenaline poured in from sources I would have praised had I had the time.

We pushed against the breaking daylight on the water, down the drive, through the eelgrass, along the Strand Road to a break in the sand and out to the cliff, Devil's Peak, known for its deep diving pool. Devil's Peak. I gave no thought to the name or the indignity of what I was doing as I stopped the barrow on the precipice. Angling it on one wheel the way one might lower a load of dung onto a bed of roses, I dumped him—down the cliff into the sea where his body splintered the water and sank. *Swash!* came the sound to me again and again then and in memory for all my life afterward. *Swash!*

In the pink light I saw that Aunt Emma had come all the way still carrying the Kodak, the lens dented and bloodstained. I grabbed for it and wondered at her strength as she tried to stop me taking it. "It's his!" she cried, but I had already pulled it away; with a fling it was describing an arc over the Indian Ocean, and sank with far less fuss and drama than its owner.

Shaking and chattering giddy encouragement to each other, we pushed the wonky-wheeled barrow along the road and up the drive to Egrets and left it by the darkroom shed. A few steps toward the house, I turned back, though, and, taking a handful of topsoil from a bag, rubbed it all over the barrow, to soak up or at least disguise excess blood.

My hands were bleached spotless four hours later as I snipped gauze at Robin Glover's request. My capacity for deception chilled me even as I knew we counted on it to save us. Glover seemed more amused than concerned by what turned out to be a surface wound, a grazing. "Had that blunt object struck bone, now . . ." he warned me, winding the gauze. But it had not, and Aunt Emma would be fine. "You women are getting a bit worked up, aren't you? Throwing around little brass elephants! How many break-ins have there ever been on Walla?" he said, comfortably winding.

I looked at Aunt Emma. She seemed very pale. I myself felt thirty feet outside my own body, a balloon filled with conflicting joy and revulsion at the events of the night, and incredulous that my behavior could disguise the terrible truth. I worked only to keep my seat and control my vocal cords as I answered in what sounded like an almost normal voice: "We're alone up here, you see."

"Borders . . . ?"

"In the darkroom."

"Oh! Well, how's it coming? I should pop in on him before I go down."

"No!" I shouted. I added, "He mustn't be disturbed."

"He won't mind, dear," put in Aunt Emma.

I stared at her. "Yes, he will," I insisted.

She was calmly rearranging her skirt.

Dr. Glover wrapped steadily and tucked the end under the last twist. "He'll be back out soon, I expect."

"I expect so," said Aunt Emma, looking only at the bandage.

"I'll give you a sling to hold all that still. No fussing about dusting and whatnot! Mustn't risk infection." He sat back and, fitting bandages, bottles, scissors, tape back inside, snapped the bag shut. We waited. He waited. A look of curiosity crossed his face, and in the silence I almost blurted out what we'd done, but he spoke first, saying only, "Take these," handing Emma a small paper packet. "Help you to sleep. Go back to bed, now."

"Oh, and Nettie's costume," said Aunt Emma, skittish. "Viola will fetch it."

He blushed as I handed it to him. "Perhaps I'll see you later in the day." He hesitated, confronted with our blank faces. "I believe, I heard ... Mr. Borders had a birthday tea."

"Well," I began. "Considering ..."

"Oh, yes!" interrupted Aunt Emma, with feeling. "We'll look forward to seeing you! Four o'clock or so. Doesn't matter when. You must come, of course!"

The house seemed lighter, rid at last—*at last!*—of the poison that had tainted our spirits for so long. I actually dozed off in the early sunlight of my room and slept well for a few hours before the heat and smoky air woke me. On that morning, I could block from my mind the collapsed figure, bludgeoned head, pool of congealing blood we'd scrubbed at with soil, our own nightclothes soaking in borax in the back basin. My tired mind felt only free at last of the grip of terror. I passed down the hall for the third time in five hours, and I was beginning to feel a numbing calm. It would have been irreverent but not inaccurate to describe the feeling, as I rapped softly at Aunt Emma's door, bringing her fresh tea, as a holy grace descending. A tiny-voiced choir in my ear dared to cheer me. We weak and captive women had slain the dragon ourselves.

"What time is it now?" Aunt Emma yawned into her pillow. "You're an angel for this tea!"

Her face seemed clear of the incident altogether.

"Going to be a nice day," I said, glad to see her so well.

"Another perfect day," she moaned. "Why can't it just rain for once?" She stretched. "Has Uncle Roddy come in this morning?"

I stared, then shook my head, appalled.

She turned to the wall and fell off again into sleep, leaving me alone in the reality of our situation and somehow, it felt, responsible.

Aunt Emma and I said little to each other that day; I watched her and could read no signs of remorse or distress. The birthday tea still, incredibly, on the books for that afternoon, we welcomed Miss Bartram at four o'clock. She rolled up in her car, bearing Tennyson ladies in large hats. Dr. Glover, too, hopped out, asking, "How's the arm?"

Fine, nodded Aunt Emma.

"Dear me," murmured Mrs. Tennyson and glanced at me with new respect and alarm. "*You* did that?"

"It's a trifle. You all must stay," Aunt Emma insisted. "Roddy's counting on it."

"Oh, yes!" chorused the Tennysons.

Glover pulled a rug up over Jenny, who smiled gratefully as she sat, slumped and pale with a low fever. Glover seemed unaware of the tension growing over his treatment of her continual ills. Mrs. Tennyson eyed Jenny with the huffing comment, "I hope at some point your constitution will strengthen. A shame to be an invalid all one's life. And *not* a good proposition for marriage."

"I'm feeling better," said Jenny comfortably.

Dr. Glover set his black bag by a little statuette of Venus and sat in a chewed-through greenish chintz-covered chair near Mrs. Tennyson. The guests smiled at each other; the hostesses, if anyone noticed, looked strangely pale and grim. "Get the cake," Aunt Emma told me.

In the pantry I placed my most recent Empire Cake on a glass stand, under a high glass dome. It looked like a museum piece when I bore it into the parlor, eliciting murmurs. I had iced it in pink with local sugar and added some of Jenny's mother's old good-luck motifs: a horseshoe, a star, and some I made up myself. Thus decorated it sat plumply perspiring under its glass, gazed at longingly by Mrs. Tennyson, who favored anything edible in pink. Miss Bartram leaned forward with interest to inspect the symbols. "You've got an unusual configuration here," she advised us. "I see love in the heart of the bakeress." She smiled up at Aunt Emma. "Of course we knew that already," she said.

"I made the cake," I said.

She turned and narrowed her eyes at me in momentary confusion. "And travel. The horseshoe. And . . . oh!" She stopped and looked sharply toward me.

"What?"

She turned to the window and took some breaths. "I thought I saw something else, but I'm clearly off today. Sometimes the messages get crossed. Well, I do hope Mr. Borders arrives back soon so we can try a piece!"

Aunt Emma sat behind the large teapot and a dozen cups, occasionally touching the spoons as if to reassure them. Harry had sent his regrets ahead. He would be working on-site; something had literally come up. "The column?" I asked Robin Glover.

He looked confused. "Maybe," he replied.

"Viola takes such an interest in the dig!" declared Mrs. Tennyson. "Quite the young tomboy. You'll never catch a man if you don't pay more attention to your hair and wardrobe and less to digging around in the ground."

I nodded, looking away, inspecting Miss Bartram, but she seemed recovered from whatever message she'd read on my cake. "I'm sure Uncle Roddy will be in soon," I told the party.

"Oh, yes," everyone agreed.

"In the darkroom, is he?" asked Mrs. Tennyson.

"Hmm," said Aunt Emma.

"Maybe not," I added.

"Viola's done yeoman's service. Baked her family's famous cake," said Aunt Emma, firmly signaling that we would not pour out, we would not give up. Otherwise she seemed more hazy than ever. I thought, watching her, the cycle was taking its toll—this lifetime of bobbing on waters of the men's operations with no horizon markers. The eight-day clock twisted left, then twisted right, then twisted left, then twisted right. Jenny and Nettie sat up attentively and emitted sober noises. Dr. Glover pulled his watch out and flipped up its cap.

"I expect you have an appointment," Aunt Emma said to him with false animation. "You have other patients, of course." It was clear that he could not jump ship without a reproach.

"Er," he murmured, blushing. "A digger, a possible quinsy throat..."

The eight-day clocked chimed the half hour.

"And I'm afraid we must fly as well," announced Mrs. Tennyson with sudden swift enthusiasm, full in the knowledge of her disloyalty. "Now, you must rest that arm. Lie down! We'll do all this another day."

Nettie and Jenny, voices rising together as though inspired, cried out, "Yes! Let's have a picnic. Next Wednesday for Dominion Day."

"Capital," said Nettie's mother. "I'd forgotten. It *is* next week."

Aunt Emma rose with dignity. "I'm sorry you're all in such a rush. Thank you, thank you." And her smile almost held out till all the guests were on the porch, then, collapsing on the divan, she stared at the wall.

Jenny and I cleared away the untouched cake, forks, plates, napkins. Jenny, who was draining the tea leaves into a little heap for the garden, said, "Men," and cut herself a thin wedge from the cake. "It shouldn't go to waste—and we certainly have enough to feed an army! Take some yourself, Vizzy! Oh!" She drew the piece out of her mouth and spat the remainder into the sink. "Well, maybe next time!" she said to cheer me up.

Still technically recovering from her fever, Jenny lay on a chaise on the verandah the next evening, embroidering a little sampler. I was working on some crocheted covers for the breadbox. I wondered, still too numbed by the previous night's events to feel danger or plan my future, if Aunt Emma would stay on at Egrets. I felt happy for her sudden release. The world was now her oyster.

Unexpectedly, Miss Bartram parked out front and stamped up the porch. She greeted Aunt Emma with loud fellowship as she unwrapped her motoring robes. "Such a heat! Mt. Walla's full of puff." She settled in a wicker chair and breathed heavily.

With a strained musical voice Aunt Emma asked, "Won't you stay for a drink?"

"Lemonade. No—tea. Why not? Roddy out of the dark yet? I think I've got a puncture. Jouncing along that bad road by the volcano. A slow leak, could go as flat as a flagstone by evening. Oh, he's still not back? Well . . ." She smiled at me uneasily as she sat. "Rest the weary carcass."

"What were you doing by the volcano?" Jenny asked. Her flutey voice hid all indiscretion.

"Social call," said Miss Bartram.

Jenny exchanged looks with Aunt Emma, who bent to pour out a cup. "And there's Viola's cake, of course," she added, giving me a timid nod.

"Oh, for four o'clock eternally," answered Miss Bartram, levering sugar into her cup and stirring waves over the saucer. She seemed indifferent to the fact that it was eight-thirty.

"I agree absolutely," I said, and wondered if Miss Bartram could be as serious as I was about stopping time. No one else was talking. "Cake, Miss Bartram?"

"Perfectly delicious, I'm sure," she said. "Unfortunately I stuffed myself so on dinner. Boiled egg. I might just take a piece home, though, if you don't mind."

"Not at all." I noticed that Aunt Emma sawed through half the remaining cake.

"Might need it to mend the puncture," Miss Bartram confided in us cheerfully. "Now, tell me about Roddy. What has happened to *him?*"

I looked down at my handwork. Jenny cleared her throat. I could hear Aunt Emma's stays creak as she leaned forward to push her napkin under the rim of her saucer. "I believe," she said in an even voice, and I was made aware once more of how little I understood of the world, "I believe he has run into trouble."

Miss Bartram held her gaze. "I peeked into the darkroom. He wasn't there, of course."

"No," answered Aunt Emma.

"He's not down at the site."

"No."

"Well, that just leaves one possibility: the white ants have captured him! I told you this would happen."

Aunt Emma, fanning herself with her hoop, objected, "Anthea, such notions."

"I'll say no more then," said Miss Bartram. "But, Viola, I'd watch out, young woman! They have a keen sense of smell, if you know what I mean. Now, I had better get back to Nuremberg and water my bird-of-paradise before the sun goes down."

I sat paralyzed, trying to concentrate on the wide view of sea and sky that was said to be so restorative, but there in the foreground was Miss Bartram's tire, softly settling into our pebbled drive like some tired beast accepting its extinction. I watched Miss Bartram climb into the car and wobble on the tire down the drive, an old lady of a species almost extinct herself, riding the last air of courage on her bumpy road to endure.

The rumors about Roddy Borders increased exponentially. Miss Bartram set in motion stories wildly detailed enough to frighten one into believing in the existence of her giant termites, whetting long teeth and circling around town on the brink of butcherous insurrection. Even Robin Glover, giving Aunt Emma more packets of medication, admitted, "There was a story of some girl carried off by the white ants. I suppose it might have happened. If Mr. Borders had wandered into their territory . . . He was fearless, wasn't he?"

Roddy Borders, handsome destroyer of women, became a local hero.

"Excellent stock," Mrs. Tennyson said, delivering Nettie to Egrets to visit Jenny. "First-class bloodlines. It comes out eventually."

The blood? I wondered.

"His mother was a Grosvenor, we hear," put in Nettie, flushed with the notion.

As Dr. Glover declared Jenny fit enough to sit on the beach, plans went ahead for the picnic. "Good to get some air in your hair," he said to her in front of us and then blushed furiously. "Lungs," he corrected himself.

"Take our minds off this business," said Harry, stopping by for lemonade and placing a hand on my arm. He gave me one of his angelic, closed-off smiles.

Late morning on a steamy Dominion Day, Jenny and I had gathered our comestibles in hampers on the verandah. Tired of failing at Empire Cake, I baked an angel food cake, but that turned out a little dry. Harry, driving Miss Bartram in her car, bounced up the drive early, and we arranged things in the back and helped Aunt Emma in. We had invited Miss Bartram, not only for her excellent company and as someone for Aunt Emma, but also, as she must have known, for the convenience of her motor car.

"Oh, you young people don't want an old lady around!" she objected, merry with irony.

When we swung by the Tennysons's, Mrs. T. and Nettie were ready with their hamper of meat pies and cream scones, things that would quickly go bad in the heat and lent, therefore, an air of urgency to our mission. Down at the surgery we honked out the embarrassed Robin Glover, bathing costume spilling from his medical bag. With head averted he took the place open between Jenny and Nettie and beamed beyond all pleasure at the blue of the sky.

The car was full with romance, chafing knee to knee. In friendly silence, Harry and I sat up front and jounced along the beach road. The forward motion seemed a good omen. It was a comfort, I discovered, to have a designated mate. When Harry asked me the all-important question, I would be ready; like puffiness before my period, I felt that it was coming on.

We spread out our rugs on the beach, high up and under some shade of scrub pines. The Devil's Peak, the site of Aunt Emma's and my fateful beach excursion, rose up some two hundred yards to the west, far enough away to ignore. I concentrated on the here and now. Hampers opened out their hearts: kidney pies, buns, a flan, cold rhubarb soup from Mrs. Tennyson, whose mother was somehow Norwegian, legs of game, aspic salad, and a pikeberry pie.

I shut out the past; I was a happy nineteen-year-old girl with a limitless future of fun. Conversation meandered pleasantly like our samplings of this feast, washed down with fizzy lemonade made with lemons just off a recent ship. I kept a weather eye on Aunt Emma; she seemed not unhappy. She was leaning against a large rock, looking out to sea, sketching a little in a small leather-bound book. Her bandaged arm hung in its sling, but Robin Glover, peeking underneath the swathing with deep blushes, had declared it to be healing nicely. She took small swigs from a bottle of tonic he'd given her. She had more color and seemed, in her solitude, more still than she'd been for weeks. I attributed the change to a certain absence. "Uncle Roddy's absence," was how I spoke to myself and others about our situation at Egrets. A small search party had gone out after clues to his disappearance but returned with nothing. The ants had taken him and devoured every crumb, went the story. All in all, I told myself, it was for the best.

Her contentment made me think of my own future as I mused seaward, sucking out the centers of deviled eggs. *Mrs. Harry Bagg.* If Emma had made a mistake in being carried away by a handsome man, I would certainly avoid it. I glanced surreptitiously at my private love. He was lying on his side, bulking large and stuffing a canapé into his mouth. He was a fascinating man to me: discreet to a fault and somehow numbed to much in the world that made me vibrate, and vibrating to currents of cerebral antiquity unfelt by me. My search for the past was particular and personal, like the search for a missing shoe; while his, I'd come to see, was open-ended and moved him into ever greater complexities. I took a deep breath and felt the salt breezes on my face that seemed to leave him untouched. I would stand by him and, like Emma Borders, I would sustain my soul on wild berries plucked at random from life wherever it took me. I trusted his perceptions. Aunt had once said that girls chose men like their fathers. Here was an architect by training, but unlike mine in every other way: surely marriage would not be difficult with someone so logical and dutiful in his role. I, in turn, not tidy by nature, could learn to cook adequately, provide a clean, neat home, produce offspring (I sputtered on my lemonade)—well, why not? And Harry's future suggested travel, adventure in places otherwise closed to me.

I called across the rug to him, "Harry? Cake?"

"I'm busting," he answered, pleased, and tapped his hand against his middle.

"What do you think you'll do after the dig?" I asked.

"No idea."

Robin Glover was smiling at me, I realized, recognizing this expression by the contortion of lip on his lower face. It was meant to look pleasant, but some people are just not natural smilers. I realized he, too, was enjoying the outing, the easy company. I smiled back.

"Heard you found a Viking helmet, Harry," he teased.

Harry took up the interest as serious. "Pretty good shape, too, horns and all. A jewel or two still encrusted around the brim. Lovely little thing."

"Surely not genuine!" Robin insisted.

Disliking his droopy smile, I ventured casually, "Why do you doubt it's the real thing?" I looked over at Miss Bartram, but she seemed to be dozing with her back against the rocks.

"Read your history. Impossible for the Vikings to sail around this way." Then he blushed at his forcefulness.

I was not ready to concede, however. "Couldn't the tide wash things in, from long distances? Miss Bartram . . ."

Miss Bartram turned vaguely at the sound of her name, and Harry surprised me by interjecting, "Currents are capricious things. Didn't grow in the sea, did it? No."

"A child could see it's a fake," Robin answered, surgically severing us from the discussion. At his either side Jenny and Nettie grinned at their medical man.

"Come on, Harry," I said forcefully, "Let's go find some Viking bones."

Harry obliged with a light heave-ho, righting himself on his good leg and brushing off the sand.

"Glover's rather full of himself," I said as we strolled together.

"Bit of a fool," agreed Harry softly.

That exchange marked for me a magic moment, a meeting of the minds. What a relief to find someone to complain with. I felt suddenly airy and glad, as if we'd just spoken our wedding vows. And I determined to help Harry along in that direction. "Isn't it beautiful, here, today?" I said, and looked romantically out over the calm water, waves flapping over each other in quiet abandon. I thought it would be nice to be proposed to near a small outcropping of rock—cool rocks symbolizing stability and permanence, the right kind of background to get him started. I spotted some seagulls flying about. Birds would be good, light yet homey, with their nests. A few tufty clouds threading through the blue. I hoped I looked fetching enough in my hat. It flattered my chin and neck.

"Hmm," said Harry. I could hear his nervousness. He spoke again more loudly. "Rather!"

One of the birds picked this up and shouted, "Rather! Rather!" while I prayed for some miracle to move us along. "At such moments," I tried, "one feels so grateful for good friends."

"Oh, yes," said Harry, "friends are terribly important, aren't they?"

"Aren't they just?" I said. Edging closer to the rocks, I took Harry's hand, and straining against the pounding of my heart at such boldness, and wondering at the dry scaliness of his palm, I pressed it hard.

Harry gave a jump. "My gawd!"

I started, too, from nerves. Then I saw what Harry had already spotted: out in the shallows, not two yards away, a large object, floating. An arm swung suddenly upward by a dark-haired head, bobbing, pushed closer toward us with each press of the tide. We stepped backward like two cats retreating in a slow-motion fight. As we stared, the body, pulled and pushed and pulled by the water, finally beached and twisted. The face was turned away but we could tell from the chalky pallor that something was wrong. Devil's Peak poked into my peripheral vision; heart knocking around my throat, I understood.

I hung back, paralyzed, as Harry stepped forward again to inspect the stilled corpse. But what I expected to see—the full extent of Aunt Emma's whacking—I did not. Surely her blows that wild night had removed the top of the skull. But no such violence showed on the symmetrical, once beautiful face of the corpse. He looked, instead, just bloated, with a small bruise at his temple. Alarm swept over me. Rising bile burned my throat as I tried not to cry out.

Harry, wading in and taking hold of the shoulder, began dragging the body up to low water. I turned aside to be reminded of normal life and spotted the picnic party at a distance like a theater set painted on the beach: Miss Bartram dozing, face up like a sunflower, Aunt Emma shaded and leaning over her sketching pad, Nettie and Jenny tossing an enormous colored ball to Mrs. Tennyson, wearing a bathing costume that showed off black-stockinged legs surprisingly fine, Robin Glover reaching for something more to nibble with his contented smile. Their innocence appalled me.

"What the . . ." Harry was murmuring. I forced myself to look back into the sea. It was horrific what death and water did to a body. This one seemed larger than I'd remembered—fat and battered. Harry let go as a wave suddenly tossed the corpse over and sent us like a backdraft up the beach.

Harry's face was pale, the muscles in his jaw tensed. He was looking at me. "What do you know?" he demanded. For a terrible moment I went deaf with fear, and the wind and the waves crashed around me without sound, then noises returned as I saw that the question had been asked in innocence—rhetorical, not suspicious. I followed his glance down the beach where Aunt Emma, composed, was resting. "Poor lady," he said. "The price of marrying a hero."

"It's horrible!" I cried out, to make him stop. Until that moment I had thought how lucky it was that Aunt Emma had not seen the thing come back up to haunt us, then realized that of course she must see it, must identify it officially, must risk an investigation. "Harry," I said slowly. He was pulling the corpse by the shirt up on the sand, clear of the water. We both looked over to our little party, which we had now to bring to an end.

I had meant his name as a plea for protection, but he took it for direction. "Yes," he said. Without hesitation, he started up the beach. I glanced again at the body, its hands clutching channels down into the sand as the water streamed away. Then, head down, I followed Harry up the beach, feeling for the first time truly afraid of what Aunt Emma and I had done.

In the crosswind, I could not hear what Harry said, but the threesome stopped their frolicking, and Mrs. Tennyson tucked the cheerful beach ball under her arm. By the rocks, Miss Bartram squinted with happy oblivion from under her floppy hat. Slowly Harry approached the widow, obliged to shake her by the shoulder to rouse her. Her face looking up seemed shadowed with foreknowledge. She struggled to her feet, turned to me, cried out like someone parched, "Viola! What have you done?" and abruptly fainted into Harry's arms.

Accessory to the crime was the phrase that pounded in my mind, though no one paid much attention to her accusation but me. I stood rooted while Harry piled the picnic into Miss Bartram's car. He took my arm to help me in beside him, whispering, "It was shock, was all." I nodded, and nodded again to seem very normal, then prayed I hadn't overdone it.

Harry first dropped Mrs. Tennyson off to organize a recovery party down to the beach, then drove on to find Kinver. Robin Glover stayed with us to see to Aunt Emma. At Egrets, Miss Bartram, Jenny, Nettie, and I waited together for news on the verandah. I could not join in their nervous chatter. Silently I prayed just to get the whole thing behind us. I gave private thanks to Miss Bartram for her stories. *Roddy Borders drowned at sea, in pursuit of the white ants' gold. He hit his head on a rock. End of story.* That was what they would, *must*, think. Then the incident would give way to newer news, a boatload of mail and fresh lemons would distract everyone, and Aunt Emma and I need never have to think of the thing again.

Some two hours later, one of the diggers drove up in Miss Bartram's car to collect Aunt Emma. The body was in the san, which was serving as a temporary morgue, and she was needed for formal identification.

I went quietly into the parlor to fetch her. She looked small, lying on the chesterfield, but her face shone with a beautiful dignity. "Come on now," I said, to let her know I was there with her, for her.

Seeing me, she pulled away. "You!" she cried. "What have you done!" Shock, I told myself, avoiding her sharp look. The tiny mouse-paws applause I had allowed myself at being rid of her tormentor, now fell silent. We were all confused. *Swash!* came the recording in my brain. I handed her the things she needed and spoke no more as I closed her into the car.

We got details from Harry, who came up to the house that evening, returning home the silent, stricken Emma. He told us, quietly, how when she had gone inside, she had been made to watch the sheet drawn back from the body laid out on an examining table in Dr. Glover's back office. I imagined her eyes traveling over the unclothed form: broad, flat chest, sleekly muscled arms, trimmed nails on tapering fingers. She had withstood all this, Harry said, as if reviewing a parade, no expression crossing her long face. "Is this your husband, Mrs. Borders?" Dr. Glover had quietly inquired. Her eyes had seemed to retract into her skull. She looked cloud white, Harry said; he had held her waist against collapse. The perspiring young doctor had requested again, "Just nod that it's Mr. Borders."

Harry said, "She finally gasped just one sentence: 'I'm so sorry,' and draped herself in a faint over the unrelenting coldness of the body." I sat pondering this, Harry's phrase, Emma's reaction, suppressing high in my throat a desire to scream.

Nettie asked, "Why do you think she was sorry?"

A wave of terror washed over me. "She'd just lost her husband," I snapped. "Wouldn't *you* be sorry?"

Harry pulled his upper lip. "Glover's given her a sedative. She lived for her husband, didn't she? He was everything to her."

I found I could not move the muscles of my mouth to argue this.

Nettie suggested stoutly, "I think we should collect for a memorial. A big statue. Him putting down an ant. St. George and dragon sort of thing."

"A halo would be good," said Jenny.

Only Miss Bartram and I remained silent.

Miss Bartram drove herself home. The others wanted to walk. Jenny and Nettie went to see Aunt Emma for a moment, leaving me alone with Harry. We stood, shoulders touching, on the second step of the verandah. After all the talk, he looked somehow stricken. I saw he was in no fit state to discuss anything more, but seemed at a loss, and not weak but needy—of me, maybe, of anyone who would be tender. I assessed his condition: things at the site had gone wrong, and now the accidental death of his photographer. It was an ill omen. Kinver would surely pack the dig up. I had never known him so despondent. In the dark, by guess and faith, I stood on tiptoe and pressed my lips to his. His jaw was unhelpfully tense but I persisted. I had made up my mind: I would have things my way on this island. I had no knowledge beyond my readings, but I thought this should do for our first kiss. Harry opened his eyes as I drew back. He looked at me with hazy surprise. "Will you be all right here?" he said, voice creaking.

"Fine," I whispered back.

"You and Jenny and your auntie?"

I nodded and smoothed his hair back, amazed at myself. "Mrs. Tennyson asked Jenny down to their place, as she's been feeling unwell again. So it's just Aunt Emma and me." In the dark I had begun to calm down and felt strangely talkative. "I can manage."

"I believe you," he said. He swallowed. "The volcano seems to be acting up."

"We'll be all right," I said. *Swash!* echoed in my mind.

"Good night, then," he said and clasped me abruptly.

From fatigue, from the complexity of the day's emotions, I gave way to tears. "Thanks, thanks so much. It's very, very kind of you," I sobbed.

He tightened his hold. "Listen," he said. "We've known each other a little bit, anyway, haven't we?"

"Yes," I said, not moving, unable to clear my thoughts. *Swash!* Harry drew a long breath, glanced toward the house. "Glover told me that Borders drowned. He must have fallen from the cliff at the diving hole. Devil's Peak."

"Yes?" I was scarcely breathing now. "Devil's Peak?"

"Which makes no sense," he continued. "Terribly afraid of heights and couldn't swim. There was no reason for him to have gone there." He gripped the back of the rocker and tried to balance himself on its tilt. "Unless *you* would know of a reason he might have been there?"

My breath came too fast. The world seemed to be darkening like a fast-action sunset. Harry was studying me hard. With painful clarity, I heard him say, "You're afraid, but you're not unhappy."

I grabbed his hand and felt reassured by its returning pressure. "I'm very unhappy. Why shouldn't I be? Aunt Emma's lost her husband. Jenny's lost her uncle. And Uncle Roddy was such a kind person to have us stay here."

He circled his fingers around my wrist. "When we were driving back, your aunt told us . . . things. I won't ask you . . . But you should know."

"Oh," I whispered, trembling, and turned with utter terror at the sound of Jenny's voice calling from the garden to Harry to walk back with them. "What things?"

Harry studied my face as though piecing together papyrus fragments. "Go to sleep now." He patted my hand hard, like a father wishing but unable to punish a child.

"Harry? You believe I'm . . . in the clear, don't you?" *Swash!*

Nettie's and Jenny's light voices moved up on us suddenly, around the corner of the porch. "Let's go," Nettie called out.

His smile held in it a flicker of annoyance. "Some things just don't interest me much," he said to me.

I watched him, a tall figure striding down the Strand Road, my friends on either side, light with ignorance, and gave some broken-wristed waves. I stood on the porch, past seeing them, unwilling to go indoors. Thoughts I could barely allow myself preyed on me. It seemed I was no longer an innocent abettor, but the potential perpetrator. That terrible night played itself over in my mind like a nightmare caught in a loop. Even explaining myself would not save me. I called out in my mind to my accusers: *He was already dead! The heap on the floor was a corpse! Aunt Emma told me so! He never moved, never made a sound the whole way to the diving ridge. Surely, surely he was already dead when I dumped him into the sea!* The only answer my brain offered: *Swash! Swash, swash!*

Slowly, deliberately, I bolted doors and windows, then, in bad need of human comfort, went to check on Aunt Emma. I found her flat on her back, however, lying unnaturally, like a corpse herself in the moonlight, and I was only reassured of her being alive by the flutter of her night-gown's lace as her chest rose and fell. I closed her door and tiptoed through the house, distrustful and distanced from myself. Being still alive and young, I thought, somehow I would have to endure.

I sat and rocked on the verandah till long past midnight, unsure if Harry were now enemy or friend. I distrusted his thoughts, and found that in the cloud of my mind, my fear gave me a new respect and distress. If I were a murderess, should I refuse to receive Harry? Or would he break off our friendship first? Harry must not, I told myself without mercy, *must not* link himself with a young woman under suspicion. But then, that young woman being myself, I felt bereft and adrift and more than ever in need of his comforting silence.

The Moment to Decide

I WOKE EARLY THE next morning and spent a dark hour thinking about the mess I was in. Had I murdered him? And did Harry believe that? To both these questions I prayed silently *No.* Harry was my hope, the north star in my night sky. I did not want to lose him. Yet, his avoidance of the issue also struck me as a bad omen. I worried over what it meant.

Stranded by Aunt's death, my father's abandonment, it seemed I'd fallen in love with a man whose vision tunneled centuries backward, who refused to take a stand on what I myself most grievously had committed. His neutrality appalled me even as I knew I should be grateful. I cursed my fate. I cursed patriotic songs that lilted through my brain. I cursed the unknown soldier whose tumble had sent us lurching out to sea. Most of all, I cursed my recklessness. Had I really not seen that I was rushing live cargo on that adrenaline-powered wheelbarrow run to the Peak? Could such a terrible oversight be true? My breath came short and fast at the thought, and my waking prayers strained toward some future in which my current life would be buried. Time might layer over this moment like an oyster's pearl. I vowed in that gray hour, watching the flames licking upward from the rumbling Mt. Walla, that if I should get out of this mess I would move on with utmost caution.

My plan for living was to practice restraint, squelch desire, screw the lid down tight on impulse. It would not be difficult. My spirit dangled like a snapped string on a violin. Every morning I tested myself by trying to make a fist. I could not, and was not able to for years, and, instead, lived through each day with a kind of rote response. Spontaneity was dangerous. I heard in my mind my lines before I spoke them. Every conversation was rehearsed and put through a ten-second delay. It was safer that way. I had had enough surprises for a lifetime.

Though my thoughts spun around, my own troubled conscience rendered me mute and numb. The next morning it took me all my strength to greet Aunt Emma as she trailed in cotton nightgown from bedroom to parlor. She looked at me as if at a stranger intruding on her meditations and whispered in a new, low hiss, "Unthinkable. Unthinkable."

"Aunt Emma . . ." I began.

"My love, my only, my dearest!" She broke into a howl.

I leaned on the wall for support in this confusion. "But," I whispered, "I know what he did. I know what he was really like."

"Get away," she whispered back. "You know nothing." Tears overflowed down her cheeks. "What will become of me now?" She pulled her legs onto the chesterfield, there to sit out the day, facing gulls and water, face veiled by the billowing curtain.

I secluded myself on the verandah, rocking with Browning's *The Ring and the Book* like a verdict on my lap, unable to read, unable to bridge the chasm of doubt that separated me from the woman I had sought to defend. When Mrs. Tennyson and Nettie, with Jenny, ambulatory, climbed up the Egrets hill to pay condolences, perspiring heavily under their hats, I just stared without words. I didn't know what they might have heard, what thoughts about me they kept carefully from their pleasant nods. They did not stop to speak, but moved directly indoors, accepting somehow my self-appointed outcast state.

In that timelessness, as I creaked in the rocker and tried to read, Harry's accusation, so mildly stated, repeated itself endlessly, like a coiling worm, turning over and over in my ear: "You're afraid but you're not unhappy." Was it true? I had not wanted his presence, yes, but had I actually drowned my host? The idea left me panting with breaths too hectic and shallow to bring sufficient air to my lungs. I swayed with faintness and relied on the rocker's rhythm to restore some order to my mind. Had I rashly, selfishly destroyed what I could now hear Emma wailing to the Tennyson group had been the joy of her life? Had I misunderstood it all? The yellow bruises? The photographs on the porch? The leers? The pressure on my waist? Had I got it all wrong, every bit?

When Robin Glover found Emma's pulse too weak that afternoon for her to withstand daily life, he transferred her to the sanitorium over his clinic, where a skinny ex-corporal was assigned to make her bouillon and toast. As I could not stay on alone at Egrets—a house whose name began to rhyme with "regrets" whenever I heard it—the question arose of where I was to go. Viola—the dispossessed and homeless houseguest now catatonically rocking. The Tennysons could have made room, as they already had for Jenny, in their spreading bungalow, but no offer was forthcoming from that quarter.

"We have Jenny already, you see," I overheard Mrs. Tennyson explain to Harry when they met on the verandah for the last visit to Egrets.

Harry took charge, proving himself, as with the recovery of the body, capable if awkward in logistics of the quotidian. He drove me and my suitcase down to Nuremberg Cottage, to sleep in Miss Bartram's back room. "Will you mind?" he asked. I shook my head. It made no difference to me, really, where I was. And, anyway, I felt at ease with Miss Bartram's eccentricities.

Miss Bartram herself gave my arrival no notice. Busy practicing scales and predicting the volcano's eruption with her cups of tea, which she felt obliged first to drink, she seemed oblivious to me or my peculiar situation. If she resented the imposition, she was gracious, offering boiled eggs at random hours. I tried to return the kindness by baking another Empire Cake. Of course, it flopped—overly moist, the texture of rice pudding. But I felt I was making progress. Miss Bartram declined to try it, though, declaring herself too old for sweets.

"But you keep at it," she remarked. "That's the important thing."

"Is it?" I asked, washing up the cake pans. "I'll never get it right. I'm as bad as my aunt back in Bremen. She was notorious for burnt offerings."

"Well, there you are. It's in the genes," answered my hostess, and the idea exploded in my brain like a tiny Dominion Day rocket: I was like Aunt. Not success but failure linked me with her, the present with the past. It was almost a comforting thought. "Miss Bartram," I cried and embraced her hard.

"Let's have tea," she said, loosening me after a moment.

As we poured out second cups, I complained, "What should I do? I'm in a tight spot. What's to become of me?"

Miss Bartram pressed her cup against her chest. "That's the kind of thinking that will get a person taken by the ants," she warned. "Never let them see you at a loss. Never let them smell despair. Remember Odysseus. He narrowly missed the ants and made it safe back to Ithaca. The ants have given you this journey. Put more sugar in that tea, my dear. You must keep up your strength. We all must. You know," she said, "I was once almost taken by the ants myself! No one knows this, but I'm telling you—because of your special history."

"Oh," I said. My mind had been on other things—whether Harry would drop by—but I was brought back to attention. "I don't think I have such a special history," I insisted.

"Yes. Once many, many years ago, I was out bird watching, as I had heard the call of a piliated stork the night before. Somehow, my foot slipped on loose rocks and I took a nasty fall on the cliff. I lay there unconscious for hours, and when I came to, the ants had placed me upright under a boulder that shaded me. And my head had been repaired, though I had a raging headache, a real migraine."

I frowned, unsure whether or not I should cut the conversation off. "What do you mean, exactly, they had repaired you?"

"It's like piecing together a Christmas jigsaw. I had hurt my head quite badly. I figure the ants had a bit of that Samothrace statue about and just stuck in the missing part, a piece of the forehead. Fit exactly— ha! Hardly shows the seams." She leaned forward, lifting her hair up off her forehead. I inspected the smooth hairline. She smiled. "Good as new, eh? Better, really, as it doesn't corrupt. Although I suppose I am prone to lichen."

I tried to take all this in. I felt limp. "Does the Louvre know about this?" I said, in part to tease her off the subject.

Her mouth overfull, cake crumbs dropped onto her lap as she replied in all earnestness, "It's none of their museological business, if you'll pardon my French. You can't get bogged down with keeping everything together, or with who owns what. That is the whole problem with the modern world—ownership. Look at me! And the same is true of your dear mama the empress, just more so. Something old, something new, something borrowed, something blue. That's how she was wed to the king of the ants. Here's a brainteaser: how much must be the original to call it real? Who can say how much is Catherine the Great or the Victory, and how much is not? Things are in constant flux, my sweet. A child like you always assumes the world stands still while she grows up. Terrible error! Creatures in the Arctic—oh, dear me! No one can prepare you for the drift in continents even as you walk upon them. You could take a train from Victoria, heading toward Chichester and find yourself in the south of France. Look what's happened to the Austro-Hungarian Empire! Witness, likewise, the African nations. Do you think Ethiopia is going to lie still while the Great Powers—and who says they're so great anyway?—try to fit those fractious parts together? Then you're quite naive, dear girleen from Ontario Province. Which brings us to the French. Those Quebecois don't like being taped onto Anglo-Canada, not one little bit, now, do they? Just what do you intend to do about that, eh?"

"It's hardly my problem," I reminded her.

"But it *is* your problem! And when the German states try to glue themselves and the whole world together with the wrong cement, we'd all better make it our problem! Yes, I've seen it in the tea. In our lifetime, too. My cup runneth over with disaster. You can go around demanding that the white ants wrap up the head of the Samothrace statue and send it parcel post to its other half in the Louvre, but you have no idea of the amount of material that gets washed up here every month. The small ants have to chew down twelve pounds per diem each just to keep the planet spinning on course and not capsizing or colliding with the moon from the weight on Walla. Ovid, old fool, thought *tempus edax rerum*, Time the gobbler-up of things, but he visited Walla late in life. No, it's the termites you may thank for consuming everything, for cleaning up the detritus and debris of so-called civilization."

"But..."

"Yes?"

"You're supposed to treasure the past. That's why we have museums. That's what the dig is all about—discovering the secrets of the people who lived before us."

"Let me make a distinction for you," Miss Bartram began, and with a cake fork drew two lines onto her napkin. "This line is Long Time. This is Short Time. Long Time is the most grand, most cerebral, most detached and detachable. In Long Time, empires fall, dynasties collapse, Zeus is reconstituted as a man, not a god. Harry Bagg works in Long Time. Short Time is harder to grasp, probably because we live in it. What does a fish understand of water? I've never mastered the art of being where I am at the time I'm there. Have you? Short Time has us losing earrings into the grass at picnics and falling in love with self-absorbed musicians and repapering the parlor and giving way to tears at the Toronto *Globe*'s account of the coronation, and making up with a friend who drops dead the next day in the post office. Borders caught Short Time with his camera and made it long, but Short Time was his specialty; he was unrelievedly part of the here and now. And you, my dear? You could take a lesson from all this: 'The world is weary of the past, Oh might it die or rest at last.' Shelley. Oh, yes," she concluded with a resigned sigh, "of course one must use the past."

"But how do you suggest doing that?" My sarcasm I regretted as I wanted to get to the bottom of Miss Bartram's mad logic. I thought of my unhappy lot—the yearnings that had brought me to Walla, my dis-appointments here, the terrible thing that had happened. I had wanted most of all to make some small life for myself, respectable and safe, and I feared more than I felt I could ever admit to anyone what acts I'd com-mitted. I asked Miss Bartram, who was pulling off a bit of cake and still puffing after her lecture, "What do you do with a past that's not happy? How can you use that?"

"History is liquid," came her cake-muffled answer. "Perfectly mu-table. All the scrolls and maps and," she swallowed, "and poison pen letters and billets-doux and miscast statues and masterworks of im-prisoning empires; when they wash up, the ants chew them down. The chewers pass the stuff on to the gluers. A Constable watercolor masti-cated thoroughly and mixed with the right proportions of excrement and saliva makes for wonderful building material." She smiled like a pixie. "Their walls are as hard as rock. They're not a garbage heap— they are a perfectly organized little colony, in the very best tradition. So successful and constantly outward-pushing as to bill themselves as an empire, actually. But the word of choice should be *utopia*. Look that up in your *Webster's Unabridged with Canadian Supplement.*"

I stared. I wondered how far I could go in risking rudeness.

She added, "Of course, they do glue things back together, too. They're famous for their skills at restoration. They have the whole of the library of Alexandria down in the volcano, scrolls intact."

"Alexandria? The *lost* library?"

"Found. And beautiful little Hellenistic statuettes and Incan jewelry, pretty little turquoise things. They love it all, what they can preserve. Very dexterous. The whole is greater than the sum of its parts." Her strident voice actually grew warm, as if in sympathy for my innocence, as she said, "You and Harry expect to find happiness by stopping time. By what right should you be happy? But that's a question we could debate tomorrow. Right now, just understand, little girl, that time doesn't stop, and neither can we." She fit her cup into her saucer and, sitting upright, drew her hands together and began to sing with a sweetness that surprised and moved me. I recognized the hymn:

> *New occasions teach new duties,*
> *Time makes ancient good uncouth;*
> *They must upward still and onward*
> *Who would keep abreast of truth.*

"My aunt sang that," I said, when she came to the end.
"Wise woman."

At that moment I realized that I'd come to regard Miss Bartram as my one real friend on the island, and why? Because she sang the same hymns as Aunt? Perhaps there was something of that to it, but more because I sensed that she wanted truly to help me, and, mad as she was, she exposed herself in her candor. She wasn't immune to the world, but more sensitive to it than the rest of us.

She added, as a kind of caveat to her song, "Keep abreast, unless one is *uninterested* in keeping abreast of truth. Some people are. They live by theories instead. *Viz* your Harry Bagg . . ."

I smiled, thinking with relief that she was a crank after all, only much later considering her words, played back in memory, as prophetic. Had she been warning me? On that summer day, I did not give her statement much thought and asked instead something more immediately troublesome to me. I pursued information about the ants in a kind of self-laceration, a reminder to myself of my motherlessness. "Miss Bartram, why do you suppose the ants fixed your wound but did not kidnap you like that other woman? Aren't you afraid?"

She cocked her head. Her cheeks flushed with the first puffs of explanation. "I have never thought of leaving. Actually, I inherited a rather nice place outside of Boston, built before the American Revolution—two rooms downstairs, two up, watch your head on the staircase, and an attic, kitchen added later. The locals put it on their annual historical tour. Would you like it? I'd be glad to deed it over. But perhaps your tastes run to the medieval." She narrowed her eyes at me. "You admire Rossetti, I suppose?"

"Not especially," I lied, brushing at a tea stain on my skirt.

"Oh, you do! And why not? A romantic-natured schoolgirl. Why shouldn't you believe that our age is inferior to that murky, incense-dusted, asthmatic-climed time when pallor in the female cheek inspired great chest-clutching madness in the male and maybe a little squirt of poetry to boot?"

"I think some of their work is quite pretty."

"No, you don't! You revel in it! You yearn to have thick, golden hair! Excuse me—tresses. You long for cloaks and wooden carvings and candlelit embraces and hokey mysticism that portends everything and means nothing."

"No," I struggled to explain. "I've given up on things like that. I don't believe in emotions anymore. I don't want anything. I want just to stop myself."

Miss Bartram was not listening. "I know you so well, my dear, because that was me. You have the good fortune of a clean, honest face, but Time betrays Beauty, and Man betrays Time—by trying to stop it. It can't. The pretty lie, Art, can't save it, either. What goes is gone, and your past will get you without prompting and certainly not as you expect. Don't play the fool. No age is greater than your own. And don't look back with sighs and longing. No—push forward! History is a cunning beast of prey, a roving lion that stalketh about, seeking out whom it may devour and who shall remain steadfast in their fate, if I may paraphrase. I'm telling you, you must remain steadfast, Viola, with blinkered eye against its bright, candle-flickering seductions. If the past corners you, take the ants' advice: eat it! Before it swallows you."

"Then you admire the termites!" I cried.

Miss Bartram's smile went lopsided as she tucked her napkin under the edge of her saucer. "How could I possibly admire them? They're savages. Now I must go and read some Shakespeare before I expire."

Later, when we were forking up triangles of toast in an old-lady meal of scrambled eggs, Miss Bartram remarked, "You don't miss Mr. Borders at all, do you?"

"Well . . ." I slumped against my wobbly chairback. "Uncle Roddy was very dear to Aunt Emma."

"Harry Bagg says you shoved him off Devil's Peak."

I sucked in ragged breaths. "Harry says that?"

After a moment of eyebrow-raised waiting, Miss Bartram brushed some crumbs from the table into the palm of her hand. "Well," she said, "I'm sure I'd have done the same, given half the chance." She paused, appraising me with a jerk of her head. "One is safe here with you, one hopes? You're not going to take a notion to shove me off a cliff, are you?"

I shook my head hard, fighting tears that rose in my throat.

"Oh, good. Because," she continued, brushing the crumbs onto her saucer, "one has enough on one's plate with those termites, you know."

"You're perfectly safe."

"There now," she said, sliding her napkin through its ring. "I believe I have eat sufficient." She pronounced the word "et," as I had not heard it since Aunt lived with us. In the midst of all the unpleasantness, I experienced a sudden sharp nostalgia for the tidbits of my childhood. Miss Bartram studied me with her ringed eyes. "And now," she said, "we must make haste lest that young man catch us washing up. He'll be coming 'round tonight, I expect."

Exhausted, I didn't even bother to brush my hair for Harry. In some ways, I felt I was his captured pet; what I did or said or how I looked now would be of little consequence, as it must be my character under review.

"Hello, hello," he greeted us, softly opening the front door, not waiting, I noticed, to be asked in.

"What news?" asked Miss Bartram, bringing out a heap of tea things.

"No news. Your aunt sends love," he directed at me.

"The volcano's about to blow!" Miss Bartram declared, setting his *topi* on top of a bust of Dante. "I've read about it in every cup since ten this morning."

"They're monitoring it on the mainland," Harry said. "Not with tea. Glover's been on the telegraph machine. There's a cloud over us."

"It is overcast," I agreed.

"Overcast!" yelped Miss Bartram. "That's ash in the air. Hot, life-extinguishing volcanic ash!"

I apologized, "I thought it might just be the beginning of the rainy season."

She shook her head strenuously. "No. No."

"And now," said Harry, as if he were not chatting with a mad woman and a murderess, "I think you'll be amused by what I have brought— a little piece I transcribed myself. See if you can guess what key it's in."

Miss Bartram plunged onto her chesterfield, causing an updraft of dust, and clapped her hands. "Oh, goodie!"

Harry stooped inside the tin anti-ant box. We heard him run along a scale and test the bottom and top notes of the keyboard for accuracy. Then, satisfied, he started in. As he played, the neat structure of the music organized my thoughts. Either Borders had been bashed by Aunt Emma or truly drowned by me. If bashed, I was innocent; if drowned, I was guilty. If the former, I was just accessory to the crime. I was shielding Emma Borders—a good and right thing to do—and Harry had no reason to save me. If the latter, then Harry's silence would shield me, but was that also a good thing? I could not rid myself of a sense of moral indignation. Crimes must be punished, not covered up. Was my shielding of Aunt Emma wrong? I thought not; she had been brutalized and tormented far too long—hadn't she? Even that seemed suddenly unclear. I should turn myself in, declare my complicity and guilt— except that I didn't know for sure if I were guilty, and any explanation of that night's events would bring more trouble down on the unstable head of Aunt Emma. I should just keep quiet, perhaps, and be glad of Harry's continuing interest in me that said to the world I was innocent.

As it was, though, Harry's silence was freeing me in public, but hobbling me in private, as I could not bring myself to speak to him about my situation. My own cowardice had trapped me.

I felt as if I were riding a wave of Fate, washing up and gliding out with the tide, abandoning myself. This was new for me. Until then I had been described by teachers as alternately headstrong and determined. "She knows what she's about," Miss Faith had said to encourage Aunt. "She'll succeed in whatever she puts her mind to." Now my fate was out of my control, but rather than frightening me, I enjoyed the freedom from plotting my course. What was the point in planning? I had lost my mother, my father, my home, beloved Aunt, my best friend; I'd become dishonorably entangled with an ex-officer, and participated in, possibly perpetrated, a heinous crime for which I felt guilt and astonishment tinged with pride. I was worth very little. And now it seemed that I had fallen into a safety net after all. Harry Bagg could save me. Exhausted from the strain, I gave myself to the small sensual pleasures: the sweet scent of jasmine on Miss Bartram's table, the charming ups and downs like popping corn of J. S. Bach as played by Harry Bagg on Miss Bartram's well-tempered harpsichord.

Harry stuck his head out the door and signaled me inside. "It's easy. You read notes, of course?" He bent warmly over me as I sat at the bench and placed my hands on the keyboard. "Like so. That's it. This is such a pretty piece, I want to hear you play it." Enigmatic, with a hint of affection that encouraged me, Harry turned the wick on the lantern to its brightest height and latched the door behind us. Light and shadow loomed large and doubled back against the silver sides of our box.

As I picked out the more difficult measures, I lost my self-consciousness. I became so absorbed in the music, in fact, my first practice since grade ten piano with Miss Faith, that I jerked when Harry put his arm confidently around me and fingered high above my right hand on the keyboard. "You're a wanted woman," he remarked into my hair as we played. I felt my breath stall, the hair on my forearms rise. "In every sense," he continued. Goosepimples slid up my spine. A vein in my ear thrummed. My fingers relinquished the keys to his, and I sat, hands in lap, staring at the lines where the notes hopped.

Harry's low voice continued, "Robin Glover has been seeing to

Emma Borders, narcotics and such. He tells me she's talking her head off. Some of what she says is, well . . ." He turned to look at me but I kept my eyes fixed on the score. "Not pretty," he concluded. His voice betrayed nothing.

I didn't dare move. I seemed frozen while all around me the world moved—Harry's fingers trilled and stepped over the keys, his arm brushed against mine, his thigh pressed my thigh as he reached for a high note. "Now," he said softly, "what are we going to do with you, Miss Monroe? Ideas?"

I felt my hands shake like leaves in night wind. What game was this? How could I trust a man who would associate with a murderess and ask no questions? Had he no moral conscience? Or, head buried in his excavation like an ostrich, did he not grasp what he was saying even as he spoke the words? Or, even—my mind was racing around corners blindly—did his lack of interest reflect total, remarkable, loving trust in me?

As his hands reached the top of a tricky chromatic passage, he said, "I think I shall marry you. That should stop their talk." My blood seemed to pool. I felt like a shirt he was buying, pressed flat, bodiless in a box. I didn't even have enough substance to feel anger, but then his composure broke, revealing his bluff, and I trusted him again in a rush as he turned, blushing hotly, pressed his face to mine, and—eyes closed— kissed me on a trill.

Above the tiny $^{C\#}C^{C\#}C$, Miss Bartram's tenor voice called, "It's starting to fizz! Mt. Walla's going to blow!" We opened up the tin door of the box to find the sitting room dark with smoke and the ashy world outside aswirl.

In that dark heat began our exodus from Walla. We scrambled aboard rescue boats with assorted baggage, books, and boxes of arti- facts. When we were a mile out in the water, the top blew: fire rocketed into the sky like a heart exploding. I stood watching beside Harry and Jenny, just as I had on arrival months before, but now it was Harry to whom I cleaved and Jenny who was the stranger. I sensed over- whelmingly the change in myself; conventional Viola with lively humor existed no more. Depleted, I was riven with love that had woken my mind and given me mental companionship, but had shaken my self-confidence and frozen me with doubt. Harry and I lasted over ten years, but the separation had begun already on that harpsichord bench, at the moment of his proposal, enclosed in tin, when I sensed the amorality, which I read also as untrustworthiness, of the man I loved and to whom I owed, by virtue of compromising the truth myself, my freedom.

4

Losing Time

Gypsy Years

❦

COUNT WALLA AMONG my losses. The volcano's lava flowed like a low but persistent tide of black glass over the island right to the western end, covering the Strand Road, all but the top of the domed club, its once landscaped and then excavated lawn, filling in like paving tar the pits where we'd stooped for long hours unearthing crocodiles millennia dead, glossing over white ant, automobile, harpsichord, corpse of Roderick Borders lying straight out in the san's cold storage. The volcano rendered the island's horrors moot and with a blast of fiery momentum catapulted me into the new decade without a past.

Suspicion—if only my own—hung like a storm cloud around me. How do you live with guilt unexpressed? You fool it into darkness. You hide it like some stolen object at the back of your heart's closet and make a point of never looking there, thinking that negligence will make it disappear behind the umbrellas and shooting sticks and, like a child's misplaced dread, the problem will resolve itself. You never say the name Walla. You never reminisce with Harry about the island, or your own father's marble masterpiece, or the dig. You break off correspondence with Jenny Abbott even before her annual Christmas letters start to arrive with the stair-step children's pictures. You read books on topics unfamiliar to you—primates of East Africa, a biography of Caruso. Anything touching on your former life—news from Ontario, the publication of Sir Robert Borden's diaries, radio broadcasts of patriotic songs of the home front, painted eggs in store windows at Easter, headlines about lost continents—from these you turn. Thought requires comparison; you stop thinking.

You pull a shade down and start again. Like some cheap wind-up penguin, you waddle forward. Of your old self, only your mismatched feet carry on, challenging your balance and direction daily, but, hobbled, you persevere. You stuff the toes of your outsized shoes per usual and keep to a narrow course. You strike people who meet you as naive, inexperienced, unsure; you were, it seems, born yesterday. Still, you hold your own in a world of mechanical breakdowns, appointments, traffic backups, and leaky roofs; you raise your daughter to adulthood. You do not consider if your life might have been richer.

We survivors were for a short time local heroes on the mainland, and in the flush of narrow escape, Harry and I were married, in a double-wedding service with Glover and Nettie Tennyson, the young Quincy Kinver in sailor suit standing, relatively still, as ring bearer. The Glovers set off with many good-byes for a honeymoon in Ceylon, and we escorted Mrs. Tennyson to the boat bound for England, Jenny under her wing as far as Southampton. Strangers to each other now, Jenny and I kissed stiffly on the gangplank.

Some shabby-genteel English ladies befriended Miss Bartram and Aunt Emma, who joined their ex-pat household. In parting, Miss Bartram handed me a marmalade jar with the deed to her Boston house inside.

"I won't be heading that way," I objected.

She ignored me. "Just write ahead and shoo the renters out when you need the place. And keep it painted or the historical society crowd will fuss." There being no choice, I packed the deed in its jar into a padded corner of my suitcase. Years later, like a crystal ball, it did direct my fate.

Rootless, Harry and I traveled on with the roly-poly Kinver and son to the Hebrides, where he determined suddenly that those islands were the lost Atlantis. The Kinver nanny, a spindly American woman whom I had never come to know better than to ignore in passing, suffered a nervous collapse during the trip, quite literally spilling red jam right down her pinafore one breakfast time as she slid to the floor, possibly more from the strain of tending to young Quincy Kinver than to the eruption. After two weeks in an Aberdeen hospital, she booked passage on a boat back to America, from where we received one small postcard of the Knoxville, Tennessee, courthouse and, too embarrassed to respond, heard from her no more.

Young Quincy became my charge. Trying hard to keep myself in check as Harry's wife, with woman's work and woman's talk, I took over the tending of house and child. Quincy was a nice-looking little boy, small for ten, with richly abundant gold hair and neat limbs, but beyond control, and once we had finished the struggle of washing, buttoning on his sailor suit, and getting some porridge down his throat each morning, I mostly stayed out of his way. He was an imp, always busy putting salt in the sugar bowl or rigging buckets over doorways. I confess I was sometimes amused by him, more often exasperated, but otherwise not much interested in children. Dashed hopes of finding a mother had spun my compass toward Harry: my newfoundland.

The wet Hebridean wind stirred up dissatisfactions in all of us that autumn. My job was seeing that Quincy came to no harm and cooking up a meal for the day's end. Both these I performed half-heartedly, spending much solitary time in the hut, thinking. To belong to a group, I reflected, hacking some large root vegetable or stoking the Aga, one must share beliefs, in things, or people, or places. I could not attach myself to objects; believed only in Harry, and then with reservations; and Wallawalhalla had turned out to be a mirage, just a trick of possibility unfulfilled. But what, after all, I asked myself, made a place? What made the grass along the Swiss border any more Swiss than the grass a foot away, growing in France?

Sam Kinver engaged me in this debate one evening when we were all freezing around the tiny coal stove. Quincy had already collapsed into his trundle bed, unwashed, one leg sticking over the side, still in his rumpled suit but quiet, and the hour in the evening before turning in was the time I savored. Official tea maker, I had brought a pot to the table to warm us up. We seemed to expand at night, we three, and ideas flowed to fill the void of our daytime frustrations.

Looking into his tea as if it might be a small pond with fish, Sam Kinver asked me suddenly, softly, if I considered myself Canadian. Hearing that I did not, he proposed, with relief, that I become a Yank, my birthright from my mother's side. It would root me, he said. But somehow I didn't feel the need of rooting. "I'm an artist," I said, to tease

Harry, who was dusting something bronze. "I weather the political winds." I grinned in Harry's direction. "I'm transnational."

"No," Harry interrupted, laying down his brush. "It doesn't work that way. One, you're not an artist. And two, you're holding out on yourself by not feeling Canadian."

Kinver's face puffed up with the excitement of debate. "Art must be rooted," he declared. "That's what it's for, right? To tell people who they are—Americans, Chinese, anyone. Every country needs its traditions. It needs Art. Human beings instinctively try to trace themselves back as far as they can to their origins. Everyone wants to know he's unique."

"Harry wouldn't agree," I said, watching him, head bent to his task. "He thinks art is universal. And we all share the same aesthetic sense. And since everyone has the same needs, art and buildings should be the same everywhere. It's a very democratic idea, don't you think?"

"Well—democracy. It's a great notion," said Kinver, "but I don't think it has much to do with art. Personally, I send my son around museums to put him ahead. I want him to know he's got an edge. In America, life's competitive, but you can win. And I know, Mrs. Bagg, you'd feel a lot happier being American. It's a great history to get onto."

"Just suppose, Mr. Kinver," I argued, "suppose my mother were Korean, my father Hindi, and I grew up in Swaziland but chose to live in Paris. Does that make me Korean, Hindi, Swazi, or French?"

"Ha," he said, and chuffed a little. "Ha," he said again, when he saw I wasn't joking. "It all depends." He took a quick sip of tea.

"On what?"

"How you feel."

"Suppose I can recite the sagas backward in the original and know Loki's favorite flavor of snow cone—am I Icelandic?"

"No. Well, it's better if you are born there."

"Then we move back to Korea, where, of course, I look like everyone else, and know the language."

"Okay, if you look Korean, then you are really mainly Korean . . ."

"Why? What about migrant workers, and refugees? Where do they belong?"

Kinver fitted his cup into the saucer. "These are trick questions," he said. Exhaustion disfigured his face, and I regretted my pushiness.

We both looked at Harry to rescue us, but in dusting, dusting, Harry would not take part.

Some pottery, silver coins, a few cannonballs, and a ninth-century brooch turned up, the weather dampened morale, and the local boys recruited to move the dirt returned to their families' fishing boats for surer employment. Sam Kinver, undeterred, chugged off with Quincy in a freighter bound for Alaska.

Harry and I returned to the East, settling for a time in Delhi, then Hong Kong, then Bangkok, partly in circumspection of the political crisis in Europe, partly because we had lost something there we needed. Pope must have known people like us:

> *Round and round the ghosts of glory glide*
> *to haunt the places where their honor died.*

We were like amateur diggers sweeping metal detectors over the surface of battlefields. Cups, keys, coins: nothing we turned up rewarded us with peace of mind.

We disguised ourselves as Moderns. Mies van der Rohe and the Bauhaus were Harry's best subjects. He took up his former profession. Architectural broadsheets arrived in a bundle of many months' worth all at once. He would closet himself and emerge hours later, distracted, feverish, impatient. "Berlin," he'd say with every gesture, his eyes focused at long distance, as if on that vulgar city's skyline. In 1931 we moved to Berlin.

Every marriage carries around it, I suppose, a kind of Atlantic graveyard of sandbars through which one attempts to steer and occasionally comes to ground. Our craft was tipping when, in a French-windowed, mote-filled Berlin examining room just off the Kurfürstendamm where I had gone with a bladder complaint, I heard news that unnerved me. "Are you sure?" I demanded of the Herr Doktor, who was a small man with kind eyes. My pulse registered alarm. I think I even blushed. I understood as never before the energy exacted by my less-than-ideal union, and I worried, taking the doctor's leaflet about prenatal care, how I would ever even tell Harry, man of the past whose urge was ever to cut back and hone down, that we were about to increase and multiply.

Finding myself pregnant after more than ten years with Harry was like discovering someone else's love letters at the back of a bureau drawer. It felt improper to untie the ribbon that bound them, shuffle through, pull out the scented pages, dwell too closely on particulars. The news, though radioactive with intent, seemed unrelated to me. Harry and I, who had never discussed having or not having children except in the remotest way as a pleasant diversion when traveling, for instance, were suddenly faced with the presence of a third party, a new, hard ball, pressing its way outward from my middle, about to demand all manner of care and consideration, joining uninvited in our lives forever. For a long time I just let out the gathers in my waistbands and tried not to think of what it meant.

Not that Harry and I were not by then a seasoned twosome, but our union was precariously welded and required constant vigilance at the seams. Harry complained I was too much ruled by illogic, and I did feel guided by forces that I understood but could not quite explain without losing out to his reasoned arguments. He remained in marriage as beforehand—elusive, mercurial. Harry drew inward, sheathed his sword, gave himself to cerebral pleasures. His thoughts pinballed too fast for me to catch on, so I made a niche for myself as pleasant homemaker. I did the cleaning, the ironing of clothes, the buying of bread, the arranging of flowers, called for taxis and porters. I read dutifully through the stack of *Times*es that arrived in a pile at our address every month, but my mind stopped short of analysis. When you're living with someone, you camouflage a little, for survival, and after a while, your camouflage fools even you. I believed myself to be complete as hausfrau. I developed a kind of Geiger counter for things that needed to be done, and I did them, and let Harry reach for glory.

At the time of the birth he was away, looking over the land for a villa outside the city. On that bright, freezing-cold March morning, with basket half-full of the day's shopping on my arm, I felt wetness trickle down my leg. In memory, the street seems to have darkened and all I saw was the long way down the tunnel to a taxi, which I knew I must somehow signal, though I suddenly felt numbed in the lower abdomen and conscious of leaving a liquid Hansel and Gretel trail behind me.

It was all very medical and seemed to have to do with other people; I was only along for the ride until, with throbbing lower parts and achy head, I found a baby fitted into my arms—a yellow, squash-faced, ancient brand-new replica of Harry, so light as to be almost weightless. It just lay there, eyes closed, mouth a small pink button, chin invisible, unmoving in its tight flannel blanket. "Hmm," I said, chilled suddenly.

I felt afraid of it, that little baby, what it would make of me. I might as well have been asked to take care of a wild raccoon or 'possum for all I instinctively knew about this creature. I reached up and fingered its face, loosened the blanket under its chin, opened up the gauzy undershirt on its tiny chest, let my hand travel down its long, thin arm to the starfish hand and felt with surprise the fingers, stronger than I could believe in so small a thing, pulling on mine. I was sobbing as the nurse closed the baby's wraps and pulled it away for me to rest. Her expression, bearing that child to the nursery where it could be properly looked after, suggested what I already feared: that I was unsuited to motherhood. In the dark, too miserable to sleep, bereft, I lay awake, awash in the newness, sinking.

When they let Harry in, he pulled flowers from out of his satchel and hunched over the edge of my bed. He looked exhausted. "What did you name it?"

"Marjorie Petunia—your mother and my aunt."

"Sounds like a prize flower." Under the comforter his hand squeezed my thigh, but he did not touch the baby or meet my eye for long; his happiness seemed abstracted, as if I had produced not his own first child but the first panda born in a zoo.

I knew only the vaguest of guidelines: not to spoil the baby by fondling, to give it lots of fresh air. I obeyed both the spirit and the letter of the law. I think back with regret on those early years with Marjorie, when I felt mostly burdened by the baby that clung to my neck like a vestigial appendage or, at best, an opossum. I wish that I had imagined it differently. I resigned myself to her, endeavoring to keep her warm, dry, and fed with the correct quantities of nutrients, to weigh and measure her accurately and record her first steps, excursions, accidents. Harry and I didn't own a camera, skittish as we were in committing ourselves to paper, but when friends gave us occasional photographs, I dutifully glued them onto pages of the baby book sent us by Harry's mother. I have forgotten her first words. I learned about teething creams, parks, the zoo, riverboats. I aimed at control—of my child and myself. I bought new foundation garments to pull my figure in. I drank cocktails at occasional parties, but what did I know to talk to architects about anymore except remedies for diaper rash and teething pain? I had become that kind of caged creature, not unhappy but very much confined.

A high point: Harry bought from his friend Josef Albers a small glass painting called *Bright City* and hung it in the bay window, filling our front room with rainbows. I remembered Miss Bartram's story of the white ants' royal suite, lit by glass from St. Sophia's in Istanbul, and imagined it, like our high, dignified, plaster-ceilinged space, shot through with glorious reds and blues. Months of pent-up tension lifted and I embraced Harry when he came down the stepladder. "I'm glad to be here. Now I am glad we came."

Somehow Harry wangled work—commissions for private villas, modest memorials, corner stores. He mixed nicely over wine with party bosses and stayed clear of the brouhaha in which Mies, as former Bauhaus director, found himself. On the topic of Herr Hitler, Harry pressed a finger across his upper lip. "Bit of a nuisance," he said. "A thousand-year vision is fine and dandy." He bounced Marjorie on his foot for a moment. "But what grotesque blueprints. Now take this child off me, I have work to do."

Until the morning Harry stormed back home an hour after leaving for work, full of fury and uncomprehending smiles of violence. "They've closed off the Bauhaus! They have posted guards around the place! The idiots! The fools! What could they possibly understand of Art!" Still he found work. Parades, broken windows, where our grocer Herr Meyer had gone—none of this figured in Harry's Long Time. As he proudly reminded me, "Art is all."

For a while I contented myself with imagining how my practical management was my own contribution to Art. I persuaded myself that Harry, in exile, needed something to call his own. But gradually, overtired as I was with nursing Marjorie through croup and measles, something in me hardened. Seated with back aching one morning, cutting bread with a long knife while Marjorie stood on fat legs, nursing under my blouse, my defenses suddenly collapsed like Jericho's walls, and I started to sob right into the bread. "Why aren't you worried, Harry?"

"Why should I be?" Harry forked up his eggs fast, eyes on the blueprint partially unrolled by his plate. "I do excellent work. I'm completely apolitical—just your average, mild-mannered, self-deprecating Canadian genius. I don't offend. Like my buildings, I'm completely see-through. Something that's invisible can't come to harm."

But if he were see-through himself, which he was not, he did not take a look out. And even I, cleaning house, dusting around the Albers stained glass, could not ignore what was going on outside the tall windows I so zealously polished. My old spirit of rebellion took hold. In the balmy days of 1934, ready to admit that I lacked romantic imagination, I decided to leave Harry, his expedience, and his theories.

"People are people, Harry," I whispered the morning I waited by the door, all buttoned in my coat, for the taxicab that would bear me, like a hearse it seemed, into some blank hereafter. I was tired from midnight packing and repeating the arguments to myself. "Call me unenlightened," I said, bending my daughter's rubber arms into her good blue coat. Her dry *Brötchen* lay half-eaten on her bunny plate. I slipped the bread into my pocket for later on the train, and, rinsing the plate, quickly slid it between sweaters in my suitcase.

Marjorie clutched my skirt as Harry silently watched my last-minute preparations. He was sitting under the Albers, his face and shoulders striped red and blue as if by holy light. "I call you a fool," he whispered. "A small-minded fool." I admitted privately he was probably right. "With petit-bourgeois morality," he continued. "You—who've had such opportunity for travel, for mental advancement; and it comes down to this, that in your thinking you've got no farther than your old home-town! I'm surprised and disappointed, I really am!" He stared past me at the carpet, his game leg outright on top of the other, a diving board ready to spring, but he made no move to claim me back.

"I'm literal minded, I know," I berated myself for his sake. I stood there, whipped but stubborn, determined to follow through in the momentum of the moment.

His spoon knocked the side of the plate too loudly. His voice for the first time carried a high note of panic. "Don't you see—we have to think ahead. Individuals hold back the movement of time. Suppose," he proposed, and an angry gleam shone in his eye, "suppose we were to dwell on certain things that happened, say, just for example, on Wallawalhalla Island? Where would that get us?"

I stared out the window, breath coming too fast. I felt the weighty uselessness of my whole life like a lead apron against his X-ray light. My wildly naive husband had made me believe for a time on Walla myself also to be possessed, twinned with him in discovery, but I had never uncovered a thing. "I regret . . ." I began, then stopped. Down in the street I heard the taxi's barking horn.

"Marriage to me, I'd imagine," whispered Harry, looking unexpectedly so lost that I felt my heart softly crack.

"Mostly," I sobbed quietly. I'm not sure he even heard. "Mostly that I never recovered the right proportions for Empire Cake." Harry sat fast, watching in confusion as I followed my feet to the door. "Marjorie's coming, of course," I added. He stared on, and the elevator cage shook my small daughter and me down toward our future, Miss Bartram's house in a marmalade jar.

Let's call it a time capsule, those years I worked downtown and Marjorie grew up, and we lived in the blue clapboard Red Leaf House with its second-story Jacobean overhang, cross-and-Bible doors, and capricious eighteenth-century glazing that thickened at the bottom of each pane. Every May the historical society sent someone in a suit to fuss with arrangements of daffodils and forsythia in the front hall and dining room and to guide visitors through on the candlelight tour. "Welcome to Red Leaf, and mind the thresholds, which are higher than we're used to today . . ." I told them I would gladly open the house to tourists any day of the week—we lived so spotlessly.

The house had once been all but self-sufficient, with outbuildings— now piles of rotted boards overgrown with morning glory—for cooking and smithing, an herb garden from which still sprouted mint and thyme. Parts of a box hedge growing wild across the front yard shielding the house from the road, and against the brick garden wall grew lilac and rose of Sharon.

We lived in the city center of this universe, but with a growing child, it becomes difficult to hold corrupting forces at bay. When I see Marjorie press a hand on my granddaughter's head as she passes behind her, I look away, disturbed by this gesture of random affection. I know she did not learn it from me. I was not warm. I was not a pal to my child; I was her determined mother and the most valuable thing I gave her was a lesson in self-denial. She told me as a teenager, not really joking, that our family coat of arms could well be a circle crossed by a bar sinister—the international symbol of No.

I felt dangers she could not, and I took her health and safety and reputation upon myself: No climbing, no whining, no pushing, rushing, shoving, no biting, no fighting, no grape juice, no name-calling, no roller-skating on walls, no rushing at trouble, no walking through puddles, no asking for treats or chocolate sweets or extra flavors or special favors, no biting nails, no picking up snails, rocks, feathers, no canvas sneakers, no tap dancing, no interrupting, no saving dead squirrels in the fridge, no yelling from windows, no walking on the roof, no overdue books, no painting your ears, no tears, no chewing gum, no muddy knees, no splashing at boys, no cannonballing off diving boards, no skirts without slips, no throwing shoes, no snakes in the house, no talking to soldiers—nothing in short that encroached on others or led my own child down the garden path of expectation. It was exhausting, let me tell you, rearing a willful daughter single-handedly in dangerous times.

At sixteen, Marjorie left home. She had good grades and graduated early from high school, rushing off to a college where she earned her own way and altered her opinions to such a degree and so quickly that her return visits threw us both into confusion. Her clothes looked ill-bred; her manner of speaking seemed lowbrow and unfamiliar. I hardly knew her after a year or two, and at twenty-one, my daughter launched her career; by day she clipped poodles and by night, tutored gypsies for the G.E.D. This is what she wanted to do, she told me, which was news to me. I had always imagined marriage for her, or a job in personnel since she seemed to get along with strangers. Her handwriting on occasional cards home looked large and round, like the new Marjorie herself, who had put on some weight, grown her hair long, and in all senses seemed to have spread out; she had friends who came and went, she took excursions, kept cats, drank homemade beer, was escorted out by several young men whom I seldom met. She moved around, following people who shared her interest in social causes to Lexington, Kentucky, then to Richmond, Virginia. On rare visits, she explained to me what she was doing, but I mostly stayed out of her way. As much as I loved her, raising my child had turned my hair white, and I felt the burden of her upkeep and care now lay with her. Sink or swim, my friend Mr. Pomeroy across the back fence advised, and that is what I did.

I had supported us by working for lawyers, my closet shorthand from the first war coming into its own. I learned good typing, was neat and punctual, performed my tasks with dispatch, and was a pleasant member of the office. My personal life I kept simple: no groups—church, choral, quilting, social, or helpful. No office parties or dinners out, no dresses costing more than I could make them for, no new winter coat for ten years at a stretch, no presents bought except on sale, no trips anywhere. I might have married again. My friend Mr. Herbert Pomeroy, who lived in the house behind me, was a bachelor, a gardening enthusiast, and perfectly nice. Over drinks on his terrace he proposed. I was free, divorced from Harry years before, but I told him nothing of that. I said just that I wanted to keep my life simple, which he sadly accepted. Upon retirement I looked things up for the historical society. I was quite the perky old thing in my rain hat down at the courthouse, checking through land deeds and census records. I often bumped into lawyers there whom I knew and would spend a moment chatting.

Then, like an elephant, Harry Bagg came home to me to die. Leaving behind the woman whose picture I never saw and whose name I never learned, with whom he'd spent the middle years of his life, he had negotiated his way from Hong Kong across the Pacific by airplane and from there transcontinentally to me. When I opened my front door without warning to him, thin, full of trembles, I saw like a ghost the sweet smile of 1920, a ready-for-life Harry, grime-streaked under tropical sun, still standing tall with that posture of impatient energy, as if the rest of the world were foot-dragging. I touched the sleeve of his raincoat, the only covering he'd needed in the East, and smelled what seemed the history of the intervening years—dust, salt, chalk, ink, smoke, ash, earth, wind, rain. There was always something ascetic about him, as if he could never find the way toward comfort, or didn't approve of it. Or happiness, either. It had once made me respect him but at eighty I wanted to take him in my arms like a boy, which I did. I embraced him hard, and his hands spreading out along my back returned the pressure. He did not let go. We stood on my porch in silence like that, cleaving to each other, as wordless as our shared life had always been. My heart fairly cracked in two.

Forty-six years apart, yet we seemed utterly familiar. I took him in, grateful for the second chance at companionship, strangely uncaring about our other past. I could no longer find much use in blaming him or myself for our failings. Our argument seemed a cerebral conundrum that had little to do with a friend seeking rest in his last days. I did not quite forgive him; I just thought about other things. And we shared two quiet years, with a bittersweet regret of what might have been. In the final analysis, hadn't I won the argument? You can't live a life on theories; you can't ignore the people who seem to get in your way. Well, you can, but you bruise yourself against them and make little headway if you try.

Invitation to Patriotism

ONE OF THE HARDEST trials in the world is to get out of bed every morning too early to greet with cheer a person whose life is slowly disintegrating and not show too great a pity, nor too little an understanding. To be available as if by chance, as he struggles out of bed, to appear casually with a glass and pills, as if we all took pills for little physical ills, to plump up pillows the way one might straighten a lampshade, with a disinterested gesture at tidiness, so as not to suggest too much concern, too much consideration, to avoid drawing attention to one's own physical health, to curtail any semblance of shock at the other's appalling, humiliating, demoralizing downward slide.

I called him H. the second time around, from a need to be jaunty, or perhaps as a way to keep my distance from him and his betrayal and his dying. Of course it was easy to have Harry in the house. His green toothbrush dropped neatly beside my pink one. His brown walking shoes lined up nicely beside my own brown walking shoes. Without thinking, I boiled his eggs to specification, I read his moods, and I took a pleased interest in seeing what he chose to do with his day, how he alphabetized my file cards, dried the dishes, polished the brass, dusted the lintels and even behind the pictures, meticulous to the end. For many months, he seemed well, except for his whispery voice and diminished breath. He could pass me my breakfast coffee with no more than a rattle of the cup on saucer. Bit by bit all of H. started wobbling.

His well-being seemed suddenly a test of my own ingenuity and resourcefulness. I was the one now in charge of the story of our life together, part two. It gave me a grave pleasure to study up the workings of my old husband's body and talk to doctors about him as if he were an important find. I was unearthing the past, and hoping to discover the treasures we had buried there alongside so much broken crockery. I watched Harry for any clue. I dusted down everything I found.

"Just leave the details to me," Harry murmured, holding out a shaky arm for the phone book.

"I've already got them on the line. I'm on hold. Vivaldi."

Our local specialists put me in touch with a doctor in Chicago interested in Parkinson's. It seemed right to address our letter for help to someone living in "Ill." The reply came promptly, quite illegible, scrawled on a prescription pad. At our mail carrier's suggestion we took it to the druggist and he, in fact, was able to decipher: *Interesting case. Refer to colleague Dr. Grady Schneiderpungs, Dorf Clinic in Dorf, Georgia.* I found it on our atlas: Dorf, situated deep in the Appalachians, population 312, "an agricultural community settled by Germans in the middle of the last century," explained the atlas. It sounded peaceful and picturesque. I had visions of the Brennekes's farmyard, Cassandra the hog munching down corncobs, knee-deep in mud, Christmas houses made of gingerbread. I got excited at the prospect of visiting a place like the prewar nation of Felicity's adoptive family. I heard the doctor's name in my sleep like a mantra.

It perked H. up quite a bit to think of himself as an interesting case, to imagine himself perhaps the toast of Dorf, Georgia, as physicians moved their pointers up and down X-rays of his vertebrae to instruct each other at prestigious conferences. At least this was what he said.

We packed up for Dorf in late summer, and feeling as though this might be a trip across the River Styx, I sat by our bags in the front room, keeping a weather eye on H. and waiting for the taxi. He was choosing to find it a jolly occasion. "A real honeymoon for us," he whispered. I checked but, astonishingly, found no trace of irony in that galumphing remark. H. had decided to rewrite history. Fine, I thought. I could go along with that, I decided, wiping the spot of wet off my eyes. I got the taxi man to put an arm strongly around H.'s waist, and, holding onto his arms, we eased him down the stairs. It was like managing a mutinous marionette.

We bumped in the air, then spent a difficult three hours in Atlanta, waiting for the bus to Dorf. Being in transit with him again brought back memories, chiefly of my anxiety and anger with Harry in those days. He was presuming that I would follow him to all corners of the earth. As he was now, with the difference that he needed me as never before. If I once stopped my attentions, Harry would be lost. H. thanked me often, for arranging his seat belt, for getting down a light blanket from the overhead locker. "Angel of mercy," I said modestly. I felt buoyed by an adrenaline high of graciousness. And I knew, too, that what I felt was dangerously like being in love.

"I've put you through a lot," Harry mumbled one night as I lent a shoulder to his trip to the loo. "You never thought you'd be doing this."

"I'm glad to be doing it, Harry," I said. "I truly am." I left at it that, afraid that if I said more I might cry. My true pleasure was too personal a triumph to share politely. The trip to the clinic in Georgia seemed our private chance to change history; me in charge rather than Harry, and the goal of our travels a Germany of my preference, not his. I felt we were being given a second chance at a peace accord, now that a site had been chosen. Saving his body seemed a way of healing history.

When at last we arrived at the sheet metal–roofed bus station in Dorf, midafternoon, a lady filling a machine with cheese crackers sold me some right from her box. "Royal Connaught Motel?" she asked. People accustomed to foreigners usually didn't smile so much. "The Mullers run the motel and restaurant. Just past McMaster Mall. Turn right at the Spanky's and go over the bridge by MacDonald's. You'll see the Connaught. Petunias on barrels out front. There's no taxi," she laughed, "with the Wisenheimers on vacation in Quebec. Quickest way . . ." She pointed to a large motorcycle with sidecar parked by the bicycle stand. "It's mine. I'll get my son to pick it up later if you leave it behind the motel."

Smiling my head off in the bright sunshine, I lugged my H. behind, like an oversized teddy bear. "I'm going to like this place," I told him, my decision having been made days before.

"I'm letting life take its course," he answered. His eyes lay closed and sunken in his leathery face.

"As you should do, H.," I advised, sage counselor. Every glance at him filled me with golden lightness.

"I'm not listening," he informed me. His face was erased of expression.

I managed to cram our things and H. into the sidecar and with a few slams got the thing revved. The cracker lady, directing me, suddenly pulled out a little maple leaf flag, the new Canadian emblem, from her pocket and stuck it into a tight spot on the handlebars.

"Okay," she said, saluting.

"Okay," I answered. Under my helmet, which seemed curiously like a doughboy's, I felt quite intrepid. I made a quick turn down the hill to the road signposted for the Royal Motel. Even from a distance I could tell that the houses were balconied, with steep-pitched roofs. "It's a Little Bavaria!" I called to H. in the wind. The low shopping center and construction machinery stalled on the weekend like a museum exhibit of prehistoric animals did not dampen my ardor for the place. How do you tell a happy motorcyclist? By the bugs in her dentures.

"Motel" was an exaggeration. There was no need of a motel on the potholed road beyond the golden arches. Soybeans were the main form of life out that way, and the Royal was actually a semiconverted barn, providing three rooms with one shared bath. The other rooms seemed empty at the moment. "Off-season," said the manager, a lady in shorts and purple tank top who warned against using the shower more than once a week without extra payment.

"It's an adventure for us to be here," I said, which was true, not just gush. "It's a sort of déjà vu, for us. We lived in Berlin before the war."

"You in the army?" she asked H.

"Was briefly." He tried to stick out his leg for her but tipped a little and caught my arm for support. "The Somme," he said.

She tapped the bell on the desk. "But you're Canadians, right? I just love that accent."

The tall son unlocked our room off a courtyard.

"What's that smell?" I had to ask.

"Slaughtered a steer yesterday," he said cheerfully. He added, "Tina will bring you tea."

"This is certainly very German," I said when we were alone. I was full of conflict, per usual. From friendship with Felicity and the Brennekes sixty-five years before, I had a childish delight in finding myself suddenly, weirdly, in the land of Duden, a refuge of good Germanness in the Appalachian hills. At least one could still find in Dorf the essence of something fine. National socialism had no place in this lush village of gingerbread houses and pastoral views. Yet it was Germany and German politics that had divided H. and me in the thirties, broken up our chance at happiness as much as the wall that later bricked up east from west in his one-time city of art. In some way, finding myself with him in this little German enclave, I wanted to make good on past promises, try again for the harmony of Walla. His return to me had struck me first as a sign of his own need for reunion. Only later, when Marjorie wrote something in a rare postcard, did I consider the imposition of caring for a dying ex-husband, but somehow I could not get angry; I felt too keenly our unspoken sense of loss.

In that whitewashed barn room, I wanted to cheer him up with German nostalgia. I, too, could pretend our time there had been fun; I almost believed it had been compared to what we now faced. "I'd know this place anywhere," I said. And, I considered, zipping out things from my sponge bag and setting them by the sink, it was pleasant to have one's preconceptions confirmed. From the window I could see parts of town, a view of Alps/Appalachians. "Lederhosen and oompah bands and people blowing mile-long horns for their cows—I can almost see them. Part of the crazy-quilt of Americana. By the way, H., did you notice the little maple-leaf flag at reception?"

"Sorry," said H., lying out on the bed, eyes closed.

I should have known he would pay little attention to the present.

I peeped out. The manager's family sat drinking pop on their front balcony, Alpine-perfect. "*Kaffeeklatsch*," I said, delighted to dredge up the word. On spotting my old head out the door, a stately young woman rose up with impressive posture. I noticed with interest that she was wearing a short tartan wraparound skirt, white blouse, and tartan bolero. "They grow Valkyries down here," I said for H.'s amusement, but barely got a guffaw. "Did the Germans ever use plaid?"

He seemed to be considering. "MacGoebbels? MacAdenauer?"

"Maybe she works at one of those fast-food places with a theme."

A younger boy shadowed Tina, who was heading our way with two mugs on a tray. "They're coming over," I said as I plumped H. up a little.

Tina stuck her head in. "You all drink tea, right?" She had an accent softer and more southern than her mother.

"Good heavens," I said and suddenly felt how much I needed a cup of tea.

"This is my little brother Wilfred," she added.

"How do you do?" I said, shaking his clammy hand. "What a charming name," I said. "Everything is so German here!"

"Named for Sir Wilfred Laurier," said Tina, placing the tray on our night stand and peaceably pouring out. "One of Canada's greatest prime ministers. You like Red Rose, I hope," she said, handing me a shallow cup.

"Only in Canada, you say?" sputtered the shy Wilfred. "Pity."

"Yes," I said, baffled. Only some years later, when I mentioned this to some other Canadians, did I learn that he had been quoting a commercial.

"Everything comfortable?" Tina asked.

"Jolly good," rasped H. with his eyes closed. We all looked at him and wondered what he meant.

Tina inquired, "You all *are* Canadians, right?"

"Oh, yes. We're both from Ontario. Why do you ask?"

Squaring his shoulders, Wilfred found a note—*hmm*—and, looking at the poster on the far wall of what I realized was not a reindeer as I'd first thought but a moose, began to sing, "O *Can*-a-da! Our home and *fa*-ther-land . . ."

H. opened one eye. "What's going on?"

"Good," I encouraged the boy, who blushed scarlet. Canada, in addition to the red-and-white flag with a maple leaf on it, had made up a national anthem for itself in the years since I'd left. I'd never heard it sung, though, and the words and tune filled me with a troubling nostalgia, mostly for a place I was sure I really did not know. I could not imagine that anyone in my hometown would go around extolling their country in that way. This was all new and uncanny. I said, "That's very nice."

"Thanks, eh?" said Wilfred.

"You bet," I said and hid my confusion by unlocking our case.

"If you're hungry," Tina advised in her careful way, "there's the Royal Inn. Just beside the motel."

"That will be fine. Tina," I added, tapping the enormous standing wardrobe, "may we use this?"

"Oh, I'll unlock it. The cows didn't have closets, so Mrs. Handschuhmacher put these armoires in every room."

"*Schrank*," I corrected her, smiling. She looked confused and backed off the point. "Maybe you don't speak much German at home," I suggested.

"No," she said suspiciously.

"That's a shame." I felt as if my quarter had slipped through the phone.

Thinking of a supper at the Royal Inn, sorting our little piles of undies and rolled socks into the top shelf of the enormous *schrank*, like some casket upended, I glanced out the window and could make out the mountains at a distance. While H. dozed, semirecumbent, I thought how lucky that I had brought my hiking shoes. I heard the beguiling low of homeward-sauntering cows, the clank of heavy bells, someone calling, and down on the *Strasse* a man swearing, and the caw of a crow settling its wings in the tree somewhere near our little ethnic motel. I took deep breaths and felt as relaxed as the woolen blouse I hung up nicely on the hanger provided. I imagined rising early, delivering H. to the famous doctor at the clinic, and starting off—each day in a different direction. Walking straight, up, down, through, if necessary, till I had worn myself out with discovery. Germany, having held a kind of mystery for me since my early friendship with Felicity and the Brennekes, was a country we were forbidden to love. Finding myself suddenly in its rural, albeit transplanted, midst, surrounded by *volk* who seemed ripe with mysterious life, I determined I would learn what I could. I would redeem Deutschland, if only to myself, and hope perhaps in some way to make up for the bad years H. and I had spent there together. This was our chance to rewrite our past. I imagined even during the time there, the many hours when H. might be in consultation with the clinic's expert, I could get to know locals—at the Greyhound station, in the post office, the travel agency, the restaurant. I would hear their version of history, learn from where in Germany their ancestors had come. I grew large with a zest for local history, feeling a natural sympathy as a perpetual outsider myself. I wanted to know how German everything was.

Breathing in with doubly expanded lungs, I nearly keeled over with the heady oxygen of it all. I could hardly wait and felt my skin burning slightly as if with fever as H. roused himself and I began the job of dressing him for our first excursion—dinner. "We're going to be correct," I warned H., "and order the local dishes. No fair asking for steak or a curry. They probably do things like wild turkey around here. But if they go along ethnic lines, we might have a pleasant bratwurst."

"This is Georgia," H. objected. "They eat hog's trotters and peaches and black-eyed peas." I indulged in a superior smile as we stepped out.

The air was warm and for me held the promise of the unexpected. It was like going on a blind date, in some ways, supporting Harry on my arm. I surprised myself by feeling almost romantic. Eighty years old, soggy muscled, out of puff, I felt that little coiling of inner eagerness, an extra alertness to the nap of Harry's corduroy jacket, the tuft of white hair at the back of his neck, the calluses on his hands that were still that mix of graceful and utilitarian, fingers rounded, wrists fine and muscled, that characterized so much of H. and his world. "Harry," I whispered and pulled close for a squeeze of his upper arm.

"What are you doing?" he said, but with a catch of pleasure. He glanced at me with glossed eyes.

"This is nice," I offered.

His head jerked; I saw for a dangerous moment that stuck with me and in some way made up for much of what had gone wrong, that he would cry, but he pulled off a respectable Canadian, "Isn't it, beloved?" as we stopped at the restaurant's door and he gained control of himself with a sturdy sniff.

The place was just a cinderblock annex to the motel. Our own Wilfred, malingering outside, opened the screen door for us with nervous pleasure but did not come in. "Canadians," he called into the dark interior where, stepping in, we encountered red vinyl tablecloths and webbed candleholders. Lengths of flypaper curled down like party streamers. A few diners, in baseball caps and monogrammed shirts, quietly wiped their fingers as they looked up at us. The hostess in a pink floor-length dress hurried forward. "Ontario?" she said brightly. "Let's get you all a table." Clipboard in front, she led us under a little canopy of maple-leaf flags toward a dark corner.

"*Danke sehr,*" I said. "Is there a table with a view? We'd like just a cow or two walking around out the window. Even a window with no cow."

Pursing her lips, she hesitated.

"An Alp," I suggested, "a sunset. Just distance for our eyes."

She obligingly hurried us to a new table, one with a mountain in the window, snowcapped, tinged pink in the setting sun, etc. She placed long menus in our hands but didn't give us time to study them before announcing, "I recommend the house special. My husband, Bubba, the cook, planned it for y'all's arrival."

"Oh," I said, taken aback by the Bubba, but recovering. "We'll be glad to try something local." I smiled at H., who was also looking a little snowcapped and pink tinged. "Thank you," I said and hoped how much I meant it came through. H., disengaged, reached for the newspaper left at the table next to ours and folded it out. "Put that away," I whispered gently. I had been looking for signs of something; what I was finding was a Harry abstracted, my old Harry lost in time. "You can read the news later, or maybe they have a TV in the hotel lobby," I added, just to speak to him, to keep him with me.

Our hostess at that instant swung out the padded door, full of intent. Following on her heels strode a glowing, growling chef in high white hat, balancing aloft with gloved hands an enormous tray.

"It's just like the great Canadian Pacific Railroad," Bubba whispered, and before I could answer, had set us in motion, painting the scene with his soft words: "*Chongo, chongo,* you cross the prairies, lakes, grain elevator in parlor car with etched glass windows and paintings of Banff Springs by the Group of Seven—oh, yes!—the maître d' is setting before you the head of game shot by a passenger in the observation car in passing." Modest *Ta da!* and Bubba's pristine cloth knicked over the dome and lifted it up for us to behold the treat within: a staring antlered head. It looked exactly like the Brennekes's old milch cow, Hilda, with a big soft nose and moist eyes, that nibbled sugar from our hands. This cow's eyes were grayed over and she somehow had got her head entangled in someone else's antlers. They lay on top of her head, small and brittle, like a paste tiara.

"Oh! Look, H.," I said, with my strained Christmas voice.

H. had his nose stuck in the dish. "It's a sculpture?"

"It's a *moose*." A sinking feeling overwhelmed me.

Bubba carefully draped his cloth over his arm and dipped the knife into the air like a conductor gathering up the power of his orchestra. "We imagine we are crossing Marathon, Jackfish Bay, Schreiber, Rossport, Nipigon, Thunder Bay." He began a gentle slicing.

I remarked in the silence as we watched, chastened, "Canada certainly seems to have come into its own." This was met with polite murmurs and I became aware that a group of men identically clad in khaki jodhpurs and red riding coats was gathering around our table. A short individual in a Mountie hat stepped close.

"Dwayne Schroder. We of the Phil-Canads wish you welcome." He stuck a pitch pipe to his lips. The air reverberated in a four-part hum, then broke into a hefty, *"This land is your land..."* I looked at H., gazing out the window, at our cow, waiting to be savored. They went through a long list of place names familiar to me but so little thought of as to sound foreign. *"From the Arctic Circle to the Great Lakes waters, this land was made for you and me."*

"Thank you," I whispered. "Thank you." I stuck my napkin under the rim of my plate.

Bubba patted my shoulder. "There's more," he said.

I tried a light, social laugh. "Actually, you know, I expected something German!"

Dwayne Schroder stepped up to my chair. In a voice softer than his florid face led one to expect, he tried to explain to the thick-headed visitor from Ontario, "Our neighbor to the north holds the promise of the future. And now, a glass, and let's drink to her, eh?"

I found a small lemonade in my hand as someone with an accordion once again started up the opening notes of "O Canada," a song I was beginning to feel very mixed about. As I didn't know the words, I held my glass up to my lips and pretended to sing. Why, I wondered, was I always getting caught in these patriotic displays?

To say we finished our dinners quickly would be an understatement. We were escorted out to the street like royalty; I felt like a crook. Worse, I felt as though life had conspired against us. All I'd wanted was to dust off some pleasant German kitsch. Instead, Harry and I were under cultural surveillance. Just when we might have found a shard of past promise to glue together, the whole dig mutinied. It was as if the site had pulled a joke on us, conspiring to make us the artifacts instead.

Back in our room, the crackers I had bought in the bus station proved tasteless. So much, I thought, depends upon point of view. "I just wish they'd relax a little," I said to H., snagging the plastic wrapper with a tooth. "And they've got it wrong, anyway."

"Ca-na-da," said H. carefully. The syllables sounded odd, reverberating in our prison cell. "I don't believe I've been there."

"No," I agreed. "Not their Canada, H. We lived someplace else." And suddenly sad for everyone, I realized how little we could give them of ourselves. We, so restrained, had walked through our roles and been nothing more or less than amateur stage Canadians. They in turn had muffed their lines in my imagined Bavarian passion play. I had hoped for Little Germany and got Little Canada instead, like a bad joke. I had hoped for the Harry of sixty years before and found that I still had him, as opaque as ever. The fervor for home and native land, a phrase that clanged in my ears like the train outside Bremen's Travelers' Arms Hotel in summer, disrupting our sleep with its iron insistence, had begun to break down my spirit. The failing body that stretched on the twin bed beside my chair darkened in the twilight to a small mountain range and I was just one more climber, lying beside it, camping for a time among mysteries.

Dorf led us into that uncharted land of decline and grief that had no use for anthems. The clinic's famous doctor referred us to a specialist outside Baltimore, but it became obvious that nothing would save H. We returned to Red Leaf House as shards of ourselves, no wiser about our beginnings, no more glued together, with the prospect of only our dust commingling. Hindsight distorted just as much as foresight. Time was a slippery bathmat that could spin you naked right down the hall. Once when Marjorie, our unexpected, graying daughter, came for a brief visit when Harry was still upright but hooked into breathing tubes, we all sat out on the terrace and laughed over the Dorf trip. But the ice we shook in our summer glasses tumbled about like Rubic's cubes, and the puzzle had no solution.

I nursed him for two and a half years, to the point of no return. I saw Harry slide through selves like a snake. He had been a delicate collage of ancient parts. More than the rest of us, he suffered from carbon monoxide, the thinning ozone, noise pollution, and contaminated drinking water, yet his mind in his last years was forward looking. He was a Modern. Not just one of the Canadian proponents of what became known as the International Style, he took the creed of functionality and social improvement to its serious conclusions. The doctors diagnosed old age. I could have told them it was New Age that was doing him in, a nagging suspicion that one could only escape into one's self for relief from the world's pestilence and plagues.

He developed the Parkinson's shuffle. Advised to keep him moving, we made a snail's tour of the garden every day. I'd never found time to care for it beyond planting a few perennials and weeding in alternate years. Marjorie had been interested in sunflowers and herbs as a girl, but after she left, the garden reverted to weeds, except where the periwinkle under an oak tree kept smooth the plot of ground dedicated to the Bartram dead.

"Bury me there," Harry whispered one day.

I looked where he was motioning toward the few weatherworn headstones.

"We're not Bartrams, Harry."

"Where would you put my remains?"

This shook me. Softly, I said, "I'd assumed cremation."

"What? And scatter me at sea? Or keep me in an urn on the mantel? I think not. Bones should rest in the earth. No fancy coffin. I want the worms to have a chance."

"Don't talk that way."

"And," he said, actually smiling for the first time in months, "let's not make things tough for the archaeologists."

I considered this. "You expect to be excavated?"

"Why not?" he asked, a trace of anger in his voice. "I've given something to the world. The future may well want to exume my remains. And, as for Bartrams," he continued, "they can easily scoot over and share their periwinkle with a fellow corpse. The dead practice a nice expedience."

I held H.'s arm as he shuffled daily past sunflower stalks leaning like dried bamboo and blackberry brambles coiling toward a small bench. Harry made the bench his shaky goal—there and back, then lunch—until the day he sat down for good, and our soup went stone cold.

The island took my mother; time, my child; that hard earth, beloved Harry Bagg.

5

Conflux

To Bee or Not to Bee

✦

M<small>Y KNEES TWINGED</small> as I put some boxes of Harry's clothes out on the stoop for charity. I panted on the stairs. I overwound the clocks. Small troubles panicked my hours—should I go down to the local hardware store for a washer or call a plumber? Alone amongst bougainvillea, African violets, Audubon prints, I was shot through with sad alarm at all the time I had, with no shaky spoonfuls of bouillon burning spots through pajama tops. I felt like a child on a trampoline, tossed by grief and release.

My weather-beaten daughter flew up for the funeral and touched me by crying more freely than I as we packed things up I had offered her. Dusting off a framed photograph with her sleeve, she stopped to study it and said, "Remember Daddy's impersonation of a hunter crab?"

I did. It caught me up short that she should, too. How odd to hear this stranger call him "Daddy." Harry had always seemed my own private mistake. I smiled tightly; I looked out at the stalks in the garden and determined not to succumb.

Marjorie thought I should sell the house. "Come to Conflux," she insisted. "It's warm and sunny. You'd be very welcome. Just to sit for a while would do you good. Get to know the twins."

I hunched down amid towering boxes, tired as an old mule, unable to decide a thing. "I don't want to be a burden," I declared. "And I need my independence." More truthfully, I knew, I needed my dependence. The house, which had been given to me in the most haphazard fashion, and which I had tended as a temporary caretaker, not homeowner, had been the place where I'd spent—the shock of it took my breath away—

the greatest stretch of my life. The quotidian had absorbed my given minutes, one by one by one, and yet I had never let myself settle in.

As Marjorie made plans to go back south, I felt a sad tug and realized I liked having her around. I was interested in this daughter I hardly knew. Hulking, ungainly, she wore no watch and dropped to sleep on a garden chair at any hour. Her snoring spread an unfamiliar warmth through the house. How could she have grown so old? Years of gardening in the heat of the day had given her dark crocodile skin, and her waistline had merged with her hips. Her clothes were of no discernible style, yet she wore them with evident pleasure. When I set our little supper of eggs in front of that cheerful, sark-clad giant in my Queen Anne chair, her muscle-bound forearms resting on my polished tabletop, I wondered that a pale-faced little girl had once sat at that place, chewing her bangs; I felt I was dining with a stranger. She seemed such a foreigner that her concern struck me as all the more queer and touching. Lucky, just lucky, to have such a daughter, I thought. I wanted to recover this aging child of mine; I wanted her to know me.

"Conflux," I repeated, trying to hear if it sounded right. A conflux of what?

"Rivers," said Marjorie, brightening.

More than that, I thought; I had a daughter, I had two grandchildren, and I even had a professor for a son-in-law. In fact, a family in need of a doting old relation, out there waiting for me. Images of our shared life passed before my eye: young faces aglow in candlelight as I brought in some rich dessert as a special treat; walks with the dog on Sunday afternoons; sitting with my daughter and reading library books aloud to each other in turn after the dishes were done. Christmas would bring carol singing, Easter an egg hunt around the garden, and summers in the south would go on forever. "Your home sounds lovely, Marjorie," I said.

"Come stay with us, Mother." Her dark eyes shone like points of light on a coastline.

Up stakes. When asked to take furniture, Marjorie chose only a few pieces, of marginal sentimental value—and I had those sent down to their house in Conflux. My own house, needing modernizing and a new furnace, sold below value despite its age, but I did not care; I had a sudden family waiting.

My only doubts, circling through my mind on those final, sleepless nights, concerned my daughter's choice of mate. As a child Marjorie had taken far more interest than I ever did in growing things at Red Leaf House. She put in a watermelon patch, a fig tree (which never bore fruit, being so far north of its native clime), a cane of raspberries, orchids. None of these ever amounted to much, and I began to observe in my daughter a perverse relationship between effort and failure, as though she wanted mostly to throw herself into projects destined clearly, even to her, to bring no rewards. She suffered from it, too, falling into spells of depression, brought out again only by the prospect of some new but predictably disastrous undertaking, which is how I'd always regarded her marriage to Quilliam DeForest, the niggling worry that disturbed my sleep.

DeForest taught sociology at the college in Conflux and was very brilliant, I'm sure. Tall, disheveled, too clever by half, he always made me think of some medieval woodsman. He'd troubled me from the moment Marjorie, on a rare visit home one summer, invited him to Red Leaf House to dig up a sunflower patch. She wanted the clay for her pots, and he liked the smell of the ground's decay, as he told me. In fact, they found some rather pretty old medicine bottles and broken crockery of a blue willow pattern, but they turned these over to me without much interest, wanting just to dig.

From the first I was put off by his name: what did it mean? I asked around this question with my daughter but learned only that he came from Virginia. He was wearing sandals he'd made himself, and had a long braid in back when I met him the first time. "A Manx name," I said when my daughter introduced us. "Quarles, Quigwilliam."

"Really?" he said, impressed, though with me or with himself, it was impossible to guess. His face lengthened and he rubbed his chest with a small, bitten-nail hand. "Changing my name was probably the best move of my life."

"Very self-caring," whispered Marjorie and laced her knobby fingers through his. "Bill Woods was not *you*."

Of course that explained why I had trouble remembering his

name. Its fanciness seemed somehow designed to distance one, unpromising in a potential son-in-law. The first part sounded like some exotic wildflower, and the second part like an environmental problem, which is how I came to regard him. I warned Marjorie at the time, which I discovered too late just promoted the match. And apart from his personality, I just didn't think a man ten years my daughter's junior and employed in the summer picking tobacco sounded the ideal mate.

My instincts told me that this young man was not only angry, but was a rebel without much initiative. He had a vacant expression, and on that first visit sat on and on drinking tea and drumming his fingers on my Formica table till I started sponging up just to signal him to move along, wondering why he had nothing better to do, being so bright, but on he sat. His studies gave him some built-in direction, and he followed the steps admirably, it turned out. Marjorie told me he walked in his sleep and often cried out in dreams. This seemed to her a good sign, perhaps of depth or character. To me, it sounded like trouble.

They lived together around the Boston area unwed for endless years, in tents, mobile homes propped on cinder blocks, someone's paneled garage, and once an empty storefront hung with horse blankets. During that time my daughter supported DeForest by clipping poodles, a trade she had learned through a correspondence course. When Quilliam at last completed all that education, he found a job—he comprised one third of the sociology department at Conflux College—and they did get married, in black, for reasons I could never fathom. I did not attend the wedding as they seemed not to expect me to come. He supported the family; Marjorie got pregnant with profligacy—twins. They bought an interpretation of a house, settled down, but I was somehow not surprised to learn from my daughter in passing as we packed up my things that late winter after H. died that DeForest often gave jars of honey away to women friends. She told me this with a great show of unconcern, but I knew she could not be neutral or why mention it at all? The news settled on me like a veil. Now that I had acquired a family, I wanted only the best kind of life for them.

Marjorie, DeForest, and twins cornered me like gypsies as I came up the moving corridor into the gate. Feeling lightheaded from just one tiny scotch in the clouds, I greeted them as heartily as I could: "Hello,

hello, hello," I cried, warm granny with carrier bags, hugs all around. I wondered at those creatures who were my blood kin. Their clothes were oddly matched, their hair peculiarly trimmed, one of the twins was missing a shoe; we drew stares. Yet I was determined to love them. They were all I had left.

Bags lifted off the loop, I saw we would be making the journey back to their place in a rusted minivan wired together against nervous collapse. I was glad when Marjorie squeezed in back with the children and had me take the front seat next to Quill, as she called him. Still absurdly young, with ears sticking out, at least he had got rid of the beard. He admired my suit as he strapped me in and assumed the role of chauffeur-guide, pointing out, with an enthusiasm I could only presume was false, things like unmarked police cars and dead possums as we drove along.

I pretended more interest than I felt, grateful not to have to talk to the twins. They took my breath away by looking with their angular faces and bristly dark hair like Harry in Walla days. They were beautiful creatures in their long-armed, large-nosed, thirteen-year-old way. With ratchety voices they explained to their patient mother the plot of some interminable film. I'd spent a long time in a shop in Boston selecting presents, but I suddenly knew that a wooden top and a book on quilts were going to be all wrong for these modern children. I wondered what I could ever do to win them over.

To amuse the children, I pretended to be disappointed when the drive provided no dinosaurs, but the joke fell as flat as the landscape. I felt indifferent to the scenery, as it had so little to do with me. Through ragweed and dandelions we approached my daughter's house, which they called Bee Happy. The name punned on DeForest's apiary interest; bees breezed around the grounds and in and out of the house all day. Marjorie and DeForest had converted a barn into a kind of dwelling. They had knocked down the stalls, put in some windows, and added a brick floor. Some people like it rustic, of course. "Well, lovely," I said, looking around as DeForest handed me out of the car, and I honestly tried to mean it. "And thank you all for coming to pick me up."

What I didn't know, and only realized later, was that this trip to collect me was one of their rare outings together. Marjorie's family lived singularly independent lives. When we sat down to dinner that first evening at a table laboriously cleared of a large toadstool collection and spread with one of my own cross-stitched cloths, and Marjorie lifted up her fork, with what blissful ignorance did I remark, "Let's wait for the children, dear."

My daughter set down her fork. Obligingly she sauntered in her medieval-looking robe to the bottom of the stairs and shouted, "Children, your grandmother would like to see you for dinner."

She made my expectation sound like some odd quirk. I called after her, "*I* don't want it, we all want it, I presume." I chuffed at DeForest.

"I think they're out swimming," he said, wadding into his cheek like a squirrel some bread he'd helped himself to a little out of turn.

"Oh, well then," said Marjorie and sat down again.

"Aren't they coming?"

"When they're hungry, I'm sure they'll turn up."

The broccoli on my plate looked like contraband, taken without the whole family present. Was I asking too much?

"Different drummers," said DeForest, with that tinge of irony that kept me off balance around him. "They need to follow their own paths in life," he said, drawling the phrase. He stroked his chin. I considered that it had perhaps never been the beard that annoyed me so much as DeForest's disturbing intelligence which, like some delinquent teenager in a parking lot, kept gunning its engine, going nowhere.

"We're like the Quakers," explained Marjorie, peacefully wiping one of my old silver serving spoons on her sleeve. "We believe in the inner voice."

"The inner voice," I said, annoyed with them both, "is quite another matter. I'm asking for some common courtesies." Of course, that brought a silence during which I vowed to keep my opinions in check. I did not even complain when one of the family bees landed on the tines of my fork and began to dine off the piece of chicken I was just looking forward to putting into my own mouth. I set my fork on my plate and let him have at it. My daughter had chosen her life, and this was it, and I refused to condemn.

On my own I had always stopped for a cup of coffee and a vanilla wafer at half past ten, but at coffee time on my first morning, I couldn't locate a soul, although the television in the book room was broadcasting local news loudly. I turned it off. Only a largish duck hunkered in the kitchen, straining over an egg it seemed to want badly to lay. I removed myself to the dining room to wait out her confinement, and looked out the window at all the weeds Quilliam had yet to mow.

When the duck exited, squawking, I poked around in the cupboards for coffee and discovered a cache of honey, stacked in jars, all neatly labeled. Obviously the work of my son-in-law. I lifted one out and admired its neat, even, amber tone, the slow pooling as I tipped the jar, how it recollected itself on the other side as I tipped it back. I replaced it in the pyramid. This amount of order reassured me: at least someone was on top of things. Then, remembering what Marjorie had mentioned, I felt I had discovered something nasty, like dirty pictures. I made my coffee from a jar of (stale) instant and drank the bitter stuff all by myself on the porch.

One afternoon during my first week at Bee Happy, DeForest took me, against my will, on a tour of his hives and discussed varieties of clover. He was back from a reception at the college, looking very much the part in moth-frayed tweed. I guessed the jacket was one of Marjorie's garage-sale finds. His voice was soft and sloppy. As he turned to point something out, a dragon's breath of whiskey shot into my face. He bent over a stand of daffodils, already in full bloom in early March.

"The pistil," he said, poking his finger down the purple petals. "That's for asexual reproduction, you know." He thought I would be shocked by such remarks. His laugh was low and suggestive as he stumbled along. One side of his face seemed to leer as he turned to me. The bees circled his head and made sudden dives down into the blossoms. "Atta boy, Pericles. Go for it, Lysander," he urged them. All around me garish flowers spread themselves open in a show of vulgar fecundity. Slightly sickened by the smell, unsteady, unready for so much pollination and display, I fell back and waited out the tour.

The children played Monopoly with me every afternoon when they came home from school. They were clearly acting on instructions. They systematically robbed me of all my money and made me pay rent for landing on their hotels. I paid up gladly, hell-bent on buying their affection. Silently I observed every bruise or scratch on their slim legs, noted the rise of pimples around noses, smelled their young scents of sweat, shampoo, red dust, felt their bodies' heat almost hurtfully close for the distance between us in spirit. I tried to win them with riddles and careless moves, throwing the game every time, and they seemed pleased to rake in their winnings, but the end of the game brought them no closer to building a house on Viola Gardens. They'd separate out the colored money, bend the board back into the box, and consult each other about swimming plans, sending me back to jail.

Their talk concerned me. They spoke in catch phrases and referred to television characters in whom I could muster no interest. I felt like a spy unable to crack a code. Jessica had a way of expressing herself that relied more on hand waving than words. To build up her vocabulary, I slid under her door some leather-bound editions I had brought with me: Dickens, Victor Hugo, Shakespeare's sonnets. I fretted about her education. Jerome's manner reminded me a little of Robin Glover's—a slowed-down bluffness, a style designed to frustrate demands or inquiries. It worked. Both children spent a lot of time in front of the computer in DeForest's study, pushing that thing around that made those things move.

In the beginning I blamed my daughter, preoccupied as she was with her potting. The vigor of her interest struck me as out of control. In a shed in back near the pond she showed me her wheel. She maneuvered herself largely up as if onto a bicycle and demonstrated how she kept it turning with her feet as she threw a hunk of clay in the center and pressed it into a lopsided cone.

I watched, amazed at the process. I had never actually seen how she made those pots.

"I feel like Gaea!" she cried. "Molding the earth!"

The wet mud oozed out between my daughter's fingers, spitting over her sunburnt face and matting her long hair; it alarmed and saddened me. I didn't believe in this display of joy; the world old Marjorie could mold seemed pathetically small, and anyway most of the effort, like her life in general, seemed to be spinning by centrifugal force out from between her fingers and spattering the walls, floor, me. I backed out of the shed and waded through the still-uncut grass up to the porch, from where I could see the road and wait for the children's school bus.

A family friend, Roberta Forster, phoned in the middle of an argument Marjorie was having with Quilliam over a clogged loo, to find out if I'd arrived. She was a partner in Marjorie's wildflower protection movement and a volunteer Anglophile. "Don't get on her sick list, Baguette," Quilliam warned me when I was blowing my nose, full of allergies. "She will tell you all about how Prince Philip's mother was a deaf-mute nun who lip-read in seven languages." He came at me with the plunger.

"Umph," I humphed, unable with a stuffy head to wrest up any retort, and distracted, besides, with thinking that DeForest seemed like a negative force, walking around like his bees, sucking out the pleasure in everything, full of sting.

When the expensively tailored Roberta stopped in to meet me, bringing the children home in her car from their school, where she volunteered on Thursdays, I brewed, self-consciously, a pot of Earl Grey, a tea that has always made me suspect that I was drinking perfume. Personally I am a coffee drinker but given my druthers on an afternoon in the low nineties, I would have taken off my girdle and lain on the sofa, sucking ice cubes. Still, it seemed a good thing to have the correct Roberta paying a visit.

"Char," I said, handing Roberta her cup. "Tea is one of those symbols, isn't it? Countries seem to acquire them. Russia has its onion domes and astrakhan hats and the U.S. has ..."

"Uncle Sam," put in Jerome unexpectedly, prone on the chesterfield.

"And blue-haired old ladies," I added, excited to get the ball rolling. "Perhaps that's what I should become."

"Mother ..."

"But our neighbor to the north," began Roberta.

"Mounties," I asserted. "Mounties and moose."

"As Gertrude Stein would have said," Marjorie remarked, scratching at a chigger bite under her knee, "there's no there there."

"No, there isn't," I asserted and heard my voice rise in decibels, "and Canadians don't try to cram it down anyone's throat, either."

"Well, you couldn't," laughed my daughter, pleased, spilling tea on my old dry-rotted Persian carpet.

"Canadians seem like old people," said Jessica. Her thin voice cut through the heat like a fine blade. We all looked at her, sunk down beside her brother, Coke can at chin level. In a frenzy of blushing, she tried to explain, "You don't notice old people very much, because they're mostly so good!"

Lying awake that night, as I was prone to do in that strange house, too hot to sleep even with the fan blowing, I thought about my grandchild's observation. She was both right and wrong. To be noticed, you had to have symbols—like cherry pie or Volvos—or be truly wicked. But old people were not permitted bad behavior. I wondered what would happen if my real crime were ever to become known.

Walla days returned in memory, tattered flags, as I felt like a knife stab the old yearning of that long-past summer. Now not my mother but my own daughter that I sought. And—miracle!—here she was, wandering through the house of a morning in a Japanese bathrobe tied loosely around her bulk, hairbrush in hand, first sweeping at crumbs on the tablecloth then swiping at Jerome's hair on his slide out the door. But having her present did not open her to me, and I saw that at best mutual respect, not friendship, not intimacy, would be our fate.

Despite my efforts, I felt her manner turned me away even as she offered me her house, and a chink opened onto DeForest: what man would want to come home to uncertain meals served up by a moody woman wearing the tablecloth? No wonder he sought the companionship of friendly lady colleagues, offering neatly labeled honey. The Forsters asked us to dinner, and amidst the comfort of their nice things and good food, I felt distressed by the neat figure Roberta cut next to my frumpy Marjorie. The next morning, I wrote out a check for fifty dollars and left it on her bedside table with a note: "Time to spruce up your wardrobe—buy yourself something new."

I felt encouraged to find the very next day a wet bathing suit, ivy patterned on a white cotton, drying over the shower stall. "That's stunning," I said, meeting my daughter in the hall. I pointed toward the bathroom. "You took my advice."

Marjorie looked into the bathroom and her face drew itself into a hard stare. "It must be Jessica's."

"Jessica's? It's much too big."

"A friend must have left it."

"Which friend?" I said, puzzled.

"You may just have missed her," said my daughter, adding, "Beatrice. She's elusive."

I noticed how tense she seemed and stroked her arm to reassure her. "I'm not offended, my dear. Next time you can introduce us."

My daughter gave me a thin smile that cut like paper.

Sadly, I came to see that Marjorie was looking for friends for me. I wouldn't have minded meeting the bathing-suit friend, but my daughter found me Miss Halliday instead. Miss Halliday was close in age to me, being just over seventy, and I was ready to like her, though I had trouble understanding just what she was. In dress she resembled neither man nor woman, but some creature concocted from a ragbag of ethnic garb: flat, many-strapped sandals that gave her hippopotamus-sized feet, scarves from somewhere in the Far East, long baggy trousers with a vaguely West African print. She even wore little string bracelets on her ankles, and cut her hair in a choppy way. It meant something urgent that I could not for the life of me grasp. She seemed the citizen of some country of a disturbed mind, though I had to admit Miss Halliday's mind was steel-trap quick. She had worked in the university library and now in retirement was propelled by all the interests she'd pent up during a lifetime of self-sacrificing helpfulness at Reference. She made you tired just to meet her in the supermarket, which Marjorie and I did one of my first afternoons in Conflux.

It was on my account that Marjorie finally went into town. I told her I needed a few sundry items—stockings, hand cream, that sort of thing. Actually, I was experiencing cabin fever out at Bee Happy and if I didn't see something of the civilized world I feared I might start to bee crazy. Marjorie shopped at little lean-tos where overgrown boys and girls, from a country bordering Miss Halliday's, wore ponytails and seemed to have too much time on their large and unclean hands. We'd been to one of them already to get eggs that weren't battery operated. Everything on the shelves was a murky shade of recycling. I understood all that in principle, but I missed the gloss, the brisk commerce. I persuaded Marjorie that only a real grocery store would carry exactly the kind of stockings I required. And it was an enormous relief to see the front of Conflux's only supermarket, all glass and advertisements and hanging fuschia and displays of bright green garden hose, with ten-cent gumball machines bubbling with good cheer in the foyer as we glided over the pressure-sensitive rubber rug and into the store's deep-freeze climate—it took my breath away.

And there, fumbling over the oranges, was Miss Halliday. She stuck out among the other shoppers—a small, nervous woman wound up in her too many scarves. Oversized pink grapefruit in hand, she studied my sensible cotton suit, my pocketbook held low to hide the run in my tights. Miss Halliday's mouth resembled a bird's, chewing. "You must join our group, Wednesday nights. We can't escape the world we live in."

"True," I sympathized and glanced at my daughter for help. Marjorie was patting the long, wet, fur-covered nose that was poking out of Miss Halliday's handbag. It seemed to be smelling the straw cherries that bobbed on the side.

"How *is* Edward?" Marjorie asked, handing the nose a grape.

"Better, better," said Miss Halliday. "A headline caught my eye: *Dinosaur egg hatches in museum, attacks guard.* Prehistory coming to our rescue? I'm off. Happy equinox," she added, and with a wave of her billowy arm she was off, bag sagging on her hip.

"Poor creature," I murmured.

"Edward had bronchitis," said my daughter.

"Marjorie... she's not *all there.*"

My daughter pushed off toward the aisle of sundry items. Like a well-behaved child, I trotted alongside the cart and tried to find refreshment in the bright cartons and cans that promised every purchaser a wonderful life. As I rode home, I thought about Walla. My mission back then had seemed hopeless but straightforward; I had found no clues to my mother, but had every possible stone to turn over. Now turning over stones produced slugs and gave no hint at all to the nature of my daughter's world, or to my place in it, which is what I needed so desperately to know.

In my moonlit fantasies, in bed, while the fan blew across my face, I imagined myself tête-à-tête with my daughter, someplace light and airy, plenty of time on our hands and a trust that kept us talking. I would try to explain what was bearing down on me hard in Conflux, how I had once known where I was, how it felt to be myself back then, when the world was of a piece, when my friends and I and the people we knew were cut from the same cloth and that cloth was a tapestry of shared allusions, from Jack Sprat to Ivanhoe; and customs, from rice pudding in the nursery to a dime in the Christmas pudding; and beliefs, in the rightness of attending church on holidays and writing thank-you notes and wearing pearls of a length to suit the time of day. It had all been lost, and so easily! A tidal wave might have reared up and taken a bite out of my coastal country, leaving barren ground in its wake, so irretrievably was it gone. What Marjorie and DeForest and their friends were planting in that ground devoid of topsoil made bloom an utter mishmash that held no comforting patterns for me. Yet they seemed to take pride in their inventions, self-inventions, and struggled at maintaining the edifice of illusion, like so many ants in the mound, as if artifice with enough effort might become real; it was poignant, disturbing. Was pride in an illusion their hope in the world as it had become?

In this move south, which was supposed to have been a rebirth, instead, like some premature infant, I failed to thrive. I regretted the loss of my old house, despite the rising maintenance costs, the battle against the termites, the leaking pipes. My chest began to compress on me like some swollen drawer that I could no longer open and shut. When I woke, my fingers were so stiff I could hardly move them till after breakfast. But the problem was not something I felt I could broach with my daughter. She had little understanding of physical or mental distress. She could be insulted, ridiculed, besmirched, but she would fall instantly asleep, ready to take on the morrow.

Odd things unbalanced me, such as the occasional visit of my daughter's elusive friend given to leaving her clothes about. I met her in person one evening. Marjorie was such a believer in the "solar dryer," as she called it, that my things always felt a little stiff, so when everyone was out, or so I thought, I took the opportunity to do my own laundry. I strolled in, my mind busily concocting a shopping list for the coming week, and there she was—Beatrice, I knew at once—a full-headed blonde; she was leaning against the laundry-room wall, looking at the dryer (swishing, clinking) as I stepped blithely in.

"Sorry," I said, staring, alarmed. She was dressed only in a long-sleeved, pea green blouse with mother-of-pearl buttons and a black nylon slip with lace at the hem, no skirt in view.

The woman glanced without presenting me her full face, knelt speedily, and opened the dryer door. I noted her long and muscular legs in their good stockings, the huge feet in flats of a pea green color that matched the blouse. "My skirt," she mumbled, voice reverberating inside the dryer's drum. "I spilled something."

I hesitated. "Beatrice, isn't it . . . ?" The back stiffened. "I'm Marjorie's mother."

"Hello," said the voice.

"I expect Marjorie will be back any minute. I would put something on, Beatrice," I advised. "There are people about."

"Thanks," said the voice and held up a long hand.

Taking that as a sign of farewell, I obeyed.

At the door, I stopped, though, and was needy enough to risk asking her, "You're a good friend of Marjorie's. Do you feel my daughter is happy?"

"What?" reverberated the voice. It seemed almost to squeak for a moment. "Very happy. Nice husband."

"Do you think so?" I asked. I felt blocked somehow, speaking to the dryer, but I added, "Why don't you take Marjorie shopping with you some time, Beatrice? She needs help in that department, and I'm out of touch with the fashions."

The hand went up again, waving.

Miss Halliday had invited us over the next evening for drinks and encapsulated whatnots, as she termed them. To make conversation she happened to ask me if I'd met many other of Marjorie's friends. "Yes," I said, relieved to bring it up. "Just yesterday, Marjorie, I met your elusive friend."

"What elusive friend, Mother?"

I watched their faces closely: Marjorie's passive and steady, Quilliam's eyes on the plate Miss Halliday held out.

"That attractive person?" he asked, choosing something crisp. "What's her name?"

There was a pause.

"Beatrice," I provided.

My daughter seemed on the verge of either laughing or crying as she said to Quilliam, "She's really more your friend than mine, isn't she?"

"She was certainly well-dressed," I pointed out to my daughter, "apart from missing a skirt."

"Missing a skirt?" asked Miss Halliday, conversationally.

"That's all right," my daughter said, rumbling her ice.

I thought no more of it till one morning soon after, I discovered a shoebox next to the toaster. I peeked under the lid: red sequined high heels. "Don't tell me," I said to Marjorie when she wandered through in her robe and accepted the cup of coffee I'd just brewed. "Your friend's been by again."

"What friend?"

I held up one of the shoes. "I know her style! But why did she leave these? What is this all about, undressing, scattering her possessions?"

Marjorie sat down hard. Fear raked through me. "Is Quill...? Tell me the truth." I lowered my voice. "Are they *involved?*"

My daughter gave a disquieting little shriek. "No," she said and laughed again. I looked at her and understood something was clearly amiss. Another, even more disturbing idea occured to me and I broached it cautiously. "You've been under stress, Marjorie. When we're under stress we sometimes do things, we sometimes come under the influence of people..."

My daughter stared at me. Her face twitched as though she might suddenly erupt. "Are you asking if I'm having an *affair*, with *Beatrice?*"

"Of course not, Marjorie. Quite the shopper," I added. "Does she attend such dressy functions? Does she teach at Conflux?"

"Drop it," my daughter whispered and lowered her head on her arms.

Numb, a stranger in a strange land, I fitted that enormous bright shoe into the tissue paper and closed up the box, adding only, gently, "Perhaps she could take you along one afternoon."

Quite by surprise that summer, and to my delight, I became a Canadian. The twins followed me around the side of the porch in their snorkling gear one afternoon, when I was collecting mint for our salad. "You're from Ontario, aren't you?" Jerome asked accusingly.

We went into Quilliam's study to look at the map. There was a white cotton cardigan with pink embroidery around the neck bunched in his chair, but this I dropped into the wastepaper basket before the twins noticed. On the wall map I pointed out my old hometown. "Bremen," I said. "Now called Balmoral."

"Wow," they said. My spirits fluttered up like goose down.

They wanted stories for the class. We sat for a think on my old Boston sofa, which they'd put out on the porch. The April evening was cool. The scent of mown grass wafted in breaths about us. I thought back, unsteady, but eager, too, to milk the moment. "Your classmates would enjoy hearing about the Brennekes's pig, Cassandra," I began. "She had long whiskers and beady eyes."

"No animal thing," Jessica tried to explain. She was using the back of the sofa for support in a plié.

"Or perhaps the time the snow reached the roof and we had to escape through the window?"

"It has to be about you," pronounced Jerome, bouncing a golf ball.

"*Me?*" This tasted like water in the desert.

"Yep," said Jessica. Arms outstretched, she sank into a split.

History does not happen for our amusement. I thought, though, perhaps my grandchildren's school friends would like hearing about my misadventure with Jenny Abbott in the car. Jessica brought out her cassette recorder and had me talk it into a microphone. Her eyes trained on the switches, it was impossible to tell if she were listening. As I pieced the story together, Jerome looked almost amused. I did my best. With my own grandchildren engaged in weekend typing, me bringing them milky drinks to keep up their strength, I found hope in forward momentum.

They decorated my room. Jessica stuck together styrofoam balls to make a little snowman, which she set by my reading light. Jerome brought back a pair of snowshoes from a garage sale. "Bet you used these a lot around the old camboose, eh?" he said as he lugged them up.

"Ah, the camboose," I repeated, trying to remember if that meant a camp.

"That's, like, Canadian?" said my granddaughter. "They talk that way?"

They hammered into my wall beams long posters the teacher had ordered from the Canadian tourist board: people in summer hats looking happy at the Shaw festival, a lady hurrying to hang up some tattered-looking laundry in the Maritimes, and my favorite: a moose in a reflective mood in Algonquin Park. We stood back and admired the effect. These scenes were as unfamiliar to me as to the twins, and I wondered at how little Americans actually knew of Canada—how little I myself knew.

"Are you ever homesick?" Jerome asked. I noticed when he looked at me directly he had Harry's fierce concentration.

"Homesick?" I whispered. Why should I confess that Canada seemed a foreign country to me? How could I disappoint my only grandson when his concern filmed my old eyes with tears? "Oh, gracious," I told him. "Thank you, children!" I laid my hands on their strong, narrow shoulders. My loneliness like cloud cover thinned.

The great railroad expansion, Meech Lake, Niagara Falls, bilingualism—even if I knew nothing about them, they put me on the map. "My grandmother," I overheard Jerome say on the phone, "is an actual Canadian." He might have wrapped a shawl around my shoulders, I felt that revered in my new role as Canuck.

Even Quilliam got interested. "Lorne Greene," he said coming downstairs one morning, reeking of something chemical.

The twins were spreading peanut butter on waffles, pouring chocolate syrup on top of that. I didn't even try to argue about it. "Who?" they asked.

"A lot of them are actors." I noticed him slip a jar of honey from the cupboard into his knapsack.

"Peter Jennings," said Jerome.

"Robert McNeil," added Marjorie, who was hefting a pot through the hall. She never had breakfast, explaining that she preferred the purity of hunger in the mornings when she worked. It did tend to make her cranky. "What's that smell, Pine-Sol?"

"After-shave." He buckled up his knapsack fast and hoisted it on his shoulder.

She persisted, "Are you impersonating a tree?"

"Raymond Chandler," he answered.

"Ross MacDonald," Marjorie countered. I felt caught in crossfire.

Jessica picked a brown egg off the floor, newly laid by Mildred, and broke it into her juice. "And they get away with it," she announced, "because they look just like us!"

With much coaxing, I got Marjorie to take me into town to find the twins a historical atlas of Canada. In the bookstore I located one immediately, but had to stand around holding the heavy thing while Marjorie poked through books on the sales table. She held up an illustrated guide to the Carolinas. "Not interested," I said through a yawn. "I'm trying to ignore where I am." She unearthed a cookbook called *Southern Delights*. I shook my head. "I know how to cook. You'll have to make your own jambalaya." She gave me a hard look, but I would not be coerced. Being newly Canadian was too fragile a thing to risk losing.

As I waited for the twins, I leafed through the book, picking up facts about eighteenth-century homesteads, Indian camps, river meanders, enjoying the pungent odor of authority it emitted from its glossy pages, feeling that in its great weight the book bound up all the stuff of belonging.

I wandered nervously into the kitchen and found Marjorie chopping up Indonesian things. "You know," I said, "we should take the children up to Bremen."

"Should we?" Her voice caught on the words; she hung her head over the sink and sobbed. Slumping into a kitchen chair opposite me, she just buried her face in her hands.

"Well," I said, trying to lighten the mood. "The lunch smells nice."

My daughter's long, pink-splotched face rose up and rebuked me. "He's all I have." Then her steam ran out; her face fell slack. She sighed and fingered the tablecloth. I felt truly shaken.

"Marjorie," I said. "Tell me how I can help." My eyes swept over the clutter of broken casserole pots stacked in the cupboards, the sink of gray water where knives lay submerged, the mess of potted herbs spilling soil over the cutting board by the window.

Calmer, she attempted a smile, and wound her hair on top of her head, then with a small sighing laugh let it fall over her shoulders. "I feel better," she declared.

Lunch was a hard little occasion. Marjorie, lost in thought, or in breathing exercises, failed to rise to my attempts at conversation. After a while I gave up and maintained a trim-lipped silence. When I could get away I climbed up to my room and sat chastely on my bed. I looked at the moose. I had caught the scent of her loneliness, felt her imperviousness to past and future, her determined potting, her acceptance of the chaos about her, her door politely latched to her mother.

The twins, dusted from the dirt roads like chicken breasts for baking, banged through after four.

"How did it go?" I asked. Atlas in hand, I followed them into the kitchen where they stuck their heads into the fridge. Their nods seemed tired.

"Ta-da!" I produced the book from behind my back.

Jerome turned around, and peeling open an orange with his teeth, read the title. Jessica squinted at me. I opened the pages up to a photograph of Banff, best sales pitch. "It has just fascinating facts about log cabins."

"Thanks," said Jessica. Her small eyes behind her glasses studied me, and in a new tactful voice, she said, "The grading period just ended. We're done with Canada."

"Oh," I said. I hid my face in the book's heavy smell.

"Nana," Jessica said as kindly as she knew how, "were you ever, like, in the Far East?"

I swallowed. Mt. Walla's eruption spouted high in my mind's eye. The possibility of selling my past flung open and just as quickly closed. "Never," I lied. "Certainly not."

Volcanic described my emotional state in the next few weeks. Interest in me had been redirected with the new grading period toward the region I least wanted to revisit in memory. My daughter turned inward after our short-circuited kitchen conversation and would not speak to me of the past or herself or anything more than domestic essentials, and I did little in that direction anyway, not wanting to intrude. DeForest impelled me, as if he were some large unfriendly sniffing mutt, to seek other rooms when he appeared. And, even for pagans, it was Lent. Out of habit, I gave up meat and chocolate. Life felt paltry. My daughter was throwing clay all over herself in the shed. The children plunged in and out of the pond masked, disguised as frogs, or traipsed through the kitchen in flippers, dripping wet, pawing cabinets and fridge in an approximation of meals. The Bee Happy alphabet read: A for horses, H for himself.

Easter Day itself, which I had imagined as pasteled, serene, in a state of grace, I spent tediously looking up phone numbers for Marjorie, whose head crooked sideways to keep the receiver from slipping off her shoulder as she wrote down names of recruits for a showy orchid yard sale, while Quilliam, stretched on his back and growling, tossed blue exam books across the floor as he graded them. Jerome beeped through a video game in the study, and Jessica bravely boiled some duck eggs silly. This was no place for a nice granny. Like Mary in the Bible, I had a lot to ponder but kept of it out of view, in my heart.

That organ, of course, eventually gives way. The hospital staff on the night of my entrance in a wheelchair through the emergency door diagnosed angina. They gave me a bottle of nitroglycerine, which is what I thought people blew things up with. The doctors said it would make me better. When it did, I packed my things up to start afresh at the Sunset Home.

Home Truths

*I*WANTED QUIET and I wanted climate control. Fully air-conditioned, the Sunset Home squatted on a hill out near the small airport, neighboring some warehouses and clearance centers. It looked like the by-product of a bad argument between architects. The result: long glass walls topped with comical Palladian fanlights and a mini-Monticello widow's walk around the roof. It would have been interesting to poll the inhabitants about which style they felt characterized the place. And would the answers have divided along the same lines as those who let care to the wind and heaped their plates with waffles on Sunday morning and those of us who had the corn flakes and yogurt and a single prune? For me, Sunset was above all sunlit.

As one of the ambulatory residents, I was given a private room in the section called Goldenrod, outfitted with bath and kitchenette. I brought over some of the chairs I'd given Marjorie. "Clean lines" was such a credo with H. that it had been all I was worth to get a chair into the house. But, I argued, let's be practical: you have to sit down. And a little memorabilia never hurt if you didn't take it to heart. So I stuck into the mirror's corner a picture Miss Bartram once sketched of the white ant empress, made with the light filtering through her stained-glass window. On the bureau I propped our silver-framed official wedding photo, taken in a tiny walk-up studio in Bombay. My old clothes, stinking of volcanic ash, I had thrown out, and I am wearing a white cotton dress so new that the seamstress was following me down the street on the way to the office like an attendant, pulling out the basting as we hurried. I loved that dress with its dropped waist and veil that hung to my knees. In the picture Harry stands tall beside me, one arm lightly behind my waist. I think back on us as a sensible pair, but in the picture we look as young and happy and vulnerable as any couple in the newspaper. We actually seem beautiful: radiant and open-hearted. Perhaps if we'd had family around, witnesses to remind us of ourselves from the outside, or if history had not goose-stepped into our path, we might have survived. Who knows?

I scattered some of Anthea Bartram's own lace antimacassars like cobwebs over the arms of the room's small chesterfield. Over the toaster oven I tacked up that mosquito-plagued moose in Algonquin Park. He looked steadfast and stupid but by now so familiar, I couldn't just roll him up and stick him away. Otherwise, I respected the room's leaning toward monochrome and subtle angularity. Fresh statements of color and style derived from a boldness of spirit I lost on Walla. A lifetime's habit of reconsideration and reflection mostly invalidated bright oranges and pinks.

On my first morning, I sat up in the heavy, scratchy purple-emblemed sheets and enjoyed the symmetry of the decor; the beige wallpaper diamond patterned, the blinds nicely vertical. I had a view of the highway, which I liked. The constant movement of cars reminded me that I could always hitch a ride out of Conflux.

Marjorie brought my things over later that day. Sporting an old cloche straw hat with red-checked ribbons hanging in her eyes, wearing sandals that laced up her leg, she sat in the lobby looking eccentric and skeptical. "Do you feel real here, Mother?" she asked. I chose not to hear her aggression.

As she spoke, an electric clock in the hallway clicked and a young woman wheeled a cart into the room, offering coffee in Styrofoam cups. "It's included," she explained, handing me my whitener. The coffee was neither bad nor good, its acidity thinly diluted by a stirring-in of dried creamer or sugar from a packet. Its taste was of all institutions run on a minimum budget for maximum value. I was one of the many recipients of equitably distributed dollops of care. One sip and I felt comforted.

"I'm an old woman," I told my daughter, blowing across the coffee to hide my pleasure. "It's best that I stay here." At least, I thought, I'll be accorded some respect. "*Lebensgefahr*," I said to Marjorie.

"I beg your pardon?"

"In Berlin just before the war I saw a sign on an electric fence that translated *lebensgefahr* into English for stray tourists as 'danger of life.' The danger of life, Marjorie, is that you can hum along quite happily and then discover all at once, with a thousand-volt jolt, that the world has changed. And in the new world, you're invisible. Visibly invisible."

"I don't know what you're talking about."

I took a long breath. "People can't be seen anymore until they advertise themselves. Maybe that's what I mean. And you advertise by putting yourself in a shop window. Glass gives everything a fantasy life. And keeps it out of reality, too. I don't know how to advertise, you might say."

"Of course life changes, Mother," said Marjorie and stared at me with strong feelings I could not read. "Look at all you've lived through just in your lifetime: cars and air travel and the space program and antibiotics."

"It's more than that," I said. "It's a question of attitude; demeanor. People's faces. We used to look more sober and serene. Nobody smiled in photographs. And nowadays they even walk in a different way, more from the hips. It's true, Marjorie. People speak without the modulation I grew up on. And so much faster. They smile harder. Those things are stranger than moon walks or cellular phones. It's good for me to be here with my own kind, in a refuge for endangered species." *Doomed, actually,* I thought, but kept that back.

"People haven't changed at heart, though," my daughter argued. "What changes is what we use as the anchor for our lives." She smoothed her hair and pulled out a twig that had got tangled in her braid. "Quill and I lean on the stability of the natural world—our grove of honey locusts, the gnarled mulberry that's a mecca for cedar waxwings, the succession of spring flowers: snowdrops and crocuses, forsythia, daffodils, azalias, peonies, roses."

It sounded lovely, but I cut her off. "Nature will get you nowhere, Marjorie. You're deluding yourselves. You and DeForest aren't from Conflux, after all, are you? Do you consort with natives? In Bremen, when I was growing up, life wasn't ideal, but at least we knew each other. Even living in a hotel as we did, we had steady friends. We spoke to people on the street. You and your family are just floating. You might be on a life raft somewhere in the South Atlantic for all the anchoring you have."

"People come and go," she answered softly, as though this news might bruise me. "But we've tried to become one with the *place*. I stop at local graveyards by the road and study the family names."

"Theirs are not yours."

I approved of the way she ignored me. "We've walked with the children along the river, east and west, learning the topography by foot."

I waited this out. How could a daughter of mine, of Canadian parents, born in Berlin, raised in an old house outside Boston, drop anchor in little Conflux, N.C.? She had gravity.

She was saying, "I stop by the roadside stands instead of the grocery stores where the produce is trucked in from the West. So what if the beans are a little wormy? The tomatoes are magnificent! As warm as puppies. And it seems right to buy from people on rush-seated chairs, who spit full of pride into the grass, halfway into a story about their children, smart as whips, on their way to college. In a big world, we need to keep rubbing shoulders with each other."

"Rubbing shoulders. Do you think the way you get yourself up, you actually blend in? You look like someone from Pluto. And this attempt at simile, is this supposed to be local speech? It misses, Marjorie. It misses by a wide country mile."

Hurt hardened her face, and something deep in me wished I could take it all back. She was stronger than I'd realized, though, and wanted me to know, "As for close friends, we're lucky in the Forsters, Clyde and Roberta, whom you've met, they're always sending us clippings and suggesting outings together, and Miss Halliday, whom we've known for fifteen years. She gave us her old dining room table and chairs when we moved here. Then I have my potting and lady's-slipper friends, and Quill has his beekeepers, and," she paused, "and the children have their 4-H pals."

I changed tack, determined to score points. "Why, Marjorie? Tell me, why does everyone have an official function? That's what I find so strange. You all belong to clubs. Life used to be a nice jumble. Now there's no mixing. Even DeForest. It was such a gentlemanly profession once upon a time, academics, and now your husband and his kind seem so single-mindedly *driven*. Except for his bees," I said and paused, seeing my daughter's expression change, "which is just a charming little sort of hobby. But, at heart, he's in for the kill. Your father didn't have to explain that he was an architect but had got enthusiastic about archaeology for a time; people were people back then, no matter what they did. Well, go home now, dear, to your little hideout, away from it all, and make a daisy chain for your hair and fancy yourself an organic part of the landscape."

My daughter leaned forward and snapped like a dog behind a chain-link fence, "You deserve your loneliness, Mother, with your snobberies in this bleached-out nowhere-land."

"Shh," I pleaded. There were some ladies looking up from their chat at the other end of the lobby. Their alarmed faces softened as they saw my daughter stand and kiss her mother stiffly.

Marjorie's visit had depressed me, but I remained firm about living at Sunset. Institutions like that expect no company loyalty, raise no fuss about esprit de corps. Anonymous and all but invisible, I relied on routine to pull me through. I rose at six to the quiet whistle of water through the pipes in my east wall. By nine I was dressed and ready to step into the elevator heading downward to take part in the social life of the institution. The two buildings, Goldenrod and Woodbine, connected by a glassed walkway, housed about a hundred old people, so there was always plenty afoot: games in the lounge (cards on Wednesday morning, bingo on Tuesday nights), television, twice-weekly bookmobile, vans into town, and, well, surely that was enough. By a sunny window, to the honk and ping of video games, I'd read. I took up *The Ring and the Book*, started long ago on Walla. It reminded me of those balmy teas with the Tennysons, but when I realized its subject was murder, old anguish rose up to the surface, and I laid the book aside for lighter fare.

Occasionally other residents, overwhelmingly old ladies like myself, approached me with comfortingly rhetorical politeness, but I declined invitations to accompany them to their various churches. They looked happy, almost girlish, spruced up with newly blued hair and thin lipstick, tying scarves around their necks as they waited in the lobby on Sunday mornings for the van into town, but I couldn't see my way to joining them. Walla had cured me of any inclination toward worship. "I'm Canadian," I would say by way of explanation, and that seemed sufficient to step them back once again into a nodding acquaintance, and to blend me into the wallpaper.

I had little contact with others as I did not look at the television or attend the bingo games. One morning, however, I found in my mailbox a folded note on excessively heavy paper, scrawled with a leaky fountain pen:

I will be in the front lounge after one. E. Ypsilanti.

Reading it over, I took it as a simple statement of fact. But "after one" contained some veiled semblance of threat—after whom? I didn't know whether I should feel insulted or impressed. I was, however, intrigued.

After a small, nervous lunch, wondering in the cafeteria if I were being watched by the note sender, I hurried back to my room and changed into my second-best outfit. It was a clever arrangement of skirt and blouse, both in Black Watch tartan, so that it gave the impression of being a suit though it was much more comfortable. Even so, the waistband seemed snug; I vowed to cut back on cafeteria fish sticks. I sat down and talked to my moose. My bougainvillea waited beside me, soaking up its water. At exactly one o'clock by the hall clock, I pushed for the elevator to take me down.

I spotted her at once in the lobby: a petite woman in a dark green cotton pantsuit and carefully lacquered hair, overly black, smoking a long cigarette. I had seen her before, often in conversation with gentlemen or young people. Her eyes, giving nothing away, stayed on me as I hobbled down the hall. She tapped her ashes into the metal stand by her chair, pulled her lips into a kiss as I approached, then blew a perfect smoke ring. Something provocative about the gesture made me lose nerve for a moment and consider taking up a magazine and pretending to be someone else. But it was too late to become invisible; she had dug the cigarette into the sand.

"Ypsilanti," she said. Her voice was smaller than I'd expected. "Sit down." She smiled dryly at me and fingered the chains around her neck. "I understand you're Canadian."

She looked expectant. I wondered if this was her reason for summoning me. "I spent many years abroad," I answered, to be on the safe side. "And lived the second half of my life outside Boston."

"Oh!" Her face went slack. "Were you never in Dalhousie?"

"Dalhousie?!"

"New Brunswick."

"I know where it is. I haven't actually been there."

Mrs. Ypsilanti smiled sadly with long gold teeth. "I suppose not," she said. "What strange jest of fate, Mrs. Bagg, has brought you to this mecca of tobacco and pine?"

Trying to ignore the chair's lump of stuffing like a fist in my back, I said, "I came to join my daughter." When Mrs. Ypsilanti lifted a hand up to the room around us and rolled her eyes, I explained, "I prefer my independence. I see them on weekends. Saturday, Sunday." I leaned toward a more truthful answer. "Their lives are a bit helter-skelter."

"I have a daughter," she said. Her sigh fluttered her scarf for a moment. "In Dalhousie. I haven't seen Persephone in twenty years. Twenty? Thirty. Almost forty. She's more precious to me than life itself. We'll have a round of chess since you're here. You play, of course." She produced from behind the dusty palm tree a traveling board of mahogany and brass, also a marquetry box. "A gift from an admirer," she explained. "Between the wars."

We set up the ivory figures and began a game. "You're infirm?" she asked.

"Certainly not." The left foot that should have been the right had recently started aching in the morning when I first put weight on it, and I saw the future ahead: painkillers many times a day, a walker, then a wheelchair. But why should I confess to my creaks and cracks, to my deformities?

"Arthritis? Cataracts?" she persisted. "You limp."

"Perhaps some stiffness," I conceded, feeling myself redden. "Some murmuring of the heart. Otherwise, fit as a fiddle."

"*Eh bien*," said Mrs. Ypsilanti. "For now." She added, "You may be thinking that my eyes are failing, but my squint is a touch of myopia, which I inherit through the Phanariot line. My family descends from Byzantine aristocracy."

I did my best to blink without enthusiasm.

"If you think you'll catch a husband here," Mrs. Ypsilanti said suddenly, shifting a knight, "you'll find the pickings slim. Those who are mobile just stare at the flicker box and swat flies. Frank Thwaite—'Sibelius,' I call him—might propose, of course, if you show any interest in Scandinavia. Don't be alarmed when it happens. Let it blow over. He has no short-term memory. Oh, look: checkmate!"

"Good gracious," I murmured, annoyed with her and myself. I felt the need to make myself plain. "But I have no such interest at my age."

"Haven't you? Oh." Mrs. Ypsilanti, with a kind smile, gathered up the pieces. She latched the lid. "We'll have another game tomorrow. Unless you're busy," she added with a glance at me below eyes hooded with irony. I felt as captured as the men in her box.

Self-worth. I had dismissed the term as faddish. Freud never trickled down much to my generation; we were already saturated with Gibbon and Darwin. My little self-worth, then, a fixture I'd previously not believed I possessed, now felt to me at Sunset something like a helium balloon sinking in my chest with a futting sound.

There were ways to last, I thought, by believing, for example, in one's personal beauty so that each waking moment represented a tribute to the world by way of color coordination, chiaroscuro of scarves, titian hair tints, matching handbag and pumps. Nettie Tennyson had been like that; even a morning's excursion to the excavation site to see the latest dusty shard entailed an hour's preparation, as though the artifacts, in their hour of unearthing, deserved that celebration. The irony, to me, was that Nettie was quite plain: slopy-shouldered, a too-short nose with wide nostrils. Had these features been my own, I would have lost hope, but not Nettie. She spent her spare time grooming. Like Pope's Belinda, she worshiped at the altar of her dressing table. But I didn't mock that, as she had survived as long as I, and I knew from her Christmas photo with her godson that she looked more decorative at eighty than I ever had. Somehow I lacked that leap of faith into fascination with my own reflection.

Those persons with mental gifts who managed to struggle past middle age without losing their energy for new ideas had, I considered, an unlimited range to their interests. Unless their field changed, and the foundation upon which their temple was built crumbled into one more antique tourist trap, leaving them ghosting round the columns. Which was not quite the problem with Frank Thwaite. A history teacher retired early with heart troubles and little memory for the present, he was only too eager to join one at lunch and turn any conversation into a eulogy to Finland where he'd spent a Fulbright year in 1952. Nothing could get by Frank without reminding him of his life's shining moment; the cafeteria fish sticks alone were enough to set him off: Finland's fishing industry, problems with the Lapp minorities, border struggles with the Soviet Union, Finland's utopian solutions to social ills. He knew all the medical statistics: infant mortality, deaths from cancer, etcetera, for that important time he'd spent, thirty years previous to the conversation. No one could get away from him fast enough when he pushed along the cafeteria line, looking no more than fifty with his bristly crew cut, full of righteous energy as if he'd just mown the lawn; walkers tripped up walkers, knives clattered off trays and Jell-O cubes jumped overboard onto the linoleum floor when Frank Thwaite came cheerfully through the line, font of Finnish facts circa 1952.

Professor Herbert Keslar, by contrast, I observed, kept his learning updated and private. No one knew him. Wheeled around with bags and tubes hooked all over his chair, he always wore a suit, polished shoes, always had a book on his lap and his thick hair groomed to perfection, as if, with all his limbs and organs failing, his head were more lively than ever. He talked to no one, just sat where they parked him and read his volumes through trifocals, which earned him a reputation for snobbery. I learned from Howard, one of the favorite, chattier nurses, that Prof. Keslar had taught French at the college. Apparently he sent politely written requests for certain articles and newspapers to the bookmobile staff. I leafed through his pile there once. What was literary theory, and why was Prof. Keslar reading it? On Sundays we watched him work his way through the whole of the *New York Times*, even the business and sports news. "Why does he bother?" I heard Mrs. Rotweiler whine to Howard, on whose arm she leaned as they passed him, absorbed and uncommunicative in the lobby. I knew why he bothered: it kept his head alive and his hair thick and combed.

I had a good mind, too, I considered, though untrained. What I learned about history and architecture from Harry might have earned me college credit, but my education was spotty, rich in certain areas, deficient in others, and I had always relied more on conversation than books to nurture my opinions. The problem in Sunset was finding anything besides gossip and cafeteria starch to feed on.

A few of the older ladies in the home, the same ones who had invited me to church, sometimes went to plays and music at the college. They approved of all they surveyed. They came back from these events in a twitter, leaning their canes against the wall as they helped each other off with their coats, declaring, "Aren't they marvelous!" and "Such wonderful costumes!" and "We certainly enjoyed that!" I envied them beyond words their hopefulness and spirit. How could they be so full of good feeling, so positive, at seventy-five or eighty, when bladders were unsteady, eyes dimming, tumors growing, feet creaking, incomes dwindling, and relatives visiting less often? It seemed mostly a matter of genetics and temperament if one could march on at eighty. I was not a kindly old thing and would never be able to fake it.

Having successfully suppressed Wallawalhalla for sixty years, now, with little else to occupy me, its memory began to loop around my mind. I would overhear a smatter of conversation behind the desk and think of Jenny Abbott's sweet voice. Mockingbirds by my window in the morning roused me with the expectation of seeing seagulls. I started thinking back to the white beaches, high cliffs, lapping waters, how glad I had felt every morning, waking with hopes of discovery. Walla seemed, relived in memory, a fine place, yet who could point to my island on the globe in the bookmobile? Among the video games and thirty-second laugh track issuing from the mammoth television in the Sunset lounge, I felt myself at sea. Who was I really in the scheme of things? Just one more flawed body passing through an expensive, hygienic, and dietetic purgatory on its way to dust.

My Greek acquaintance did not share my fatalism. Mrs. Ypsilanti was a local celebrity, a self-styled VIP. At least once during the course of our chess game someone would come through, someone from outside, usually academic and male, neatly dressed, vigorous, whose energies and brain power had not been sapped by Sunset air. He would greet my opponent in one of several languages. "Just nonsense, pardon me," she'd say by way of excusing herself. Then she'd look over some papers handed her, scrutinizing them with a hard squint and scribbling notes in the margins. Watching, I could not concentrate on the next move. I wondered about the envelope the visitor handed her. They'd joke in a foreign tongue, and Mrs. Ypsilanti would resume the game, explaining only, "Just checking up on some translation. Polyglots!" And she'd open her handbag and stick the envelope carefully inside. They gave her money, I realized. With Medicare, that's how she got by. It couldn't have been easy for her, but she knew how to survive.

Like Nettie Tennyson, Evangeline Ypsilanti believed in style. Erect, overdressed, overly made-up, she kept herself visible among us. Even carrying her tray shakily to a table and passing a group spooning up their banana pudding, Mrs. Ypsilanti would be waylaid and asked to sit down, encouraged to repeat some anecdote. She was a favorite with her stories. From my place alone across the room, by the window, I could hear them: how Evangeline had been kissed by General Patton, the private lives of the Greek royal family, and—a favorite in the community— the time she'd disguised herself as a shark to escape right-wing soldiers and had nearly been captured by the zoo.

Like all her languages, stories spun out of Mrs. Ypsilanti unchecked. And while I disapproved of this exhibitionism, she was my closest thing to a friend, and I suspected I was dull. I felt constrained to justify myself. I decided to change my image. On a Wednesday chess afternoon, I tried to tell her Harry's humorous anecdote about hunter crabs in Malaya. "They were so big," I told Mrs. Ypsilanti, who was studying a configuration of pawns on the board, "and so strong that the men strung them around their waists and used them like a tool belt to carry things!"

Mrs. Ypsilanti, moving a piece, looked up. I raised my arms. "My husband used to do an impression of a crab." A shadow of confusion passed over her face and she grunted politely as I let my arms fall to my sides again, all enthusiasm punctured. "It was very amusing," I added lamely.

Mrs. Ypsilanti opened her bag for a cigarette. "I'm sure it was."

Her light yawn irked me. I studied the board but inwardly resolved that she should know that I too was a figure of note.

On a whim I searched for and uncovered quite easily the address of Nettie Tennyson Glover, recently widowed in Singapore, with whom

I had continued, for no good reason, a haphazard correspondence over the years. Odd how it is that sometimes it is the least important people with whom one remains most easily in touch: I stopped writing to Jenny and was always losing Harry's address during our years apart. I wrote Nettie a long letter, describing my present happiness and hoping the same for her. I was not altogether cut off from the exoticism of my youth, was I?

On my next meeting with Evangeline, both of us spruced up after our naps, I turned the conversation to the engagements to which I had been invited since arriving in Conflux. I was conscious, though, that I had not been anywhere in months. With some surprise and interest, in Mrs. Ypsilanti's presence, I heard myself adopt a condescending tone. I described the Forsters, who, I had to admit privately, had been very kind to me when I arrived. "Their house is a monument to Anglophilia. Roberta brings out their chipped china service, rosebuds washed off by their electric washing-up machine. She serves cornish pasties or shepherd's pie, or some other inedible tourist contraption."

Mrs. Ypsilanti arched the muscles in her back for a moment. "I know those long evenings. Conversation that pirouettes from tax forms to house paint. They invite you, of course, to relieve the tedium." She blew smoke from the corner of her mouth. "They're feverish about foreigners. That's the dirty little secret we Europeans have on them. They expect one to come in a toga, bearing a suitcase full of slides for their Rotary Club. I had to give little lectures and wear the most abominable corsages that pulled at my blouse, making me look quite risqué in those photographs in the paper."

Before I could stop myself, I had asked, "You were in the newspaper?"

"The mayor invited me to 'lunch' with a member of a Tunisian trade delegation." She gave a tiny laugh. "That man later sent me a whole crate of blood oranges. We still exchange birthday cards."

Up in my room, counting back on my calendar, I confirmed my suspicions: there had been no drinks with Miss Halliday or tea at the Forsters's for a month and a half. And the last time I'd been invited, I'd noted some alterations. Roberta Forster had offered a commercial interpretation of a torte, only partially defrosted. I had been obliged to crumple myself into a canvas chair on the porch and drink, not Earl Gray, but iced Lipton's from a jelly glass. This denoted a cooling of enthusiasm, I felt. The cowl of mystique that had first enveloped me was drying up. I was, in Roberta Forster's own comfortless phrase, almost like one of the family. And while I felt myself shrivel into obscurity, I saw Mrs. Ypsilanti casually brush off gestures of esteem as "bread and circuses," and remain perpetually exotic. In the drama of exile she knew none of the sadness of becoming old news.

Evangeline's charm, spiderlike, captured everyone. She worked by embellishment. I doubt she ever confided much, especially in men; she thought of the truth as a kind of second-rate conversational topic. Even Jackson Pancake, my mailman pilot friend, when he eventually made her acquaintance, defended her, saying, "My great-aunt always said, 'If you cain't add nothing to it, a story ain't worth the telling.'" At that, Evangeline blew smoke right into his face.

She offered encapsulated versions if her life with a grandma's-hair sugar spin. Someone not high in her hierarchy, I was offered details like broken crackers after the party. She never appreciated how I thought back over what she told me as we moved chessmen around the board. In my Sunset isolation, details were creating sharp shadows. I needed badly to know what sense other people had made of their lives, what they deemed their birthright.

Evangeline had come to the U.S. ten years before. "I had to leave Greece," she explained, picking off a pawn. "I had been living on a shoelace. In the war, I lost everything. I was divorced then, too, twice over. First because my father made me marry, when I was quite young. I couldn't bear the brute with his poppy eyes. And that in nineteen twenty-five. Then, between the wars, I married Yannis. He drove a taxi in Athens and read Nietzsche. Not Our Class, Dear, as you say, but fascinating to me, a rebel intellectual. And Persephone was born in 'thirty-two."

"'Thirty-two?" I said. "The same year as my Marjorie." This fact drew me up short. It seemed odd that the two of us should both have had but one daughter so late in life, and in the same year. "March?"

"May." She seemed unimpressed. I supposed it was part of being sophisticated not to get too worked up over coincidence. She refused to let it bind us. To herself as much as to me, she said, "Pretty girl,

Persephone. Not bright, not intellectual. More like her father, with his attractive hairline and soft sneeze. I was sad to lose him in the war—he died a prisoner in Italy—but Persephone kept me company. She was always lively. Afterward, I tutored French and a little English. But my bracelets, my dining-room table with the set of sixteenth-century leather chairs, the Louis the Sixteenth samovar, everything had to go—for a few tomatoes and bread. During the civil war, I survived by teaching French and English. Persephone learned dressmaking. I didn't have the money to send her to high school. She met a nice Canadian fellow. Why shouldn't they get married?"

"The young are stubborn," I said.

"I'm stubborn. It was the child's only chance." Primly, she added, "They have a nice life in Dalhousie."

Dalhousie, I thought, and could only imagine gray bricks and sooty rain. "What do they do there?"

"Her husband's a self-made philhellene, bless him. I rescued him with a guidebook from some street urchins. He had saved up for years to see the antiquities and had no idea how to negotiate modern Athens. He was almost run over in traffic his first day. I spotted him, suggested coffee, and learned he'd actually taught himself some Greek—modern vocabulary, ancient pronunciation. Quite amusing."

"And then he met your daughter and they hit it off?"

"I had to prod a little. But at last I had the pleasure of waving them off at Piraeus, on their way to Gibraltar for a little honeymoon before sailing on to New Brunswick and good old safe Canada. Persephone looked quite fetching on deck in a polka-dot dress I had bartered for her from a friend in the trade, and Sam was squinting beside her, holding her handbag."

I pictured them. "Not unlike Harry and me."

She laughed as if I'd been joking, which hurt. She continued, about herself. "There are always people who need tutoring in foreign languages. And then, when I'd all but forgotten how to flirt, I met Professor Brendle. Bucktoothed Ernest, almost fifteen years younger than I was, spending the summer of 'sixty-seven in the National Library. We met when he asked me for directions on the street, and I just couldn't let such a sweet man go off on his own in Athens. We drank lemonade under every café awning in the center city, right through the afternoon when everyone else was napping. He'd read Kazantzakis and talked to me of passion. I was a little bored. He had no notion of what passion meant, poor man, but he loved the idea. He was charmed by Athenian rudeness. Luckily he couldn't understand what people were shouting. One of his life's highlights he told me later was dancing like Zorba at our wedding. I looked forward to married life with him; it promised to be so easy. I packed my complete sets of Balzac and Hugo into a steamer trunk bound for Conflux, N.C. He more or less comprised the entire English department here. Poor Ernest—stone dead within a year. I killed him. *J'ai le fait.* With my passion. Ernest used to say, 'You tire me, Evangeline. Won't you please do things more quietly?' Dear man. Dying was his only way to get some rest, I suspect. And I, again no money. He'd bungled the will; everything went to Harvard, that over-protective alma mater. I lived on my own for a while, tutored French. Sunset looked plausible. I was prepared to amuse myself. I had not ex-pected such a depressing view of dying pine trees around the place. Lapland would have provided more joie de vivre. Oh, I shouldn't men-tion Lapland or we'll get Sibelius over here. Let's say, a monastery would have more esprit de corps."

"Americans can be very discreet," I agreed. "They're polite." I tried myself for discretion as I asked, "Do you manage all right?"

"Welfare and whatnot. Not so bad. You meet the natives."

I winced at her snobbery, though I had to admit I did not envy her rubbing shoulders, as my daughter would have put it. "Then you took citizenship," I said. It occurred to me with a wormish pleasure that my opponent, if naturalized, was not rightfully foreign.

But Mrs. Ypsilanti objected, "*Mais, non!* I am Greek and remain so to even the tiniest toe bone of my corpus. Would anyone *choose* to be American? What a dreadful, vulgar notion." She slammed down her queen.

I felt an unhealthy attraction to her. She struck me as someone who had lived a vulgar life herself, making all the wrong choices, valu-ing wealth and misrepresenting herself in a manner I considered repre-hensible. So why did I continue to meet her for a weekly game, which I invariably lost? Why did I allow her to make me feel so second-rate in comparison, that my own life had been curtailed? Loneliness, surely, was not least among my reasons. A sense that she was right. Interest. Admiration, even, at her daring. And on an afternoon of enduring her tiresomeness, I was touched greatly by her surprise gift of a small red figure-ware vase. "A good copy of an amphora by Exekias," she said, turning it in my hands to show me details. "Circa five-fifty B.C. Do you see? It's Ajax and Achilles playing chess." I looked closely. There they sat at the edge of square seats, Ajax helmeted, spears in his left hand as he moved a piece with his right, Achilles likewise elegantly bent toward the board, ready with spears while intent on the move at hand.

"Thank you. It's lovely," I said, not quite believing she meant it for me.

Her wide smile broke straight through the crust of all my resentment. We sat together for a moment in silence, I, examining the vase, as flushed with pleasure at the gift as she was with the giving.

"I've had it for years," she said simply. "It needs new eyes to feel appreciated."

I set the little red vase on my entrance table where it made me smile whenever I saw it, thinking of Evangeline and me as supple warriors intent on our game. More personal and generous a present than I would ever have expected, the vase honored Evangeline's engagement with the world.

We did not invite each other up to our rooms nor seek each other out in the cafeteria, but we met every Wednesday in the private corner of the lobby and played with considerable gusto. I seldom won. Actually, I never won, but left every match feeling a little bit bruised and stronger for it. My opponent aroused in me a fighting spirit. Sometimes I would be woken up the night before a match by the grinding of my own teeth (*mostly* my own). At noon on Wednesdays, I prepared myself carefully, like the warrior my vase implied I was, fastening on my firmest girdle, clasping Great-Aunt Eustacia's cool ambers against my throat for, not luck, but breeding—my *instrinsic worth*, which I was struggling so to recapture. With Mrs. Ypsilanti, I was in danger of straying, of becoming infatuated with her as I have done all my life with the wrong people—Aunt Emma, Roddy Borders—of positing myself as a passive, corresponding part and taking on her attitudes and mannerisms, for instance, or, worse, placing myself in diametrical opposition, alienating my only chance at a friend by cool behavior, as I seemed to have done with my daughter.

In the elevator, going down to the match, I steadied my breathing. Concentration was all. Taking my seat in our corner of the lobby, I focused on the black and red and chatted to relieve the tension. Without knowing exactly why, I often talked to her about my daughter. Perhaps the role of mother lent me authority. Perhaps having a daughter close by gave me a leg up on Evangeline.

"Marjorie made a healthy match in Quilliam DeForest," I told my opponent. "It's a Manx name, you know. The mixing of the gene pool strengthens the stock."

Mrs. Ypsilanti glanced over her eyeglasses. "You speak of your family as if of chicken soup."

"I meant only . . . Well, I wasn't sure it would work out with an American, you see. They met at a musical event. They have always shared an interest in music."

"Hippies," said Mrs. Ypsilanti.

"Marjorie was a beatnik," I corrected her, glad to be in the know. "He was a flower child."

Mrs. Ypsilanti leaned over the board, her long scarf mowing down some pawns. She would never put her glasses squarely on her nose, but held them, folded, to her eyes, like lorgnette. Very proud, she was, as though anyone really could be fooled by rayon scarves and a foreign accent into overlooking the stiffness in her bones, the creases in her cheeks. Retirement homes, I was discovering, were as relentless as the seventeenth century for memento mori; all one saw were old people getting frailer, more stoop-backed and more confused, their ears and noses continuing to grow till their faces became caricatures of themselves. Dotting on my lipstick in the morning, I noticed how my mouth was beginning to tilt; one half bent slightly up, and my nose, soft and lumpy, looked more and more as if it had been stuck like clay onto my face by a not especially artistic child.

"Marjorie throws pots in the back garden," I said. "Pasta bowls, mostly. Bird baths. She's enormously strong in the shoulders." As soon as I'd said this, I regretted it. Mrs. Ypsilanti's own daughter would no doubt be the sort to glide around in silks. "Marjorie's getting quite expert on wildflowers, too," I added. Persephone, I just knew, would roll up fine little suppers in grape leaves on a terrace and converse in chemical equations. And write perspicacious notes to her mother about Life. She was everything my warm-hearted, lumpy Marjorie could never be. And Persephone's children, unlike Marjorie's poor waifs, would win violin competitions and lip-read three languages and excel at mental calculus. Envy as hard and mean as gallstones pained me. In my mind a scene by Marjorie's pond played across my thoughts with an uneasy insistence; I had seen the twins, waist deep in green water, reflected like playing cards from the waist up. They had been staring down, waiting. Why? For what? For some image of themselves to emerge like a print in a photographer's bath? I could have warned them: the camera only lies. Beware the shifting nature of the water's reflections. Look deeper than your mother did to find your life's rewards. I saw them as genetically already doomed.

Mrs. Ypsilanti, breathily scooting her rook toward my careless knight, said, "Persephone is childless. And she's all I have. And here we are, a thousand miles apart."

Envy's knife withdrew, leaving only a dull ache—for my friend as well as myself. No children for Persephone after all. After a moment's thought, I said, "Why don't you go to your daughter?" I jumped my other knight away.

"Impossible."

Oh, I thought. I pressed on, too curious to check myself. "Surely, they'd make some room." But my opponent lifted a pawn without comment; the piece wobbled a fraction in her hand before she managed to set it squarely down. I did not know what it meant, but I felt my own armor open a crack as I saw this chink in hers. I studied her closely, glad to have discovered a reason for sympathy.

When I came down to wait for Marjorie one Sunday noon, Mrs. Ypsilanti was sitting in the lounge dressed up in a white pantsuit and reading something French. The lounge was a quiet place on Sundays, with churchgoers not yet back, and many of the residents taken out for the day by family, but my friend's peace was disturbed by Sibelius, sitting near the window, swatting at flies. He had no family and looked up with happy expectation as I entered. I gave a wave but aimed for Evangeline before he could detain me. She tucked a blue airmail envelope into the pages of the book and closed it softly on her lap.

This, however subtly done, annoyed me. My opponent seemed always to be dropping exotic correspondence around on the floor. I had received a foreign letter, too. Nettie Glover (née Tennyson) replied to my note, writing to me from Singapore in pristine script, describing her current life without reference to our shared days. I carried the letter around in Mrs. Rotweiler's purple bag like a talisman. No matter what we lived through, the long-ago seemed always more real, even if left undiscussed. Nettie's note was now my only link to that time and my defense against Evangeline's unvoiced insinuations that I had no past worth mentioning.

"Persephone's written?" I inquired.

Her face, lifting for a moment, fell again in swags of gloom. I sensed I might be heading right into trouble so asked briskly, "And what's on your agenda for the day?"

"Oh." She pulled a face. "Someone is coming by to have me check over his Aeschylus translation, to admire it, really. A. R. Fenway in Classics. Do you know him? Hairless. It would be like sleeping with a fish. He reminds me of a vacuum-cleaner salesman who once chased me around the Plaka. He thought I was being coy, but really I was terrified of having to talk to him, the old windbag. This Fenway could be his cousin. No romance here, I'm afraid, though he has pots of money. I think he calls his stockbroker every morning at seven. I can never get through."

"Still, that will be nice," I said. I meant it. I envied her usefulness to someone; I felt all too keenly my daughter's charity.

Mrs. Ypsilanti shook a cigarette into her mouth. "He thinks I'm the last of the ancient comedians. Can't get it through his pea-sized brain that we Greeks do not descend in a vertical from Zeus. But one does what one must for a date. If I have to speak in ancient Greek to amuse him and claim I learned Homer at my nurse's breast, I will. Why not? It's as good a use of the past as any. And for him, better than his own, poor pale Anglo-American. *Et tu?* Same old thing?" Her smile, while attempting to seem indulgent, looked a little wistful, I thought, with the cigarette drooping from one corner.

I checked the driveway and tried to cast my excursion in a picnic light. "My daughter is that rare sort of person whose thought processes are so intense, she really oughtn't to drive while she's talking." My friend seemed interested for once. I told her, "DeForest is very clever. He's one of those beekeepers. He has hives right near the house, so he can watch them, and of course, they keep the doors open anyway because of the ducks. Mildred prefers to lay her eggs indoors. Which makes it so convenient at breakfast." I unclasped my bag and checked around for nothing in particular. I was surprising myself with my strong line of defense. I mostly believed what I heard myself tell her. "Marjorie has a creative flair. Economical good sense. You should see the nice furniture some people throw into those dumpsters on the highway."

Mrs. Ypsilanti looked surprised, not uninterested, but offered me no help in understanding my daughter's ways. I felt as though I were betraying my family, though, for the sake of her esteem and could oblige no more. Silently I watched out the window for the car.

Mrs. Ypsilanti asked, "You and your daughter fight much?"

I pulled my skirt sharply over my knees. "Heavens."

"Persephone and I had some gorgeous brawls when she was a girl." She blew a smoke ring. "Wouldn't turn down her little socks when she went to parties. Unbraided her hair along the pavement." She stopped and looked vacantly at me. "We liked the tension, Persephone and I. We thrived on the venom. We bared our teeth at each other and snarled and locked jaws and dripped foam down each other's throats—"

"Now where can that Marjorie be!" I interrupted. "She's always late—such a busy life! It's tea, this week, I believe, with the Forsters. Oh, here she is." As the rusty minivan pulled up and tooted, I hiked my scarf around my neck in an action worthy of my friend. "Well," I said. Mrs. Ypsilanti opened her book without a nod as I hurried out into the open air, which was baking with summer scents and sunshine.

My daughter looked like a sea lion, with her long hair plastered flat against her head. She was wearing a nondescript bathing suit—not that attractive white one I'd seen—and it had dripped a large dark puddle like a shadow under her. On the backseat, perched on one of my daughter's pots, leaning forward to rest her head on Marjorie's shoulder, was Mildred the duck. "We've been swimming," Marjorie explained. "Mildred wanted to come along for the ride." She added in an undertone, "I think she's depressed."

I resisted this nonsense. Something in me was beginning to rebel. I would not be their sweet, passive Granny. I complained, "How could a duck be depressed, Marjorie? Is she lonely? What ambitions could have possibly been thwarted?" I buckled my belt on with a locking of metal that sounded decisive. "Is she frustrated for want of friends? Did her hatchlings neglect her? Could she regret her own nature?"

My daughter glanced back at the duck and then at me, confused. "Mother," she said. "Is everything all right at Sunset?"

"Fine. Fine. I'm disappearing into it, which is what happens at the end of the film, isn't it?"

I hardly paid any attention to the small houses we passed, which always looked flimsy, being wooden. The yards were mowed down like the crew cuts of the children who played beyond their fences.

"You're always welcome back . . ." my daughter offered, missing the point.

"Thanks," was all I said. "Thanks, Marjorie."

As Mildred honked at dogs, and my dripping daughter related bits of news, I saw the day moving like a treadmill toward me. My thoughts turned back to my own predicament. Had I made a wrong move in leaving Red Leaf House? Should I have stayed on, alone, free to bore myself and indulge my geriatric habits? Something in me, the sensible face of my grown-up self, nodded in sad concurrence, while a younger voice somewhere sprang up in opposition, with hope: I had a family in Conflux. Surely I'd been meant to come—in the nick of time—to help them straighten out their lives.

I tried to work out a plan as we drove. Smash the television (accidentally) and compel the family to read Dickens together? The notion pleased me briefly, then reality set in again. The superficiality of my presence mocked me at every turn. I might scrub their kitchen floor and polish some silver. Then darn Jerome's socks. I'd reread my letter from Nettie. DeForest would come home, drink his beer with some bees around his head, and make jokes that I'd pretend not to grasp. On

Sunday afternoon, having accomplished nothing but boring everybody, I'd be sent off with a jar of honey in my hands, something sweet and heavy to hold, like an apology for not giving me their affection.

"Mother?" said Marjorie. "It looks as if the gardenia's going to bloom *again*."

"Lovely!" I cried on cue, as Marjorie, satisfied, turned a sharp left onto their dirt road. Was experience the traditional method employed by the old and wise? Not for a moment did I want to burden my descendants with the complications and messy emotions of my youth. Besides, they would never forgive me. They might have had me hand-cuffed and marched down to the Conflux jail.

After a lunch of lentils topped with mustard sauce, enjoyed by mother and daughter on the picnic table beneath the mulberry tree, I settled myself, as predicted, into a rocking chair on the porch, socks with holes on lap. Marjorie, in a muddy apron and that awful red sweater-vest, trudged in rubber boots out to the shed. Some of the family bees circled around my head as I darned. One, landing on my finger, began an obscene gesture with its lower parts. They all had names but I'd never been able to tell them apart. I had to whistle that particular individual away with some cost of breath to myself. Meanwhile, I finished two holes and tried to rest my eyes on the scenery, which my daughter praised for being untouched. I had never accustomed myself, however, to Nature. I didn't trust its benign exterior. I looked out to the pond where Mildred and a few grayish ducklings were floating mindlessly in circles. One shook itself hard up over the water, barking as something surfaced in goggles and breathing tube. "Helloo!" I cried down to the creature. "When did you get back?"

Hand flapping, a call of something I didn't hear. An identical frog-man popped up close behind and amid some ripples and laughs both dipped down again underwater. They were fish, I thought; no wonder I could not talk to them.

I opened Nettie's letter with its lavender-scented pages, the treat I'd been saving. Nettie had a style carried over from school days, much given to ellipsis points. A bee, maybe Pericles, circled tediously near my ear as I read:

Vizzy dearest,

*Sorry to hear about Harry's death. Widows aren't anyone's idea
of fun at a dinner party, are they? You know my husband died ten
years ago this June. He hadn't Harry's brains but he was an
angel. I'll never forget our wedding day—you and Harry seemed
such an old couple already, so calm while I was fainting all over
the place. I live with Beverly, my elder son, in import-export. Hope
he won't export his old mama! At the moment am sipping lemonade
at the Club rock garden . . . My driver parks there, as it's Free. Am
collapsing . . . Just found something to wear to Circle luncheon. We're
first tasting some Chinese food (looks like boiled rubber on a stick)
and then a little speech about Progress and then the mahjongg.
Am practicing a bit of the Español with a lady from Majorca. Do
write more about the mad woman in your hotel who can't play
chess. Delicious! Lizards are running over my shoes. I feel like
Daphne!! Must fly,*

All love,
Nettie

I let the letter lie loose on my lap as I observed the ducks brain-
lessly pecking at each other in the cattails. I had spent the better part of
my life working under fluorescent lights in an office, getting by, while
Nettie had *lived.* I, too, might be playing mahjongg with internationals
rather than creaking in a chair looking at ducks, forgotten by Marjorie's
friends, with only a Wednesday chess game on my calendar—for the rest
of my tedious life.

Wallawalhalla . . . I thought of the moonlit Strand Road, Egrets, the
crumbling club, the shirtless men digging down to ancient remains
in the earth, how I had picnicked on the beach with Harry. *Swash.* It
stopped my thoughts for but a moment. That echoing *swash* sounded
ever more faint. Apart from that unpleasantness, my summer there had
been one of the best of my life.

Marjorie climbed the steps of the porch, covered in mud like
someone just dug up. Three small ducks bounced in the grass behind
her heels. "What's wrong?"

"Nothing's wrong, nothing. Except that I'm too old. And have probably wasted my life."

"Nonsense, Mother. You've enjoyed your life." She shook the mud from her hands into the grass, which caused more bees to rise from the bushes like hovercrafts. Lowering herself into the rocker beside me, she pulled off her boots. Her bare feet were streaked with algae that clung between her toes. "I want to raise orchids." She spat some clay out of her mouth. "I'm thinking of hiring someone to help me build a greenhouse, since Quill's not the hammering type, right over near the beehives. Nothing big, maybe thirty by twenty with space for a fish tank. And we could fit it out with solar panels, to heat the house."

"Why would you do that? All that effort and expense?" Her projects tired me. "Why make your life more complicated, Marjorie? Why not clean up a little, not expand out even more?" My daughter looked away to hide the hurt I understood too late. "Of course," I backpedaled, "you might make some money if you went into business with orchids. Corsages and such."

"I'm not going into business," came her muffled reply, directed at the porch floor. "I'm not trying to make money."

"No," I said, quickly changing tack. "The children would gain so much—educational experience."

"I'd do it for *me*." She looked up with smoldering eyes.

"Oh, dear. I am a Bear of Very Little Brain." We fell into a trapped silence, and watched the children surface and disappear in the pond. I knew that once again I'd stepped right into it, flattening my daughter with my misunderstandings. "Apropos of Wallawalhalla," I said, surprising myself. "I'm going back."

She patted my knee. "Mildred! Din-din time!"

Over dinner Quilliam lectured me, as though some intellectual uplift should come with the package. "I'm writing an article, which I'm calling 'The Culture of the Looking-Glass,'" he said with a modest flourish of his knife as he skewered a potato across the table.

"On vanity?" I guessed.

"Close. On the modern narcissistic search for self. We are all out to 'find ourselves,' and 'discover our true identities.'" His little clawing gesture, putting all this in quotation marks, irked me, but I listened, perplexed, embarrassed for him. Was this all a boast or a confession? "We lack a center," he was saying. "We have no organizing principle, few shared sentiments and beliefs other than the notion that we are each the captains of our destinies and must discover our true inclinations."

"We do, of course, believe in Nature," put in my daughter, cracking walnuts together in her palm.

I said, "I thought you heard a different drummer, or some such thing."

"We do," said my daughter. She seemed abstracted.

DeForest continued, "We each embark on a self-tailored and ultimately artificial construction that we call our life, and we struggle to keep afloat despite our suspicion that it is all unreal and meaningless."

"How awful," I murmured. He seemed to be waiting for my opinion. "Well," I said. "I suppose that explains why I feel so disoriented." I was trying to keep it light. "Personally, I've always found comfort in rules of etiquette. I think people should learn from an early age how to stand up straight, shake hands, say thank you."

They were both looking at me with detached interest. "That's just outer trappings, Mother," my daughter reminded me gently. "Quill's talking about the big things. How to live your life."

I felt unfairly rebuked. "That's a distinction without a difference, Marjorie. What everyone needs is family around, of course. Then you'd have plenty of guidance and advice. And good examples to follow." DeForest studied me harder than I cared to be looked at. "Not that I did," I admitted. They were waiting. I concluded lamely, "Heritage is all."

"Heritage," repeated DeForest.

"Yes." I wasn't even sure what I meant, but I was prepared by then to defend it to the death. "History and the past and tradition mean nothing if they're not brought to bear. You can't put time under glass and treat it like an object of art; you have to live it."

DeForest nodded gravely. His face seemed sadder and more lined than ever. He offered me grapes, then opened his mouth to take one, and I saw all his jawful of gray teeth, discolored as if by smoking or a general lapse in hygiene, and their disarray let me in on a secret: DeForest, for all his objective understanding, was lost. I thought of his stockpile of honey. He was giving in, too, it seemed, to personal fulfillment.

Marjorie cracked another walnut. "Oh, shoot, it's all moldy inside. I'll throw it to the birds."

Weren't things designed to mold and disappear? What my son-in-law had so plainly presented churned me up with the knowledge that I, too, was succumbing to the chaos of this modern world. I, distinguished by left feet, of which I was both ashamed and proud, scorning the organizing principles, had knocked for eighty years against the closed door of fulfillment and was in danger, at the end of my life, of being no use to anyone. I chewed carefully on some grapes, got the seeds out before they did damage under my dentures, and thought of my return to Sunset, disappearing into Goldenrod, where we were all mostly widows, supposedly resting after long, vibrant lives, encouraged to indulge ourselves, in some television, say, to sit in front of that enormous kaleidoscope of a screen in the lounge. On a Sunday you'd find us there, vacant eyed, hunched over on osteoporitic spines, knocked out by medication for arthritis, asthma, you name it; we really didn't care if the station were tuned to football or, as one thoughtful visitor suggested, a Fred Astaire movie, something more to our tastes, whatever they used to be. No, football or wrestling was just fine; we would watch anything in color. The pictures blinked for us and kept us awake until it was time for medicine and sleep. Some had been football widows all their lives, and now were widows of their own selves, having lost their transmitting station and given over the controls to the cork-soled Sunset staff. I knocked my knife against my plate in staccato percussion, thinking these things. I felt trembly enough and feared tears if I didn't gain some control in a minute.

Wallawalhalla. The island, I'd heard rumored, had come up in the world. A new town had grown on top of the lava flows. I saw it all so clearly: I would wear tropical white and a big broad-brimmed hat to shade my face. I would drink gin and play old popular tunes on the piano and people would gather around and join in the singing. I would be happy there. I would have lunch with the mayor. Mrs. Ypsilanti had nothing on my old connections. And, then—and this was the part my mind lingered over—once a year I would return to Conflux in triumph. I, too, could win at the game of exoticism. I would paint myself bright with the eastern sunrise; I would be an International.

As I helped my daughter scrape dishes in the kitchen, I was thinking about Evangeline. In a funny way I would miss her. She had come closest of anyone I knew to Harry's cerebral authoritarianism, with her snobberies and attitudes and pronouncements. It seemed to be part of my nature to fall victim to such colonizing forces as Empire and Harry Bagg and Mrs. Ypsilanti. Even in my small rebellions, I had failed to break completely away from someone else's control. A return to the past, newly and brightly reconstructed, seemed suddenly an excellent gamble for freedom. I would, symbolically, stitch a little Betsy Ross flag for myself, to sew to my trip's luggage. Was I nervous about leaving? Would independence undo me? Any neck adjusted to fit its yoke, I supposed, remembering Miss Bartram saying something of that kind to me when I was too young to understand. Any creature felt its freedom with a certain agitation. Even babies preferred to be swathed at first and cried if left to the air, didn't they? I determined not to become complacent and servile. I sighed deeply as I closed a cupboard.

Marjorie said with annoying tact, "The children should be back soon from Miss Halliday's. They're feeding her goat while she's in Tibet. They'd love to play Monopoly."

"They've had enough of Monopoly, I suspect. Did you know I have a regular chess date?"

DeForest overheard, hefting out the refuse for composting, dropping orange peel on the floor I'd have to mop again. He declared with a lot of front teeth, "It's that man from Finland!"

When he was out the door, I confided to my daughter, "Mrs. Ypsilanti. She seems perfectly happy all alone here. She hasn't seen her daughter in over thirty years."

My daughter looked distressed at the suggestion in my non sequitur. She reached an arm down the disposal and pulled up a silver spoon. "We'll invite her to lunch."

"What would we do with her here?"

"The usual," said Marjorie, considering. "People at gatherings seem mostly to laugh and tell anecdotes."

"You wouldn't like her," I backpedaled.

Later, however, drying a platter, I reconsidered, thinking that perhaps a nice tea with almond cake might cheer my daughter up. Also,

I confess, I considered how impressed Mrs. Ypsilanti would be with DeForest, snake that he was, and the bright-eyed grandchildren—if I could get them to take off their snorkel gear and shake hands. I fitted the platter into the back of the cupboard. "Tea, Marjorie. Tea is the absolute most we'll do."

Over knight's gambit on Wednesday, Mrs. Ypsilanti alluded to the plan. "Lovely voice your daughter has," she added. "Musical, lyric mezzo."

My tapping antennae picked up no sarcasm in this observation, which surprised me. "H. was musical," I answered. "Played the harpsichord." I added, "Casual dress for Sunday," though she hadn't inquired.

My brain was jumping around, full of my own travel plans. I had had the staff bring Harry's huge leather suitcase up from storage and I had begun sorting out my clothes, what suits needed dry cleaning, which hats required blocking. I felt the nervous excitement I'd known as a girl in Bremen when Jenny Abbott and I were first setting out. Then I'd been looking for my mother; now, well now, I supposed—how modern!—I was searching for my self.

The next weekend, I spent Saturday night worrying, and was up early Sunday at work in the kitchen. From my frayed memory I pieced together the ingredients of an ancient almond cheesecake, invented circa A.D. 230 and passed on to me by Miss Bartram, who claimed to have found the recipe near the termite's hill on Walla. It tasted of eternity. I wrote out notes for Marjorie on how it should be baked and set out to cool. This was an important step for if it were left in the oven too long it could become hard and the whole effort spoiled. I wouldn't have time to oversee the baking myself, as I was driving in with DeForest to pick up our guest.

Still in apron, I checked on Marjorie, who, at my suggestion, was clearing Jessica's toadstool collection out of the dining room. Apparently the humidity suited them there under the south window, but the odor of fungus was rather overweening. I found the carpet sweeper under the chesterfield and tried to get up the small feathers the ducks had left on the rug overnight.

"We could collect for a down comforter," Marjorie suggested

brightly, setting out plates. She was trying to be cheerful, but I distrusted her mood.

"We'll have to keep the doors closed," I said. "And not the best plates, beloved. She's not royalty. And we certainly won't require all these forks." Stepping backward, I tripped over a duck, shaking itself awake and frowning.

"Shoo, Mildred, honey," Marjorie said to it. "Roberta and Clyde will be coming, Mother. They are planning a little trip around the Mediterranean in May. They'll have lots to ask your friend."

I hadn't reckoned on the Forsters, and the idea of their Anglophilic presence with Mrs. Ypsilanti made me uneasy. "Clyde may be good-looking but he's awfully dull, don't you find, Marjorie? When he opens the door he always looks as though Roberta just hit him on the head with a stack of dishes—Wedgwood, of course."

"Mother," laughed Marjorie. "Catch him in a frivolous mood and Clyde can be quite amusing."

"As for Roberta," I continued. "All that backtracking. I admire people who decide what they're going to say and then say it, not the other way around."

She must have been tired; for once my daughter didn't rush to someone's defense but let the remark go. "I told them three o'clock."

"Three! The cake needs time to meld!"

"It can meld while we chat. We have to get you home by quarter to six, Mother, or you'll miss your dinner," and with that one remark all the routines of Sunset, right down to the smell of the cleaning fluid, deflated my mood with their inescapable certainty. My daughter continued, "I made shortbread. Quill should sit next to you or he'll spill everything on Roberta. He always manages to sit right against her knees." Her face opened for a moment but closed down again fast.

I didn't know what to say about what she wasn't telling me. "Shortbread!?" I complained. "You never made shortbread for me."

"This *is* for you. Do you see this glorious creature I found near the muskrat's grave?" She set a large mushroom with red spots on its hood in the middle of the table. "It might stain. I should put it on a plate."

I stared at the toadstool. "Marjorie, you should know that I'll be leaving soon."

The duck gave a crude squawk.

"I cut out an ad from the paper, Mother, for a bus tour up to the Niagara Valley, Balmoral included."

"I won't go to Balmoral."

"Then let's drive out to Hayfields House one day. It dates from the Revolution. You'd love the brick. And they have some beautiful embroidery, one of a ghost."

"I'm not interested in ghosts."

She patted my hand with a smile. Then she dropped it in order to right the mushroom that had toppled over. And that was all the notice she gave her unhappy mother. Or her mother gave unhappy her.

DeForest and I found Mrs. Ypsilanti waiting under Sunset's awning, shading her eyes with a small gloved hand. She had flagrantly disregarded my suggestion of casual dress. Rather than her standard pantsuit, Evangeline was decked out in a slender yellow linen suit so new that, when DeForest stopped the car abruptly curbside, the air around her reeked of sizing. A tiny pair of matching yellow high heels lifted her up, and gold teardrop earrings pinched at her wrinkled earlobes. Even her tight little purse was yellow. She looked stuck down and eager, like a canary stepping out of a bath.

DeForest shook hands, solicitous and pleased. He liked chauffeuring his children and their friends around and regarded his duties on that day as roughly the same. "What do you think of this weather?" he said. "Humid for June. Have a garden?"

Mrs. Ypsilanti allowed him to take her arm.

"Baggie," he said with a grin he considered boyish, "if you'll squeeze in back ..."

I heaved open the sliding door and stepped into the duck-smelling back of the van. I had to shove a pile of recycling out of the way, move a pot, and brush feathers and cracker crumbs from the upholstery. "Put on your belt, Evangeline," I instructed. My own safety belt was covered with sticky dust and impossible to untangle. As I struggled, DeForest clipped Mrs. Ypsilanti's neatly into the catch. He bounced up the engine as I was still tugging at the twist in my belt, envisioning my unprotected person hurtling through the windshield.

As DeForest pulled out to the road, I gave up the fight and leaned forward. For the first time I noticed a beige plastic lump behind Mrs. Ypsilanti's ear. "That's a smart frock," I shouted.

Mrs. Ypsilanti touched the device. "No need to shout—I'm not senile. Just bought the suit on sale. I took that bus that runs to the mall. Eighty-seven dollars, on sale from one hundred thirty. It's a new silk and ramie mixture. Pretty, *n'est pas?*"

"Oh, my," I said, pleasantly embarrassed to have my opponent talking money.

When we pulled up the dirt road I saw the Forsters's old black Daimler parked by the potting shed and Roberta and Clyde waving from the porch as happy as Hollywood farm children—in coordinating white cotton cricket uniforms, hers with a skirt. She set down her drink to help Mrs. Ypsilanti up the steps. "*Kali-mera,*" she declared.

Mrs. Ypsilanti smiled and bobbed. "*Kalimera. Ti kanete?*"

"And this is my husband! Stand up, Clyde."

Clyde shuffled himself together and stuck out an arm as long as a broom handle. "*Eimai andras.*"

"He means, he's my husband," explained Roberta in her small, fluty way.

Marjorie waddled out at that moment with Mildred under her arm, her gait impeded by her choice of garment—a kind of brown sari wound around her middle and pinned in various places with large safety pins to keep it decent. I was dismayed by the many wilting daisies glued to the skirt. My daughter whistled out of one side of her mouth at a bee and wiped her hand against her hip before holding it out to Evangeline. A few flowers dropped off. "Mother made the most exciting cake. Unfortunately, I burned it, but I did find something in the freezer. It's just defrosting."

"Park yourselves," DeForest said, genially rubbing his hands together. My continental guest raised her chin and looked poised, lowering herself nicely into the chair Clyde Forster pulled out.

Roberta, eyebrows high, started explaining their itinerary. "We're beginning in Athens, the cradle of democracy . . . My Scottish cousin Cyril . . ."

I hurried Marjorie into the house, furious, and rightly so. "What's happened, Marjorie? How could you have burned the cake? It was already out of the oven! I left such careful instructions! And what is this thing you're wearing?"

Marjorie flapped the wide sleeves. "Isn't it fun? The children are into daisies. I'm truly sorry about the cake, Mother. I put it back in the oven to clear some room on the counter, and I guess I'd forgotten to turn the flame down. I'm hopeless." A look of panic swept over her and she collapsed against the counter, disturbing more floral design on her robe.

I saw all this but I could not stop in my anger. "We have a guest on the porch who's descended from an Ottoman or something, their silverware rivaled the Hapsburgs, and you go around in a bedspread. Oh, Marjorie, Marjorie." I pulled at my amber necklace and walked in circles.

Marjorie combed her fingers through her hair. "*Deep* breath, Mother." She opened up several packages and slid brown wedged-shaped frozen objects onto a metal tray. "Now, *breathe* out. Fine. And again. I think your friend won't mind in the least what I wear. Or that our flatware rivals Howard Johnson's."

"Oh, you don't know her."

"And, Mother, it was you who said not to use the best china."

"But I don't want her to think we're peasants." My daughter had taken a cleaver and was hacking up a large watermelon. "Where are you going with that?" I asked. "Watermelon in June? It can't be any good."

"I suppose not," she agreed. She arranged the bleeding slices on a platter. "Probably from Chile. Just something to nibble on." She searched under the sink and drew out a one-minute sand timer.

"But we're having tea in a minute," I objected, "You can't serve fruit now!"

Marjorie blew a kiss and carried things toward the porch. Following in my heavy shoes, I paused a moment to inspect the table again, reluctant to go out. I propped up the mushroom with the red spots, which had sagged into the butter; poor thing looked as lumpy and irrelevant as I felt.

Out on the porch Mrs. Ypsilanti was remarking to my daughter, "Watermelon is the national fruit of Greece. I feel at home here."

Everyone looked charmed with her and pleased at their success. It hardened my heart. Taking my seat, I announced, "I'm returning to Wallawalhalla Island. It's my homeland in many ways."

"In what ways?" DeForest asked, making trouble.

I thought for a moment. "A homeland is where what's there becomes part of you, too. And Walla was the place I grew up, all in a summer, and my views will always be shadowed by it."

"Grendel's mother," said Clyde suddenly, and leaned back grinning, satisfied.

"That was Valhalla," whispered Roberta. "And a monster."

"A homeland," said Mrs. Ypsilanti, and everyone turned to hear her, "is a nice idea that someone must have thought up, I suspect, to get people to war with each other. The invention of women somewhere, to keep the men out of the house."

"Mm," someone murmured, maybe the bee that had landed with a skid on the slice of watermelon Marjorie handed me. DeForest saw it and warned, "Pericles ..." as it embraced the fruit.

Mrs. Ypsilanti looked up, removing a seed from her lips. "Is that a significant nomenclature?" I nearly choked, but it struck me guiltily that Mrs. Ypsilanti truly appreciated the outing, that she wanted the hospitality of my family. My darker side suspected privately, too, that she was hoping to usurp their goodness with an overdose of foreign charm.

"I give them classical names. Their lives, dramas of intense order protected by pain, intent on sweetness." DeForest shook his finger at another bee that was circling down for a landing. "Thucydides ... And they make the perfect food—liquid amber. Harmony under glass."

"Drama," I said fast to get my foot back through the door of this conversation. "That's what the world needs. On Walla, we all lived in a state of suspense. Things were on the brink."

"Of eruption," put in Clyde.

Mrs. Ypsilanti's guffaw blew little shreds of fruit about in the air.

Roberta shifted in her chair. Her voice sounded tight as she said, "I think we need to reaffirm our English heritage. Williamsburg would be my choice of homeland."

"*What* heritage?" said Mrs. Ypsilanti. "The beauty of America is that you have no past. Your children, Marjorie, have no burden of comparison."

Marjorie looked troubled by the compliment, and DeForest rose to the challenge with a faked lethargy meant to disarm. "Heritage, of course, is not to be confused with history. The country has a relatively short history, about four hundred years, but in the short term we do pass down some small measure of ourselves. And I agree with Viola, place is part of it. Real places."

"Oh, no," laughed Evangeline. "In America, you get to invent yourselves. It's what makes the country bearable."

I sucked in my breath and announced so loudly that even Mildred on the steps straightened up, "This time next week, you may imagine me on white sand, between blue sky and green water. This is my farewell."

No one spoke for a moment. Marjorie reached for my hand almost as if to pull me back. I felt myself escalating to some position of prestige, from bargain basement up to ladies' lingerie, erect, purchases tied up with string.

No one spoke till, drawing a cigarette out of an embroidered case, Mrs. Ypsilanti leaned toward the match DeForest lit for her and said, "We'll miss you, dear heart." My son-in-law dropped the matches into his pocket, extended his arm around the back of Evangeline's chair, and smiled at her profile.

In the pause, Marjorie turned the timer upside down. "Mother has always been self-reliant. And fearless. She's even ridden a motorcycle."

"Marjorie! Just that once in Georgia."

"When she had to eat a cow dressed up as moose," put in DeForest, making me uncomfortably unsure if he were paying me attention or telling tales at my expense.

"I rode a motorcycle once," interrupted Mrs. Ypsilanti. "It was during the war. I met the pleasantest American fellow in a bar on the Plaka. He was stationed in Athens. Said he'd give me a lift. *Pourquoi pas?* I thought. We ended up in Sparta. Lost his directions."

"Why didn't you tell him the way?" I asked.

"Too much wind in my face."

The others smiled. Clyde, face unmoving, offered, "I spent a summer at the British School for Archaeology."

"Lovely marble floors," said Mrs. Ypsilanti.

"Dried up my allergies."

"That reminds me," Mrs. Ypsilanti began, flicking a bee away from her watermelon. "I once was involved—*romantically* involved—with a pearl diver, and one night we were in an exclusive restaurant, starting our oysters, when he leaned across the table and pulled out of mine a whole pearl necklace!"

I looked at Roberta and Marjorie laughing and DeForest's happy smile and refused to condone that kind of nonsense in my daughter's house. "This is my necklace," I let everyone know, holding out my amber strand. "From my Great-Aunt Eustacia."

They leaned forward and studied the beads.

"The insects trapped inside once led lives of greater formality and complexity than our own. You would think them just flaws in the stone, though, unless you looked sharp. What does that mean?" I felt Marjorie's squint on me but refused her eye and watched one of the bees, Pericles, most likely, hovering four inches over my arm. I wished him nearer and nearer my hand. "Of course Aunt Eustacia's ambers did not arrive in a dinner like a prize in Cracker Jacks."

"Mother," Marjorie shushed me. "Roberta's telling us their itinerary."

I wasn't listening. I was watching as my bee visitor closed in over the spot of scent on my wrist, landing with a tickle on my exposed skin, and stepped lightly on the blue and fragile covering that was my skin, twisting inside his little striped fur coat. I imagined it: a pinprick, a jab of pain, then a huge welt mounding up, pills and telephone calls, and Quilliam with cold compresses and Marjorie with baking soda, and the anxious faces of the Forsters . . . Were they even paying attention?

Roberta was asking, "And Mrs. Ypsilanti, where in all the world would you most like to travel?"

"Of any place, I suppose—New Brunswick."

Everyone looked startled. Clyde queried, "*Canada?*"

Evangeline explained. "I have a daughter there—Persephone. My eyes!"

The bee's six legs executed a grand plié on my arm. He touched along my skin in toe shoes.

Evangeline tapped a new cigarette on the arm of her chair. "I was going to live with her and her family, you see. In 'sixty-seven. After I fell and broke my leg. When I got free of the cast and could walk again—it took weeks of therapy—I packed up, sold off what I had in Athens, and was all set, but what should happen? I met Ernest! Love in Conflux."

"But Persephone writes every week," I prompted, watching my bee tap at a hair. Something mean in me wanted to test how far Evangeline would go.

"Will she be coming to visit you here?" Marjorie said.

Pericles, if it was he, was now turning his little triangular head to the right and left in a nearsighted attempt to locate the scent. I jerked my arm. A miniature sword punched down hard and hot.

"Ah!" cried Mrs. Ypsilanti at the very instant I cried, "Oh!" Glancing up with surprise I saw my chess partner sliding down in her chair, her eyes staring out at the ducks, her face a blotched blue, her mouth open and slack. Marjorie, sitting next to her, grabbed her by the arm and tried to pull her upward. "Are you all right? Mrs. Ypsilanti? What's happened? What's wrong! Quill, call for help!" He'd already rushed into the house.

Tears of pain spilled over as I inspected my own damage. The little mound on my wrist had risen into an angry red hill and Pericles, unable to withdraw his blade, had detached it from himself and fallen like a ball into the grass where he lay twisting. The punch throbbed and stung and the stinger moved back and forth like an excited second hand. From my private pain I watched as the Forsters surrounded Mrs. Ypsilanti, loosening her collar. Roberta took off the yellow shoes and lifted the stockinged legs up on the table, saying, "What tiny feet she has." Clyde, standing up, wet his lips and jingled coins in his pockets, waiting for instructions.

"I've stung myself," I told him. I held out my wrist.

He blinked over it. "You have," he said helpfully.

"Mother," cried Marjorie. "Is your friend ill?"

I looked again at Mrs. Ypsilanti, now with her eyes open. Whereas before she had seemed dark, now she looked gray and white. Her eyes had lost their shine and glinted dimly like a baby's, the color of gunmetal. She was swallowing with difficulty. "I don't know anything," I whispered, limp with remorse and fear.

Marjorie patted the stiff hairdo. "Help is on the way," she told Mrs.

Ypsilanti. The eyes showed no sign of understanding. "Relax," Marjorie insisted, her voice seesawing with panic. "We're all here with you."

Before I had time to lose all hope, the rescue squad arrived, in a cloud of red dust, in the persons of two lightly moustached and under-nourished boys. They instructed each other as they lifted Mrs. Ypsilanti onto a stretcher. "Stroke," one said to Quilliam. Marjorie climbed in the back, pulling her bedspread up behind her, and sat on a metal seat with one of the young men. The other one closed the back door on them and revved up the engine and lights. DeForest and I, stepping through the flower beds, followed in the minivan while Roberta and Clyde, open-mouthed, holding pieces of watermelon heavily at their sides, waited on the front porch, the telephone in the doorway for news. "Ring us the minute you know anything!" Roberta called.

"Tell Mildred we'll be home soon," Marjorie shouted back. "And the twins, when they get back." Everyone stared straight ahead without waving.

At the emergency entrance at the hospital, a scuffle of white-clad staff pushed and pulled on my old chess partner and called in the aid of various chrome-and-black devices. I stepped back. I watched as they wheeled her on an oversized ironing board through double doors.

Holding my stung wrist up with my other hand, I let DeForest and Marjorie lead me to some plaid chairs and smudgy magazines. It seemed odd to be panicking quietly in the middle of what looked like a stranger's living room. An old man, hairless knees poking out of a loose bathrobe, feet unmoving in new slippers, a bag of fluid hanging from a pole like the windsock at the airport, stared at us, hopeful of diversion.

I had no words, imagining Evangeline under the many hammering hands: late of Athens, without a family, having no real home. My chess partner needed her daughter nearby, now and forever more. "I'll write to Persephone."

Marjorie gave me a luckless smile.

"Poor old flapper," said DeForest.

A young intern passing brought himself to a halt in his enormous white shoes and leaned over my arm. "Left the damned stinger in," he said and, with tweezers produced from a chest pocket, pulled it out. He applied salve.

Marjorie intervened. "Could you give her a tube of that stuff? She's going off to the Far East."

Stunned, and angry with my daughter, I added, "And I may not be back."

6

Walla-Bound

Points of Departure

꙳

WOBBLY BUT DETERMINED, I booked a flight and checked off the practical considerations of departure: travelers' checks, vaccinations, muffin-sized malaria pills. I took my moose off the wall and rolled him up. I piled my suitcases in the center of my room. A taxi would call for me around six on the morning of my departure. I preferred to do it all alone. It was my own adventure.

I spoke to the girl at the travel agency three or four times; it flustered me to hear Vivaldi abruptly between her brusque questions whenever she put me on hold. Sunset by taxi to the airport, then through New York to Frankfurt, to Athens, then on to Bombay. The last leg, I admit, had not been booked. Were there even boats over to Walla anymore? My hands went clammy; I had an image of my girl-self rocking, white frocked, on the front porch of Egrets, but so much must now be under the volcano's glassy ash — what would I find?

"I have a place," I assured the agent. "A private address." I had no such thing, just a sense that I would find what I needed.

Through all this my mind spun around the problem of Evangeline. I put off visiting her until I was ready to leave. Something warned me I would lose my nerve if I hesitated for even a moment. Near the last day, when my favorite nurse, Howard, passed in the corridor, perspiring lightly with the effort of pushing a tray of steel things, I followed behind him into the elevator and down the beige halls into Woodbine where octogenarians in bathrobes sat at school desks, as if sent out for misbehaving.

Howard, panting, brightened when I asked if the rumor were true that he was getting married. He launched right in with the details, and, listening, I realized I would miss the end of this drama: would they decide on peach or turquoise for their color scheme? Would his bride's divorced parents reconcile for the occasion and be seated together? I apologized, "I'm going away, you know."

"We heard that," he said, as if offering condolences.

We stopped outside a darkened room. A television in the ceiling celebrated without sound the passions of some people in heavy makeup.

Howard pinched my elbow. "Go on in."

Sheets gleamed blue in the murky light. Bumpy under the blanket lay my chess partner, looking like a cardboard cutout of herself, hair flattened on the pillow, eyelids swagged shut, a tube snaking through her nose. I thought of Harry towards the end.

"Respirator," Howard called cheerfully. "Just for a few days. Ms. Ypsilanti? Company!"

One fragile eyelid lifted. Evangeline raised her chin as Howard tied the strings of the nightgown together at her wrinkled throat. "She's lost some use of her fingers. And some speech. Could have been a whole lot worse, though, couldn't it, sweetie? Here's your friend."

"Hello," I said, overly bright, as Howard rolled off with his cart. I thought Evangeline looked anything but lucky.

Her mouth pulled together strangely, the two halves no longer symmetrically meeting. The words sounded like groans. Her hand appeared from the side of the bed, turning like a flipper. Making a guess, I picked up the sweating paper cup on the night table. She grasped it and pushed the straw down between ice chips that swished. Some dead French poet seemed to grip her tongue: "*Je ne viens pas ce soir vaincre ton corps . . .*"

I laid a hand on my friend's arm. "It's me," I said quite firmly. "Viola. I speak about three words of French."

Evangeline blinked slowly and rolled her eyes. Her mouth came together. "*Ich,*" she said, listened, then stopped. "*Je,*" she tried again. "*Ego.*" It was as if someone had ransacked a house and dropped the contents of all the drawers into one big heap.

"It's all right," I said. I reached for her hand and stroked it. It lay cold and hard in my hands. "Ssh," I whispered. "Just be quiet."

Massaging the chill fingers, I closed my eyes and hoped to gather some direction in the silence. *Things will get better,* I wanted to tell her, but it sounded so flat that in the quiet of the room, I tried to imagine myself in my friend's place. In the darkness before my mind's eye, I saw the outline of a young woman. I instructed Marjorie to go away and leave me to think, but the girl, some girl, remained in flimmery outlines, insistent, and in trying to recognize her, I thought of Mrs. Ypsilanti's daughter, Persephone. The dutiful Persephone of Dalhousie should be notified. *I will write to her,* I thought, relieved. My friend had this relation, just a plane ride away. *I must tell her to come at once.* I breathed hard with new resolve and direction. I opened my eyes and found Evangeline's searching my face. She was trying to force my attention downward, I realized, over—here? there?—to her bedside table. The keys? Yes, the keys. Her expression relaxed. I closed them in my fist. "I'll look after things," I assured her.

A small surge of pleasure, about the wattage of a reading light, rushed through me. I whispered, smiling, "You'll be fine. I know it. I'll come see you again before I leave." Her hand tried to grip mine but the muscles could scarcely close. Only her eyes seemed alive, overly dark and bright. "That's fine," I said, softly pulling my own hand out from under the fingers. "That's fine." She watched me out with two sets of smiles—one up, one down.

As I walked back to my half of the home, I felt marked. I had the sense that somewhere in the sharp corners of the corridor, crouching behind wheelchairs and potted palms, a sniper was pulling the trigger to shoot doom into me. What right had I now so agilely, overflowing with resolutions, to cross the walkway from the sick to the well?

The sun had shifted along the dust balls on the lobby floor. Sibelius, sporting crisply ironed blue seersucker shorts and knee socks, leaned against a window. He held up a pack of cards in greeting when he saw me; he cheerfully lost all games. I almost stopped, wanting badly to talk to someone about Evangeline, but I couldn't trust myself not to break down, so I just raised my hand and passed on, clouded in grief. By what right, by what grace was I upright in the elevator ascending?

Without hesitation I turned the key to her room and went in. Charged with a mission, I hastened to perform it. Without looking around except to note the quantity of library books piled on valuable counter space, I walked to a table where I spotted two bottles of ink at the ready. I sat on the hard, needlepointed chair and was pulling a sheet of writing paper toward me when the telephone rang. I froze for a moment, then got up, lifted the receiver, and whispered, "Hello?" A click closed me off from the caller. As I stood there, phone in hand, though, I had an idea and paged through the directory until I found an area code for New Brunswick. The operator obligingly read out the number for Sam Samuelson. Heady with this quick victory, I dialed. After a few rings, a recorded voice screeched out a Tarzan call, and I nearly hung up but clung on till a Donald Duck voice then asked me to leave my message for Sam or Jan. At that, I replaced the receiver and sat down, winded, at the desk. Technology held far too many perils for me. I squared the writing paper and chose a pen. The old-fashioned postal service would have to deliver my message. I wrote:

> *Dear Persephone:*
> *Please allow me such familiarity as I am an aged friend of your*
> *mother's. I am writing to let you know she is unwell. She seems to*
> *have suffered a stroke, a few days ago, and we all agreed you would*
> *want to know at once.*

A quick hunt through the drawer of the table produced an address book, out of which, as if on cue, fell a letter addressed to Mrs. Ypsilanti, with the return address of "Samuelson, 96 Maple Drive, Dalhousie." This I copied out carefully onto an envelope and searched around for a stamp. Then, before folding the letter, I reread what I'd written. Suppose, I considered sadly, some stranger had to inform Marjorie of my grave condition? My chest tightened. Thinking to find the correct phone number that might gain faster access to Persephone, I pulled the letter from the envelope and opened it. The message surprised me, being, as I deduced quickly, from Evangeline's son-in-law. In neat italics he described a wet summer, late roses, adding that Persephone was off for a week, hiking in Quebec. The date—a shock—May 20th, 1952.

Confused, I pried further where I had no rights, pulling out all letters from her lidded box, scanning the address book for clues; there were no other notes from Dalhousie. Communication seemed to have ceased at that point—1952. I sat, trying to understand what this meant.

Had Evangeline, in truth, no contact with her daughter? What of her stories? Self-deceptions? I felt a minor earthquake erupt from my heart, with shock waves of anger and frustration traveling through my limbs. I'd been had. I sat for a while, absorbing it. Of course, uneasily, I had to acknowledge my own deceptions, and thinking of Frank Thwaite forever trapped in the Finland of 1952, I began to admire the ease with which Evangeline had moved into each decade. I was glad I had written, but my one practical worry was: would my note, thirty years later to ninety-six Maple Drive, actually reach Persephone?

When I stood to go, everything felt harder and sadder than when I'd come in to write the letter. I felt disinclined to leave, as the things of the room, though merely small and hers, now seemed charged with loss and uncertainty. They spoke of a long life now struggling to continue, in a bed more mobile than its incumbent, and tended by healthful girls who had never heard a French poem. I felt bowed down with an understanding, by the fear I sensed alone in the room, by the burden I was assuming; I seemed the only one, just an old woman, but the only one who understood what years meant. I looked at the black-and-white framed photographs on the walls and spotted Evangeline—slimmer, brighter— in sunglasses, leaning on a column of the Parthenon. The paintings, the pictures, the handmade rugs, the embroidered cloth framed under glass—these should not be left alone. They needed tending as much as my friend herself. I wanted to guard them. Until Persephone arrived, I told myself, I would put off my trip.

This resolved, a troubling thought occurred to me, and from my handbag I withdrew my checkbook. I wrote out a check for two hundred dollars and added a postscript to the letter: *Please let me assist in the cost of the flight.* Then I folded everything into the envelope and took it down to the outgoing mail. Addressed, stamped, and ready to fly, it made me both envious and tender. Somehow I would find Persephone and bring her here. I touched some saliva to the stamp for good luck as I sent it down the chute.

Within a week the letter was returned, check inside, with a note explaining that I'd made a mistake, no Mrs. S. D. R. Samuelson at that address. It was a regretful card with a hand-pressed trillium from a retired

Admiral Jessup, who suggested consulting the police department for changes of address. I moved a blouse off my chair and sat, trillium in hand, breathing hard. I could not now leave Conflux. In the next few days, I rearranged everything I'd spent the previous weeks planning. I said nothing to my family, because I was not actually canceling my trip as I saw it, just postponing it, detouring for a while.

I discovered that, since I had given notice, I was expected to vacate. A Mrs. Dobbs with a brassy daughter-in-law had already puts dibs on my own room, and there were no vacancies.

"We have a waiting list," offered the housing director. "About two years." She was not.the woman I had checked out with, but a younger, more official personage.

"What about two-o-nine?" — my friend's old room.

"Ypsilanti," she said, checking a Rolodex.

"She's in Woodbine." Speaking into a small hole in the glass that separated us — were there octogenarians with bullets about? — I said, "I'll pay the rent until she's well."

The manager blinked, defensively, then marched into a back office. When she returned, she said in neutral tones, "What name?"

I paused. Above all, I thought, Marjorie must not learn of my change of plans. I could not bear to go on as her poor, dull, benign, incarcerated mother, tolerated and ignored. It was of the utmost importance that she believe me happily returned to my exotic island roots. To accomplish this, I realized, I would have to cover my tracks. I thought of the old statues turning to dust at the bottom of Mt. Walla, and decided to reconstruct myself along classical lines. "Terra cotta," I told the manager.

Terry Carter, as the name went up on my mailbox, moved into 209, into the long room of anxious African violets and basil that Evangeline tended on the windowsill, into the scent of her perfume, the reds and oranges of the her decor: a Josef Albers abstraction, a Max Liebermann portrait, both sharp, unexpected reminders of my unhappy Berlin past about which I now felt almost nostalgic. I put my own X-rays and the twins' poster at the back of the closet. I hung my clothes up on one side of the closet and spent a moment fingering through my friend's suits and blouses. They were all new, stylish, kept in plastic against the chumbling of moth. Tucking my underthings into a drawer I noted with pleased surprise her variously colored petticoats: dark red, beige, black. Who would have guessed? In her medicine cabinet, a box of bleach, the secret of her gold moustache. I checked my own. Perhaps I'd try it . . .

Everything at last in its place, I sat down on the bed and bounced. I breathed in and out therapeutically. Then, lifting the red phone, I dialed, and spreading a handkerchief over the mouthpiece as I had seen done in the movies, I waited. After ten rings, Marjorie came on, out of breath. I guessed she'd been out in the garden, pulling things up. She sounded distraught. "You're *there*? When did this happen, Mother? We wanted at least to drive you to the airport! When did you leave? Do you have an address?"

I steadied myself against emotional blackmail; I had come so far. "Things all right your end, darling?"

"Fine. Mildred's . . ."

I couldn't bear to hear it. "I'll write when I'm settled, my dear . . . !"

I set the receiver down and bounced some more on the edge of the bed, strangely excited. The sun had turned a corner on the building and threw a long shadow into the room, cooling it. Out of Evangeline's window, I had a view of the airstrip belonging to the private aviators' club nearby. I could see small planes bouncing down along the tarmac, pink light angling off their wings. "Well," I heard myself sigh out loud and caught the sound of my own breathing—regular, purposeful—as if it belonged to some stranger sharing my wagon-lit.

When you are in hiding, to paraphrase Proust, an author I found on Evangeline's shelf (in translation), it is as if time has tucked you away in some fold, some backwater, where past, present, and future paddle in disoriented rings. All the joy and terrified pleasure of subversion gave way to fatigue. On my back I stared at the ceiling: a jigsaw of plaster cracks and water stains. What was happening to my life? I, who had always been the model of patient decorum: now a deceiving, runaway octogenarian. What would my daughter think if she knew? I puzzled this over, but failing to interlock any bits of sky, I grouped shades, as it were, and pondered generally the malcontents of parent and child. Why could Marjorie and I never fit together? What bothered me most about her? Her good-hearted disregard of *me*. And the grandchildren seemed to feel I was a creature from the moon, occasionally interesting, mostly translucent. And, moving on, I asked myself: why was I caught in such a tangled web with Mrs. Ypsilanti? Why was Marjorie's warmth too hot and Sunset's promised glow too cool? Why, in fact, were things never what they seemed? But, that, of course, was the overbred question that had yapped at my heels all my life.

In the twilight, with the sound of rain knocking along the metal pigeon guard on the window's edge, time played me tricks. Sounds and smells of my own distant past flooded my mind, unbeckoned. Funny how, lying on my back in the dark, cut off from all but Mrs. Ypsilanti, I felt the same frustrations and confusions I'd known as a girl when my only friend turned her back on me, and rightly so. These memories caused me great fatigue. I was a colony still, the recruited consort—to Harry, Marjorie, now Evangeline. I had failed at all the important things: I had never found my mother, I had lost my father, I had left Harry and lost him to death forty years later, I had thrust my own child from me and failed to bring her back. My job seemed to be to declare independence, but for that you needed some nice confidence-building myths, those Paul Bunyon–Paul Revere tales that feathered the nest. And for myths, you needed a leap of faith. Owing to my feet, I had in my life seldom leaped.

I felt an unexpected kinship with those people in Dorf, living a mishmash. It struck me with a little inward guffaw of recognition: Viola Bagg, eighty-one in August, felt the strains of being herself. I, too, needed a national anthem and a flag with a picture of a leaf, needed a Mountie hat and stories of giant loggers and promise of buried treasure on a storm-beaten coast. Old age gave independence, as my friend Mr. Pancake later said, referring to his plane, but with independence came struggles of a new and exhausting kind. I felt like a stranger, neither a local like my grandchildren, nor a cosmopolitan like Evangeline; neither enemy nor friend but someone stateless and displaced. Commercials on television I'd glimpsed with the twins showed grandmothers in cardigans proud of their effervescing dentures. I spied us graying into the wallpaper in medical waiting rooms, edged to one side in supermarkets, left smiling meekly and overmedicated in the corridors of Goldenrod. Knowing where you came from gave you some protection against invading forces, and we were being invaded. Statehood at least gave you a border to guard. That's what I needed, and I was not the only old person in the world with this problem, either. Perhaps there was an entire diaspora like me. Where were they? Out there, each struggling to write a declaration of independence, each treading water against obscurity. I lay on top of the coverlet on Evangeline's bed for a long time, wondering how to map our little nation-self.

Without turning on a light, I readied myself for bed, thrown off balance by the arrangement of Evangeline's rooms, made uncomfortable by the nap of the shag rug that divided bedroom and hall, tickling my soles. But I had a capacity for sleep that trouble augmented, and I was almost somnambulant as I bunched my underthings on a bedside chair and rolled into cool sheets. In Evangeline's bed that first night I dreamed hard but forgot all details by morning.

I woke early. Lying still and alert, I began to feel pleasure in my odd situation. I was entirely free, I realized, under cover of a new name and address. In the early years with Harry, on waking to some new building site, I had felt this same kind of excitement. I had unpacked first the cleaning gear and the picnic plates and cutlery. I stirred up milk by adding boiled local water to powder from a box, presented my family with a good breakfast on our first morning, instant coffee for him, milky tea for baby Marjorie. Then Harry would go off to work at his high, tilted drawing table, and I would get down to cleaning.

Never one for daily maintenance, I enjoyed the pioneer work of scrubbing away disagreeable signs of life left by former tenants. I was squeamish about stepping on a floor in bare feet that might have been covered in pet rabbit droppings. I would sort through the traveling bags, placing everything around me in the middle of the floor (usually the furniture arrived days after us), and then designating the function of each room. "Choose your view, Harry!" I'd tell him as we looked around on those first mornings all over the world. North, south, east, west, Hong Kong, Addis, Jakarta—the view kept shifting but we stayed the same: two creatures out of sync trying to draw straight lines to each other, invariably striking only tangents. No wonder, I suppose, we spawned a child who chose to live with a wild man in underbrush.

That first morning in Evangeline's room at Sunset, I had to choose *my* view. A nagging voice in my ear asked: was it failure of nerve that had made me cancel my trip to Walla? Yes, I had to admit, it was. And yet, I considered, and I was determined to be truthful, I was not just temporizing when I found that truly, *truly* I was reluctant to leave Evangeline. Knowing this, I got out of bed, eager to put this altruism into action.

As I dressed, a blouse in the closet caught my eye. Just for fun I tried it on—a pink cotton-linen mix I'd never seen Evangeline wear but which suited me and matched my seersucker skirt. It was, I had to admit after the first moment of excitement, too small. I took it off and put on my own cream cotton blouse that made me look more like myself than ever: a cranky old woman at a loss. I resolved then and there to buy some new clothes.

Hanging up the blouse again I noted a hatbox on the closet shelf. Inside—wasn't I looking after my friend's things?—I found, to my shock, a dark wig. I lifted it out and held it at arm's reach: chestnut brown with an auburn tinge, styled in a full curving swing around the back with a hint of fringe over the forehead. In front of the bathroom mirror, I pulled the thing on. It constricted my scalp but spruced up my face remarkably. Well, I thought, looking and looking. Of course, one wondered how such a wrinkled, pink face could sprout such thick, shiny hair. Be that as it may, I twisted a curl down in front of my ear. I liked the energy and moral fiber of the elderly lady who smiled back at me with polite attention. The wig was *me*. And, as my mailbox reminded me, I was now Mrs. Carter.

As I made my toast, I resolved to visit my friend as my first act as the attractive, full-headed, extra-brunette Terry Carter. I stalled a little, tidying up around the room, fussing over the placement of the boxes on Evangeline's dresser. As I locked the door behind me on that first day of freedom, I felt a coiling and wildness. I walked through the halls disguised as my own person.

My old friend was sitting up in bed, looking drawn, her black hair uncurled but combed straight back, white at the roots. She took my hand with a bright smile.

"What have you done?" she asked, noting my hairpiece.

I touched it. "Just changed my do."

"Whatever, you paid too much!"

"Hmm," I said, thinking how to let her in on my situation. "Evangeline," I said. "It's important to me that you not mention to anyone that I'm still here."

She leaned toward me. "Why?"

"I'm incognito. My daughter thinks I've gone to Walla."

"Haven't you?"

"No. I won't be going."

"Ah. *Une petite tromperie.*"

"So please don't tell them you've seen me. I'm now Terry Carter."

"Good lord." She yawned. I could see she was alredy bored with this topic and wanted to return to her own concerns. "Now, tell to me minutely," she said, "how is it that you came to this country? I'm asking after legalities. I don't want an editorial." She chopped into her ice with the straw. It took a moment for me to understand her blurry words, but I was moved by her vigor. She sucked at her straw from the more mobile corner of her mouth and said, "I might become a citizen."

"An *American?*" After all her dismissive talk, I was truly startled.

Evangeline smiled her new, crooked smile. "Yes, why not? And you must help me!" She waved her hand loosely toward the night stand.

Howard, passing on track shoes, squeaked over to my friend's bedside. He glanced at me. "Hah," I said, in a stagy Southern accent. He grinned perfunctorily, as if at a stranger; my disguise was working.

Time lightened. I woke with the sun striking Evangeline's violets. Opening the window as I dressed, I could hear the distant acceleration of aircraft, tipping as they spun along the airstrip and wobbling upward into the sky. For the first time since arriving in Conflux, no one except Evangeline knew where I was—or who I was. Even the friendly staff treated me in my wig as a newcomer. I had energy.

Evangeline needed me, as Harry had in those last years, in a way less evident and unexpressed, but, then, it seemed she would deteriorate more slowly. Plotting her deceptions improved her health. She had learned that as a citizen she could sponsor her daughter over to Conflux to take care of her. "Persephone will come in a flash," she informed me, rustling her forms. "I can't wait!"

I just nodded, kept my mouth firmly shut, and went on with my hunt for her daughter. When Jessup of Holland Road, Dalhousie, answered my first secret letter with his polite trillium in the negative, I went down to the public library in town, on the bus especially for us old people. While geriatrics pushed by on their walkers, holding large-print mysteries and dropping heavy bestsellers on the carpeting, creaking their bones to retrieve them, I sat tensed at the large reference table. I pored over columns of names in phone books, searching every major city for a Persephone Samuelson, her married name, or any Samuelsons in New Brunswick. There were twenty-seven. I wrote down each carefully on a long legal pad. I swore that every day I would write to three; I had the time. It was an expense, what with postage going up, but Terry Carter would find her. I said nothing of this to my friend; knowing we each had our deceptions gave me a certain boost.

Meanwhile I marveled at all the ways Evangeline had found to make herself comfortable, that I'd never considered. And why not? Why should one highlight one's own deterioration and ignore one's creature comforts? I admired her for that particular kind of self-centeredness. I thought I should work on cultivating it myself, and found that Mrs. Carter took to comfort fast. I broke out guest soap in the medicine chest (pine scented), hung up fresh hand towels (imprinted with some Greek letters that looked like the name of a hotel), made coffee in Evangeline's small espresso machine. Under her stockings in the bureau's top drawer I found cologne that I dabbed on with a heady sense of power. And daily I sat at her table and pulled another piece of stiff writing paper toward me, fountain pen poised.

A curious note from Dalhousie arrived a week later:

Dear Mrs. Carter,
Your letter was misdelivered to the residence of my friend here where I am visiting. Myself hailing from Tennessee, but Merce and I go way back, flying buddies even before the war. I'm buying a plane and am coming south to visit godson's nephew who is a Professor at Conflux. Small world — but zip coding is still important. Am retired mail carrier, would like to meet and assist in

your search. Arriving Saturday, will call Sunday at Sunset, if I
may. Will be wearing running shoes (recent foot surgery).
In anticipation of our meeting,

Your friend,
Jackson Pancake

P.S. My hair looks like a toupee but isn't.

I opened this in the lobby and sat down on the sofa, appalled. I had written off a formal inquiry and now I was getting a man in return—a mailman who declared himself, with his toupee hair, my friend. I looked up, but no one seemed to be paying me any mind. Howard squeaked past, holding Mrs. Rotweiler by one of her chicken-bone arms, but didn't even turn to say hello. Of course, he had not recognized the new heavily brunette me. No one seemed able to do anything about this odd—terrible?—situation. A man, coming to Conflux, to visit his god-son, no—his godson's nephew—would call on me on Sunday.

To meet Mr. Pancake—and what kind of a name was Pancake, anyway?—I decided Mrs. Carter must have a new suit. It was the least I could do for her in her time of need. At the front desk I got instructions on the van that drove out to the mall. I had never been there before, always relying on Marjorie for sundries and nightgowns, and I sat on the edge of the seat behind the driver, watching him shift lanes and helping him spot the signs on the highway. "Sears is north, Belks is south," he told me at the mall as he handed me out onto the sidewalk. It seemed like a lesson in the poles of a new planet. "They have wheelchairs," he added.

"I'm not that far gone," I let him know.

I felt slightly feverish at the sight of so many shops and no one to guide me through them. I followed a well-dressed woman into a specialty store that sold imported sweets. I looked at striped potholders and cookie cutters till I felt oriented. On a shelf I spotted Turkish delight. It was the sweet Harry had brought me on those courting afternoons. I hadn't tasted it since. Not that I would offer any to Mr. Pancake, but Evangeline might like some. Carrying two pounds in a white bag with handles, I continued down the central corridor, more upright, justified by the parcel in my hands.

I passed a shop with Chinese exports and stopped in. Displayed prominently on the counter was a game like dominoes but colored with green and red blocks of ivory on bamboo. I felt my heart wake up in my chest and take a leap forward as memories of the Egrets verandah swept over me. Hadn't we played mahjongg, Harry and I?

The salesgirl, an Asian whose eyes curved like Cleopatra's toward her temples, waved a hand over the pieces. "The favored game of the old emperor," she whispered. She made the entire store seem like a tourist trap. Still, I weighed a piece in my hand. It had a pleasant, familiar smell, a chill to the ivory.

"There are instructions, of course," I said. I thought about teaching the game to Jessica—and then had to check myself.

"Of course," said the salesgirl. The pieces clicked against each other softly as she pushed them across the glass. The sound itself seduced me, and I gave no thought to price as I signed a traveler's check.

"I'm from the Far East myself," I explained.

The girl yawned lightly into the back of her hand.

Waiting for her to wrap up my purchase, I received a shock: examining something in the show window of the shop were Jessica and Jerome. I thought at first they were admiring the kimonos, but then I saw, wouldn't you know, they were staring at some lighting effect made with tinfoil and streamers. Seeing them, on their own, alone together, foreheads pressed to the window, against the backdrop of the shoppers, I recognized them as somehow belonging to what little I claimed in the world. I just wanted to go out to them. I wanted to speak to them, to say, "You are good, dear children, but you must find better things to do with your time than hanging around shopping malls." But, of course, I couldn't; I wasn't there anymore. I watched them through the earrings, chatting inanities to the salesclerk, till they moved on, satisfied with whatever they'd wanted to know about the display. They hadn't seen the old lady on the other side of the glass.

Outside the window displays, I began to discriminate, entering only with some intent. If you wandered, you were easy prey to the clerks. In one high-priced store where the saleswomen looked like overbred afghan hounds, I spotted an elegant pine green suit. I fingered the linen, admiring its polished strength. The outrageous figure on the price tag might have sent me right out of the store, but somehow in the wig, as Terry Carter, I felt challenged: why shouldn't I wear such a suit? Yes, I told the saleslady in a commanding voice, yes, madam would like to be shown to a fitting room.

I was flushed with my daring, and happy with the fit; there seemed ample material around the hips, always my figure concern. I stepped out of the fitting room in my stocking feet to have a look in the larger mirror. The person I had heard moving about in the cubicle next to mine stepped out at that moment, too. We politely shared the mirror, I gauging the shoulders of the green suit, she turning to check the swing of a long black rayon skirt. Then, uncomfortably, I recognized her as Marjorie's shopper friend Beatrice and wondered what to say. I was standing aside, noticing her height, strong forearms, large feet, when I had a shock: the person in the black skirt was unmistakably Quilliam DeForest. He glanced up in the mirror, and, meeting my eyes, a smile froze on his red lips. We hedged, silently staring, he at my big auburn wig and expensive suit; I at his craggy face overlaid with pancake makeup, neither wanting to give ourselves away for sure. After a bad pause, we scuttled back into our respective changing rooms. There, ringing hangers, heart overbeating, I gave him a chance to clear out first.

I emerged, at last, flustered. I had heard of men doing such things, and it wasn't really illegal, but seemed such a peculiar occupation for his time. Poor Marjorie, who must have known. It must have depressed her, to have a husband who looked better as a woman than she did. I trusted they kept all this from the twins, but my imagination balked at unpleasant ponderings on the more personal aspects of the arrangement.

Needing to dawdle, I let the saleslady talk me into a cream-colored silk blouse with tiny pleats down the front. Spending money for beautiful things had a way of calming my nerves. I even bought a broad-brimmed cream-colored straw hat, of all things, for a "total look," as the able saleslady described it. I smiled privately as I adjusted the hat over my wig. Would Jackson Pancake make the Harryish joke of saying I looked totaled in the outfit? Somehow I felt he would talk that way—direct, unsentimental, ex-navy. Well, I consoled myself, at least I had a Jackson Pancake for my new persona; he would be coming in six days' time, and

I'd wear a slimming green suit for him. Mrs. Carter would not let her end down.

Wearing suit, blouse, and hat, I carried my old clothes in the bag along with the mahjongg set and the Turkish delight. Glimpses of myself in the mirrored posts astonished me and renewed my confidence. I had to admit that Quilliam's other self was alluring and attractive, if overly made up, but I looked like the kind of person who would raise money and sound authoritative about some cause when interviewed by Inez Parsons-Mueller on channel ten. It occurred to me: perhaps I was such a one, my cause being the reunification of Persephone and her mother. I smiled, considering what a feat, to restore Spring to the withered earth.

When I stepped into the van, I felt as charged as any Berlin airlift reporter. The driver must have noticed; he whistled! An attractive man, with strong hands and gray hair, he returned a smile that I read with surprised comprehension, like a dead language from a planet where I once had lived.

Looking out at the scenery I felt, though, too, how shrunken I was inside my crisp new clothes. As I waited and watched the other old bodies helped into the van, I thought: awful lot of people dying at Sunset. Old people always died first. The director seemed more interested in preserving life beyond natural limits. He wanted geriatrics, not corpses. He almost encouraged one to be feeble, as though we might leave if we felt too spry. And bad health was contagious. Once one person on a floor caught poor circulation, everybody had it within the week. Someone discovered a heart murmur and everyone was in to see the cardiologist. Lead poisoning in our youths became a favorite theme, a way to explain our mind's wanderings. We checked our toothbrushes for dampness to know if we'd brushed or not. But I think my mind wandered even when I was young. In fact, I'm sure I was less alert in those days. Had things improved with age? What was I doing, I wondered, at the front of the van on that May day, my hat blocking everyone's view and constraining the movement of my head as it scraped the window and seatback?

The van had some trouble getting through the cars all leaving the mall at the same time, and as we waited, nudging along, I watched the people going in and out of the hardware store at the end of the row of shops. People were choosing watering cans and inspecting the impatiens and petunias for sale in peat pots all lined up on the walk outside. I watched one couple maneuvering long thin boards through the double doors.

"They staking giant tomatoes, you think?" said the old lady behind me, a churchgoer I recognized, also observing them.

"Building something?" I suggested. They struck me as gardening types, the man, youngish and rough and ready in worn blue jeans and work shoes, the woman carrying the planks on hefty shoulders.

"You think that's her son, or what?" said the old lady's voice in my ear now as she scooted forward. "Wish I had that girl's muscle!"

I caught back my breath and clutched the window's edge to steady myself. That girl was Marjorie. There she was, heaving two-by-fours into the back of that stranger's pickup truck parked close to the doors, swinging around heavy construction material as if she were not fifty-one years old, for goodness sake, and trying to keep a young husband. I was creating my speech when to my surprise she stepped into the man's cream-colored, mud-spattered truck, got right in on the passenger side. The young man, with a flush of hormones spotting his chin, looked up at our van as we passed, waiting to get clear into the exit lane. I sat there as we moved by, leaving my daughter to her chosen fate, trying hard to understand what was happening. I felt breathy with distress: my daughter trafficking with builders and not a thing I could do to stop it, being now disappeared.

Dead Letters

⋘⊗⋙

MY MAILMAN'S IMMINENT arrival threw me into a moderate, not unpleasant, tailspin. I kept imagining conversations with him. Why did he mean so much even then — a stranger, an American? I was lonely. More, I was looking for anything as a guide through my thicket of deceptions. My quest for a daughter had been foiled at every turning, it seemed, leaving me as downhearted as a beached whale. Departure always looked like a good option, which explains, I suppose, why a mailman with an airplane seemed to hold out promise.

I kept back from telling Evangeline; Terry Carter was going to hoard her gentleman caller, and until he arrived I was counting the days and dusting. Meanwhile my other notes cast out in search of Evangeline's daughter were reeling in replies. On Thursday I received a dispiriting letter, typed on a balky machine:

> *Dear Mrs. Carter:*
> *My wife left us fourteen years ago in August. Friends tell me it*
> *may have been the heat. I have no forwarding address, and she is*
> *not the one you want, anyway. She was not a happy person, walked*
> *around the house most nights. She qualified to teach math, so I*
> *guess that's what she's doing. Roger, our son, sells real estate in*
> *Bathurst. Stop by if ever you're in N.B. There's room.*
>
> *C. Samuelson*

I felt in some ways I'd opened a dead-letter office. There in the lobby I sat down to study three snapshots that fell out. The first was a school picture of a young man with a faint moustache, squinting seriously for the camera. Roger? The second was a young couple—he in his forties, she in her early twenties—standing on the steps of a brick building. The picture dated from the fifties, I guessed, from the pageboy cut of the woman's hair, not unlike my own in those days. She was short, dark, not plain, but practical faced, clothes serviceable. The stoop-shouldered man stood properly beside her, holding a bottle of milk. Just visible in the shadow of a bush was a baby in rompers, not smiling, pulling at grass, starting his real-estate career early. Happy was not the word for this family. A small corner of my being applauded the wife's desertion as I stuck pictures and letter into my handbag, and then I just felt depressed for us all.

Evangeline put down an INS booklet when she saw me and smoothed the coverlet, ready for a game. "*P'ung!* I'll get your dragon this time!" She spoke almost without slurring now.

"We'll see about that," I said. I unwrapped a piece of Turkish delight for help. "You just wait." Always gaming, Evangeline and I never risked roles.

Evangeline drew her face into an acute stare. "What is that jacket you're wearing?" she asked. "*Très orientale.* Have you gone bush?"

It was one of her own, but I was spared answering by the entrance of a nurse whose burnt smell gave away that she'd just smoked up a storm on break. She was new to me, walked like a man, and evidently was not paid enough to include a smile with her announcement, "Visitor."

"Hell," said Evangeline, "and I was just about to ask you to get me to the ladies'. Who is it?"

The nurse checked a slip of paper in her hand as she lumbered out. "Margaret."

"But if you wouldn't mind first... the old water works are a bit..."

I shot up from my chair. "Marjorie!"

"Oh, yes. She's bringing me biographies of the founding fathers. I have to learn all that for citizenship."

"What'll I do?"

Evangeline's good eyebrow edged up an uneasy fraction. We stared at each other for a moment, then Evangeline glanced toward the closet. Without stopping to gather the mahjongg tiles, I turned the door handle, pushed back the clothes, and stepped in. I pulled the door as tightly closed as I could. The air inside was for storage, not human breathing, and I found barely enough space to perch on a humidifier. I hoped Marjorie would not want to hang up whatever table linen she was sporting.

Pushing between Evangeline's negligees, which clung like cobwebs to my face, I could hear my daughter's horse laugh as she spoke to the nurse down the hall, then recognized the flopping tread of rubber boots. "Evangeline?" She sounded startlingly young.

Mrs. Ypsilanti made a throat-clearing of welcome. "Orchids. What beauts."

"Showy lady's slipper. Dave and I have transplanted some from the river to the greenhouse, to try to replenish the natural supply."

"The old greenhouse effect," quipped Evangeline. I could have done as well, I considered.

My daughter laughed pleasantly. "They are saying now that the greenhouse effect may actually have some positive consequences. And if our region turns into a tropical haven for orchids, they won't hear any complaints from me."

"Did you get the books?"

"Evangeline, I remembered them at a stoplight coming here. The red reminded me there was something. Oh, mahjongg. Mother used to play this. We're all winds, aren't we? Blowing, shifting directions." Big sigh from Marjorie. "We haven't heard a word from her."

Click of ivory on ivory. I tried to calm my pulse enough to hear the talk. I considered that Quilliam would probably not mention his dress-shop sighting of me.

"Quill says we upset her. He says she still lives in a world that never was."

Evangeline spoke thoughtfully. "She reminds me of that elderly person who flew in an airplane for the first time and, when he got out, claimed he'd never put his full weight down."

Marjorie took this nonsense seriously. "Mother never put her full weight down. I think you're right. I don't think she ever considered Conflux or our life here, the twins, or Quilliam very real. She sort of levitated around the house like a spirit, never landing."

They both laughed quietly, at my expense. Then Marjorie said, "Evangeline, what does an elderly person want?"

"Scandal, but that's me."

Marjorie's voice had a smile when she answered, "You know we tried to get her interested in watching soap operas. Quill loves them. But she's too moral. She said, 'Those people just stand around looking depressed and talking about each other behind their backs.'"

Evangeline added, "Listening at keyholes must have appalled her."

Marjorie laughed lightly, as I sat mortified among the negligees.

"Mother has denied herself all her life. I thought that Nature would bring her out. Whenever I need to think through a problem, I go potting, and somehow as my mind spins, answers just seem to build up into a shape. Do you have a hobby like that?"

"Nature is not for her creed. I don't really think your mother believes in anything."

"Hand towels," my daughter said. "Meal times, a cheerful manner. We failed her. She doesn't worry about God, but she does believe in Emily Post."

"She seems to have believed in your father," Evangeline said, always ready to steer the conversation toward romance.

"He was an idealist, far-sighted, one of the truly great of his generation. Mother said *no* to him, too, of course."

I stiffened during the uncomfortable pause that followed and tried to forgive my daughter, so engrossed with her inner life, who rarely paid her exterior enough notice to comb her hair.

"I was under the impression," said Evangeline in a protected way that told me she was miffed by my deceptions, "I had somehow understood that your parents were together till the bitter end."

"They were together right *at* the end. They had separated in Berlin. I suppose art was his last chance at utopia. He was obsessed with the work of an architect named van der Rohe . . ."

"Mies?!" Whinny from my friend. "Lovely style."

"You like those glass walls?"

"I meant his kissing. As a man, authoritarian — bullheaded and mole-blind."

"Where, exactly, did you . . . meet . . . Mies?"

"Ah! Hmm. The answer to that will no doubt swing around the curve in just a minute, but we'll have to wait till it does. So they had a parting of principles. How luxuriously moral."

"Unlike Mother, I am good at falling in love with the wrong people. Or, maybe *like* Mother . . . I never thought of that."

I squinted hard through the crack. Evangeline was sitting up, looking at the wall with her bifocals. She started a story by way of reply. "In Athens, before the war, right after my first divorce, I met a young man from Cyprus. Dmitris was working for a shipbuilder. I'd meet after work. We used to argue politics back and forth, sometimes till three in the morning. I found him more fascinating than anyone I'd ever known, the only man I ever really respected—but he was married."

"They always are."

"Unhappily married, being better educated than his wife. Anyway, a woman spotted Dmitris and me one evening at a café and sat down. He didn't blink, just went on talking, ignoring her. 'Who's this?' I asked finally. 'Toula,' he said and paid her no more attention. I wasn't jealous, seeing how he ignored her. She just leaned her head on her arm and watched me. When he got up for cigarettes, she gave a sad smile and said, 'You're in love with him, aren't you?' 'It's mutual,' I told her. We started talking—of this and that. I quickly came to see that she knew nothing of politics, didn't read poetry, hadn't even been to high school. In short, she was completely unspoiled by other people's opinions. She wanted to walk. When Dmitris came back with his cigarettes, he found an empty table.

"Toula and I saw each other every day for a week. Dmitris was sputtering with jealousy. 'What's the big problem?' I teased. 'I just like your friend.' 'She's not my friend,' he snapped. But I didn't have time for him because I wanted to be with her instead. I found an elasticity in her reactions to life that enchanted me—no ranting, no anger, just a village wisdom that looked struggles straight and somehow continued, despite. We tried shopping together but hardly bought anything, we were so busy talking across the produce. Toula never wanted to go home. I asked her once about love, and she told me, quite simply, that she was married—it had been arranged—and her husband got distracted easily. I read: other women. Still, she believed in him, she said; she believed in marriage and knew she must stay with him even if he didn't love her. 'The rat,' I said. I was moved by her loyalty. I had never liked women very much, but for Toula I wanted happiness. And her situation gave me qualms about Dmitris's wife. When Dmitris came by, revving his little motorcycle's petrol engine outside my window, I put him on ice.

"Then, about a month later, I was in his district and on a whim thought I'd drop by. I thought, if his wife answers, I'll say I rang the wrong doorbell, that's all. She wouldn't know me and would be none the wiser." Evangeline paused a minute before continuing. "Who do you think opened the door? You've guessed, of course. Toula, with a cigarette, reading a circular from the church. I was stunned, then the pieces fell into place like a combination lock. We stared at each other. She tried but couldn't smile. Sad and calm and maybe a little sly, too, she stood there sucking in smoke. I don't know why she seemed like some version of myself, but she did."

I could hear Marjorie stacking ivory tiles.

"Soon after they returned to Cyprus. She died of cancer in 'sixty-four." Evangeline coughed slightly. "I've lost the point of that story. Except to say that if something works, it's right. I once had a friend. You may not think that possible."

My daughter made a comforting murmur. I could tell that like me, she was caught off guard by all this. "Of course you had a friend," she said. "Why would I doubt that?"

"I don't always treat people as I should, Marjorie. I'm selfish, and vain, and want the limelight all to myself." A smile lightened her voice. "Don't call a priest. I'm not dying. Today I wanted to confess to you."

"I absolve you," said my daughter solemnly. "Of course you are forgiven."

In the quiet, I held back angry tears, at Evangeline and my daughter for undertaking such earnestness between themselves. I would have liked some forgiveness, yet here I was, stuffed away in a closet, bearing awful witness as someone usurped my rights.

Some shuffling sounds and Marjorie's multicolored T-shirt passed inches in front of my nose. Evangeline asked in a smallish voice, "That little button on the left. Push it, please." A mechanical grinding raked over the conversation. "Thank you. It cheers an old woman up to have a visit. When one's children are so far away . . ."

"But your daughter will come soon, won't she?" Marjorie paused. "I wish . . ."

"I *am* fortunate. Of course, your mother is also lucky to have you close at hand."

"That's why she went off to Walla! Well, I'm glad she's done something so self-caring." There was the sound of someone near the closet. My sudden shift of alarm at discovery set off a dance of hangers, but Marjorie didn't hear the ringing. Almost out of the room, her sad, tired voice haunted me afterward as she stopped and reflected, "This time of day takes me back to my childhood, when we were all together in Berlin." I could hear Evangeline yawn again, but I had my ear against the door. "I would be going to sleep, listening to my father playing his harpsichord, while my mother in the back of the apartment threw pots around, resigned to getting a meal together. All I had to do was wait."

Inside the closet, I sagged, hearing my daughter remember what I myself had so long ago forgotten. She made them sound almost happy in a way that saddened me to the core. I wondered at my own tough resolve then: had it all been, in Evangeline's words, just mole-blindness? I knew what it was for Marjorie to sit out her escape, like the negligee waiting dutifully on its hook.

New sympathy for my daughter felt like a bruise that ached when I was reminded—by Evangeline, by my now unending weekends—that I was completely on my own. This changed with the landing of my pen pal, Mr. Pancake, retired of the U. S. Postal Service, on Sunday in his little plane.

"I want details," Evangeline said, sitting up when I walked in on Monday. "What's going on?"

Terry Carter was a methodical, feminine sort of person. She settled carefully on the plastic chair and crossed her legs. "How do you mean?" she asked.

"Your mouth isn't quite its normal line of the equator. Is that a new lipstick? Something's up. Good-looking? Rich?"

I couldn't get away with it, evidently. Glad suddenly to talk, I admitted, "Handsome in a conservative way. Sears," I added with my new mall experience. "Tall. Government pension. The best kind of American. Honest, soft-spoken. He could almost be Canadian."

"Shame."

"His name is German, he told me. The funny thing is," I said, then paused. "He knows Wallawalhalla."

"Does he know you're there now?"

I felt myself steam up. "I'm not really deceiving him. I'm under an alias. And my alias has the same past as me. More or less. Walla in the twenties. Far East, Germany. There's no deception!"

"What did you do with him?"

"He came over around four. It was cool enough to go outside, so mostly we walked around the grounds. He liked the plantings. He said that spiky thing out front is called Spanish bayonet. And he told me about his little plane—he's just bought it—and I talked about myself a bit. Then we had dinner in the cafeteria. Spaghetti and beets and peach cobbler, which he liked—we had to dodge Frank Thwaite—and then he went into town. He's staying with the nephew of his godson, or something." I didn't tell her that I'd explained about my search for Persephone, that Evangeline in a strange way had brought Jackson Pancake and me together. Apart from my pact with myself to keep her in the dark for her own sake about my hunt for her daughter, I didn't want to give her the satisfaction of playing matchmaker, nor convey the certainty I felt already that Jackson was on more than a milk run in Conflux.

Though I had fretted like a cat waiting for him in the lobby, wondering what to do to entertain my first date in maybe forty years, I relaxed within minutes of meeting him. He strode into the lobby and greeted me with a smile of quiet respect. Something so sincere and kind in his manner, so trustworthy, set me immediately at ease; I felt at last I had found a compatriot, someone who held the same principles that I did. It was a feeling I sometimes had with Harry, though our history made it edgy. Mr. Pancake, knowing only the best of Terry Carter, smoothed a way for us as easy as the yellow brick road.

I had worn my "Terry Carter: Capable Older Lady" disguise and carried it off with more aplomb than I'd thought possible. I had Terry herself to thank; she gave me the confidence. Jackson looked as he'd described, like someone in a toupee but tall and handsome nonetheless, walking gamely around the property in giant-sized Adidas, large hands rubbing leaves as we talked. "Mrs. Carter," he called me in his mountain voice. "Mr. Pancake," I said, without a smile, like a seasoned diplomat. In my new green suit and fake hair, I'd felt just fine. And for his part, Mr. Pancake had seemed perfectly at ease, with a spark of wit I'd not expected from so honest a demeanor.

Walla came up quite unexpectedly. We were standing in front of Sunset, watching a Carolina wren branch-hopping in the pine tree, and I just casually said, "When you see birds in the air, they do seem to be swimming, and the whole theory of Lemuria almost makes sense." He hadn't heard about Lemuria, the reversal of land and water, so I explained it, adding, just for the sake of conversation, "I heard that from an odd lady on an island called Wallawalhalla. I bet you couldn't find that on a map."

"Walla!" He turned to me with an astonished grin. "When were you on Walla?"

"When were *you* on Walla?" I countered.

It was like finding out that we were cousins. We almost embraced with our enthusiasm, which is strange, given my own peculiar and terrible history on that island, but the past can touch itself up, it seems, when it's all you've got. It turned out he'd been out much later than I had, during the Second World War. "It's a volcanic mountain," he said. "I wish I'd seen it pre-eruption. My mother's cousin once spent a summer out there. In nineteen-twenty or so."

"Who?" I whispered, my breath stopping. "What was her name?"

"Victoria Sayles."

I scanned my memory but came up blank.

"She was working as a nanny. Didn't last long, apparently. Dreadful little boy kept putting crabs in her bed. When they made her go to Scotland, she fell apart."

"The nanny! Quincy Kinvers's nanny?!" That gaunt, put-upon woman had had a name—erased from my mind utterly—and obviously had also had a life after her breakdown in Aberdeen, for here, so many years later, stood her tall, aging nephew. Despite myself, I felt my face crumble, my knees loosen at the bolts. "How about that," I blubbered. Mr. Pancake's eyes shifted in sympathetic confusion. We reached together for each other's hand. "I'll be all right," I whispered. "Really, it's just such a surprise."

"Walla," yawned Evangeline and opened her eyes. She was feeling for her American history books, but I wanted to say one more thing before she cut me off: "He's the best kind of person. Open-minded but nobody's fool." I smiled as I remembered, "He carries an embroidery bag with him and did some stitches while we talked. It was a reproduction of a Williamsburg sampler, on a hoop. He knows all about the history of stitchery."

"That's nice," she said, then tried to cover up her boredom by adding, "You seem happy."

I couldn't stop myself. "He says now that we've met, he might stay in Conflux all summer."

Evangeline peered at me. "To finish his sampler."

I reached for one of her books. "Where do you want to begin," I asked, "presidents or battles?"

"Battles. Gunfire always perks me up."

We rehearsed Valley Forge and I forced myself to think about something besides Jackson. I felt at odds with myself, proud and guilty at once. Catching a whiff of how it worked to change one's persona, Evangeline's sudden evangelical turn toward American democracy threw me into gyrations of conflicted admiration. Become a citizen and sponsor your daughter over to take care of you. Her approach seemed so casual, yet brilliant—an answer to her problems when no one else could solve them, but disturbingly deceptive, as bad as marrying for a green card. To reconcile myself, I tried to remember that her citizenship was also a self-deception, there being no known Persephone on the scene. Did that little detail make her crime less offensive?

Terry Carter, as a deception, took on a stronger presence every day. Looking starchier than the usual Viola in new clothes, younger with full hair, I felt as much at sea suddenly, as full of risk and promise and lost compass points as when I was twenty and newly wed to Harry. And something of the same sense of being under suspicion. For me there had always been at the base of our understanding and respect a niggling worry: did he or did he not understand what I had done on Walla? Being Terry brought back the taste of those times: silence and fear of discovery.

When I just needed to think about my own problems, other people's distress kept arriving by mail. Some were repeats, like C. Samuelson's:

My dear Mrs. Carter,
Your kind words of encouragement did me good. The offer of hospitality still holds, but you'll have to decide soon, as my son is bringing his new wife for a week in August. Hoping to have tomatoes by then,
Sincerely,
Cedric Samuelson

Some were new:

Dear Mrs. Carter,
You can't find anyone this way. And I'm not it. Give up. Maybe she won't want to be found. Thought of that? Maybe she is Dead.

E. Samuelson, Vancouver

Dear Mrs. Carter,
You're doing a fine thing, hope you find your Missing Person. Wish I were "The One" but I'm not, being Ninety-Six and Bedridden, no one to help me even with getting my Medicine except the Milk and the Postman Mr. Teasdale "bless him"— he "looks in" Once a week when he Brings my Cheque. "Sonny" died last winter, aged seventy-one, from heart.

Wishing you "Good Luck,"
(Mrs.) Esther Samuelson,
46 Milton's End, Halifax, Nova Scotia

Madam:
We regret we are not them. We lost our only boy Lem, aged fourteen, last January, through the ice. Body never recovered. But it has to be somewhere, right?
Sincerely,
T.H. Samuelson Family, The Ridge, Fredricksburg

They filled my mailbox and occupied my thoughts, those replies from wrong Persephones. I cried over them, from sorrow that I had no answer for them but my own regret, and something like guilt at having bothered them with extraneous worries. I was surprised at the candor of those replies. I kept the correspondence in Miss Bartram's family tea caddie, one of the things I'd brought down with me to Conflux. And in the midst of my own busy inquiries, I felt all the more spurred on not to let Evangeline slip away without a reunion with her only child. I had kept H.'s death all to myself; had I mistaken bravery for selfishness? Even Marjorie's grief then had struck me as strange.

Like Dante, I was beginning to see how death had come to so many. I was getting to know so much about people, merely by stating my problem. It astounded me. Canadians—writing so intimately to a stranger. I could hardly believe it, and the critic inside called them foolish, yet their stories touched me all the same and I worried for them. How could I throw away these notes? *Think globally, act locally* was one of the many tattered commands keeping the bumper glued onto Marjorie's car; perhaps I should stick it to Mrs. Carter's bumper, too, I considered. I started writing back. Terry Carter was a woman of compassion.

> *Dear Mrs. Samuelson, This is just to hope that all continues as well as possible with you. Count yourself fortunate to be on your own, still. I gave up my independence and have not enjoyed it. I'm very sorry about your son.*
>
> *Yours sincerely,*
> *T. Carter*

To the Samuelsons of The Ridge, I fretted long over my reply. I, too, had once fallen through the ice. My body had been recovered, but other things lost. I knew what it was to live for a moment on the dark side of the mirror. I doodled on the edge of writing paper too heavy and expensive to waste in scrappy thoughts. But I could not get started, thinking back always as soon as I'd dipped the pen into the ink Evangeline still affected to use, of the chill wind that had frozen me as I surfaced into the air, of the scowling, thankless silence I had kept at my rescue, my mind's eye shadowed for days and weeks after with the vision I'd had of a tranquil kingdom under the ice. I wrote to the Samuelsons:

*Death is a terrible thing, but a drowning death may be imagined
as something like sleep, into which the soul escapes to peace. Life's
path is always toward invisibility; our bodies are never recovered.*

Reading this over, I was struck by Terry's style, which was both
more direct and wiser than my own. She appeared more an agent than a
force unto herself. To be like that in real life seemed a worthy goal
among others I was amassing. I hopped over to the mirror and checked
my face: which did I more resemble, the wrinkled visage I couldn't see
on this side or that smooth, matronly face watching politely behind the
looking glass?

When the coast was clear, I visited Evangeline. We built up the
pieces to form the wall for mahjongg and sucked on Turkish delight given
me in a silver box by Jackson Pancake. By coincidence he liked it, too.

Evangeline pried a finger around a tooth. "Bloody Turks," she mut-
tered. "Revenge for the Big Idea of nineteen twenty-two!"

I reminded myself to be patient. "What are you talking about now?"

"Asia Minor catastrophe. We wanted only to have back what was
ours. And they came by droves, those people dancing like dervishes and
claiming to be Greeks!"

"Hmm," was all I could manage, bewildered by all this old news. I
thought back to 1922; I had spent a lot of time playing croquet with
Harry among sheep in the Hebrides, only dimly aware of the crisis in
Greece. My thoughts had been on beating my husband who was taking
undue pride in his swing.

Evangeline's cheeks worked up and down on the candy as she continued, "Gounaris, Protopapadakis, Baltazzis . . . At the trial Venizelos
was let go. You think they were traitors? No!" Some ivory pieces slipped
off the wall.

"Well," I said. "Empires decline. That's history, isn't it?" Yet I wondered what made that so. Why didn't a good idea work forever for people the way it did for creatures in the wild? The answer seemed to be a
problem of parts and the whole. To ants, for instance, individuals were
just parts. "But people want what they want before they die, don't they?"
I asked my friend. "You want your daughter here. You want friends and
applause. And I want, well, the respect and recognition of *my* family. And

I want them to straighten out the mess they've made—and to see them do it in my lifetime. We want *happiness*, which of course is our right."

"Life, liberty, and the pursuit of," said my friend. "Breezy Enlightenment notions."

"But that's what you Greeks wanted, wasn't it, with the push into Asia Minor?" I could be as clever as she.

Evangeline was only half-listening, though. She laid her head back on the pillow. "The poems we read then the way you eat bread and jam. Who remembers?"

"That's another thing," I said gently, clearing my throat. I cast about for some distraction, noted complicated flowers in a pottery vase. "Has Marjorie been in?"

She was counting on her fingers. "Palamas. Cavafy. Sikelianos..." Eyes closed. "Ypsilanti . . ." She whispered so softly that I hardly heard the words. "All gone. All a dream. You find it now only in words, but you don't feel that it's true." She turned her head toward the flowers. "Sir Quilliam-of-the-Forest brought those. Your faithful Monsieur Crêpe stopped by with library books and *Le Monde*. Ha! I said to him, 'He's got the whole world in his hands,' but I don't think Mr. Pancake knows any French."

My mind was still on that summer long ago, and the mention of Jackson Pancake brought a sudden rush of sensations. That seemed the way my memory worked these days—in wholesale quantities of stuff I hadn't ordered. "Did you know," I asked my friend slowly, for speaking about it seemed unnatural, and I could only speak of it as if it had happened to some casual acquaintance, "did I ever mention that I'd lived through a volcanic eruption?"

Evangeline's eyes, trembling and dilated with some new medication, came to rest for a moment on my face. "Who did?"

"Me. Summer of nineteen twenty."

"I saw this already on television."

"I'm telling you *my* history!"

"Well?" She paused. "What happened?"

"It changed our lives, Harry's and mine. We started afresh and tried to believe we had no ties to our past."

"That's nice. What happened about the volcano?"

"Nothing. It just erupted." I was suddenly sorry for having brought it up at all, for Evangeline had already lost interest. She lay back and rubbed the red dragon with her thumb. "Clean up this mess," she said. "I have homework."

"We think too much of ourselves," I reproached her as I began to stack the blocks.

"And who's going to if we don't?" she cried. "Do you think anyone cares who you are?"

My heart felt tired of beating, as though mired in mud. "Then what's the point?"

"There is no point." She looked at me with amusement. "The battle lines are drawn from the start. We work off antagonism. Love is just another word for contempt—men and women, old and young, Greeks and Turks. Expect no favors from the ones in control. Just try to work the system to your own advantage."

Confusion swept over my thoughts. I sputtered, "But you married for love, surely. You loved your husband and your daughter."

"It's better when you don't, you know. Better to be the beloved, that's the trick. Fewer bruises. Pick your man to see you forward. Men are so *predictable*. Show them a pink sunset and they decide, 'Sunsets are pink.' They have to project certainties on everything. Women flow. They don't generalize or theorize or categorize or make grand hypotheses; they just notice and flow. But," she added, pausing to appraise me, "you had a truce in your marriage battle."

I looked down at the bleak gray tiles of the floor, scuffed and dusty. "I did." The delivery truck had just dumped a load in my yard. I remembered Harry with sharp emptiness. No one ever again would dare tease me about my feet. No one ever again would assume I'd nurse him in his final days. No one ever again would kiss me on a trill. Nothing more would happen to or be asked of me. I had never found my mother; I would never recover my daughter. I could only offend my own kin, never advise or console. What was it all for, staying alive now? Just a habit? I reached for the flowers and sniffed.

"They have no scent," said Evangeline.

"Pretty, though," I apologized, straightening the vase.

"From the new greenhouse project. I like Quilliam's long finger-nails, don't you?" My friend arched the eyebrow that still arched. I ignored her and took care fitting each bamboo and ivory rectangle into the box. "Marjorie and a curiosity called Miss Halliday came by earlier, as well. The twins had been camping, she told me, and had a close encounter with a black bear. But a ranger rescued them in time."

"Oh, good," I said, determined to mask my alarm. "Must water my plants now."

Hobbling along the hall, I felt like a table setting, still rattling after the cloth had been pulled out from under me by some unpleasant conjurer. My friend Evangeline in some ways had pulled such a trick; she'd taken over my family. Depressed, I gave up vanity so close to my room and took off my wig, which was heavy and itched.

As I waited, the elevator's doors opened on Jackson Pancake, screwing in the button panel with his Swiss Army knife. He folded the blade against his thigh and dropped it nicely into his pocket as, hiding the wig behind my back, I panted, "Providence! You're like a taxi, Jackson, when a person needs one."

He stepped out. "How sweet of you, and likewise," he said. His eyes traveled over my hair—which was my own flat, gray mop, I suddenly remembered—and my old blue suit. "Mrs. Carter, I presume?"

"Well," I said, touching my head, "that proves that you look at my face, not my hairdo."

"How about a Coke, Mrs. Carter?"

"I'll just spruce myself up. Come in for a moment, Mr. Pancake."

"Women are always doing that to me," he joked, waiting, looking at the photograph of Harry and me, the pot from Evangeline. "Changing into something less comfortable."

On our way to the snack bar, he said, "Didn't find you in. I've been playing chess with that gentleman history professor."

"Oh, we call him Sibelius."

He pulled at his ear and remarked, "Don't believe I'll ever get to Finland."

I laughed, the stiffness in my neck relaxing to his mild warmth. "You've been to Walla," I reminded him. "That's enough." How much easier it was to be with Jackson than with Evangeline. The power of helping could give you a private tune and a whole new attitude, though a counterpoint in a minor key played through, reminding me of the ugly views of my friend. She swept one into her emotional whirlwind—demanding, extracting, judging endlessly —while he, stolid old boy scout, gave quiet consideration to what he encountered, dismissed what he wished but all without fuss, without the intrusion of a bony and bruising self.

I wanted to discuss with Jackson my thoughts on Bee Happy, but when we had paid for our soft drinks and sat ourselves by a window in the lobby, he pulled out of a flight bag his Williamsburg sampler. He sat working an eagle in blue thread, lending such a veneer of calm to our encounter, I decided to keep my troubles to myself. It was Jackson who surprised me by asking, apropos of something in that morning's paper, "Did you ever hear about the murder on Walla?"

"Goodness," I said, churning my straw hard in the ice.

"My aunt told me about it. A man called Roderick Borders. Got himself pushed off a cliff. Though the jury's still out."

My hand paused in its churning. I couldn't find a place to look or an expression to hide the dread that felt like something oozing from my pores. My lungs took some extra little breaths before I managed, "What is all this about?"

"It was during your time there, before the eruption?"

His trusting baby blues were trained on me with all their acetylene power. I noted his face lengthen as his jaw slowly dropped. "Don't cry," he whispered. He pulled a soft folded handkerchief from his hip pocket. "Don't cry about it now. Did you know the Borderses? I apologize, Mrs. Carter. Whatever..."

"Jackson," I said. "I'm as much a fool now as I was when I was young." The dam was about to burst. I folded the handkerchief back up, smoothing down each crease. "I want to tell you," I began. Then I stopped short. He waited for a long minute, then pulled a thread through the cloth. Fear locked my jaw and I sat on. I finally managed, "Have you been up in your plane?"

"They're building a student union at the college," said Jackson, darting toward this new topic with rare animation, like a rabbit running scared. Soon he had me smiling again, inanely, just from sheer relief, at the details of goings-on, as seen from the air. It felt unreal, though, like a double exposure, to be sitting over a Coke at Sunset, talking about Conflux, when the Walla past kept breaking over me in cold waves.

Greenhouse Effect

S TILL ELUDING MY FAMILY, bearing resentment, pinning my hopes on Persephone since I could not reach my own child, I was getting letters from people who seemed like acquaintances by now. So many old people out there! Looking for spring, I encountered perpetual freeze.

> *Ms. Carter: People don't want to be found, thought of that? Do something for your community if you need a hobby, visit old people, read to the blind, march against the greenhouse effect— we're all going to disappear through that hole in the ozone one of these days. Stop wasting paper on this search. You are not the center of the universe. Considered counseling, for yourself I mean?*
>
> D. Samuelson, Montreal

> *Mrs. Carter:*
> *Wrong party. My wife's family comes from Balmoral, by the way. Can you take a half-Siamese kitten, eight weeks old? Tabby got into the bloodline, very good-natured. Could box and ship.*
>
> A J. E. Samuelson, Red Deer

Such was my mail the next morning, the first of July, a sunny day in Conflux that marked the anniversary of that fateful Walla picnic when Harry should have proposed, except that a body washed up. The first note left me, frankly, a little shaky. Was I selfish in my quest? I'd thought of it as altruism. Maybe disappearing was what Persephone had wanted—as I had, at Sunset. I filed it in my tea caddy. The second, a sunset postcard, I stuck in the edge of my mirror and admired the sandy beach. I thought about the kitten. Any home-seeking creature distressed me; I'd come that route myself and never forgotten what it meant to need protection. But a cat had too long a life expectancy for me, past eighty.

The quality of mercy is not strained, and on that summer day in the Sunset Home, filing away my notes from strangers, all caught up in their lives' hardships and wrong decisions, in a search I somehow knew was futile, on what might have been something of an anniversary had I not joined the band of underpaid, stigmatized single mothers, had H. not died one spring previous, I might have been able to forgive myself my unspent life. But mercy, like most things in my life, was coming too late to matter. The timing was off.

I pulled on a new extra-strength girdle and best green suit, though, and went to see my friend. She was sitting up in bed looking alert and ready for the world. "Two phone calls for *you*, Mrs. Carter, here in *my* room!" she cried. "Am I become an answering service in my dotage?"

"Who from?"

"Someone in Nova Scotia."

I started and swallowed hard. "How odd."

She continued, "I expect he'll phone back. You were not in your room."

"Having coffee."

"Ah, Jackson. Decaf, of course. You like a solid citizen."

"As opposed to a fraudulent one."

"Ah! An arrow has pierced my heart!"

Despite myself, she made me smile. I sat, ready for our game. "Where's the board? Where are the pieces?"

"Oh. I think I gave it to Howard, for their wedding. What a shame. I don't know what got into me. I liked those dragons."

I made no comment and did not really mind. Let Howard and Debi enjoy it. There was no use hanging on to things after eighty.

We played cards instead: Old Maid, a game from my childhood that I lost easily, being on edge. I couldn't help noticing that Evangeline's night table and bureau were transformed into a hothouse for my daughter's new hybrid orchids and the great lopsided things she threw on her wheel. "What are those things? Spittoons or chamber pots for bedridden elephants?"

"Don't be snide."

"I'm not snide." I was envious. Where were my tokens of homage?

Day by day Evangeline's color had slowly returned and her speech was clearer, though she had lost her hold on languages. She slipped and slid, unable to stay on any one given grammar. The therapist insisted she get out of bed every day. She leaned on Terry Carter's competent-looking arm for a slow stroll down to the vending machines and back again. "It's my little penance," she explained to me, tucking her tiny aqua-veined feet back under the sheet. "Now I can relax again. I've always done my best work in bed." With an INS brochure at her side her mood was high. "The examiners are coming down tomorrow," she confided.

I was caught by surprise. "Tomorrow?"

"Yes. They sounded so pleased on the phone. They said, 'Yes ma'am, we'll make you a citizen!' I'm the oldest person ever to do that in this state, they said. I may get some coverage."

"Insurance?"

"Media. Their office is closed on the Fourth of July, but they're timing my conversion for Labor Day."

"You mean Independence Day."

"Whatever."

Dealing another hand, careful to keep my cards close to my chest, I said, "Little do they know."

"Know what?"

"Well, you'd hardly be accused of patriotism."

Evangeline, not listening, interrupted. "They're going to send a reporter down to interview—maybe Inez Parsons-Mueller from channel ten, the one who always wears a scarf. She's covering a tracheotomy, I believe. Probably choked on a fish bone. That happened to Britain's Queen Mother, you may remember." She looked at me hard over her glasses. "As for patriotism—I'm as patriotic as the next individual."

I shook my finger at her. "You just want to sponsor your daughter so you'll have someone waiting on you hand and foot. I truly believe you would become a Fiji Islander if it suited your interests."

"How jaded the idealist."

Her vehemence, and my own confused discretion, silenced me for a moment. My so-called idealism—what did it mean and where had it brought me? "After Walla," I began, not wanting to slip too much into revelations, "I grew up into a careful sort of person. I think I have lived beyond reproach, since that time."

"While, of course, remaining cheerful," she added, in an aside that hurt. I had always regarded dark moods as intolerable self-indulgence. When nursing Harry I prided myself on my heartening phrases, recognizing them as clichés, but then I have never been a sophisticated person. I cannot read a scene, strike a pose, seduce with a flash of a butane lighter, rebuff with a one-liner, hear an argument and know what is not being said. I plod and ponder and stick to the rules and miss most of what's under my nose, I suppose. And foolishly, preoccupied with supporting myself and daughter when we arrived in the United States, I seldom considered what I might truly think and feel, which is where Marjorie had room for complaint. But we of my generation were brought up to have control of ourselves, not to flash our mood rings, not to consult our biorhythms.

I pulled a jack from one of Evangeline's discards and, making a pair, said with a force that surprised me, "I don't think Marjorie should blame me for getting her out of Berlin before the war. Think of the alternative."

Evangeline held up her glasses to examine me.

"Harry," I explained. "Expedience was all; Art in and of itself justified the means. Those were his phrases." I considered for a moment. "There was Harry of the Past, whom I met on Walla, whom I married. In the eruption a cinder blinded his left eye. He had to have it out when we got to Scotland. An Edinburgh doctor replaced it with a glass one. He showed us several, like jewels in a velvet-lined case."

"Honey, this is a most *peculiar* tale . . ."

"We chose a slightly darker blue but a good match for the slight hint of irony around the pupil. Except Harry's views had undergone some changes, too. He turned into Harry of the Present. You know with one eye you lose your depth of vision."

Evangeline's own eyes were glazing over as so often happened when I talked about myself. "Views are always mutable," she remarked.

"They shouldn't be."

"'A foolish consistency is the hobgoblin of little minds.'"

"Expedience breeds contempt."

"All's well that end's well." My friend smiled like the Cheshire cat. "Oh, how nice to feel it coming back, my poor old mind—Swiss cheese. But *sharp* Swiss."

I wouldn't detour. "Where would we be without standards?"

"Flags, aren't they?" she mused, sorting through for some new quip, I imagined, but she seemed serious when she said, "Every little nation has its standard, fluttering in the breeze at the airport. You can choose whichever one you want at the ticket counter."

"No," I said. "You have to decide beforehand where you're going. And you have to buy the ticket and stick to your route." I continued, "Lastly there was Harry of the Future, who came to be looked after by me at the end of his life. Left his little Singapore mistress—well, she must have been in her sixties—and came back to old, stodgy Viola. By then he'd given up on what he called Art's redemptive powers. He was just plain self-absorbed, turned all inward, and even looked like a bathrobe someone had stepped out of too fast. He sat in a tiny chair with scrolled armrests in the living room, not comfortable, more like someone waiting for someone to arrive, and he listened to endless tones of gamelan and synthesizers. He burned candles and consulted minerals in the middle of the night."

"Yes, he always struck me as dull."

My friend chewed her cheek and looked over her hand as I sagged on the side of the bed. There seemed no point in arguing. The memories were hard enough to bear without trying to defend myself to a woman who survived by rules she made up as she played along. I drew another card that made a pair in my hands, laid it down, and tried to read through the backs of the two that trembled together in Evangeline's hand. My friend did not need to tell me what gray face stared out from her remaining card. I picked the Old Maid and shuffled it briskly into the pack.

She remarked, head down, "You never danced!"

"Because of that bullet."

"*Paithie mou*, I would have kicked him in the leg just to explode the damn thing!" She broke into a flashy laugh interrupted by the phone pipping by her bedside.

"Your daughter," said Evangeline, bending her cards.

"You can't just let it ring . . . !"

She closed her eyes. Panicky, I picked up the receiver and spoke in Southern. "Hello? Evangeline Ypsilanti's room."

"Mrs. Ypsilanti?" At first I didn't recognize the small voice.

"Uh, well . . ."

"Oh! Is that . . . Mrs. Carter?" My heart skipped a few beats. I was perspiring nervously with the notion that it might be Persephone on the line.

"Yes. Yes, it is. How may I help you?"

"My name is Jessica DeForest. My grandmother was friends with Mrs. Ypsilanti."

She waited. Of course Terry Carter always came through, with efficiency and a bad accent. "Jessica. I've heard so much about you. How is your family?" She seemed to buy the act. "Your mother?" I wondered if I should have said *mom*. "Greenhouse coming along? I'm a great friend of Mrs. Ypsilanti's, you know, and she talks about your grandmother . . ." Evangeline's accordion eyelids flickered open briefly. I patted her arm to silence her.

Pause from Jessica. "Did my grandmother die?"

My heart lurched. "Oh, no, not at all. She's not the type."

"My brother and I looked on a map, and we couldn't even find that island. I just wondered if Marjorie was covering up . . ."

I was about to tell her not to call her mother by her given name and to use the subjunctive when I caught a reflection of myself in the chrome headboard and had one of those Terry Carter moments of revelation. "Old age is the sloughing off of what is unnecessary until we finally slough off even ourselves. Your grandmother's gone into exile."

"Exile," Jessica repeated dreamily. "She seemed like someone from the twilight zone, walking around the house in black and white. She'd lived through so much."

"It's the nature of aging."

"I found a picture of my grandfather—kind of flat-faced, standing in the middle of a hole in the ground beside a yardstick, holding up a dead crocodile."

I remembered the shot, one on Roddy Borders's last developed roll.

"My mother said something happened out there," Jessica continued.

The walls seemed to be crowding in. I scanned Evangeline's face for help but she was dozing. "Did your mother . . . say what it was?"

"No. My mother says if my grandmother's guilty of anything it's for what she didn't do."

In a pause too long, trying to swallow, I felt my throat swell. "Meaning? What is it she didn't do?"

Her voice brightened unnaturally. "I'll call back. Thanks, Mrs. Carter. Hope your liposuction goes all right."

"*Liposuction?*" I gasped, but she had hung up. Evangeline's lips were curling even as her eyes stayed shut. I slumped on the bed, watching her breathe in and out of a mouth that had once spoken eight languages. It was alarming—all the things that got lost. I was fighting crosscurrents of emotion. It angered me to think of Jessica waiting to phone back, to fill her in, perhaps even to ask advice from Evangeline, who had no rights to my family. The phrase *sins of omission* suddenly bobbed up, while waves begun by Jackson's small queries tugged me down harder, dragging me toward the bottom of the sea. How had I ever let memory slip me a mickey, as they say in old movies, about Walla? I once heard a glib young man in the Sunset lobby say something to Howard about his father's "good old days that never were." My hackles rose at that phrase, but wasn't there also truth in it, necessary truth? Didn't we need to gloss over, ever to keep on? Can't you admire the electrical charge from polishing? Isn't that the secret of amber?

7

Back to Conflux

Back to Conflux

ROCKED BY THE SHOCK WAVES of these conversations, I found it hard to leave my lair. Terry Carter's indomitable spirit went AWOL. I sat around, wigless, in my bathrobe and twice ignored the ringing phone. I suspected it might be Jackson and somehow I felt too much was expected of me when next we met. I couldn't face him. I didn't go down to meals; I grilled cheese sandwiches in Evangeline's toaster oven.

A note found its way under my door Tuesday afternoon. I left it open on the table, where it took up space like a visitor waiting for a chat until I finally read it:

> *Dear Terry — may I?*
> *I have looked for you, for coffee or a Coke, but I can't ever find you in. I'm sorry if the reason is me. Was it what I said about the island mess? Since it was family history—my Aunt Victoria Sayle's employer's photographer—I really wanted to know. I am sorry if the story disturbed, as I would least like to cause you pain of anyone I know. I have been thinking about us. Are you ever going to come out? I'd like to fly you over to Hayfields House—for a picnic? I want to check some embroidery. It's not far. Think about it.*
>
> *Your friend, truly,*
> *Jackson M. Pancake*
>
> *P.S. Also, I have something to discuss with you, (not about the past) and you may guess what it is.*

I sat in silence by the window, looking out at the planes, while the letter lay there, waiting for my response. What he wanted to know about

Walla, what he wanted to discuss with me—perhaps in his mind these were not connected, but to me they inevitably were. I had happily become friends with Jackson. Terry Carter had given me the courage to advance step by step on the dance floor, with light swings and changes in direction that we accomplished with agility, I think, for persons of our years. I respected him for his discretion, duty, courtesy, an interest in others that seemed to go along with the vocation of delivering mail. I did not know many things, though, that a person would know before moving on to a two-step—must learn or risk an explosion.

And, I considered further, unsnagging my bathrobe sash from under the foot of the chair where it had got caught when I scooted closer to the window, Jackson, whether he realized or not, obviously felt there were things about me that needed some clearing up. There were. I didn't blame him—I just hid from him. What other choice did I have? Lie, and live a deception for the rest of my life? Tell the truth and lose him and all we had come to enjoy together—the small jokes, the shared memories, the life we seemed to authenticate in each other?

Sitting there at an impasse by the window, I found no revelations in the scenery, no sudden messages in the highway's cars or the planes that rose up at steep angles, glinting like slivers of mirror. I might have been stuck in my self-imposed time capsule had it not been for Howard's loudish knock at the door, and his insistent, "Ms. Carter, Ms. Carter."

"Who is it?" I called back, feigning confusion.

"Ms. Ypsilanti's about to do her citizenship. You coming?"

I'd forgotten. "Yes," I said. "Tell her I'll just be along, Howard."

I got myself together—wig, makeup, green linen suit—and felt stronger on the outside, anyway, though inside I was marshmallow soft. At the last minute I took my ambers from their box and fastened them on. They looked fine against my pea green blouse. They were serious beads, with a simplicity of purpose that made me feel all the more the silliness and triviality of much of my past weeks. I resolved to come clean.

I met Jackson at the doorway to Evangeline's room. He gave a shy nod, which I returned, likewise skittish as we walked in together. Evangeline was sitting on her bed, her tiny veined feet kicking over the edge. She was already dressed, except for knee-highs and shoes. I thought her choice of sequined sweater in red, white, and blue obvious to the point of mockery, but Evangeline was adamant.

"I want them to know they're dealing with a zealot," she declared, clipping on an enormous red earring. "Besides, it will show up well on the news." She explained to Jackson, "Channel ten is covering us, and the *Star*. Some of my polyglots promised to come root for me."

Mixed as I was about this conversion, meanness got the better of me. I said, "Then you'll have to wire Persephone. You can start the sponsoring process tomorrow." Of course, I regretted this remark at once.

Evangeline fumbled her watch around her wrist, trying to thread the strap through the buckle. "Yes," she said. "Absolutely. Call her back from the underworld."

Jackson looked over at me, pulling an ear, warning me, and I gave a nod that promised good behavior. Privately, I wondered how I would ever stop my correspondence with potential Persephones. I would miss it. What had begun as a purely altruistic task of reconnecting Evangeline and her lost daughter had grown into the strange pleasure of being confidante to the intimate sorrows of strangers. How could Terry Carter ever not respond to C. Samuelson's invitations, or T. H. Samuelson's anguish at his son's death, or Esther Samuelson's bedridden attempt at cheerfulness at ninety-one? Unwittingly, I had found myself moved by these letters. They had reminded me, disoriented as I was, of the need in this world for charity. I had not yet found Persephone, but I had rediscovered something of myself.

As Evangeline got her feet into her shoes, two young men in camouflage jackets tiptoed in, bearing bunches of red carnations. "Here come the dead languages," she gurgled. "Expecting a battle? Those are very pretty, those red things—what do you call them—flowers," she said. "Take a seat, dears. Latin, Coptic, don't loiter in the doorway. Howard! Nurse!" Latin nudged grinning Coptic into the room where they both pushed up against the wall, looking vibrant on our planet of old people.

Jackson pulled up a chair beside mine. "You all right, Mrs. Carter?"

"Fine, thank you. Please—Terry."

"Well, thank you." He sat and clasped his hands between his knees, foot bouncing. He cleared his throat. "Except rumor has it that you've been operating under a *nom de guerre*."

My heart skidded. I glanced hard at Evangeline, who was busy stroking some orange powder on her nose. "I can explain it," I said. I heard my stutter, my voice shift out of Suthren to my old Ontario clip and back again. "I meant no harm. I just childishly wanted to prove a point by leaving, and I found I couldn't. Terry Carter would never have done that. It was silly Viola's idea."

His eyes looked so hurt, I nearly started to cry. "I don't know how we can be friends after this. Will you ever forgive me?"

He hesitated. "I'm finding this very unusual. Viola. I considered Mrs. Carter..."

"I haven't committed mail fraud, have I?" I interrupted.

"I'm not sure. That's not the point."

"I always seem to do the wrong thing."

"Well," he said, tense but trying to smile. "I had my suspicions. For one, that accent sticks out fake a mile."

We chuffed once together. "Speaking of out," he said, "my Cessna's across the street." Before I could answer, he called over to Evangeline, "First president?"

She stuck a slim cigarette between her lips and accepted a light from Latin. "Booker T. Washington. He could throw a cherry pie across the Potomac. Oh, Howard, good, you brought the chair! Is he here yet, the INS man? Help me into this contraption. They wouldn't flunk a cripple, would they?"

Jackson turned to me softly. "We're the cheering division."

I accepted his hand pulling me upright, and thought how he always made me feel as if the world could be tamed. Through my mind played a song from Morcombe days: *Where e'er you walk, cool breeze shall fan the glade*... And yet I was still stirred up about Walla when I saw him, but decided that mention might dampen the mood. Lemuria made sense: some things were better kept down to give others a chance to rise up.

Thinking this, feeling myself on his team, I was pained to see Jackson bend low over Evangeline in her wheelchair. "Don't smudge me," she commanded. Sidelined, I thought, *He kissed the less dishonest one.*

I felt a little giddy with uncertainty as the elevator, with customary agitation and rumbling, sank us down to the lobby. Along the way

Howard explained the latest wedding snag: his mother-in-law-elect's allergy to gardenias. He seemed excited by the setback.

On her best behavior, as her chair bumped over some electrical cord, Evangeline pretended to listen, but her eyes were searching for the man from Immigration. I saw her spot him right off; too dressed up for Sunset in his dark blue suit, he was inspecting the undersides of things in an attaché case open like a TV dinner on his knees.

"God save the president," she called, with a lift of her better hand.

He had a bland, good-natured, red face, with the sort of expression you'd expect from the government. "Douglass," he said. His very blue eyes seemed not quite to focus as he stood and shook hands with us all.

Jackson and I sidled around the pair and took up seats in the lobby behind the plastic dieffenbachias. Mr. Douglass pulled a list from the case and gave a nod.

"Could you hold just a minute, Doug?" Evangeline asked and smiled coyly. "Channel ten is sending a camera crew. You don't mind."

It seemed Mr. Douglass did mind. He thrust his left arm out beyond his cuff and checked his watch. Three nurses and the dietician were gathered near the entrance to the lobby, eavesdropping.

"They just phoned," Evangeline persisted. "They'll be here in five minutes."

Mr. Douglass's eyebrows wiggled. I noticed Jackson's bent head, as he smoothed a crease in his trouser leg.

"All right," she gave in. "Shoot at me."

Mr. Douglass read the first question slowly off his note card. It was one we'd practiced over and over, but I could tell she was eyeing the entrance, not listening. "Why do we celebrate the Fourth of July . . ." she repeated. "The Fourth. That is the day of our treasured declaration, courtesy of Jeff Jackson. Jack Jefferson? Such neat handwriting . . ."

"That's fine," said Douglass. He really was a nice man. "President who freed the slaves?"

"Could you repeat that, Doug?"

Perspiration was beginning to glaze Mr. Douglass's chin. Jackson reached over and squeezed my hand, but I could feel my insides tying knots. To see her behave this way to officials, to know she had no belief in the things she said or the grace to suspect she should—it wasn't right.

It was all just a means to an end, prompted perhaps by jealousy at my having Marjorie close at hand. She had suddenly craved this lost daughter, must find her, must see her, must *sponsor* her, as if there were any good reason for Persephone to leave Canada. To this end, at eighty-two, she drew the personal attention of the whole Charlotte, North Carolina INS bureau, and here we sat listening to her declarations of loyalty, Persephone still at large. It struck me as very unworthy. It also made me want to spring-clean my own deceptions.

"Honest Abe," said Evangeline. "Tragic marriage. Too attached to his mother."

"It's not necessary to answer more than the question," Mr. Douglass advised.

An energetic slamming of doors and hard mechanical noise broke over us as channel ten pushed their equipment into the lobby.

"Light's bad," someone said to Mr. Douglass, and I recognized her at once: Inez Parsons-Mueller herself. She'd just had a baby boy and used cloth diapers instead of plastic ones, which were so harmful to the environment. We watched her all the time. It was thrilling to see her life-size and up close.

"Roll her by the doors," Inez told a cameraman with a ponytail. He swiveled Evangeline over to a domed trash can.

"Not the garbage," my friend started to object, but someone else wrapped the rigid fingers of her left hand around an American flag. She fluttered it like a duster.

"Break a leg!" Howard said, and catcalled in high spirits.

"She's not a game show," I whispered to Jackson.

Inez personally angled Mr. Douglass's head down to get him closer to the microphone as he asked, "Mrs. Ypsilanti, why do you want to become an American citizen?"

Evangeline inhaled so deeply there was static. This was her big line. Just as she began to speak, though, Inez snapped, "Bulb's blown."

Mr. Douglass had to ask the question again. The lights made Evangeline perspire, clumping mascara on her cheeks like bruises, but she answered with vigor: "Doug, I love the freedom and democracy of the United States!" Howard clapped and Evangeline swung her flag around for the cameras.

"Mrs. Ypsilanti," continued Mr. Douglass, consulting his index card. "You are the oldest person in the history of our state to become an American citizen. You are assuming the duties and obligations inherent therewith." Her hearing aid whistled over his last words but, once the battery was fiddled into submission, the cameras whirred for a close-up and Evangeline turned her head to the right and to the left, showing her Athenian profile to advantage. Hardhearted skeptic that I was, full of self-recriminations and comparisons, still for a moment I found myself caught up and proud.

"Am I going to be on TV tonight or not?" Evangeline demanded.

The cameraman swung his spotlight off her. "Seven o'clock, unless there's a fire."

"A *fire?!*"

"Makes better copy."

"He shouldn't have said that," I whispered to Jackson. "It will just give her ideas."

"She is already on fire," he answered. I looked and saw that it was true; she glowed.

Mr. Douglass was lifting her hand gently. The corners of her mouth tipped up, and I could just see her thinking: *how unexpected, how charming, a kiss from the INS.* But, no, Mr. Douglass was rolling her index finger first onto a stamp pad and then into the neat square of a standardized form. Then he closed up his papers in his attaché case and stood. "Well," he said. He gave us all a smile as open-faced as a cheese melt.

"Thanks," we said.

Evangeline had been saving up her big American line. "Have a nice day," she called after him. Then she rolled herself over to Jackson and me.

"Here she comes — Miss America," Jackson sang quietly. I was studying her face; I'd never seen Evangeline look so full and satisfied.

She remarked, "Mr. Douglass is so honest, almost enigmatic. Persephone would marry such a man, don't you think?"

"Might," I said. Persephone, if we ever found her, would be in her fifties and quite likely past such undertakings. Her mother still pictured her as a young girl. But then Evangeline thought of herself that way, too. Her time was caught in a loop.

"She'd be a star-spangled little wife, working in a bank," Evangeline continued. "Some place cool and federal. Three children. Two boys and a freckle-faced girl. They'd chew gum and carry firearms." Evangeline patted her hairdo with inky fingers. "It feels *good* to be an American. I should have done this years ago!"

We waved as she rolled toward the elevator, on her way to the video lounge to oversee the little buffet she'd arranged in her honor. Somehow she seemed to have made a leap of faith. I *knew* her motives were purely selfish, a formality, that she'd never taken any pledge of allegiance or national history seriously, yet I had to admit she looked satisfied somewhere deep. I envied her.

"Jackson," I whispered, "does Evangeline seemed *changed* to you?"
He nodded in slow agreement. "It just goes to show."
I nodded, then asked, "What, exactly?"
"Life doesn't stop. We keep on learning and growing."
"Hmm," I said, considering the paradox: there were some men, like Jackson, so strong and silent in their masculinity, you started confiding in them as if they were women. They were so prone to clichés that you failed to notice it after a while and began to share those sentiments without self-conscious censure. I'd always heard that American men were like that: naively trusting, protective, slow to reveal themselves. Finding those traits in Jackson, I felt they were more durable than cherry pies or statues of liberty. I wondered if Evangeline felt comfort in joining the company of such people, like travelers on a ship all facing starboard. "My granddaughter," I told him with a laugh, "thinks old people are all good."

Jackson's hand wrapped around my wrist. "Feel like a spin, Mrs. Carter, Viola?"
I raised my eyes to him full and caught a deep breath. "There are things you need to know, Jackson."
He studied my face from his height. "No Christmas rush."
"I will explain. I promise."
"Let's just get airborne."
After more fussing over Evangeline and shoveling some celebration sheet cake into my handbag, we did—which was how we happened to tour Hayfields House, how it was I came up against my personal ghost:

the face in the framed embroidery, the beguiling face of a long-dead Roddy Borders, invisible to the direct gaze but, when studied in the landing mirror, all too apparent as an angel in a tree.

The full force of my guilt wracked me. I sat as lifeless as a mannequin with Jackson's fake money and metal soldiers on my lap as we flew up again, and all I could consider was the perspectives of angels when I looked down again at the land below and saw a boundless puzzle of interlocking parts. Just before we nosedived into my daughter's pond—had Roddy Borders cursed us with his evil eye?—over the engine's hum, I shouted to Jackson, "From up here Conflux looks so easy."

Then we went down.

Jackson must have flipped out, but I went down, Bagg and baggage, like airdropped potatoes, like a spy behind enemy lines, like Miss Bartram's submerged Lemuria; I went down like nobody's business. And at the bottom, water-bruised, muddy, I was nervous and panting the shallow breaths of labor, trying to save on air, but I did not panic. Sunken treasure, I flattered myself, as I waited for rescue or whatever was going to come. The failings and gifts of my ancestors had crossed to my descendants over the land bridge that was me, but I had become for a time invisible; me: the Bering Strait. I had been through reversals before. Clearly, as if someone had snapped the reel into a projector, my mind's eye watched with sad alarm the events of my life in early spring 1914, when skating with my first and very best friend in the world, I had cracked straight through black ice.

The war had driven a wedge between Felicity and me, and that morning was one of the last times we met. We had trudged the mile and a half to the pond without speaking. At the fallen stump, I looped up the laces of my skates, binding them around and around at the tops, and set off, hurling myself onto the mercy of winter's glass. The Brennekes's pond, shaded by cedar trees that grew up close to the water, seemed as grave and sequestering as the interior of a chapel. Icicles hung from every twig like drippings from candles set alight by the sun struggling to keep its head above water.

When you are pressed against something so hard and yet so invisible as convention and prejudice, and a rift opens, you have no choice but to go through. Aiming toward the center of the pond, I heard a splintering and my skates pulled me suddenly vertical, tugging with cruel abruptness toward oblivion, and air became an element of the past.

The silence underwater was even greater than our human silence above, but kinder. The freezing water itself embraced every part of me with absolute possession. Below, the world was thick and murky with slow-shifting silt and complete unto itself. Through the film that separated me from life on top, I could see, or I imagined, waxwings settling on branches, bouncing juniper bows, clouds rushing in patterned darkness and light that worked to ease my guilt.

When a rope snaked down at last—years after, so it seemed—snagging my waist and shoulders, jerking me up into the wet wind of the world above ground, I resisted, gulping, crying out, tears running over my face faster than the rivulets of pond water down my hair. It felt crueler than death itself to be brought up into unnatural air.

Mr. Brenneke's stubbly chin raked over my cheeks and mouth, insisting on a kind of kiss that repulsed me. The suspected spy had stuck his fingers into my mouth, snagging out grass, had pressed his coffee-bitter lips hurtfully hard on mine and forced his used-up air into me. I remember retching into the mud of the pond's edge. Later, waiting for Aunt and my father to fetch me, bundled by the Brennekes's woodstove, naked and dazed beneath three blankets that chafed my skin, while the Brennekes moved around me, light-footed with relief, I had no sense of owing anyone any thanks. The world underneath, I had discovered—and was rendered for a long time afterward dumb by the secret I could not reveal—the world underneath offered grace, salvation, was endlessly still.

The last thing of note in my handbag, the small flyer from Hayfields House, I opened—hopeful, fearful—of running against that face. No. It was not featured. Instead, my eye slowed over a description of the land: "area built on Triassic basin . . . site of extinct volcano." *Volcano* caught my attention. Conflux was after all, I thought, a real place with a volcano, too, and a past going back as far as time, and I was sitting on it. I tried to feel myself really there. I deliberately pressed my hand, flat-palmed, into the pond's muddy bottom and noted the cool soil with its slip of algae, scratch of rock. Pressures and sensations clarified my mind. No one had touched me in years, and here I was, caressed by blood-warm sludgy water, shot through with cooler currents. I felt with peculiar pleasure the slinky seduction of algae that waved over my knee. Wrist-high in pond bottom, I shuddered with a pleasure I'd known on the Walla dig.

I could not rid myself of *swash* and Roddy Borders, but that overly-defined ghost face that stuck in my mind now seemed to offer neither rancor nor accusation. Ever the archaeologist, as clearly as if from the ground itself through my hand into my head, he seemed to be sending me facts as news about this plot of earth called Conflux: raging waves and continental rupture, volcanic fires that shot into the night sky brighter than noon, creaking ice that shoved the mountains up and rippled these horizons, fearsome heat that pressed common rock to diamond, ruby, emerald, the trudging reverberations of dinosaurs, the night scuttle of oppossum with a shifting cargo of young, deer droppings like toy cannonballs and hoof prints like victory signs imprinted with piston speed, projectile points and chipped shards and folded bones thrown unsentimentally by kin down garbage pits a thousand years ago, pots or pipes close at hand, treasures unearthed by planters breaking up field gone to pine scrub, or skulls crushed to silent screamers by tractors running above, row by blazing row, soft-shelled black snake eggs in warm clay holes, pin feathers dropped by mockingbirds in song, flitting from shaded branch to branch, human sweat and blood, turtles waiting in hard sun to stir, waddling quail, tarry pines snaking down roots through the paths of nematodes and night crawlers, termites and ants, and the entrails of moles caught and digested long ago by stoop-backed turkey buzzards suspiciously landing, honey locust, dogwood, and mimosa trees wound up in trumpet vine, spreading shade for daffodils, dogtooth violet, lady's slipper, Venus flytraps and pitcher plants, John Deere harvesters clearing acres as geometric as a Grecian urn, termite-laced tobacco barns buckling back to earth while quarried granite was set stone on stone, and hard-drinking kudzu shooting up streamers overnight, squeezing cedar trees to death, and among the ivories and ochres, vermilions and violets of petals yielding into clay red from the ferrous oxide of hematite and goethite, a million seeds waiting for the word to spring up and try their luck, and, I added, it was, for a brief time, also the story of the hand and body of Viola Bagg,

Canadian born, much traveled, who would soon brace the soil with her acrid ash but until then resolved—I found strength in the mud!—to grasp hold of the few last things left her on earth.

I was underwater less than half an hour, they tell me. The frog twins held onto the cables that heaved off my bubble as the emergency team, goggled and snorkled, lifted me in a rescue harness right up and out into chill air that knocked at my chest. Wind rushed across my ears; I felt attacked on all sides by sound: voices, strange and kind, motors, birdcalls, the clomp of boots. As I was borne from the water on a stretcher, I noted that the Cessna lay in parts by the bank like some Loch Ness monster uncomfortably beached; it was disdained by the ducks. Oxygen tanks leaned in abundance pondside, and at the water's edge, my daughter and son-in-law stood ankle-deep in cattails, arms around each other's waists, faces strained. "Are you all right? Are you okay?" their voices seemed to shout at me after all that silence. The most I could do was breathe and my exhalation roared.

Heady with oxygen, like an imprinting chick, I found everything gloriously real, double 3-D: sunlight, pine trees, house up the hill, hum of bees, flutter of ducks. Jackson—to my exhausted relief—lay on a blanket by a rescue van, propped up on an elbow. He lifted a hand up to his face mask when he saw me. My royal wave was something closer to the shooing away of a fly.

Strangers propped me under blankets on the bank and made me breathe some bottled air through a mask. The girl in charge motioned Marjorie back to give me space while they checked me over with their instruments, talking, talking all the time, with words that flowed over me without meaning as the air roared in my ears. Calming down from the ordeal, but not able yet to pay attention, I watched duck Mildred and her brood bobbing out. They were rippling old feathers behind them over the seamless water where I had been, sitting tight on the glassy reflection of sky as if it held neither danger nor desire.

According to Miss Bartram's law, continents sank while ocean beds rose up to form dry land, with leftover artifacts shredded by white ants. Likewise, it seemed, I had lived through a steady up and downward, where glass gave hope and took it away, while empires rose and fell. I was going nowhere. For better or worse, I was a fixture in Conflux, now and forever. And Conflux, I was coming to see, was a fixture in me. Its fields and roads, its houses and people, its sky, its mud and ducks—they were all making claims on my literal life.

Marjorie, frowning, came with a towel and sat on the grass by my legs. "You're all muddy," she said, rubbing them.

Yes, I nodded.

"Mother, Mother," she scolded me gently. *"Where* have you been?"

She untied my Nikes and pulled them off. There they were, exposed for all to see—those feet that had walked me through my awkward life—but she washed them tenderly, attentively. She poked the towel between my toes. Of course, I should have known my daughter was not such a person to blink at shameful secrets.

On the stretcher, drying, with kindness all around me, I felt solid and ancient, ruined and very real. I closed my eyes and just let the sun bake the top of my head for a time, like an old piece of Parthenon.